The Major Arcana

An anthology of short stories inspired by the tarot major arcana

THE MAJOR ARCANA

Copyright © 2024

All rights reserved.

Published by Arteminion Books 2024

Hull, United Kingdom

No parts of this publication may be reproduced, stored in a retrieval system, or transmitted in any form or by any means, electronic, mechanical, photocopying, recording, or otherwise, without the prior written permission of the copyright owner.

This book is sold subject to the condition that it shall not, by way of trade or otherwise, be lent, resold, hired out, or otherwise circulated without the publisher's prior consent in any form of binding or cover other than that in which it is published and without a similar condition including this condition being imposed on the subsequent purchaser. Under no circumstances may any part of this book be photocopied for resale.

This is a work of fiction. Any similarity between the characters and situations within its pages and places or persons, living or dead, is unintentional and co-incidental.

Paperback edition ISBN: 978-1-8383786-3-9

E-book edition (Amazon) ISBN: 978-1-8383786-5-3

E-book edition ISBN: 978-1-8383786-4-6

Cover Art by David M. Simon ©

Generative AI has not been used at any point in the creation of this book.

Contents

Editor's Note

These stories are written in a mixture of British, Canadian, and American English.

This has not been changed in order to preserve each author's own voice and style.

Please expect discrepancies in spelling, punctuation and language accordingly.

Content Warning

It's important to protect yourself when reading. Content warnings can be found below. If you're the type of person who would rather not know in order to avoid spoilers, please skip ahead to the next page.

Below are warnings for the stories containing topics that are typically considered triggering:

0: The Fool – *mutilation*

I: The Magician – *gore, death*

II: The High Priestess – *gun violence, unreliable memories, gaslighting*

III: The Empress – *death, murder, pregnancy*

IV: The Emperor – *suicide, murder*

VII: The Chariot – *murder*

IX: The Hermit – *death, incarceration*

XII: The Hanged Man Reversed – *reference to child murder, suicide, blood*

XIII: Death – *plague, mass-death, mention of suicide*

XVI: The Tower – *reference to rape, pregnancy*

XVII: The Star – *violence, murder*

XVIII: The Moon – *murder*

XX: Judgement – *death, blood, body horror*

XXI: The World – *sexual coercion, suicide*

Prologue

You're plunged into near-darkness as you pass through the velvet curtain into the small room beyond. The air is heavy with incense, the scents of cedar, vanilla and clove mingling in your nostrils. It's intoxicating.

As your eyes adjust to the gloom, you make out a circular table in the centre of the space, with two high-backed chairs facing each other on either side of it.

"Sit, please."

The voice seems to come from all around you. It's rich, melodious, inviting. It flows over your body like silk, caressing your skin. You comply, feeling your way to the nearest chair and lowering yourself into it. The cushions cradle your body perfectly. In fact, you don't think you've ever been so comfortable.

Light fills your vision for a moment as an array of candles burst into life. They line the shelves which adorn each wall of the enclosed space, illuminating ancient-looking books, bottles, jars and vials of all shapes and sizes labelled with illegible writing, and even occasional skulls and bones – none of which you recognise as coming from any animal you're familiar with.

"Shall we begin?"

Your gaze snaps back to the table in front of you, where a figure sits opposite. A slender woman of indeterminable age lounges back in her chair, a small smile curling on her plump, red lips. Large, hooped earrings hang from each ear, and a multitude of gold and silver bracelets and bangles adorn each wrist. You vaguely wonder how you didn't hear her sit down, but the thought disappears as her warm, golden eyes settle on yours, immediately putting you at ease.

"I understand you would like a reading, correct?"

She holds up a deck of long, thin cards. Has she always been holding them? You suppose so, and the question fades from your mind as quickly as it came. The woman raises an eyebrow; she is awaiting your response.

You nod eagerly. A reading – that's why you came, right?

She smiles, flashing a set of sharp white teeth. Something tugs at the back of your mind – a warning, perhaps? – but it disappears before you can pinpoint what it is.

You watch as the strange woman places three cards face down on the table in front of you. Your chest tightens; there is nothing more important to you in this moment than the identity of these cards.

The woman runs a sharp fingernail over the cards, and your stomach lurches. "Before we start," she croons, her voice soft as velvet, "know this. Each card comes to you with a story. A fantastical tale through which you will gain a deeper understanding of its meaning. Some are lighter, some darker. Some are plain, some more complex. But each is imbued with the essence of the card. Let it guide you as you see fit."

She lifts the corner of the first card, and you hold your breath.

"Are you ready?"

You nod, nervous excitement thrumming through you.

Her grin widens, and she turns the card over.

"Let's begin."

0: THE FOOL

The Fool's Gold by Imelda Taylor

The moon shone on a provincial village, away from the city's chaos. Its light spread across the rice fields. The shadows of the coconut leaves danced on the ground and the banana bloom was ready to transform someone's life. Pedro hoped it would be his.

It was the night he had been preparing for, the night he proved that a scrawny, sickly boy with a defective heart could conquer the extraordinary. Elders warned him and mocked him that his ambition was foolish.

Yet, he held onto his dream – the dream of living a full and long adventure-filled life. His family's lack of money to pay for his treatment meant whatever future he imagined would remain a mere dream.

He could never forget the first time he heard the story from his grandmother. Six o'clock meant it was time for the *orasion* – that few minutes of prayer always felt like hours for Pedro, his siblings and his cousins. As a reward, their grandmother told them stories of fairies, elves and creatures that shared our plane but not our world. One story stuck in Pedro's mind more than others:

"A banana tree is not all that it seems," Pedro's grandmother started. "On the night of the full moon, at exactly midnight, the banana bloom releases a magical pearl that can give any person who catches it with his mouth supernatural powers. Alas, only the worthy can keep the pearl and the power it brings. The Tikbalang, a creature with the head of a horse and the body of a man, will test those who wish to claim the power. Whoever holds the pearl in their mouth until dawn will possess the power."

As Pedro grew into a young adult, he kept the story close to his heart. His siblings and cousins forgot the story of their grandmother. They forgot the magic, but Pedro learnt whatever he could about the Tikbalang, his future opponent. However, his body became more frail. Born with a weak heart, his family thought they were lucky to see him reach his twenties. But, as he grew older, the stench of the Grim Reaper became stronger and he had nothing to lose.

Time seemed to have stood still as Pedro waited for his folks to fall into deep sleep. He needed extra time to allow room for any unexpected happenings. However, leaving the house felt like his first feat. Every step on the bamboo floor made a creaking sound that stirred his parents. Pedro found a bag of berries on their table and filled it with more things he might need for his quest. As soon as his chance arrived, he crept towards the door. He must not be late. It was the moment not to be missed.

"Pedro, what are you doing?"

Pedro jumped at the sight of his half-asleep little sister brushing her jet-black hair off her face. A smirk appearing on her olive skin meant she was up to no good. At other times, Pedro wouldn't have minded her mischief. While everybody else treated him like delicate china, Tintin never spared him. Although she was half his age, she was the only one who made him feel normal.

"Nothing! What are you doing out of bed? Go back to sleep!" Pedro commanded, his heart still racing.

"Or else what?"

Pedro was speechless. He knew he couldn't threaten to tell their parents.

"Look, you better be quiet before we both get in trouble," Pedro whispered.

"No, *YOU* will get in more trouble if you don't tell me what you're up to!" Tintin demanded, enjoying the panic on Pedro's face. "Where are you taking that bread?" Tintin noticed the bag Pedro was clutching – and *her* berries. "Hey, those berries are mine! I just picked them."

"Let go! I'll replace them tomorrow." Pedro tugged the bag back from his sister.

"What is all this noise!" Pedro's mum caught both of them as they were tugging the bag.

"Do you have any idea what time it is?"

"I just want a snack?" Pedro said. He knew his mum wouldn't stop him from eating. His illness often made him lose interest in food and his mum usually encouraged him to eat. Hearing that Pedro wanted to eat was something she had been hoping for. Although Pedro's little sister knew he played his card well and accepted defeat, she threw him a glance that promised revenge.

Pedro went back to his room. When all was quiet, he snuck out of the house from the window to avoid another encounter. Onwards, he headed to the field where wild bananas grew.

As he passed by an acacia tree, Pedro took extra caution when he noticed an anthill. "Pardon me, just passing," he muttered. He had been taught by his elders to give respect, as it could be a dwelling place of a Nuno, a dwarf-like creature that possessed supernatural powers which could bring ill fortune *or* good luck.

He was reminded of the time he overheard a few men from the village talking about how one of their drunken neighbours disappeared.

A drunkard was on his way home late at night from a drinking session when he answered the call of nature on a mound where it was thought a Nuno lived. The following day, the man's genitals began to itch uncontrollably. He scratched until blood could be seen under his nails but it didn't stop the man from scratching, for whenever he stopped, the itching became more and more intense. Frustrated, he started bashing himself with anything he could reach, a shoe, a ladle, but nothing could bring relief. Out his kitchen window, he noticed the jungle knife he was using to chop some wood. At that point, one of the men asked for the story to stop. It was the Nuno, they speculated.

Time passed and many of his peers stopped believing in its existence, but they carried on with saying 'pardon' as part of the tradition – or maybe, just to be on the side.

***

"Psst!"

Pedro momentarily stopped at the creepy sound, but remembered he should ignore such noises in case it came from something malevolent.

"Boy! Got any food or water you can spare for an old man?"

A hunched little man appeared dressed in rags, loose and draping as his wrinkly skin. He tipped his hat like a bowl, showing his balding head.

Pedro reminded himself to keep focused. It could be a trap. Besides, the food he had was his offering to the Tikbalang.

Yet, he couldn't ignore a plea from a vulnerable old man and offered what food he had in his bag.

Pedro carried on his way without an offering for the Tikbalang. He wasn't sure how he could pull his quest off now he had to turn up empty-handed. He tried to remember his grandmother's story when he passed by a familiar landmark. He once again passed an anthill next to an acacia tree.

"It can't be..." Pedro thought. He knew the way to the wild banana field by heart and there shouldn't be any other acacia trees, especially if it had an anthill identical to the one he passed by a few minutes ago.

Psst!

That noise again. Pedro turned around, but there was nothing there. Once again, Pedro reminded himself to keep focused; he couldn't afford further delays.

He moved as quickly as he could but his breath became short. *Must move, can't stop! You can do it!* Yet again, he passed by the same spot: anthill and the acacia tree.

Damn!

Psst!

That noise again. He realised that someone or something was playing a trick on him. "Please let me get through. I'm running out of time," Pedro pleaded.

"You're forgetting something, boy!" said a familiar voice. As soon as he heard it, Pedro slightly regretted helping him. He should have trusted his instinct that the old man was a Nuno.

"I'm here to help, boy," said the voice again. "Wear your shirt inside out," the Nuno suggested.

How could he have forgotten? Over the years, Pedro's grandmother instructed the children to wear their shirts inside out whenever they got lost. *"It will ward off the spirits,"* he remembered his grandmother saying. As soon as he took off his shirt and wore it inside out, a rope landed in front of him. It was coarse and as black as shadow. "You'll need that to tame the Tikbalang. Now go!" said the voice firmly. Pedro wasted no time. With his heart racing, onwards he continued.

At last, he arrived. End of the road. Pedro was greeted by uneven dry ground with roots crawling like the veins on the Nuno's old wrinkly skin. This led to a weeping fig tree. Feared by the villagers, it was believed that this tree housed spirits or demons, a portal to a world from which no mortals returned. Past the gigantic tree was where the wild banana trees grew.

Out of breath, Pedro slumped on the ground, but upon seeing the moon, he knew it was not time to rest. Of all the banana trees around, there was only one with a flower and it was starting to open. He had to hurry. He stood under the bloom, ready to catch the magical pearl, if it even existed. As the moon aligned itself with the tree, a glimmer of a white substance appeared at the very tip of the flower.

"It's now or never," Pedro muttered. He opened his mouth and hoped that he wouldn't miss. Time stood still. Everything moved slowly. His jaw ached. With a pounding heart, he felt he was going to pass out. Then, he felt something touch his tongue. Could it be? Yes, he got it!

Tempting as it was, he tried not to swallow or spit it out. He needed to hold onto it until daybreak. He heard a loud thumping on the ground that made the dirt around his feet fly. He turned, and there it was. A beast with a horse's head and a humanoid body, but with long muscular arms and hooves instead of feet, towered over him. Its mane, thick and black, rested on its shoulders and ran down to its back. Pedro caught a glimpse of hell as his eyes met with the beast's – fiery red and resembling a pit to the abyss.

The beast's nostrils flared and it bared its teeth, speaking in a low monstrous voice. "Prove yourself worthy!"

Without further notice, the Tikbalang charged at him. Pedro might have been weak, but his brain was quick. As the beast charged, Pedro rolled away. The Tikbalang might be from a different dimension but the law of physics still applied to him. With a body so heavy, he couldn't stop quickly enough to grab Pedro.

While Pedro caught his breath, he watched and waited for the Tikbalang's next move. This time he wasn't quick enough. He felt himself flung up in the air and kept his mouth shut with his hands to stop the pearl from falling. However, trying not to swallow it was much harder. Life flashed before his eyes. He wasn't sure if it was worth holding onto, for as soon as he hit the ground, he knew his body would shatter.

Instead, something caught him. Pedro looked around. He was still high up but alive. The banana tree seemed to have caught him. Confused, Pedro looked for the Tikbalang. He was way down below wearing a sinister grin. Before Pedro's next thought, he was tossed again by the banana tree, this time towards another. For what felt like an eternity,

Pedro was thrown backwards and forwards like a shuttlecock. The beast laughed in the background.

He remembered the rope that the Nuno had given him. "You need it to tame the beast," the Nuno had said. How, he had no clue. His head spun. He felt his entire body jolt as he hit the hard ground. Nearly, very nearly Pedro would have swallowed the pearl if he hadn't tucked it in between his cheek and his gum. He struggled to get up. The bag! Pedro looked around, but it was nowhere in sight. The Tikbalang stomped its hooves while laughing. He felt like a cockroach about to get squished. His heart raced. He was out of breath but he couldn't open his mouth to gasp for air. The elders were right. It was foolish of him to believe that his life was going to change – that this would extend his life.

As he scuttled backwards, waiting for the Tikbalang to stomp on him, he saw a familiar object. His bag! He wasn't sure if there was enough time to grab it, but the Tikbalang seemed to be enjoying watching him in agony. Pedro lay on his side and rolled instead of getting up. He was glad that he was right to expect the Tikbalang would be amused by his suffering.

The bag was within reach. He took the rope and instinctively threw it towards the Tikbalang's legs. When the rope wrapped itself around them, he pulled and the beast fell. Something about the rope seemed to weaken it. The Tikbalang hit the ground with a loud thud. When it was down, Pedro took his chance and charged towards it. With a quick whisk of the rope, it was loose from the Tikbalang's legs. Swiftly, Pedro climbed on the beast's back and wrapped the rope around its neck. It tried to shake him off, but Pedro was determined to hold on. The Tikbalang's mane was coarse and felt wiry between his legs. Its stench was something he hadn't smelt before, like burned hair soaked in murky pond water.

Pedro had no idea how long his battle lasted. The beast slowed. The sweat coming from it made the cuts on Pedro's leg from the monster's wiry mane sting. When it finally stopped, he saw the golden strand of hair, the strand that would put the beast in his power. Pedro's grandmother's words echoed in his head. *He who seizes the single golden strand of hair from a Tikbalang becomes its master forever.* Pedro plucked the golden strand, and with a final neigh, the Tikbalang managed to throw Pedro off its back. But this time, it didn't attack.

Daybreak was in sight. Pedro was glad to see the sky turning light. Time to swallow the pearl.

"You are worthy," said the Tikbalang. "You are now my master and I your servant. For as long as you hold my golden mane, I will be at your service."

"Oh good. Thank you. I'm so tired, can we get some water?" Pedro asked. The Tikbalang scooped him off the ground and took him to the nearest creek where fresh mountain water ran. It tasted sweet and refreshing. He asked the Tikbalang to have a drink as well. Aware that the Tikbalang could only come out at night, Pedro asked if it could take him home.

From that day on, for the rest of his long and healthy life, every full moon was a special time for Pedro.

I: THE MAGICIAN

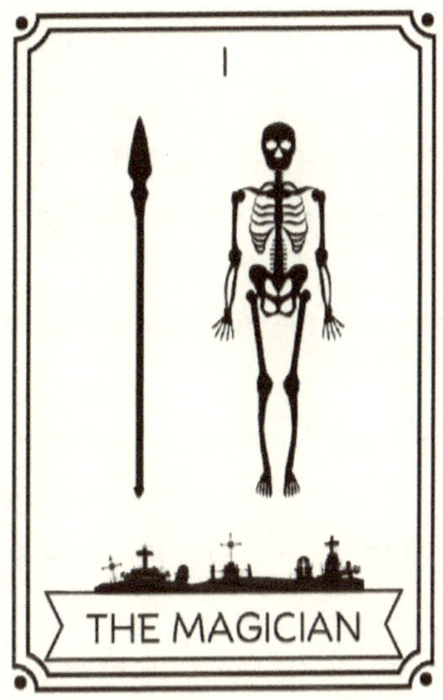

Manifest Necromancy by Emily Ansell

We descended into the sepulchre on high alert.

"Okay everyone, stick to the plan. Let's do this," Galawin muttered. He had become something of an unofficial leader over the course of our journey. He'd even *almost* relaxed a bit, as much as a paladin ever did. But now his jaw was held tight in concentration. As if *he* was the one here on personal business.

He wasn't. He was only here because his holy oaths said something about opposing necromancers and the undead. Perhaps it was more 'honorable' than Jev being here for money, but Jev was upfront, and less of a dick. And it wasn't like Meridwen and Doni didn't have their own, noble reasons.

But for me it *was* personal.

"The Stone itself is permeated by necromantic energy," Doni murmured, touching the walls as we walked. "I will need to call deeper when we fight."

"I'll take a sample for later." Meridwen pulled a hammer from her belt and chipped off a small piece of the wall, which she popped into a glass bottle.

Galawin glared over at the two women. "Okay, fun's over. Get ready."

"We *are* ready, Galawin. The Stone is filled with dark energy, but it still speaks to me. There is no threat between us and the necromancer himself. A small moment for a sample will not doom us," Doni replied, ever serene.

"If the Stone is corrupt, how can it talk to you?"

"It may have the power of the necromancer within it, but my people are born of the Stone. It is our mother and father. Even afflicted by disease, it still knows me."

"So there's no one waiting to ambush us in this hallway? A perfect choke-point and nothing?" Jev raised an eyebrow. "Why not?"

"I do not know. The Stone can read the hearts of the dwarven, but not of the races of Man. We will have to find out when we get there."

The door at the end of the hall opened into a large, yet rather homey-looking study. Mage lights hovered in the air instead of torches, and shelves of books and scrolls lined the walls. But in the center of the room, waiting for us, stood the necromancer and his small army of minions. Skeletons, mostly, but also some zombies and even a revenant of some kind.

Jev immediately melted into a shadow, drawing his knives. Meridwen pushed a button in her gauntlet and a mechanical, spider-legged machine sprouted around her, pushing her gnomish height up to almost human-sized. Doni set a totem down before her, holding a hand above it to invoke the spirits at a moment's notice.

Though this had all happened in seconds, the necromancer was the picture of boredom, as if we'd prepared for hours. He studied his long, crimson nails for a moment before asking, "Are you all ready now? You break into my home and don't even announce yourselves? It's a good thing I heard you were coming, *and* you walked right through the door ward and let me know you were here. Such ill manners you adventuring types have!"

"Good, then you know why we're here!" Galawin snarled.

"I don't, actually. But I can guess." The necromancer pointed us out, one by one. "You, Sun Elf, are here because you're a paladin and that's so very dull. The gnome is likely here for research, the Deep Dwarf sensed my presence through the Stone, the nightblade in the shadows is here for wealth, and the Moon Elf... oh, I know why she's here."

"So you do remember?" I ground out the words.

"I needed a piece of Light Wood from your Tree for my work. It was a simple experiment and I was willing to pay for it and everything. I did not start that fight. Yet you are here to kill me. What is your name?"

I drew my bow, aiming an arrow at him. "Elynisi. You killed my brother and sister in that fight."

"Well then, at least you'll have company when you return to your moon goddess. Or, maybe you won't."

After those words, everything happened all at once.

Galawin charged, only to be brought up short by the swarming skeletons. He began to cast some sort of holy smite, but they piled on enough that he couldn't finish. Meridwen waded in to help him. Jev flew backward in a cloud of purple, necrotic magic, narrowly missing the gout of lava that sprang up as Doni sang a deep note over her totem.

But none of that mattered to me. I ran, swift as moonlight, around the fracas. The necromancer didn't see my arrow, blessed by the goddess Tinatu herself, until it buried itself in his chest.

All his breath went out with a wheeze. Twisted, purple magic flowed out of his body, slamming into my chest. I flew backwards, just as Jev had done. But when I was brought up short by a stone wall, everything went hazy. I felt a rumbling beneath me. Doni, perhaps? That was good. I'd struck a deep blow, but they'd have to finish it without me.

The last thing I heard were shouts and deafening crashes, before blackness overcame me.

***

Awareness returned slowly. My shoulder throbbed, pulsing up my neck into my head. It was quiet now. The magelights were gone and it was dark. That had to mean the necromancer was dead. But, thank Tinatu, as one of her children, I could see in the dark the way other elves could not. And I could see that I was trapped.

The bookshelves behind me seemed undisturbed, as if the whole place hadn't crashed down around us. In front of me, chunks of stone and other debris had completely blocked off the rest of the room, and the exit. I was stuck, unless I could dig my way out. Or unless someone could dig me out from the other side?

"Hello? Is anyone out there? Meridwen? Doni? Jev? Galawin? Can anyone help me?" I swallowed hard. What if they were trapped, too? Or what if they'd been crushed by all of this? I shouted louder, straining my voice to be heard through the debris, but no one responded from the other side. Coldness stole through me. What if they'd left me behind? Perhaps they thought *I'd* been crushed, and left. It didn't seem outside the realm of possibility. We'd been strangers before meeting at an inn in the windswept city of Weatherpeak, and none of us really owed any allegiance to the other. Sure, we'd become friends on our journey, but if the necromancer was dead, then all of that was potentially done. Whatever the reason, it was best for me to assume that there was no one on the other side who could help.

"Time to dig, I guess," I said out loud, studying the cave-in. I wasn't going to be able to move some of the larger chunks of stone, but there were places where the debris was smaller, and I could probably clear a space big enough to squeeze through.

"Lady Tinatu watch over me." I made the sign of the moon in front of me, then bent to my work. My shoulder and up into my head still hurt, but I did my best to ignore it. Staying in this little corner wasn't an option.

The dirt and stone moved easily and things were going well until I hit a large boulder. I pushed it as hard as I could, inching it slowly forward. It fell into an open space, but that brought more dirt down. It hadn't erased all of my hard work, but it reburied enough of it to be frustrating. Still, I couldn't give up now. There was obviously a way out!

I began to hear chattering from the other side of the blockade, and as I dug further, a skeletal hand burst through. I yelped, and the hand retreated. What in the name of the moon was that? But the dirt was falling away faster now, and soon there was a large enough hole that I could wriggle my way out.

The cave-in hadn't affected the rest of the room as badly, other than a fine layer of dirt coating everything. There were a few large bits of dislodged stone strewn about, but things seemed mainly intact. Including the six skeletons and the tall, lanky draugr waiting in a loose semi-circle. My heart began to race. I'd lost my bow when the necromancer had flung me across the room, and I could hardly take them all on with just a dagger and an injured shoulder. The skeletons didn't have any weapons, but the lot of them together were more than a match for me right now. My only hope was to take a couple of them down with me.

Before those thoughts could go any further, the seven of them bowed.

"Missstresss, you are free!" The draugr spoke in a hissing voice as brittle as its remaining skin.

A chill went through my body, gooseflesh washing over my arms and legs. "I'm... I'm not your mistress."

"But you are, Missstresss!" the draugr insisted. "Can you not feel the link between usss?"

"How? How is this possible?" I demanded. "This makes no sense! I'm not a necromancer! And... and you were bound to that other guy!"

"But he isss dead. And now we ssserve you. We have found what is yoursss, asss a token of our loyalty."

The draugr swept his hand at one of the skeletons. It came forward, holding out my bow. A choked cry fell from my lips.

It was broken in half.

The skeleton put the pieces gently in my hands. I held them against my chest, already sobbing. The wood of the bow was dull, the spark of Life that had hummed through it gone. A sacred weapon, made of Light-Wood from the Great Tree of our people, blessed by a priestess of Tinatu... broken.

"How?" I cried. "It was supposed to be indestructible! The priestess told me it was indestructible! How can it be broken?"

I reached up to my amulet, preparing to grip it tightly. It was made of the same Light Wood, from the heart of the branch that had made my bow. But it too was *wrong*. I pulled it off; the gold setting remained but of the wood, only a piece of charcoal remained.

I fell to my knees. "Lady Tinatu? Are you there? Can you hear me?"

Nothing.

I spoke the ritual words that would bring her blessing and voice to me. Instead of that familiar warm glow, there was only an abrupt cut of the connection. Like a door slamming shut in my face.

I cried even harder.

***

My undead companions let me cry. They stayed close, watching but letting me process my emotions. The bones of the skeletons clunked softly as they shifted, and the draugr wrung its bony hands as I wept. Oh, wouldn't Meridwen have loved the chance to study real elf tears? I wished suddenly I had one of her ubiquitous little bottles to collect the drops of silver that spilled down my cheeks.

Eventually, the draugr stepped forward again. I looked up at it, defeated. "I don't understand."

"We know only a little of sssuch thingsss. But our former massster chose you asss hisss heir. Hisss power isss now yoursss."

"Why?"

"We do not know. We only felt the link move to you, Missstresss. You now have the power, and we will ssserve."

I looked at my hands. "I've lost my connection to the goddess of my people."

"Yesss. There are many who ssspurn thossse who wield necromantic powersss, even among the godsss. I am sssorry, Missstresss." The draugr reached out, putting a gentle hand on my shoulder. "What may we do to ease your dissstresss?"

"There isn't anything to do about that. I'll just... have to accept it. Unless there's a way to get rid of these powers?"

"I do not think ssso, Missstresss. Not without death itssself."

"Dark side curse it!" I sighed. "I do have one more question, if I may?"

"Of courssse, Missstresss. We will anssswer if we can."

"What happened to the others? The ones I came with?"

"They left. The bright one... accursssed bright one, he led them out. When the othersss wissshed to find you, he told them you were dead. He knew the truth, Missstresss, he knew you lived, but lied to the othersss."

"Galawin..." Bitterness rose in my throat. "So your damn vows were more important than friendship? Than *my life*? Of course they were, weren't they? I'm *evil* now, aren't I?"

"You are asss you wisssh to be, Missstresss." The draugr shrugged its bony arms. "And we will ssserve."

I held up a hand. Deep purple tendrils of magic rose from my palm, just as they had from the necromancer. "You know, I really don't like that."

The tendrils engulfed the skeletons and the draugr. They barely had time to raise their arms in defense. But once it was done, the skeletons began to chant.

"Mistress! Mistress!"

"What isss thisss?" the draugr asked, looking at itself.

"You can just call me Elynisi if you want. I don't like this whole 'serving' business. My people really don't believe in that kind of thing. We don't do slaves. I've taken that part out, given you your free will back. You can remain with me, if you wish. But as companions, not servants. If you wish to return to your rest, I'll respect that and help you get where you want to be."

"The ssskeletonsss are animated by your magic, Missstresss Elynisssi. The sssoulsss who inhabited them onssse are long moved on. They have asss much intelligenssse asss you allow them. I will ssstay, by my choissse. I wasss a ssscholar in life, who ssstudied necromansssy academically. It isss how I fell under the thrall of the former massster. I can help you learn about your new powersss."

"Thank you! Oh, what is your name? If you're going to stay, I must know what to call you!"

The draugr sketched a bit of a bow, "I wasss called Draxsss the Younger."

"Well met, Drax the Younger." I held out my hands to include the skeletons as well. "Well, if I'm going to learn these powers, I guess we'd better clean this place up a little bit so we can get to the books. Then maybe we can find a nicer place to live. Somewhere a little less dank. What do you think, my new friends?"

The skeletons cheered.

***

Three years later

"So Ely, if you don't mind my asking, what do you need books about paladins for? Aren't they kind of the opposite of what you've got going on, now?" Jev raised a thick eyebrow as he handed over the sack of books.

I shrugged. "They are, more or less. But I was always taught that in order to defeat an enemy, you have to know them. So, just like I learned the creatures of the forest I once hunted, so I'll learn the ways of those who'd come to destroy us here. I've gotten quite fond of this tower, and of Drax and the skeletons. And anyone who comes for me might also come for the rest of you, too."

"Aww, Ely, you don't have to worry about me! But I do appreciate it. And I get it, know your enemy and all that." He paused for a moment. "Do you think he'll come?"

"Eventually, yes. He'll be honorbound to finish what we started. He probably won't be the only one, either. Their vow to the Light overrides everything. They'll come because they have no choice, and eventually he'll come, too."

"Are you going to be ready when that happens? 'Cause I don't mind hanging around and helping you and Meri out if you want."

I laughed, putting a hand on his arm. "That's sweet of you, Jev, but I think we'll have it handled. You're doing more than enough already, bringing us information and things like these books."

"Well, if you say so. But if that changes, you better let me know, okay?"

"Of course! But I wouldn't have sought you all out if I wasn't confident I could handle whatever trouble came my way. But let's not worry about that right now. Would you like to stay for dinner? Meridwen was going to make some traditional dishes. It's a gnomish holiday today so we're having a bit of a party. Doni is supposed to come too, in a little bit."

"You know I'd love to have dinner with all my favorite ladies. Gives me a chance to tell you about a new idea for a poison I've been thinking about. I could use some extra input with it."

"Of course! Let's go downstairs; I'm sure Meri won't mind if we interrupt her for a few minutes."

***

Two years later

I'd know that swagger anywhere, walking up the stairs, kicking down my front door. Striding in all gold and glowy to where Drax and I waited in the receiving chamber.

I'd thought setting up a throne in here was a bit much, but Drax had convinced me it would make for a more dramatic sight when he finally showed up. I had to admit it *was* rather satisfying looking down at his smug face instead of up.

"Galawin, it's about time. I was starting to think I needed to send a personalized invitation. Or were you still trying to convince people that I was dead?"

I watched his hand tighten around the grip of his sword. "I did what was best for the rest of the group. So that they weren't corrupted by whatever corrupted you. You may still dress in the raiment of Tinatu, but I know what you really are."

"Oh this?" I stood, showing off my star-strewn purple robes. "I bought this because I saw it in the market and thought it was pretty. Trust me, the only betrayal more hurtful than yours was Tinatu turning her back on me. I don't even *look* upon the moon anymore. But that's a vengeance for another time."

"So that's why you did all this? Made yourself a target for me? For revenge?"

"Kind of. You're also the only one who didn't come visit me after I got the new place set up. Rude. Doni and I have regular tea now that we've cleansed the Stone where the old necromancer place was. Meridwen moved into my basement to research with my books and study my companions not long after we finished this tower. We had to add on to make sure she had a bedroom *and* a laboratory so she wasn't sleeping on the table with her experiments. Did you know Jev is running a spy network now? He's given me intel on you for a long time. And I see you've been the same uptight prick you've always been."

The tips of his ears twitched. "So what, you lure me here to make me one of your undead thralls like that creature at your side? Because I will not stand for that, and by the Light, I will strike you down first."

I laughed. I actually laughed until I could barely breathe, holding onto the armrest of my throne. Drax had to slap me on the back to get air back into my lungs, and tears streamed down my cheeks.

"Did I miss a good joke?" Meridwen complained, coming out of the door that led downstairs.

"Indeed," Drax said for me. "The Sssun Elf thought we would make him one of the ssskeletonsss, or a revenant asss I am."

Meridwen began to laugh, too, her high, gnomish voice bright. "Oh, Galawin! That's too funny! Imagine!"

Galawin looked less sure of himself now. In a petulant voice, he demanded, "I thought better of you, Meridwen! What is your nefarious plan, then?"

"It's very simple." I straightened, waving my hand to the wall beside me. A collection of skulls adorned it. "I have a special place reserved just for you."

His eyes darted to the wall, and this time his ears drooped as he shook his head. "Who... who were they? Are these my brethren? How many have you killed, necromancer?"

"You will be number twelve that has barged in unannounced. I am seriously considering sending a bill to the Temple of Light for all the doors I've had to repair or replace. You paladins need to learn how to knock."

"You are a fiend and a blight! We do not owe you such niceties!"

"Okay, this is very dull." I swept a hand up. Glowing, skeletal arms rose from the floor and grabbed Galawin's legs. He snarled out a holy spell that banished them in a flash. Then he grinned at me.

I grinned back, waving my hand again. I cast a spell of weakness this time, watching him slump down as his weapons and armor and even his own body were suddenly too heavy to lift. I cast again, to drain his magic reserves and take that power for myself. Not that I needed it, but it was a nice bonus.

"No. You will not! The Light... ack..."

"Sorry to cut you off with paralysis there, Gal, my dear. But we don't need to bring the Light into this. It is just as manipulative as the other gods. They waste talent such as you and I, throw us aside the moment we are no longer their perfect ideal." I stood from my throne, delicately descending the three steps to the floor. I reached out, lifting his holy amulet up from where it lay on his chest. Black smoke rose from it, and the glass holding the icon in the center shattered. The icon itself blackened and curled up into nothing. His eyes went wide, but he was still trapped by my spell.

"You see? The Light will not come, will not care. And that was only a little bit of blight." I tutted as I dropped the amulet. "I didn't want any interruptions, either. I've been waiting for this moment, Galawin, since you left me to die. And Meri and I have a wager going. I know this spell, Decrepification. She thinks it will corrupt and destroy not just your body, but your holy armor and weapons, too. I'm not so sure, but we're going to find out. Meri, you ready?"

"Whenever you are, Ely." She waved to Galawin. "See you later! Maybe we'll reanimate your skull once in a while? Catch up and stuff?"

The hate in Galawin's eyes was the sweetest sight in all the worlds.

Meridwen came and stood beside me as I cast the spell. She scribbled on her notepad faster than I could follow as patches of Galawin's skin turned a mottled, virulent green. It oozed as it then blackened, peeling away from his bones and falling wetly to the floor. He fought against it and the paralysis, but he was no match, especially without the divine link he was so accustomed to taking power from. He could do nothing against the ancient magics that I commanded. Not even scream.

***

It took about twenty minutes until the last, pustulent chunks of flesh fell from Galawin's bones. I took up his skull and placed it in the wall niche I had saved especially for him. As the skull settled into its new home, it took a huge weight with it. My shoulders lifted, my whole body lighter.

"Ely, come look at this!" Meridwen cried. She was pulling Galawin's armor away from what remained of his corpse, practically jumping up and down.

The breastplate was rent almost clean in half. Gauntlets, greaves, and pauldrons crumbled to the touch. Even the already blighted amulet had blackened and melted into an indefinable lump.

"It corrupted his armor and weapons, too! It works against divinely blessed armaments! Look at the amulet! I didn't think of it before, but I've seen these described. It's a *reliquary* amulet. The icons are painted with the blood of divinized saints. And you were able to destroy it!" She waved her hand over the mess on the floor. "*This* is our basis for the next step. This, Jev's poison, and the... item."

At the final word, a skeletal raven with feathers just corporeal enough to be visible zipped in through a high window. It landed on my wrist, bearing a small slip of paper tied to its leg. I patted the bird on the head, before unrolling the paper.

Meri must have seen a change in my expression. "Is that from Jev? Is there a problem?"

"Not at all. It's real. They found it. He's sent coordinates... I can't believe the spear is real."

"This is going to be unlike anything I've ever studied," Meri agreed. "A myth come to life. To see it do what it was meant for... it boggles the mind. It's the biggest discovery of... ever!"

"And I'll make sure you are able to study it doing what it was made for. And then it will be over, and we'll finally be able to move on, settle down and see what else we can do with our lives. That'll be nice."

"You're not going to get too important for me, are you, Ely?" Meri nudged me with her elbow.

"Of course not! You're my right-hand woman, my other half! I will gladly have you by my side and share everything with you."

"Aw, Ely, you're too sweet. And I look forward to it."

"I'm glad."

And I *would* share it all with her. And Doni and Jev, if they wished. But mostly Meridwen, who'd been steadfast all this time. Who chatted and planned as we gathered our things. Who squeezed my hand as we stood before the portal that would take us to where Jev waited, and with him the final item needed to carry out our plan.

The Spear of Divine Usurpation.

Galawin would not be the only one to answer for their betrayal.

II: THE HIGH PRIESTESS

The Runner by Amanda Shortman

The atmosphere in the stadium is electric. Sarah's already beaten the World Record for the hurdles and two hundred metres, and now she's lining up for the eight hundred metres. She's pretty much guaranteed the Gold at this point; we're all just hyped to see how many records she can beat. The crowd is full of Union Jacks, banners, and screaming fans. But nobody is as proud of her as us. Her friends. The ones who have seen her push day after day for years. This is her moment, and we're here for it.

The starting gun goes off, and so does Sarah, charging around the track like a bullet. The farther she runs, the greater the gap between her and the rest of the runners. I'm shouting so loud my throat hurts, and when she crosses the finish line Josh grabs me in a hug, jumping up and down so hard we almost topple over the seats into the row in front of us. She's unstoppable.

Until she's not. Gasps ring out around us, and my stomach drops. I let go of Josh and desperately look around, trying to figure out what's wrong. Sarah's on the track, the colour drained from her face. There's a man standing in front of her, but I can't see who he is. All I know is he's pointing a gun at Sarah. He's saying something to her, but it's impossible to hear from this distance. That is until he lifts a megaphone to his mouth. The crowd falls deathly silent as a squeal echoes around the stadium.

"You have been fooled," the man says. "This isn't normal. She's been changed. Genetically enhanced."

My blood runs cold. No. No, this can't be happening.

"The government has been testing on us for years, and she is the product of that. Superhuman powers. Don't trust, don't succumb, don't acquiesce. This is an abomination, not a celebration!"

I act without thinking. He's a threat, a risk that must be taken out. My body leaps into motion, faster than even Sarah could ever dream of, and I'm hurtling down the stairs towards the track.

"Resist, forever!" he screams, as he drops the megaphone and moves to support the gun with both hands. Time seems to slow as I barrel towards him. I tackle him to the ground, absorbing the gunshot with my own body. The pain is like nothing I've felt before...

I jolt awake, my heart pounding and my breathing wild. It takes me a moment to realise it was just a dream, and I'm safe in my bed, in the dark. What the hell was that? It felt so real. Like another memory resurfacing, yet it couldn't be. I don't know a Sarah or a Josh. And I've definitely never been shot.

Except...

I run my hand over my stomach, lifting my shirt to touch the scarred skin that rests there. The doctors all told me it was a puncture wound from the car crash. The one that caused the amnesia. And I just believed them. What else could I do? I couldn't remember anything. Not even my own name. It was like I had no life before that day. I woke up in the hospital and that was it. Day one of my life.

They said my memories should start to come back. It would just take time. And familiarity. So my friends have all been rallying around me. Taking me to places I should remember. But none of it makes a difference. It's been six months already, and the only memories I have are of those since the hospital. I can't even remember my parents. They died in the crash, but I can't grieve for them specifically, only the fact there's a gaping hole where they should be.

I feel like a shell of a person. A character whose story didn't matter enough for the author to write; my only purpose to fill in the background so that life can go on around me. It's miserable and disorientating. No matter how much people tell me about my life, or how many photos I see, nothing is familiar.

Except in these dreams. This is the third one this month. And each time they feel more real than anything in my waking life. Why is that?

My therapist says you can't take dreams at face value. They're representations of our thoughts, anxieties, and things that have happened to us, but they aren't real. Just a random selection of data wrestled into some form of a story created by our subconscious. I should believe her; she obviously knows more than me about it. And yet, I don't.

I know I'm not going to be able to sleep any more tonight. I'm too wired from the dream. So I turn on my light, grab my laptop, and open another tab. Maybe I'm paranoid. Maybe that's what happens when you can't remember a thing and have to trust those around you to tell you the truth. But that's the thing – I don't. My instincts tell me that they're hiding something *big*. And I need to figure out what it is.

I type in DuckDuckGo, not trusting a Google search even on incognito mode. I don't even know how successful I'll be in hiding my internet history, but this at least makes me feel safer. And then I start my search again, looking for any kind of hints that my dreams may be real. Because surely, if something as huge as that had happened, there must be a record of it somewhere.

***

I barely notice the light changing as the hours pass by. So it's a shock when I hear Matt and Emily's door open and footsteps along the hall. I quickly shut down all tabs, close my laptop, and shove it under my bed. Then I shuffle under the covers and lay my head down. Just in time.

"Lucy?" Emily's voice calls, as she slowly opens my bedroom door. "Are you awake?"

"Mmmmm," I moan, stretching my arms above my head and trying to act as if I've just woken up. "What time is it?"

"Seven. Matt's gonna make pancakes for breakfast; apparently, he's really craving them. So the bathroom's free if you want to jump in the shower first today?"

I smile at her and nod. Living with friends, in their marital home no less, and being reliant on them for pretty much everything has made me so scared of overstaying my welcome. I literally have nowhere else to go. Maybe that's why I'm so hesitant to let them know my doubts. It's definitely why I'm always the last to use the bathroom in the morning – I never want to get in the way.

I set the shower as hot as I can bear it. It feels good on my tense back and shoulders, even if it does make me wish I could crawl back into bed. These sleepless nights are taking a toll. I fight back a yawn as I dry myself and then move to the sink to brush my teeth. I look in the mirror and note the dark grey hollows under my eyes. Desperate to avoid more questions on how I'm doing, lest they make me see yet another therapist, I dig out my makeup and do the best I can to erase the evidence.

And then before I know it, I'm eating pancakes whilst making sandwiches for my lunch and waiting for Emily to finish off so we can head to work. She always insists on dropping me off on her way to the office, even though the shop where I work is within easy walking distance. She says it's because I'm on my feet all day and shouldn't have to walk any further than necessary. But a part of me can't help but feel like she doesn't trust me not to run. As if I have any other place to run to.

From there, my day goes as it usually does. Get to work. Deal with snotty customers and bored co-workers. Browse the High Street during my lunch break because I need to be away from everyone who knows about me and my issues for just half an hour, and none of these strangers give me even a second glance. Then finish my shift, wait for Emily to pick me up, back home to help cook dinner, and then pretend to be social for just a few more hours before I can escape to bed.

Sometimes I wonder how I ended up here. Beyond the obvious 'memory loss'. How did my life become so claustrophobic that I could scream? Was it always like this? I'm convinced it wasn't, even though I cannot remember a damn thing about my life *before*. It's like I know, in the pit of my gut, that this isn't where I'm supposed to be. And it kills me that I don't know why.

So, again, I wait for the house to go quiet, as Emily and Matt finally go to bed themselves, and then I lift up my laptop and start again. Searching for every conceivable query that might lead me to some answers.

'Sarah World Record attack'

'Sarah gold medal heptathlon'

'shooting Olympics athletics event'

'conspiracy theory genetically enhanced'

The internet takes me down some wild rabbit holes with that last one, but nothing ever seems to fit the things I can remember. I feel like I'm going mad.

***

"Hi Lucy, how have you been?"

I walk in through Dr Clarke's door and take my seat on the cushioned chair beside the window. I know this drill; we've done it so many times before.

"Fine."

"You look tired," she says, her expression soft and open. Like she just wants to help me. But I don't trust her. One wrong move and I'll be sent back to the psychiatrist for reassessment and more meds.

"It's been hard to sleep, with the heat, you know?"

"Yes, it has been rather hot, hasn't it? How has that been affecting you? The disturbed sleep, I mean."

"It's fine."

"Lucy, we've talked about this before. Getting adequate sleep is crucial for your well-being. Have you noticed any effects on your mood?"

"No," I lie, even though I know she won't believe me. I need to come up with something or she's going to know I'm holding back. "I mean, I'm a bit grumpier but it's okay, I'm managing. I'm using the techniques you taught me."

"Which ones?"

"Thinking of three things I'm grateful for each day. Box breathing when I get overwhelmed. Laying in bed and resting, even if I can't sleep." It's all a lie, but I'm hoping that mentioning them will make her move on.

"Good, good. And do they help?"

"Yes."

"And how about journaling, have you given that a try yet?"

"I just don't think it's for me."

"Well, it's always there if you need it."

I nod. She keeps on trying to get me to write a journal, but there's no way I'm putting any of these thoughts down on paper. It's not safe. I don't even know who I think might read it. Emily? Matt? Her? All I know is that my gut instinct tells me not to trust any of them. And right now that's all I have to go on. Instinct.

"So what else has happened this week?"

And so continues yet another therapy session, in which I lie through my teeth and hope to escape unscathed.

***

"Let's get away this weekend," Emily says as we're finishing up dinner.

"What?"

"Yeah," says Matt. "You've got this weekend off, right Lucy? Let's do something fun."

"I was just going to chill out," I say, wondering where this is coming from. "Why don't you go and have some time together. Goodness knows you deserve it."

"What? No!" Emily looks offended. "We love having you around."

"I'm a thirty-something friend you have to look out for every day. Come on, you're young, you're in love, go have some fun. I'll be alright for a weekend." *Please, please, please* I beg silently, desperate at the thought of two whole days alone without having to keep up any pretences.

"No, Lucy, we can't…"

"You can," I insist. "Look, you're gonna have to learn to trust me at some point. I'm doing much better – I'm keeping up with my therapy, I've got a stable job, I know all the best places locally to go for a walk or treat myself to lunch. I need this as much as you do."

I try to hold in my desperation, and I can tell that they're both unhappy at the idea of leaving me alone. But I also know that they can't refuse without outwardly admitting that they don't trust me. And they've been doing everything to avoid that.

"Okay," Matt says, eventually. "You're right. It will be nice to spend a bit of time, just the two of us." He smiles at Emily, and not for the first time I wonder how genuine it really is. It feels like we're all just playing a game of charades.

***

The rest of the week passes in a blur of normality. Or as normal as life can be when you still can't remember a damn thing beyond the past few months, and you're desperately trying to keep it together. *Just go through the motions,* I keep telling myself. *Act as normal as possible.*

Saturday finally comes and the freedom is so close I can feel it.

"So I've left the address of where we're staying, and their contact details in case our signal drops," Emily says, pinning a piece of paper to the noticeboard by the back door. "There's enough food in the fridge to get you through the weekend, so you don't need to worry about shopping. And Grant next door says just knock if you need anything."

"Stop worrying, I'll be fine. Go."

She hesitates, looking at me and then around the kitchen as if she's trying to find something, anything, to keep her here. Then she sighs, picks up her bag, gives me a quick squeeze, and leaves to join Matt in the car.

I stand at the open door and wave them off, watching the car make its way slowly out of sight before going back into the house and breathing the biggest sigh of relief.

I daren't do anything yet. Emily and Matt could very easily decide to pop back to get something they'd forgotten. So even though I'm absolutely desperate to dive back into my research, I force myself to make a cup of tea and sit in the living room, watching a movie.

***

The weekend passes quicker than ever. Saturday is lost in a blur of websites, and because I fell asleep at my desk in the middle of the night, it's almost lunchtime before I wake up on Sunday. I could kick myself for not setting an alarm. But the last time I slept for so many hours was weeks ago. I guess feeling relatively safe for once is enough to knock anyone out.

And yet I can't believe the thrill of finding something didn't keep me awake all night. Because finally, *finally*, I found it. A link to a site which led me on a wild quest to find the original. And there it was, deep within the dark web, the answer to my dreams. Sarah.

'Does anyone else remember?' the title says, above a photo of her. Her hair is down, and she isn't wearing her training clothes, but it's her. No doubt about it. It's on a forum, and someone with the username BelieveNothing404 has written a post that describes my memories perfectly:

'Everybody I speak to tells me that I'm just imagining this, and I cannot find any proof of it online. But I swear I remember this happening. Sarah Fox, an athlete like nobody else, appeared on the scene and blew every record out of the water. But then a guy tried to shoot her, and the transmission cut out. I was really young, I didn't know what was happening. I don't remember what happened next. I think I forgot all about it. But then I saw this photo of someone random on Facebook, you know how it recommends people for you to follow? And I am **sure** it is Sarah Fox. But it says her name is Samantha Brown. I asked my parents if it looked like Sarah, and they just said Who? So I told them about it, and they said it never happened. Have I stepped into the multiverse or something?'

My heart stopped when I first saw the post. And now I feel sick as I read back over the replies again. Several people say they remember Sarah but nobody else in their lives do. Some even have additional details, like the shooter shouting about genetic experiments, and it being someone other than Sarah who got shot. They all say they have tried to search for evidence of it, but there is nothing. No news reports. No comments online. Nothing. But how can we all be remembering the same thing?

I'm just about to start a new search when I hear the back door open. Shit. I slam my laptop shut, leap up from my chair, brush my hands through my hair in an attempt to make it look like I haven't just woken up, and rush into the hallway. Emily is already on her way to my room.

"Emily, I... I wasn't expecting you back until later."

"We had to come home early," she says, eyes watching me carefully. My stomach drops.

"Why? What's wrong?"

"Come through to the living room and we can talk."

"Wh... why can't you tell me now?"

"Just, come on through," she says, grabbing me around the waist and guiding me along the hall. I want to protest. I want to run back into my bedroom and slam the door closed. I want to do anything but go into that room. I just know it isn't good. But my body betrays me and I'm powerless to do anything but move where I'm directed.

"Hello, Lucy," Dr Clarke says as I walk through the door. "Sit down,"

"What? No. What are you doing here? What's going on?" I'm trying to be firm, to stand my ground. I cross my arms in an attempt to stop myself from shaking. But it doesn't work. I'm like jelly and all it takes is Matt to grab the arm not held by Emily and I'm suddenly sitting between them on the sofa.

"I'm sorry it had to come to this. Again."

"What do you mean, again?" I need to escape. My eyes frantically sweep the room, trying desperately to find a way out. But all I see are more people – two at the door, three in the kitchen. What the fuck?

"We had really hoped that this time would be different. That you wouldn't go seeking answers. That you could settle into your new life." She sighs. "But you just couldn't do it, could you? You're a tricky one. I guess that's why you were chosen in the first place."

"Chosen for what? What have you done to me? Let me go!" I'm screaming now. There's nothing else I can do. I'm trapped.

"It's okay. It'll all be over soon." Dr Clarke makes a move towards me, her hand outstretched, and I try to move away from her. But Emily and Matt have vice-like grips on my arms and all I can do is squirm onto the floor, my legs flailing as I try to find a purchase.

"Hold her down," a man's voice says. I recognise it. It's the psychiatrist who treated me when I first had the accident. The one who pumped me full of drugs and made me lose all sense of reality.

"NO!" I shout, so loudly that my throat hurts. But I can't escape. Hands are all over me now and I'm pinned to the floor. I feel his hands on my arm and the scratch of a needle, before my vision swims.

The last thing I hear before the world goes blank is, "Here we go again."

III: THE EMPRESS

The Rage of the Empress by Craig Rathbone

Jia awoke to the smell of smoke, along with the sounds of screaming, crackling flames, and the bawdy shouting of cruel men. Her head was spinning, one eye closed to stop blood dripping into it from an open wound on her forehead. She could feel it swelling shut with a black eye anyway, so at least that problem took care of itself. She realised she'd been deposited in the foot space of her carriage, seemingly thrown there by some incredible force.

The baby! she remembered with a start, fear running down her spine like ice-cold water as her manicured, bejewelled hands flew down to her stomach, where the bulge of her pregnancy was hidden by an elaborate network of layers and corsets, barely loose enough to keep her child from harm. A quick feel around put her immediate fears to bed though; she could feel a gentle kicking from within, an insatiable urge to stay alive. She knew that the child wasn't out of the woods yet, but at least they were safe for now.

Unlike their mother, it seemed. Whoever had forced her carriage off the road had intended to do so. Her bodyguard was still sitting upon the leather-upholstered bench seat, pinned in place by two wicked-looking crossbow bolts. He had been a loyal servant, one of her husband's protectors originally, but had sworn to help keep her secret when he stumbled upon Jia and Ling's tryst in the castle kitchens a year ago. She felt awful for what had happened; if he had never caught them, perhaps her poor bodyguard would still be—

No! I cannot blame myself!

Swallowing her fear, refusing to let it paralyse her, she rearranged her voluminous petticoats and dragged herself toward the open door of the carriage, cursing her decision to flee straight from the castle without stopping to change into something more practical. Not that she had much in the way of anything that fit that description; Empresses didn't tend to need hunting gear or casual about-town outfits. Ling had left a set of her unassuming kitchen-hand clothing in the stables. If only she hadn't been in as much of a rush.

Creating enough rustling to awaken the Jade Warriors of old, Jia lowered herself from the carriage, which was half in a ditch at a rather strange angle, and lowered her elegant white pumps onto the muddy hunting trail, immediately devaluing them by a sum of money no regular citizen of the Empire would ever see. Not that she cared. Her husband, the Crown Emperor himself, had never been a particularly easy person to love. It still stunned her that she carried his child in her womb, after the suffering and misery he had put her through.

If only she had met Ling sooner. Much sooner.

Hoping that her lover was safe with the advanced convoy, she looked back into the cabin with thoughts of finding her late bodyguard's blade in its scabbard. But the blade and its sheath were missing from the poor man's belt, no doubt taken by her attackers. Clearly, the fools had taken the exquisite blade as a trophy, and not to deprive her of a weapon. Their fear of her was so insignificant that they hadn't even bothered to restrain her.

She could hear their booming voices getting closer. The screams of the convoy's other members were thinning out too; Jia didn't need to be a genius to figure out why. Hoping that the brutes hadn't shaken her down also, she reached into her corset, removing a much-used, worn kitchen knife wrapped in wax paper. Ling had given it to her, a last line of protection should all else fail.

She removed the wax paper and let it fall into the mud, secreting the blade up one billowing silken sleeve. She could have tried to hide in the dark forest, but the fashionably gaudy colours of her dress, the vivid blue, silver and white palette in vogue with Imperial high society, would outshine everything around except for the intricate jewels that festooned her outfit. She wouldn't get far anyway, since her footwear was completely impractical and she wasn't as lithe as usual owing to her advancing pregnancy. So she stood and waited for her ambushers, trying not to show fear unbefitting of an Empress.

To her relief, only one attacker came into view around the corner of the trail. He was tall and grizzled, dressed in the lamellar armour and leather-padded uniform of a soldier. He was carrying a bottle of rice wine in one hand, his unsteady gait suggesting that he had been enjoying it perhaps a little too much. She knew the style of the bottle, the favourite tipple of Ling and herself, secreted away on the carriage so they could toast their escape once the ship left port. For the first time in ages, Jia found herself grateful that her husband's pointless war had sent so many men across the great desert to die under the spears and arrows of their neighbour. If this man was anything to go by, he only had the dregs left to call after her.

"What are you doing walking around, you degenerate whore?" the soldier growled, stamping over to her with his fist raised as if to smack her into the dirt. She tried to backpedal, wanting to come across as defenceless, lull the drunken sot into even more of a false sense of security, but she slipped and fell backwards onto her rear. The mud was cold and thick, but Jia didn't need to suffer for long, since the soldier hoisted her back up by her expansive collar, pulling her close to his face so she could smell his rancid breath.

"Couldn't you have had the manners to stay down a little longer? I just found a lovely roast hen back there," he cackled. "His Grace wants you back, you know. He told the captain that once the little one is born, he's going to let us have our way with you, then kill you. What you get for betraying him, committing the sin of lying with some peasant bitc—" He grunted as Jia interrupted his monologue, jamming the kitchen knife through the gap in the man's armour under his armpit.

She slipped again but managed to keep her balance this time as the man staggered backwards, releasing her and attempting to reach the handle of the knife that jutted out from his armpit, blood dripping from it like thick, red rainwater. The wine fell to the ground, and he goggled at her in disbelief, a wordless plea for clemency upon his face as he fell onto his back, the wind escaping his lungs. Jia wanted to turn and run, tear through the woods and never look back, but she knew that she couldn't. They would find her; she could hear more of them just around the corner, an unknown amount.

May as well reduce the amount by one.

She knelt next to the man and, without giving herself a chance to reconsider, pulled the knife from the man's armpit, reversed her grip on the bloody handle and brought it down hard into his windpipe. Once, twice, three times, four. She lost count of how many times she plunged the kitchen tool into him but, by the time she stopped, he was dead and she was drenched with his blood. Fighting back the urge to vomit, she got back to her feet, removed the soldier's sword belt and wound it around her waist instead, feeling it dig slightly into her bulge as she did so. The man's sword was heavy, a solid but plain steel number. The hallmark embossed into the blade had it as capital-made, but not one issued to the military. Jia wasn't surprised. Her husband was one to cover his tracks.

She almost slipped again as she moved to leave the scene. Finally deciding that enough was enough, she kicked off her pumps, throwing them into the undergrowth. The mud oozed unpleasantly through her white tights, but she would have to put up with it for the moment. Leaving the kitchen knife jammed in the man's throat, she picked up the wine bottle, taking a long gulp of the fiery liquid before dropping it back onto the trail.

"Sorry little one, I'll make that up to you, I promise," she whispered, patting her stomach as she started down the trail toward her freedom, toward the bickering voices of her attackers. Rounding the corner, she found two more of her husband's attack dogs, these two having a heated discussion about how to share the spoils they were looting from two of her handmaids – older members of her staff whose bodies lay in the blood-stained muck with their throats cut. They had been good to her and cared for her since she was no more than a child. They'd always been quick to smile, caring and patient even when she grew into a demanding and unpredictable teenager. Loyal when they found out about her affair.

And now they were dead, their belongings being picked apart by bloodthirsty vultures. The men were so preoccupied that they didn't hear Jia unsheathe their comrade's stolen blade as she closed in on their turned backs, silent on her stockinged feet. Hunched over the dead, they were utterly preoccupied.

She recalled her sword art lessons with Master Fang, remembering how the grey-bearded man had chided her for calling it *fencing* or *sword fighting*.

"Blades must never clash, Young Empress. They deliver the killing blow; it is your own awareness and fleetness of foot that deters your opponent's own killing blow. Sword art is like a dance, and the most fluid and skilled dancer always wins!"

They had practised the art for five years, every second day. Without fail. It had taught her a lot about self-defence, and a useful amount about going on the offensive as well. Letting her growing anger fuel her, she closed the gap to one of the soldiers, wrenched his head to one side by the rim of his iron helmet and, before he could work out what was happening, sawed the blade as hard as she could across the pronounced tendon of his neck, just as Master Fang had taught her. The weapon didn't cut that deep, but it didn't have to; the damage was done. He tried to stand and face her as she pulled the sword back out of his neck, only to stumble as blood jetted from the artery she had severed.

Blood splattered across her dress and finely made-up face, but she didn't care. Even as the first soldier fell into a gurgling heap next to the slain handmaids, his comrade was drawing his blade. "You *whore,* that was my friend!" he bellowed, swinging his sword at her in a crude overhead swipe with enough strength to take her head off. Therein lay another Master Fang pearl of wisdom – always balance power and precision and never let your emotions overtake your discipline.

Jia twisted aside, avoiding the swing with ease and causing the man to stagger as the impetus of his attack pulled him forward. She took the brief window of opportunity to half-step behind him and, with a feral snarl of anger, scythe her blade across the back of his hamstrings, which no lamellar or leather protected. The soldier screamed as he landed face-first in the mud, his sword landing out of his reach. Jia knew he'd never walk again, but didn't intend to give him time to find out as she straddled his waist and, throwing her blade aside, placed both hands on the back of his helmet, pushing his nose and mouth into the filth. He bucked and struggled for a few seconds, his grunts and muffled screaming growing ever more sporadic until, with a final heave, he lay still.

"At least you can keep him company on your way to your final judgement then, prick," she spat as she climbed back to her feet, collecting the blade of the first man she had killed, favouring the clean and dry handle for its more reliable grip. Unable to just leave her handmaids in such a sorry state, she knelt next to them, gently closing their eyes and crossing their cold hands across their chests. A lone tear tracked down her face, cutting through the mixed blood and vanity powders and oils. These bastards would pay. They would all pay.

A little further down the track, she found the supply wagon. The oxen were all slain in their traps, and the driver and his assistant were dead on the road. It was still piled high with the cargo she had stolen back at the castle – gifts for their new hosts across the sea and supplies for the voyage. Their attackers had started picking through the collection: several crates were prised open and the ones containing food, drink and fineries had been pawed through by greedy hands. She guessed that the man in charge of the ambush team had dragged them away, probably to finish the job of murdering everybody in her coterie.

She spotted something strapped to the back of the driver's assistant, something that she could use against the remaining murderers. A crossbow, its wooden stock smoothed with use, the metal bow pitted with patches of rust. Unable to untangle its strap from around the dead man, she used her sword to cut it loose, cradling the heavy thing in her hand. It was unwieldy and old-fashioned. No doubt the enemy had more advanced models, but it would do to kill at least one of them. Sheathing her blade and taking the crossbow in the correct shooting stance, she carried on along the trail, following the prints of booted feet.

Master Fang hated crossbows, called them *crude tools of murder, that any peasant could use to slay a man*. Jia used to tease him, saying that she would quit the sword and take up such a weapon instead. He'd always met her jibes with a laconic smile, a glint of humour in his eye. Such was the way of the sword monks of the Temple of Yumao. Instead, she'd relied on the head of the guard to teach her how to use the weapon. Though he had at first been reluctant to teach the teenage Empress such a skill, he ultimately had little choice in the matter.

Those winter evenings spent at the freezing guard tower had paid off, as Jia now felt a surge of confidence with the weapon in her hand that matched her still-growing rage. The trail twisted down a dip, the tree canopy overhead giving her some useful shadows to cling to as she approached the next group of men. These she recognised as her husband's crossbowmen. No lamellar armour, daggers instead of swords, but they were indeed wielding the faster, lighter crossbows that she had been expecting. It was probably these five rats that had killed her bodyguard back in the carriage, as well as who knows how many other members of the group.

Nothing would keep her from her beloved Ling. Her servants would be avenged.

Time for these pigs to die.

Wasting no time, she plunged her hands into the mud and covered whatever clean patches remained on her dress, hiding the gaudy colours under a layer of earthy brown in order to better conceal herself from hostile eyes. The outfit had been selected by her husband; it didn't matter what she did to it now. It was as dead to her as he was.

Keeping to the shadows, timing her movements through the underbrush to when their boorish banter had them distracted, she moved in as closely as she could. Jia knew that this could be a tough fight. The initial shock had to be complete, otherwise, she would be unable to close with them and they would simply shoot her and her unborn child full of bolts before she could put her sword to work. To her relief, they were still roughhousing with each other as she closed to within five or so paces, huddled behind a wide tree and with the old crossbow pushed into her shoulder, just like the guard captain had taught her. She braced against the stock, planted her feet among the prickling leaves and twigs of the forest floor and took aim at the closest archer.

Keeping her training in mind, she drew in a deep breath and held it, gently resting a finger against the trigger as she lined up the iron sight against the soldier's chest, a sufficiently large target to ensure that she couldn't possibly miss. She counted to five in her head, prayed to the gods that the bolt would fly true, and applied more pressure to the trigger.

The wooden stock thumped against her as it discharged the bolt, which flew across the short distance and embedded itself in her target's chest. He staggered back with a shocked yelp, the thick shaft of the bolt jutting from his chest. The other men were unable to react in time as Jia burst from the treeline like a she-wolf. She charged straight into one of them, breaking his nose with the crossbow. As he staggered back, she dropped the weapon and drew her sword to meet the panicked attack of the remaining three men.

The first didn't have time to drop his crossbow, instead discharging it at virtually point-blank range. Thankfully it was a wild shot and did nothing more than tear through one of Jia's sleeves. He tried to draw his dagger instead, dropping the bow to the ground as he fumbled, but Jia was faster, sinking her blade into his gut with a feral howl. He twisted back, falling to the ground and taking her blade with him. She needed to retrieve it but knew she wouldn't have time as the other two soldiers closed in on her, crossbows discarded and daggers in hand. She managed to dodge one with a lithe sidestep, but the other delivered a slice across her arm, making her cry out in anger as she slashed his face with her exquisitely manicured nails.

She must have caught his eyes because the man howled in pain and withdrew, clutching at his face as he stumbled into the woods. The last crossbowman pushed an attack, swinging with his dagger like he was trying to cleave meat. Jia instinctively dodged every stroke, thankful for her years of sword art training but knowing that she needed to find a way to neutralise this threat quickly before one of the less-injured men was able to get back up to help him. Timing her moment for when the fool missed with a particularly heavy swing, she rolled to the ground, clutched the dagger up of the man who she had clawed, and sunk it as hard as she could into the back of his thigh.

He howled like a stuck pig, immediately dropping his blade so he could try to extract the one stuck in his leg. Jia took the opportunity to leap back to her feet, pick up one of the crossbows, dropped by its panicking owner as she had closed to within sword distance, and used it to shoot the man square in the face. The impact snapped his head back with brutal force, killing him outright. Taking a moment to catch her breath, Jia assessed the state of the remaining men. The man shot in the chest lay still, as did the one she had run through with her sword. The man whose nose she had broken with the old crossbow had crawled to the roots of a tree, from where he was currently trying to stand, spitting blood and cursing her name. He fell back to the ground when Jia picked up the remaining discarded crossbow and casually discharged it into his back.

The last man, the one she had blinded with her fingernails, was sat among the brambles and leaves, crying red tears down his dirty face. Jia collected a dagger from the dirt and strode over to him, resisting the urge to sink it into his soft palate and kill him there and then.

"My husband sent you after me, correct?" she demanded, using her most imperious tone.

The man faced his ruined eyes in her direction, looking terrified. "Y-yes Your Grace, that's right! It was the Emperor, he sent us after you – he said you had betrayed the Empire, that you'd done heretical things, degenerate things – with a chamber girl!" he blubbered, his former bluster completely gone. Jia narrowed her eyes, her jaw set. There were those words again. Heretic. Degenerate. How typical, she mused, of powerful old men to choose what kind of love is pure and what kind is, as they insisted on saying, *degenerate*.

"How many more of you idiots are out here? Give me an accurate number and I may let you live," she hissed, "but if you lie to me, I will slice open your belly and leave you for the ravens."

The soldier nodded, eager to please his former Empress, knowing from her tone that this was no idle threat. "The captain and his officers are up ahead with the horses, Your Grace. There are six altogether. Please, please don't kill me, I have a wife and—"

Jia stopped the man's pleading by carrying out her desire from earlier, pushing the man's head back and jamming the dagger up through his soft palate. It was a quick death, her idea of mercy at that moment. "I too have a woman I love, just as much as your foul master's child that I carry. You weren't too bothered about taking those from me, were you?" she whispered, a hand unconsciously placed upon her tummy. Her precious cargo shifted within. They were safe for the moment under their mother's care.

The cut delivered to her arm was stinging badly by the time she had retrieved her sword from the guts of the dead man and wiped the blood on his uniform. She sheathed it and ripped the impractical, blood-stained sleeve from her dress to investigate. The cut was quite deep and bleeding freely, but she had no time or training to stitch it up, so instead tightly wrapped the torn silk around it like a bandage. It hurt like hell to do so, but her despair was held at bay by her still-simmering rage, her need to find the commanders of the enemy ambush and put them all to the blade almost as strong as the fear she felt for Ling's welfare. Deciding that she enjoyed the better mobility without the sleeve, she tore off her other one also, tying it around her forehead to keep her ornate ringlets from her face.

She picked up one of the newer crossbows, attaching a narrow quiver with a few arrows in it to her belt as she followed the road.

It didn't take long to find the commander and his inner circle. They milled around at a stream on the edge of the forest. Beyond the trees, a road cut across miles of pastureland before reaching a large coastal town. It was from there that Jia and her peasant lover were supposed to have made their escape. She hoped that the first convoy, manned by her most trusted soldiers and carrying her precious Ling and her family, had seen less excitement as they moved along a different, more erratic route. The carriages should already have deposited her aboard the ship, if the gods favoured them.

The crossbowman hadn't lied; six men remained between Jia and that ship. One was ensuring that their horses were taking on water, while the other five crouched around a large cooking pot that steamed into the morning air. Four of the soldiers were dressed like their dead comrades back on the forest trail, with lamellar armour for the upper torso, a helmet and leather-padded clothing underneath. The man walking the horses looked to be dressed the same, though his helmet was not on his head.

It was the final member of the group that interested her the most, though. This soldier was wearing far fancier armour, in lamellar head to toe and a well-balanced looking katana at his hip. A masked helmet sat on the ground next to him, the face protection styled like a snarling demon. This man had to be the captain that the other soldiers had spoken of before their violent ends. Jia sighed in resignation, biting back an angry curse, for she would not be able to slay these curs, not with a sword and a crossbow. The moment she fired the first shot they would be onto her, leaving her outnumbered.

At the same time, she could not bring herself to simply evade them and leave. These bastards were responsible for the men in the forest, responsible for murdering her coterie in cold blood, attempting to capture her and drag her back to her cruel husband and keep her from her beloved Ling. Perhaps worst of all, they had put her unborn child at risk. No, they had to die. All of them.

It was then that an idea dawned on her. As a young girl, precocious and nosey, she had befriended a member of the royal household that most didn't even acknowledge the existence of – the poison tester. The old woman had been responsible for thoroughly testing all food that Jia's then-future husband was given, to ensure that his many enemies weren't trying to assassinate him via poison. The woman had allowed the young Empress-to-be to hang around her laboratory and had been kind enough to show her common plants and fungi that, if imbibed, could kill something as big as an ox in seconds. She had once asked the woman why she kept such deadly samples within the walls of their royal home. The tester explained that detecting poison in food or drink was performed by way of an old seer's spell, the kind not often seen since the great war many years before. For the magic to work, she explained, a sample of the poison had to be sacrificed, its ashes used as fuel to power the incantation and help her find the deadly surprise in her master's meal.

From her current hiding place in the undergrowth, the Empress was able to see one such fungus. A few paces away, nestled in the roots of a large tree, was a growth of four jet-black mushrooms, their canopies speckled with orange spots – Deathmires. Ensuring that none of the soldiers was looking her way, she got onto her hands and knees and crawled over to them, tearing off a strip of fabric from the hem of her dress to collect them, as touching Deathmire with your bare hands was almost certainly a fatal mistake. Jia praised the wisdom of the royal tester, wrapping the deadly fungi up in the shredded fabric and placing it into a small leather pouch attached to the sword belt she had stolen earlier.

A plan forming in her mind, the Empress scurried down to the edge of the treeline, out of sight under a rather thick bushel of thorny brambles. While she had a few bolts for the crossbow, she knew that the time it took to reload would make it effectively useless after just one use. It wasn't much good against the soldiers for that reason, but it could be used to create a distraction. Looking out past the five men around the cooking pot, she examined the horses in more detail. The remaining soldier was holding all of their reins; she could just make out their trappings lashed around his wrist. Five of them had only saddles and packs, though the largest of the beasts was bedecked with quality-looking steel armour plates. This was perfect for what she had in mind.

While firing a bolt at any of the beasts would have worked, Jia had a deep hatred for those who deliberately harmed animals. Since childhood, she had kept many pets, rescued many injured animals and fed most of the feral cats that lurked in the palace gardens, so it was essential to her that she used only the captain's armoured horse as the crux of her distraction. It would be a long shot, but at least the bolt would do less damage to the horse that way. With this in mind she raised the crossbow, carefully took aim, inhaled deeply and, muttering a prayer, depressed the trigger.

The iron bolt flew across the open ground with barely a sound and, much to Jia's satisfaction, whacked the captain's horse squarely on its steel rump plate. She bit back a cheer of delight as the projectile bounced harmlessly off the armour, the impact more than enough to make the beast rear up and charge away across the field. The other horses followed it in a panic, dragging the soldier behind them across the stubbly corn stalks. The other soldiers jumped to their feet and took flight, yelling in dismay at their expensive mounts escaping across the open ground.

Jia wasted no time, jumping to her feet and half running, half sliding down the embankment at the forest's edge and quickly covering the ground between the cover of the trees and the soldiers' cooking pot. Snatching a glance, she spied the soldiers still chasing the horses away from her across the field. The Captain stood at the stream's edge, hurling threats and abuse at them between great guffaws of laughter.

Perfect.

She wasted no time in fishing out the wrapped mushrooms from her pocket and dropping them with a wet *splosh* into the watery soup. She crammed the torn fabric back into her pouch and ran as quickly as possible back to the undergrowth, sliding into the bushes just in time as the soldiers finally grabbed the reins of their horses, untangling the somewhat battered soldier that they had dragged across the field.

What followed took a good while, the soldiers taking time to tie the horses to a fencepost before returning to their cooking, the man dragged by the beasts being helped along by his comrades. Jia watched with bated breath as they dished the soup into battered metal bowls and began to enjoy their food, clearly content to let their subordinates deal with the execution of the Empress's coterie back in the forest.

But their enjoyment didn't last for long. After only a few bites, the first man toppled over onto his back, blood running from his mouth and nose as his insides began to melt. The others went to his aid, but after only a minute or so they were also down, howling in pain and clutching at their stomachs. Jia didn't scurry this time. She strode down to them, sword drawn and leaning against her shoulder, a twisted smile on her blood-splattered face. The captain saw her coming, too weak to even get to his knees as she stood over him. She was content for the other officers to simply die, but she wanted the captain to die by her hand.

Especially as the katana at his belt had belonged to her slain bodyguard for many years up until that morning.

"No. How is this possible?" gasped the captain as a fresh wave of pain wracked his body. "How did you get past my people? How are you even on your feet?"

The Empress threw the military pattern sword aside, leaning down to draw the beautiful katana from its scabbard. It was light, like holding nothing more than a feather. "I didn't *get past* anybody, Captain. I killed them. All of them. You dare to come after me? Fine, do so. Your liege is a hateful pig, so it makes sense that he'd send soldiers more akin to bandits after me. But my handmaids? My drivers? My bodyguard – my *unborn child*? You should have killed me back in the carriage," hissed Jia, her every word dripping with venomous rage.

The captain moaned and spat blood, but tried again to stand, refusing to give up the fight. "You – you are a *whore*, a *heretic* and – and a *degenerate* that lays with women. How could somebody like you ever defeat somebody like me?"

"Simple, captain. I may be a whore, I am definitely a heretic, but I am also an *Empress*. An Empress on her way to building a new life across the ocean, with the *woman* I love and *my* child. So, in my capacity as a Celestial Ruler, I request that you go *fuck yourself*."

And with those chilling words, his head bounced onto the rutted ground.

IV: THE EMPEROR

The Fall of Vrandaska by R. A. Cheddi

The flames of a dozen candles flickered, arranged in a small circle on the floor of the otherwise pitch-black bedchamber of Crown Prince Mivaan of the Vrandaska Empire. He sat cross-legged in the centre of the ring, his thin, wiry body ramrod straight and slender fingers resting on his knees. At twenty-six years of age, Mivaan looked much older than he should have. His closed eyes were sunken with dark circles contrasting his browned, sallow skin. A permanent scowl caused the skin between his eyebrows and forehead to wrinkle heavily. His once handsome countenance now consisted of hollowed cheeks, a long, narrow nose and a pointed chin with a scraggly goatee. Oily, shoulder-length hair tied into a messy bun completed his look. Mivaan wore very little save for a loincloth around his waist.

Sweat trickled down his body in rivulets as he inhaled deeply through his nose. As he did so, the candle flames seemed to pull towards him ever so slightly. Exhaling, the flames receded. With each breath he took, the fires drew closer to him. As he continued the rhythmic breathing, Mivaan willed himself to ignore the uncomfortable heat of the room, the licks of flame on his skin and the fatigue he felt in his body. Instead, he focused on his breath and repeatedly chanted a word in his mind. *Ma-Agni. Ma-Agni. Ma-Agni.*

The fire on the candles acted as a conduit between himself and the pure energy that made up the world. Atma. Absorbing the cosmic power as the flame touched his body, he felt his senses begin to expand upon uttering the eighth repetition of the word. He could soon smell the traces of honey on the wax candles. He felt the individual fibres of the thin rug he sat upon. And he could hear the excited chatter around the palace grounds. From the guards to the handmaidens, cooks, stewards and beyond, Mivaan listened to them talking about one thing.

Today was the day that his sister would become Empress of Vrandaska.

Mivaan pushed down his anger at the thought of his younger sister ascending the throne. He stowed his disgust at his father, for naming her the successor to the Empire and not him. He instead focused on the most critical moment of his meditation. As Mivaan reached the fifty-sixth repetition of the Mantra, he felt the Atma seep into his mind, causing his thoughts to speed up. He had felt sluggish and slow up to this point, but now, he felt ready for the day ahead. And what a day it would be.

As today was the day that *he* would become Emperor of Vrandaska.

A pair of arms embraced Mivaan from behind as he finished his sixty-fourth and final Mantra. He felt long fingers caressing his chest. The prince growled as a pair of shapely and plush breasts pressed against his back. No matter how much he enhanced his senses, he could never hear his Priestess' wisp-like footsteps approaching him. His skin tingled as he felt her lips against his left ear.

"How do we plan to kill her today, my Emperor?" the Priestess whispered, her raspy and seductive voice sending ripples of pleasure down Mivaan's spine.

The prince exhaled, his scowl deepening. He felt the Priestess' body press harder against him in response. "For the last year, I've exhausted every avenue to eliminate my sister," he said, his forceful, yet regal, voice low. "Assassination attempts, faulty intelligence on the battlefield, and even sabotaging political negotiations. She has survived every obstacle I've thrown at her." He stared at the wax dripping down the candle in front of him. "Worst of all, she is aware of these increased attempts on her life. I must kill her today lest she traces them back to me."

The Priestess circled and knelt in front of Mivaan. She cupped her hands around his cheeks. The skin on her heart-shaped face was ghostly pale, with a pert, upturned nose, voluminous violet lips and wide cheekbones. Long, fiery-red locks adorned her crown and spilled messily down the sides of her face and back. Wide, almond-shaped eyes tinted amber stared back at him with adoration. "You must not give up, my Emperor," she said to him. "Lord Ahmbra is guiding you on the path he has created for you. Follow it, and you will find your solution."

Mivaan opened his mouth to protest but stopped short. Honing his senses, he could hear the tell-tale jangling of his sister's treasured anklets as she climbed the steps leading to his chambers. His heart pounded in his chest, the blood pooling furiously into his veins. "Quickly!" he hissed, the muscles on his legs protesting as he stood from his meditative stance. Moving to the bookshelf on the left wall of his chambers, he pulled on the second-to-last book in the middle row. A latch clicked, and he pulled on the shelf, revealing a hidden passage. "Go! I will see you at the temple later this morning!"

Mivaan then turned back to the candles. Along with heightened senses and improved cognitive function, his Gift granted him precise control of his body and allowed him to extinguish all twelve flames in the blink of an eye. He shut the secret passage, then wiped off the sweat from his body using a towel he grabbed off the floor. Tossing it aside, Mivaan leapt into his bed and dove under the silken covers just as the portal to his chambers opened.

"Good morning, Mivaan!" Pawan, his younger sister and heir-apparent, exclaimed jovially. With his head under the covers, the prince could hear his sister crossing the room. The jarring tinkling of her anklets caused him to grit his teeth. He listened to the sounds of a curtain drawn open. "Rise and shine, bhaiya!" Pawan called, pulling the bedcovers off of him.

Bright, searing sunlight pierced Mivaan's enhanced eyes, and he grabbed a pillow to shield himself. Groaning loudly, he pushed himself to a seated position. "Pawan, could you not wait until later this morning to wake me?" he asked as he blinked away his discomfort.

"Sorry big brother," Pawan said, grinning. "I can't help it. It's coronation day!"

Mivaan said nothing as his sister finally came into focus. Despite her twenty-two years of age, Pawan was statuesque and stood a full head higher than him. Her muscular, chestnut-skinned frame was partially covered by an ornate sky-blue wrap embroidered with golden thread. The wrap started around the right side of her chest, crossing over her waist with the end draping over her left leg. Underneath the wrap, she wore a white, sleeveless top exposing her toned midriff and a pair of tight-fitting pants ending just above her calves. Thick, golden bracers adorned her forearms, each covering from her wrist to just below her elbow. She wore no shoes, preferring to feel the earth beneath her feet. Her golden anklets jangled as she paced the brightened, messy room. She carried a small book bearing the image of a golden woman with long, wavy hair cradling a green orb – the emblem of the Holy Preserver.

In contrast to her toned, warrior-like physique, Pawan had a delicate, oval face framed by wavy, auburn locks that trailed loosely down to the middle of her back. Upturned, earthen-brown eyes roved around the sizable chamber. The large gold ring pierced on her left nostril moved as she wrinkled her pointed nose. Mivaan could feel his sister's judgement radiate from her body as she tutted at the chaotic state of his room. Stopping finally at the ring of freshly outed candles, Pawan turned to her brother, her small lips twisting into a severe expression.

"Mivi, were you up just now?" she asked, using his pet name.

Snorting, Mivaan flipped out of his bed and moved smoothly to an armoire on the left side of his room. His actions only caused his sister's brows to furrow deeper.

"Bhaiya, why are you communing with Ahmbra's Will this early?" Pawan asked, folding her arms and tilting her head to the side. "Everything has been scheduled down to the second, thanks to your efforts. You don't need to strain yourself." She scoffed, her brows knitting together. "I even *commanded* you to take a break from all that constant thinking and planning you're doing and rest. You earned it."

"Pawan, you're to become Empress today," Mivaan answered tonelessly, opening the wardrobe. "I have to be sure that I've accounted for every possible outcome. Your coronation must go off without a hitch."

He fished out a hooded, white robe spun from cotton threads, a vest and loose trousers. Simple clothes were required to enter the Temple of Ahmbra, where he would seek the God of Creation's guidance for the day.

"You speak of the brazen attempts on my life?" he heard Pawan ask as he dressed. Affixing a simple leather belt around his robe, Mivaan turned to face his sister. She wore a gentle smile. "Try not to worry, brother. All of Vrandaska will be here. Only someone very determined or very crazy would attempt to kill me today." She moved towards Mivaan and mussed his hair playfully. "Besides, they would face my magic before my guards."

Mivaan swatted at her hand. "I'm off to the temple," he said, feeling a slight pang of guilt as he pulled away from his sister. He hadn't wanted to kill her, but the throne meant more to him than she did. "I'll visit Father once I've returned." He paused at the door and then glanced back at Pawan. "Is he getting better?" he asked, feigning concern.

Pawan closed her eyes and exhaled softly through her nose. Her forehead wrinkled. "No," she said. "The Healers can't seem to find the reason why he's wasting away."

"I've been assisting them with the research," Mivaan said, looking sympathetically at Pawan. "I feel that we are close to finding the issue. I'm sure we will find a cure for him soon." Despite his frown, Mivaan smiled inwardly. From his extensive studies, he knew of a few toxic substances that could only be traced by the most learned of Healers. By mixing small quantities of those compounds, Mivaan could make anyone sick for years. Today, though, he would need something more powerful.

That thought caused the neurons in his brain to fire rapidly as he remembered a plan he had formed months ago. A desperate gambit to be executed when subtlety all but failed him. With this in mind, he needed to go to the temple now more than ever.

"What would I do without you, Mivi?" Pawan said, breaking his train of thought. She had turned away from him and looked out of the window. The sounds of nature and the people beginning their day intermingled into a harmonious and pleasant cacophony. "Honestly, with your brains and my magic, we can achieve long-lasting peace for the empire," she said, breathing in the fresh air. She then opened her book, fished out a writing instrument from within the cover and started writing in it. "Our people can freely create joyous memories for the Holy Preserver to use on the Cradle. Isn't that wonderful?"

"Indeed," Mivaan answered, his jaw tightening at the sight of his sister's Memory Keeper. He bristled whenever she spoke about her recent conversion to the religion. Adjusting the belt around his robe, Mivaan opened the door. "Now, I must be going. And you have a coronation to get ready for." He stepped through the portal, but paused and glanced back at her. "May I see you... before the ceremony? At our special place?"

"Of course," Pawan said with a laugh, closing her book. "I was just going to ask you that as well." Her anklets chimed as she followed her brother out of his room. They trekked down the stairs to the eastern royal apartments, passed through the main foyer and arrived at the royal courtyard. Pawan stopped at the main gate and hugged her brother. "May the memories of old be preserved, bhaiya," she said, invoking the traditional farewell uttered by followers of the Sect of Preservation.

Stepping back and waving farewell, the Empress-to-be turned and ran back to the palace. Mivaan watched impassively as she channelled her Gift. Granted by the Goddess of Liberation, Vah-Si, a fair number of women in Vrandaska were blessed with the power to shape the Atma around them into whatever form they imagined, based on the element they were born under. In Pawan's case, she could manipulate the very earth around her. Angular, golden lines appeared on her tanned skin as columns of earth formed beneath her feet. The pillars gradually formed taller as she stepped towards the palace. They lifted her until she was level with the second-floor window leading to her chambers on the west side of the palace. As she climbed through the window, the columns disintegrated into loose dirt and piled into a heap below.

Mivaan snorted as a group of servants hurried out to the courtyard and cleaned up the dirt piles. While he had to meditate in order to channel Atma into his body, Pawan's Gift allowed her to instinctively draw the mystical energy from around her. She needed neither chants, nor bodily movements to control her element. All that was required was her mind and the boundless creativity locked within. The prince growled, contempt for his sister filling his thoughts. "Show off," he muttered to himself as he threw the hood over his head and left the palace.

***

The Palace of Vrandaska sat on an island at the centre of a lake within a massive crater. When the Twin Gods – Ahmbra and Vah-Si – clashed a millennia ago, their conflict shattered and hollowed out the land around it. The seismic upheaval of that impact formed a channel starting at a nearby lake, which widened into a river that spilled over the side and pooled at the crater's centre. Over time, life teemed within the caldera, transforming it from a barren landscape into a lush and verdant forest.

Mivaan's ancestors stumbled upon this natural fortress and settled into the crater's interior. They built the city of Vrandaska around the crater lake's island, which became the seat of their power and starting point of the growing Vrandaska Empire. Twelve equidistant bridges connected the palace to the mainland city. It was the northernmost that the prince travelled across to head into the district where the Temple of Ahmbra lay.

Mivaan threaded his way through the sea of people heading to the palace to witness the coronation that would begin later that day. With his simple garb, and face concealed by the white hood, he passed as a servant heading away from the palace. While his enhanced senses guided him around the crowds, the prince allowed himself to reflect on the past year leading to the coronation. A ritual he performed every morning since that fateful day.

When his father, the fourth Emperor of Vrandaska, had named Pawan his successor instead of him, it shocked the whole empire. But despite her age, she spoke with eminence and poise and was well-loved by the people as she projected an air of stability and security.

Mivaan remembered approaching his father the very night he made the announcement. He demanded for him to reconsider and name him successor as intended. "The first born of each emperor has taken over as per tradition," he had argued. "Why change it now?"

Despite his efforts, his father had only said, "Beta, you have been instrumental to many of our victories. But like the fires you channel as an Agnipath, you are also volatile, reckless and careless. You rely too much on your Gift. You lack the discipline needed to maintain the Empire. Pawan has proven that she is the right person to lead. While you command with an iron fist, she leads with a gentle hand. While you speak with forceful aggression, she speaks with calm authority. Her strength and perseverance are what our people need to feel safe and secure. Your job now is to support her in any way possible."

The conversation ended there, but Mivaan's despondency did not. He, more than anyone, deserved to be Emperor. It was **his** plans that expanded the empire. It was **his** strategies that brought them victory. All Pawan did was execute them. Using his brilliant mind, he could provide the same peace and stability that his sister could. *No*, he assured himself. *I could do it better than her.*

Through his anguish, he soon met the one who would be instrumental to his plans – the Priestess. She appeared in his chambers that night unexpectedly, her tantalizingly near-nude figure illuminated in the pale moonlight. Proclaiming that she was sent from Ahmbra himself, the Priestess offered to help him become Emperor in exchange for his undying devotion. Days after their conversation, the current Emperor fell ill with a sickness the Healers could not identify. As their mother had died long ago when his sister was born, the job of ruling the empire fell on his and Pawan's shoulders.

For a year, Mivaan pushed his abilities as an Agnipath to their limits, scheming in ways to eliminate Pawan so that his father would have no choice but to name him Emperor. Despite the aid of the Priestess and his genius, all of them failed. Hesitation. Distractions. Guilt. Fear. Those feelings had stopped him in the past.

Each morning he remembered the events of what spurred him on. On some days, the memories caused him to feel shame for his actions. On others, righteous fury boiled inside him, as he felt his Path to God had been denied. But on this day, he felt nothing but fiery determination well up inside his chest. Today was his last chance. He only hoped that his contingency plan would bear fruit and that he would have the courage to act.

Mivaan soon approached the temple, located near the city's outer edge. It was a small single-story building crafted of marble and sandstone. Its facade was simple, consisting of a pair of windows, a sturdy oaken door and a circular emblem carved into the stone above it. Two perpendicular lines divided the circle into quarters. In the centre of each quarter was a coloured gem, each representing one of the four Elements.

Mivaan crossed the threshold and entered the temple. He passed through the foyer, removed his shoes and then entered the prayer hall. It was a dimly lit space, the only source of light coming from the mid-morning sun that shone through the windows at the front. The hall was empty, save for an older man with a long, white beard and a woman who covered her body, face and head with a wrap and headscarf.

Mivaan stepped upon a raised, polished stone platform and moved to one of the many rows of thin prayer mats. At the back was a wall with two doors leading further inside the temple. Mounted on the wall was a mural depicting Ahmbra, the God of Creation. The depiction of God sat cross-legged on a lotus leaf floating atop a body of water. No clothes adorned his body, his bluish skin and taut muscles exposed. He clasped his hands in prayer, his eyes closed and shorn head bowed in meditation. Hundreds of smaller arms erupted from his back, arranged in a circle behind him.

Settling down on a mat near the mural with his hood still obscuring his features, Mivaan bowed, his head touching the mat. "Oh, Lord," he murmured. "I bow in reverence to you. With your many hands, you created our world and shaped our destinies. We tread the Path you formed for us. We overcome the obstacles you present out of love, to prove that we are worthy to uncover the secrets of the universe, the secrets of Creation itself—"

He paused, sensing the change in the air as a gnarled hand rested on his shoulder. Mivaan rose and looked up at the face of the kindly old priest who resided in the temple. Wearing the same pure white robe Mivaan did, the priest wore a wrinkled smile on his beige-coloured face. "My son," he said, his voice sounding like crunching gravel. "Are you well? You seem to be troubled."

He was not, but Mivaan recognized the coded message. "Yes," he responded, modulating his voice to sound like a commoner. "I fear that I've strayed from the Path."

The priest smiled and extended his hand. "Then come," he said. "Let us go commune with God and set you back on your way."

Mivaan stood up and followed the priest through the door to the left of the mural leading to the back of the temple. They entered a small room illuminated with candles. A low, square table lay at the room's centre and was surrounded by plush pillows. The priest shut the door behind them. "It is unusual to see you here at this time, your Highness," he spoke in hushed tones. "I expected you to appear after the coronation ceremony. Do they not need you back at the palace?"

"No," Mivaan said, pulling off the hood and dropping the fake commoner accent as he sat by the table. "The coronation preparations are keeping everyone busy, leaving me free to go about my business. I made sure of that."

"Good, good," the old man said, taking a seat across from him. "And... your progress?"

"Stalled," the prince replied, his scowl deepening. Placing his elbows on the table, the prince steepled his fingers together and narrowed his eyes. "But a thought came to me this morning, as I spoke with my sister. Do you still have those items I requested half a year ago?"

"I do," the priest replied slowly, bones creaking as he stood up. He opened the door behind him. "Wait here."

Mivaan felt his pulse quicken as the priest tottered off. But as soon as the door had shut, the sensation of his throbbing pulse began to dampen, along with his other senses. He swore under his breath. *It has worn off sooner than before.* Mivaan scowled as his thoughts slowed to a crawl. *Only a fortnight ago, my power would have remained for at least four hours before I needed to renew it.* He contorted into a meditative position, inhaled and began drawing in more Atma through the candlelights in the room.

A pair of slender arms encircled him from behind as he finished his mantras and his senses reawakened. Mivaan's lips split into a smile. "You're here," he whispered, twisting to face the Priestess. His eyes roved around her curvy and nubile body. A flimsy, white wrap that barely covered her ample breasts and wide hips draped over her – the same thing she wore on the night they met. Her eyes shone brightly in contrast to the dim lighting in the room.

"I've been waiting here this entire time, my Emperor," she purred, licking her plump lips. "Did you not notice?"

The prince stared at her, bewildered by her comment. "No, my love," he said, his eyebrows raised. "I did not see you."

"No matter," she said, giggling as she caressed his cheek. She then sat down on him, her legs wrapped around his waist and lips nearly touching his. Mivaan could feel her hot breath against his skin. His loins tightened in response. He wanted to take her, right then and there, in the house of his God.

"The priest has what we need," the Priestess continued through ragged breaths as she ground her hips against his. "So, how will we kill your father? How will we kill her?"

He opened his mouth to answer but was interrupted by a knock on the door. "Y-your Highness?" the priest said haltingly. "May I enter?"

The prince growled, casting a seething thought at the meddling holy man. *Another time, then.* "Meet me at the palace," he whispered to his lover as she extricated herself from his lap. "I will need your help for what's to come." He turned to face the door, waited for the Priestess to hide and then answered. "Enter."

The priest re-entered with two small wooden chests in his arms. He set them down on the table. "Were you... communing with God, Your Highness?" he asked, casting a wary eye at the prince.

"What I do alone is my business," Mivaan responded smoothly. "You know this, old man." He inclined his head towards the chests. "Open them."

With trembling hands, the priest opened the boxes. "I've been concerned for you since the day you came to this temple after your mother died," he said as he lifted the lids. "I've done my best to help guide you on the Path that Ambrah created. But, it was only when Pawan was named your father's successor that you finally opened up to me after all these years." The chests opened, he unfolded the cloth wrappings that covered their contents. "At the time, she had also publicly converted to the Sect of Preservation. Because of the adoration she garnered from the people, they followed suit. Including the vast number at our church. Barely anyone remains now." He exhaled deeply through his nose. "I was surprised at your initial request, but then I realized: God must have brought us together from the start to usher the people back onto the right Path."

Mivaan ignored the man's ramblings and leaned forward to inspect the contents. The left chest held a large tin. Removing the container,

Mivaan opened it to reveal tea leaves. Though dried, the prince recognized the reddish hue on the leaves. "This is—"

"Dinrabane, yes," the priest finished, placing his clasped hands on the table. "I've been assured that its long storage does not affect its potency."

The prince smiled as he replaced the cover and set the tin on the table. He turned to the second opened chest. Inside was an object wrapped in thick burlap. Peeling the fabric off carefully, the prince beheld a wooden dagger with a dozen jagged pieces of lucid crystal inserted into the blade. Mivaan's smile grew into a wicked grin. "Voidshard," he uttered softly.

"You should know that both of these came at great personal and financial cost, Your Highness," the priest said, his arms folded and eyes narrowed. "The church's survival now rests on you ascending the throne." He then huffed loudly and turned to avoid the prince's eye. "If you wanted my honest opinion though, we could have enlisted one of the Seers of Nuer to help instead."

"It is not worth it," Mivaan countered through gritted teeth. "Though we can afford to pay them the gold, I refuse to pay their seed fee. I cannot risk having illegitimate heirs roaming around the city unabated while I am Emperor. Seer or not." He ran a finger against the cool and smooth surface of one of the Voidshards embedded in the dagger. He dared not touch the sharpest part of the crystal. "I deal with absolutes, priest," he continued with an edge of venom. "I will not depend on sightless and fickle waifs who claim to see the future to guide me on my Path."

They sat in silence for a brief moment, before the prince spoke again. "Still, your loyalty to me and your efforts to keep these items safe will not go unrewarded," he said, placing the dagger back into the chest.

"With you as my High Minister, we will re-establish the Path as the one true religion of the Empire."

The priest flashed his yellowed teeth as he wrapped the dagger in the burlap. "Indeed, we will bring the Glory of Ahmbra to all the citizens of the Empire," he said, handing the prince the two items.

Seeing that their business had concluded, Mivaan pocketed the items, stood and made his way out of the room. The priest placed his hand on the prince's shoulder as he approached the door. "May Ahmbra guide you on your Path, my son," he said, his wrinkled lips pressed tightly in a thin line.

***

As the crowds leading to the palace thickened, Mivaan opted to journey to one of the docks lining the crater lake. He slipped a few gold coins to a boatman he was familiar with and boarded a small craft. He did not ask if the Priestess had rented a boat as well – the two had an unspoken agreement to not mention anything aside from business. Ferrying it out of the dock, Mivaan angled the vessel around the other watercraft parked in the lake for the coronation and paddled towards the island where the palace lay. What he lacked in strength, he made up for through the efficiency granted by his Gift. Within a quarter of an hour, the prince reached the northern shore.

Dragging the boat to a spot where the boatman could retrieve it at a later time, Mivaan walked west along the shoreline until he spotted a hole within the cliffside, right next to a narrow path leading up to the northern bridge. He squeezed into it and emerged into a passage within the bowels of the palace. Ten minutes of ascending stairways later, the prince emerged in his chambers through the secret door concealed behind his bookshelf.

He was not surprised to see the Priestess lounging on his rumpled bed. He knew that she would be there before him. He stripped from his prayer clothes and extracted the tin of Dinrabane and the Voidshard dagger from his pockets. As he did so, he took a sidelong glance at the soft and exposed curves of the Priestess' body. At any other time, he would have gladly jumped into the bed and sunk into her warm flesh. But today, he needed to focus on what he was about to do.

"My love," he said to her as he strode towards the wardrobe and began dressing in a resplendent crimson kurta adorned with patterns of small white crystals and a black hem lined with gold embroidering. "There is a knife on a bookshelf, next to a rock my sister gave me as a child. Take it and wait for me in the small garden in the west wing of the palace – the place the two of us would go as children." He slipped on a pair of jewel-encrusted sandals as he spoke, not once glancing back at the woman on his bed. "Once I've struck her with the Voidshard, I will signal you. You must come in and slit her wrist while I have her restrained."

"Your wish is my command, my Emperor," he heard her say.

Satisfied, Mivaan tied up his hair and straightened his goatee. He collected the tin of tea leaves, a bag of gold and then stashed the wooden dagger in the left pocket of his suit, taking care not to nick himself with the shards. "I'm off. Be sure to stay out of sight as you get to the garden," he instructed, opening the door. Without a backward glance at the Priestess, Mivaan left his room.

Mivaan returned to the now-bustling main hall and took the central stairway to the throne room. He cut to a door on his left and walked down the corridor. A set of carved and polished wood doors lay at the end, guarded by a lone sentry.

"I'm here to see Father," he told the guard stationed by the doors. The prince slipped the bag of gold into the soldier's hands. "Make sure no one – not even the Healers – disturbs us."

Snapping to attention, the guard opened the door to let Mivaan through. Shutting it behind him, the prince beheld the Emperor's private room. At double the size of his own, it was the largest in the palace. Stacks of bookshelves lined half of the room's right wall. A long table piled high with maps, charts, ledgers and other bureaucratic documents sat near the middle of the room. The left wall held closets containing the emperor's vast wardrobe. Sunlight, partially obscured by the crater's lip, shone through three floor-to-ceiling windows on the opposite side of the room.

The Fourth Emperor of Vrandaska lay in his bed, on the far right side of the room close to the windows. A Paanipath – known formally as a Healer and recognizable by his white mask and billowing white robes – was attending to his father. His glowing palms, caused by channeling Atma through water, hovered over his body. This Healer, Mivaan noted, was trying once more to identify and extract the toxins that were poisoning the ruler.

A fool's errand, the prince thought as he strode up to his father's bed. "Leave us," Mivaan instructed loudly, startling the Healer and breaking his concentration. He moved to admonish the intruder, but wilted at the sight of the glowering prince. Without a word, the Healer bowed and made his way out of the chamber.

"Who is there?" Mivaan heard his father croak out.

The prince turned to face him. The older man's pallid state belied his forty-five years of age. His waxy skin stretched over his near-skeletal face. Wisps of white hair streamed down from his balding crown. Though he was covered, Mivaan could still make out the thin and ravaged body of what was once a powerful and mountainous man.

"It is I, Father," Mivaan answered in a low voice. He then pulled out the tin filled with Dinrabane and turned to the cart that was next to his father's bed. It held instruments for the Healer, including a small burner that could be used to brew tea. Taking one of the Healer's flasks, Mivaan poured some water and began boiling it.

The emperor took ragged, wheezing breaths as he stared back at his eldest child through sunken eyes. His chapped lips broke into a smile. "Ah, my son," he rasped. "It is Pawan's coronation today."

The prince grunted, engrossed in his work. Time was not on his side. He could feel his Gift begin to wane. *I could replenish it using the burner—*

"I am proud of both of you," the Emperor continued, forcing himself into a sitting position. "Especially of you, Mivaan."

Mivaan abruptly turned to face his father, his jaw hanging slack upon hearing his statement.

"When I fell ill," the Emperor continued weakly. "You and Pawan took the task of ruling upon yourselves. Since then, I have watched you. And you have proven me wrong." He was interrupted by a coughing fit and continued once he settled down. "You are still hot-headed, but you have served the people well. Pawan leads with her heart and you complement that with your rational mind." Tears began welling in the older man's eyes. "It is as though you both share the same soul, despite walking different Paths."

"Does that mean..." Mivaan trailed off, the blood loudly thrumming in his veins. Hope had filled his heart. *I could still be Emperor without shedding any blood!*

"No," the Emperor replied after a pause, looking out the window and avoiding his son's eyes. "Pawan will still become Empress. It is too late... to change things. However—"

The hope Mivaan held had shattered and was replaced with white-hot rage. It drowned out the rest of his father's words as he dumped the entirety of the Dinrabane into the now-boiling water. The dried leaves soon steeped into the liquid, giving it a dark, reddish hue.

"Mivaan, what are you making?" his father spoke out loudly, breaking into a coughing fit from the strain.

"My apologies, Father," the prince responded tonelessly, doing his best to mask the venom in his voice. "My research into various antidotes led me to a special blend of herbal tea. It is a rare variety, since it is composed of a few plants outside of the crater." Mivaan took the flask and poured the liquid into a cup. "It took some time, but I managed to get a tin. One sip of this should begin flushing out the toxins. With a little luck, you may be able to catch the ending of the coronation ceremony."

The Emperor let out a low, raspy chuckle. "Your determination is admirable, Mivaan," he said, keeping his hands in his lap as Mivaan offered the cup. "But, you must be mistaken if you expect me to drink the contents of that cup."

Mivaan's brows rose sharply. He felt the hairs on his neck stand up. "W-what do you mean, Father?" he asked, the hand not holding the cup trembling at his side.

"That 'tea' is made with Dinrabane and a sip of that means death," the Emperor replied, calmly. His tired eyes looked directly into his son's with a fury unseen for a year. "I understand you were disappointed in my decision, but your actions now prove that I was right in choosing Pawan over you. You would be so craven to stoop to mur-GACK!"

"*Yes,*" Mivaan hissed, grabbing his father's throat with his free hand and squeezing it, cutting him off mid-sentence. He could feel the older man's fingers claw feebly on his own in an effort to pry them off. "Ahmbra set me on the Path to become Emperor. Killing you is but a means to fulfill his Will."

Mivaan then moved his hand from his father's throat to his nose, squeezing it tightly and cutting off his air supply. Next, he drew the cup of the poisoned drink close to the Emperor's lips. "The moment your mouth opens, I pour," he whispered, leaning in close to his father's ear and pinning him down to the bed as he struggled. "A long, drawn out suffocation, or a quick death. Which will you choose?"

The decision was made quickly as the Emperor involuntarily opened his mouth, sucking in air. Without hesitation, Mivaan tipped the cup, the liquid poison spilling messily in. He backed away, watching as his father stuck his fingers down his throat to vomit the liquid out. But the damage was done. Within minutes, the Emperor lay back in his bed, his body convulsing and foam forming out of the corners of his mouth.

Mivaan stood by and watched impassively as his father died before his eyes. Half a year ago, he would have been horrified at himself for this. Today, he felt nothing for the man who robbed him of his birthright. "Pa... Wa... Kn—" was the last thing Mivaan heard before the Emperor let out a death rattle.

One down, the prince thought, turning away from the dead body and raising his hand to the still-lit burner. He quickly chanted, but only felt a fraction of his Gift being restored. *Not enough flame,* he mused, gritting his teeth as he shut the burner off. *This will have to do. It should be enough for the next phase.*

Storming out of the Emperor's chambers and passing by the guard he paid off, Mivaan returned to the main hall. He cut through a passageway on the ground floor that led northwards to the inner gardens. Treading east on a well-worn path, Mivaan soon found himself at the edge of a small clearing near the southernmost wall enclosing the gardens. A large tree holding a rope swing sat near the centre of the clearing.

Pawan sat on the swing, staring at the ground with a grim expression on her face. She wore a ceremonial battle dress consisting of a thin, halter-style breastplate with flexible bronze chainmail covering her abdomen. A bespoke skirt flowing down to her knees and covered with crimson-painted plates adorned her waist. Her Memory Keeper lay in a holder on her left hip. She wore her gold bracers and her feet were bare, save for her signature anklets.

Pawan's auburn hair was styled in an elaborate, looping updo with a space atop her head where the crown would rest. Her dark eyes and the contours of her cheeks and jawline were accentuated with light makeup. She angled her head towards her brother, who entered the glen. "So, you've come," she said, her eyes turning steely.

Mivaan scoffed, a sardonic smile crossing his lips. "Well, of course I came, sister," he said, strolling up to the tree. "I asked you to come—"

"As did I," Pawan cut in, standing and folding her arms. Her imposing figure towered over Mivaan, who stopped in his tracks. "Because I know."

"Know what?" Mivaan asked haltingly, biting the inside of his cheek.

"I know that you're behind all the attempts on my life," she said, her brows furrowing into a scowl. "I have known for months."

Sweat started pooling down Mivaan's back. "Then why haven't you said anything?" he pressed.

"Because," she continued, looking away from his eyes. "I had hoped after your failures that you would give up and that you would accept

Father's decision." Pawan looked back at her brother, her glare intensifying. "But I was wrong. I saw proof of that this morning, when you communed with Ahmbra instead of resting like I told you to!" Golden lines bloomed on her skin and Mivaan could feel the earth move beneath his feet.

"You haven't been using your Gift for the good of the Empire, you've been using it for yourself!" she shouted, the tattooed lines on her body flashing brightly.

His enhanced senses were Mivaan's only saving grace as he quickly moved to the side. An earthen cage erupted at the spot he stood on. He kept moving, feeling the Voidshard dagger against his thigh as he let the vibrations of the earth guide him. *Not yet. I have to get closer...*

"You barely eat, you barely sleep and you're always angry," she continued, her radiant skin glowing as she attempted to ensnare Mivaan in a cage. "You're selfish, immature, controlling and manipulative! I even hear you talking to someone in your room. No one has seen this person come in or out of the palace!" Closing her eyes, she inhaled deeply through her nose and exhaled from her mouth. The golden lines covering her body pulsed brightly.

Without warning, the prince tripped on an upturned block of stone Pawan conjured up right beneath his feet. He stumbled and landed in a heap in front of his sister.

"You will tell me who this person is and you will cease your attempts at my life," she demanded, her upper lip curling into a snarl. "You'll be confined to the dungeons. Father and I will figure out what to do with you after I am crowned Empress. Be thankful for the mercy I've given you."

Now! Digging into his pocket, Mivaan fished out the Voidshard dagger from his pocket and slashed at Pawan. The crystalline edge tore a gash in her shin.

The warrior princess cried out in pain and stumbled back into a kneeling position. She glared hatefully at Mivaan. "You've made your choice, then," she heaved through gritted teeth as she summoned every ounce of power within her to strike.

Instead, the lines on her body faded, as though they were snuffed. Nothing happened.

"What?" Pawan spluttered as she tried to make the earth move around her. "What have you done?!"

"I've evened the playing field," Mivaan answered, cackling. "Anyone cut by Voidshard has their Gift nullified, albeit only temporarily." He stood up, his lips spread into a wide grin. "It will be long enough that I can kill you and reclaim my birthright."

Quick as a flash, Mivaan took advantage of her shock and pounced on his sister, pinning her down and knocking the wind out of her. The prince grasped her wrists. "Now, Priestess! Come out and heed the first command of your new Emperor!" he called.

His summon was met with silence.

Pawan soon recovered and pushed her brother off of her. She rolled away, creating some space and shakily got to her feet. "Priestess? Who in the Preserver's name is that!?" she spluttered.

Mivaan roared, tightening his fist so hard that he drew blood from his palms. His eyes bulged as he looked at his sister. "You were supposed to die from suicide once you discovered that Father was dead," he hissed through gritted teeth. Exhaling loudly, he hefted the Voidshard dagger in a reverse grip. "This dagger is designed for ripping and stabbing, not cutting. I was hoping to avoid a mess, but it seems my hand has been forced."

"Gift or no, I can still thrash you senseless!" Pawan yelled, charging at him despite the injury to her leg. "You'll pay for what you've done to Father!"

"He deserved it," Mivaan spoke conversationally, his heightened reflexes allowing him to dodge the incoming tackle with ease. With her back exposed, he raised the dagger and plunged it right between Pawan's shoulder blades. She stumbled and fell face first into the grass. "He stole away my birthright, as did you. I'm now taking it back." He kneeled down to face Pawan, who's life force dribbled from her mouth, her eyes angry and defiant even in death.

"Rest easy, dear sister," Mivaan continued, yanking the Voidshard dagger out from her body and watching the life fade from her eyes. "Vrandaska will be in good hands. Ahmbra will once again guide our people on the right Path. I will see to it."

"Congratulations, my love." Mivaan stood and looked to his right to see the Priestess saunter up to him. Her plush lips stretched into a wide smile. "You are now Emperor."

"Where were you?" he demanded, his face scrunched into a scowl. "You were supposed to be waiting here. You were supposed to slit her wrists!"

"It matters not," she said, shimmying her shoulders seductively and causing the thin wrap to slide off her body. She then opened her arms and embraced him lovingly. "Come, let's make love next to your sister. With her last breath, she can watch the new Emperor mount his treasured Empress."

"Yes," Mivaan said after a pause. He still held the blood-soaked Voidshard dagger in his hand. "However, you've neglected a small detail."

"And what is that?"

"I never said that you'd be Empress."

Mivaan raised his hand and brought the dagger into the Priestess' back. But instead of feeling the contact of the blade against her flesh, he felt a blinding, searing pain in his chest. He looked down and saw the crystal-embedded dagger stabbed deeply into his sternum. The Voidshard drained the Atma he had stored inside of him, leaving him devoid of feeling. The world around him slowed to a crawl as he dropped to his knees.

Mivaan looked up at where the Priestess was. The image of her flawless, near-translucent face, her flaming red hair and her perfect, nude body vanished into the ether as the Voidshard absorbed the last of the Atma in his mind.

With his Gift gone and death slowly approaching, he made a startling realization. All the times she was with him. Scheming with him. Making love to him. She wasn't real.

She never existed.

What have I done? Mivaan thought regretfully as he lay dying next to his sister.

V: THE HIEROPHANT

Mr. Hierophant by David M. Simon

Lily and Joshua stood in the shadowed third-floor hallway of a nondescript brownstone in Hell's Kitchen. The floor beneath their feet was linoleum, worn in spots to the cement beneath. The wooden door they faced was scratched and shabby, with a frosted glass window set in the top half. Centered on the glass, in chipped gold copperplate letters, were the words:

MR. HIEROPHANT, ESQ.

OCCULT & ARCANE

GOODS AND ENLIGHTENMENT

Joshua raised his fist to knock on the door, but Lily stopped him with a gentle hand on his arm. "Are you sure about this?" she asked.

He knew without even looking at her face that she was biting her lip in worry. It was just one of the many little things he loved about her. "I'm not sure, but I don't have any better ideas," he said. "I heard about this dude from those pagans in robes who hang out on the High Line by the Hudson Yards elevator. They say he's the real deal. He knows things. Maybe he can help us."

"Okay, I trust you. Let's do this." Lily smiled at him, nodded her head and knocked on the door firmly, with more confidence than she felt.

They waited anxiously, and Lily was about to knock again when they heard a muffled, "Yeah, yeah, come in."

Based on the building, with the three dingy, narrow flights of stairs they had climbed, and the hallway itself, they were expecting an equally nondescript office: Mr. Hierophant seated behind a cheap wooden desk, flanked by metal filing cabinets.

Instead they found him sitting on a throne in the center of the room, flanked by ornamental plaster columns, the kind favored by wedding planners. Mr. Hierophant wore a threadbare red bathrobe, cargo shorts, and an FDNY ball cap. His long grey hair was pulled back in a careless ponytail. He slouched on the throne like Captain Kirk on the bridge of the Enterprise, leaning on a hockey stick he held in his left hand.

Surrounding the throne and columns were a roomful of book-shelves, cabinets, and display cases, each of them overflowing. The bookshelves were crammed with a jumble of leather-bound volumes, folios, stacks of folders, and rolled-up scrolls wrapped in linen. An avalanche of loose papers spilled onto the floor. Stacked and layered on every flat surface was a jumble of curious items – jars and bottles filled with mysterious morsels floating in cloudy fluid, luminescent crystal orbs, strange artifacts and amulets, wickedly formidable ancient weapons, and apothecary cabinets with hundreds of tiny drawers. Star charts and rune-covered parchments covered the walls and papered over the windows. And everywhere, candles of every shape and size.

"Go ahead, take it all in. I know it's a lot. Sometimes the brujas in the Spanish Harlem botanicas send me their Upper East Side ladies who lunch for further counsel, and they love all the theatrics." Mr. Hierophant had an accent totally at odds with the room, a braying honk straight from the mean streets of Flatbush.

"Joshua, I don't think he can help us. Let's just go," Lily said.

Mr. Hierophant waved his hands, the hockey stick bouncing up and down. "Hey, hey, hey, not so fast! Look, I know my office looks like a Spirit Halloween store, but that's just the sugar that makes the medicine go down, if you follow. I know my shit. So how can I help you kids? You're holding hands, so I'm guessing you don't need a love potion. Any assholes at school you want to curse with a custom-built voodoo doll? Dead Bubbie you'd like to contact? Lay it on me."

Lily and Joshua whispered back and forth, finally coming to a decision. "We need advice, sir," Joshua said.

"Enlightenment, excellent, one of my specialties. Only twenty dollars, because I got a good feeling about you kids."

Lily pulled a crumpled bill from her pocket and handed it over. "Our parents don't know that we're together. If they did, they would never allow it. How can we fix this?"

Mr. Hierophant held the twenty out. "Here, take your money back. Young love is way out of my wheelhouse. Too... pedestrian."

Lily pushed his hand back. "You haven't heard the reason why our families don't approve of our relationship."

"Color me intrigued. Let's hear it."

Lily took a deep breath and shared a look with Joshua. "I'm a werewolf," she said.

"And I'm a vampire," Joshua said. "If you know as much as you say, you know that vampires and werewolves have been mortal enemies for hundreds, even thousands of years. My family would just as soon stake me as see me with a werewolf."

"And mine feels the same, except it would be a silver bullet. Can you help us?"

"Whoa, that's some deep shit." Mr. Hierophant removed his ball cap, scratched his head, and put the cap on backwards. "Let's see what the ancients have to say on the subject, if anything. To the bat cave!" He climbed off his throne, which turned out to be an old La-Z-Boy, and made his way to the bookshelves. He walked slowly back and forth, one finger tracing along the spines of the volumes. When he reached a tall stack of oversized folios, he paused, took several steps past, then returned. He rummaged through them, found what he was looking for halfway down, and pulled it out with a triumphant, "Hah!" The rest of the folios cascaded to the floor, but he didn't seem to notice.

Mr. Hierophant swept a collection of fetish dolls off the top of a cabinet and spread out the portfolio, flipping through the thin, brittle parchment pages. He lifted one sheet from the stack and spent long minutes studying the spidery handwriting that crowded the page. When he finished, he slipped the sheet back into the folio. He climbed onto his throne without saying a word, but he was grinning from ear to ear.

The two teenagers waited patiently for as long as they could, until Lily could no longer hold it in and asked, "Well? What did you find?"

"Yeah, sorry, I was trying to heighten the drama. Clearly, you're not in the mood. Okay. That folio is what's left from a grimoire published in the sixteenth century, written by Count Radu, a member of Romanian royalty who was also a sorcerer. He considered, as an academic exercise, a problem surprisingly similar to yours, and he postulated a solution. I think it could work, but I can't promise you that it will."

"We'll try anything at this point. Just tell us what to do," Joshua said.

"We love each other, so yeah, we'll try anything." Lily said.

"I just want to caution again that this may not work—"

"Tell us!" Lily said.

"Fine. Here it is... bite each other."

"What?" Lily and Joshua said in unison.

"Bite each other, at exactly the same time. If Count Radu was right, and I gotta tell you, based on my own knowledge I'm giving it a fifty-fifty chance, the two of you will become something the world has never seen – vampire-werewolf hybrids. If you're successful, I can't imagine your families will be able to deny your relationship. If you're not successful, then hey, you gave it a shot."

"That's fucking crazy," Joshua said. He turned to face Lily, took her hands in his. "Let's try it."

"I am a little hungry," Lily said, and laughed. "I bet you taste good."

"Great," said Mr. Hierophant. "Like some poet, or maybe it was Selena Gomez, said, the heart wants what it wants. Now get out of here; I have a bearded dragon at home that gets grouchy if he doesn't get his snuggles. And let me know how it goes, kids. I'm rooting for you." Mr. Hierophant waved to them as they went out the door hand in hand.

***

Mr. Hierophant was reading an ancient text on transfiguration when someone knocked on his office door. "Yeah, yeah, come in," he said.

Lily and Joshua entered slowly, as if they didn't really want to be there. Mr. Hierophant sighed when he saw their solemn faces. "Ah, shit, it didn't work?"

"Oh, no, it worked perfectly," Joshua said.

"Then why the long faces? The two of you look like someone cut the horn off your pet unicorn."

"You were right about everything," Lily said. "We have all the abilities of both vampires and werewolves. It's an incredible feeling – the power is coursing through us like electricity. And our families, once they got used to the idea, accepted us being together."

"They didn't really have a choice. We're stronger than any of them now. My older brother is so pissed off," Joshua said.

"So lemme ask you again... why the long faces?"

Now it was Lily's turn to sigh. "Because we had to promise something to our families in return. And I get it, it makes total sense, but I'm sad about it, because you helped us, and besides, I like you."

"Wait – what?"

"No loose ends," Joshua said. "We had to promise them no loose ends."

Mr. Hierophant smiled, just a little. "And I'm your loose end. Should have seen that coming. Can I ask a favor?"

"Anything," Lily said.

"Can I die by werewolf, and not by vampire? No offense, but ever since I saw Ginger Snaps, I've thought that would be a cool way to go."

"You got it," Joshua said.

And Mr. Hierophant spent his last minutes on earth, in horror and giddy wonder, experiencing something he had read about for many years, but had never before seen.

VI: THE LOVERS

The Lives I Spend With You by Mara Lynn Johnstone

I don't remember our earliest lives together, you and I. We may have been finding each other like magnets since before magnets existed, before people did. All I know is that you used to be easier to find. When all the world was contained in a small part of the globe, and no one who looked like us existed anywhere else, then it was only a matter of time. Of course I could find you. It was a game.

But then, somewhere along the line, our people traveled. And spread. Built homes. Built villages, towns, cities... and spread further.

I began having lives when I didn't find you until I was old.

Or not at all.

I remember the first time I lay dying without ever having seen your eyes sparkle or heard your laugh. Never felt your touch. I'd been alone before, but not like this.

Where were you then? I never did find out.

The next time I met you, it was like old times; we had roaring adventures together, traveling farther and exploring more of the world side by side.

I knew that we were only helping to spread our population further. To make each other harder to find. But I brushed the thought away, packing it deep inside the goatskin bag in the back of my mind where my earliest thoughts live, from before goats and sheep were different creatures.

We spent that life well, seeing unfamiliar sights and new sunsets and old stars. It was grand. We even died in each other's arms of the same illness, grown white-haired and frail like we used to. Together.

Then in my next life, you were nowhere to be found. As soon as the memories in the back of my mind became conscious thought – at a reasonable age, this time around – I set out to find you. I wasn't about to die alone again.

I was a young woman from a small village, strong of limb and stout of heart, with skin the color of fresh-turned earth. My family wished me well in setting off to seek my fortune at a larger settlement. Opportunities would be better there. I would surely make them proud, and might find a husband who wasn't one of the dozen familiar faces I'd grown up with.

I didn't tell them that I was looking for a familiar soul instead. Previous lives had made it clear that there was little point in telling other people what you and I shared. It didn't matter. I would find you, whether or not anyone else knew.

The dull ember in my chest – the one that always glowed to life when we met – hadn't stirred yet. I walked to the big town and kept going, catching a ride on a merchant cart, weaving ropes and bracelets to sell as a means of paying my way.

I prodded at that ember from time to time, hoping for a spark, but felt nothing as the miles and years passed by. The traveling merchant taught me the ins and outs of the trade. Eventually I inherited the business, and made a fine life for myself with all the luxuries my cart could hold, yet always on the move. I visited my family a time or two. They were sad for me and my solitary lifestyle. I told them I was waiting for the right person, and no other would do. Then I showered them with gifts and left for the final time.

I took on apprentices as my joints grew stiff: a pair of orphans with quick fingers and paler skin than was common back home. They blossomed with regular food and words of approval. We traveled north. I didn't tell them why.

I tried not to despair as my hair grayed and my vision worsened. I wouldn't need sharp eyes to recognize you. I spent many days riding at the front of the cart with one youngster or the other holding the reins, silent as I listened and *searched* with all my heart.

It was only when the youngsters were a pair of fine adults in their own right that I felt a flicker of heat.

I gasped out loud, worrying them both, but explained nothing. I simply pointed to the road I wanted to take, and they obeyed. My hearing wasn't the best by then either, and my heartbeat nearly overshadowed what was left, but even so, I could make out the sounds of battle.

You were there. Among those shouts and sword blows. Alive and so, so, near.

The horses shied back when we passed through a clump of trees to find bloody chaos. My apprentices expressed dismay, wrenching the horses away from all the wildly swinging blades. I slid from the cart. My knees barely held up as I hit the muddy ground, but that didn't stop me, and neither did the worried cries I left behind.

The ember in my chest glowed with eager warmth as I stumbled across the field. You were there. Which one? Not either of the two yelling at me to get away, or that one raising a sword to me, only to be cut down from behind. I ducked past and moved as quickly as my aging limbs would let me.

There.

Gray hair, pale skin, and eyes of the most vivid blue I'd ever seen. A uniform with a fancy hat. An expression of wild, distracted joy.

I shouted the name you'd worn a century ago, and dashed forward just before a spear sprouted from your chest.

My scream was lost in the clamor. I charged, ignoring impacts of several kinds, finally sprawling in the mud two arm lengths away.

Our fingers nearly touched. "I'll find you," I whispered, meeting eyes that were already blank and empty.

You were gone. And moments later, so was I.

***

I was pampered royalty in my next life. Even with all the wealth and opportunity to travel to any corner of the empire, I couldn't find you. It may have driven me a little mad. I ignored the whispers about instability and unsuitability to inherit, and I called for every sorcerer and cut-rate diviner that could be bought or threatened.

They knew many secrets, and told more lies, but none could tell me what I wanted to hear. An unfortunate number of these charlatans met unpleasant ends when they displeased me. Only the honest ones were spared, especially if they could point me toward more promising magickers.

None of them were promising enough.

It became clear to me that none of the regular mortals had untangled the mystery of reincarnation, even the ones who thought they had. I would have to do it myself.

I dove into my studies, sending soldiers to ransack knowledge hoards in search of anything useful.

I had barely begun to unveil the mysteries of endless lives when the assassin hit. Absorbed in my books, I didn't hear his approach until blood spilled from my throat onto the valuable pages.

I turned to get a look at him as I fell.

He wasn't you.

***

After that was a long string of lonely lives, peppered with tantalizing glimpses of you from afar. Time ground by while humanity spread to every corner of the globe and delved into sciences that would have been unthinkable several lives ago.

Sometimes I cared. Sometimes I didn't.

Sometimes I buried my old memories so deep that they might not have surfaced even if you'd kissed me. Maybe you did. I'd never know.

Other times the desperation flowed hot to the surface, and I set off traveling by any means necessary. I didn't know if you were searching for me too. I hoped so.

Then one life, out of nowhere, I woke as a toddler to the realization that the child next door had been my friend for an uncountable number of years.

The air was full of summer joy. We played together on the lawn that both houses shared, while the adults spoke in words we hadn't learned yet. We used words that they never would. Our playacting held special significance, and every embrace made my chest glow like a bonfire.

Then your family moved away.

I wasn't old enough to ask where you'd gone. All I could do was cry and tear up the grass in my tiny fists, while the adults clucked sympathetically at my tantrum.

By the time I learned enough words for the conversation, you were long gone and the adults hadn't kept in touch.

That life, I'm sorry to say, was a short one. I won't burden you with the details. It wasn't your fault. All the blame lays on whatever forces of fate kept ripping us from each other's arms, and the growing number of families you could possibly be born into.

***

In my next life, I was a brilliant scientist who made strides in the field of contraceptives. It didn't help.

***

I started to wonder, as science advanced, whether the magic tying us together was fading. Other magics certainly seemed to have disappeared from the world, some to the point where I doubted whether they had ever been real in the first place.

But not this one. The truth of this was something I could never doubt.

Well, never in my well-balanced lives. There were times when my senses couldn't be trusted, or my memory. But even in my darkest confusion, I could fall back on that ageless certainty that you were out there somewhere, waiting for me. It was a comforting bedrock to anchor my sanity. Looking forward to holding you again had gotten me through many hard times in the past, and doubtless would again in the future.

All I had to do was imagine myself running fingers through your hair – springy and coiled, thin and silky, even cloudlike wisps of fading age – all versions were a joy. As were your smiles: I'd had so many to cherish. Cocky and cheerful and ready to lead me gladly astray, or calm and wise, or bashful and saved for only me. I loved all of them.

I couldn't wait to see which kind you favored next.

Bringing the advanced sciences into my search felt like a route worth taking. Humanity had made so many astounding breakthroughs, after all. Surely this one could follow suit.

But again I was stymied, this time by a lack of grant money and willing subjects. With thoughts of recreating some of the fortune I'd had in that one life, minus the assassination, I mingled and schmoozed and married rich: an heiress who left me for a movie star before my 'quaint little hobby' could get off the ground. I hadn't even persuaded any investors yet.

I tried several other money-making schemes, but gave up when I realized that the test subjects were more of a concern than the funding.

All I really had was me. The others were all double-blind placebos, hoping or deluding themselves that some recurring dream was significant. I couldn't learn anything from them.

And as far as science had come, it hadn't yet acknowledged that ember deep in my chest that told me when you were near.

Not yet. I could be patient.

I had to be.

***

It was during one of my scientific careers that I suffered a catastrophic injury when a prototype hover engine exploded. I woke to find you grinning at me from the next hospital bed.

I definitely tore something new in reaching for you, but it was worth the pain, and also the scolding by the nurses. You laughed over your own broken ribs while I was wheeled off for more surgery, promising to still be there when I returned.

And, in one moment of shining joy among darkness, you actually were.

We didn't have a language in common from this lifetime, but we didn't let that stop us. It had been too long for either of us to be interested in playing by mortal rules. We simply pretended that we had both studied Sumerian and met online, clamming up when concerned relatives visited who would have known we'd done no such thing.

It was such a simple deception, childish and full of mischievous smirks, that I could just imagine we were back in any number of childhoods, keeping secrets from the grownups again. As soon as they left, we spoke of Mesopotamia and Mars.

You died of your injuries before dawn. I woke the entire ward screaming curses in every language I knew.

***

For the next few lives, I fell back on traveling, aiming to visit every population center on the map. I let everyone else think I enjoyed sightseeing, or creating lists of the best places in the world to ride a hovercycle, or studying the patterns of people in crowds from a drone's-eye-view. Sometimes I did enjoy those things, at least to some degree, but even at their most rewarding, I was always thinking about how much more fun it would be to have you by my side, flying along with me.

I did anything I could to travel. Well-funded artistic tours to sketch passersby from every subculture in the world. Conspiracy theory census counts to see how many people above a certain height were left-handed. Manhunts on both sides of the law, fleeing after the crimes of repeatedly stealing identities, and bounty hunting in every exotic location I could find.

In one life I became a borderline religious figure for my 'attention-seeking stunt' of living in a small hovercraft, criss-crossing every large city in a grid, only dropping low enough to buy food through the windows. Apparently that sort of thing had become enough of a curiosity that the general public took an interest. For a while there, a cloud of camera drones followed me around, seeking interviews. I finally told them the truth, thinking that you might actually be able to find me this way.

You didn't, of course. But a whole crowd of supporters did, offering to help with no practical way to do so. It was aggravating and irritating and heart-meltingly kind all at the same time.

Eventually people lost interest. The drones peeled off from the flock in search of fresh excitement, and crowds no longer gathered below me.

When my hovercraft lost power and crashed into a bridge, only the rescue teams came.

You weren't among them.

***

I'm afraid I gave up for a while after that. I drifted, apathetic, doing nothing to search or to make a name for myself, for several lives in a row.

What did it matter? Even when I did absolutely everything in my power, canvassing the entire globe, the odds of finding you were growing smaller every day. I fantasized about causing some grand catastrophe to bring the population down, but I could never take that sort of thing seriously, no matter how devastated by loneliness I was.

You wouldn't forgive me for it. And I wouldn't be able to get over meeting your eyes again, only to see them harden in disgust at what I'd become. You had always greeted me with delight. To poison your joy would be infinitely worse than never seeing you again.

So I drifted. Took unimportant jobs, or easy ones, or none at all. I pretended to be unable to speak for one entire lifetime. It was kind of peaceful, though I was ready to give up the charade by the time it ended.

Speaking my first and last full sentence as a devastating insult to the family member who deserved it sent me laughing into a heart attack that was a better ending than if I'd planned it.

I felt a bit better in my next life. Not ready to rush off full-tilt again, but ready to be adventurous once more. I dabbled in the sciences, did a bit of backpacking with friends, tried out hobbies and kept myself fit.

I deliberately avoided thinking about you through most of it. The thoughts were too painful. I didn't test the ember for warmth, or untie the leather strings of that goatskin bag. I pretended they weren't even there. Not burying them like I had before, but letting my attention skitter away like a frightened animal whenever it drifted close by.

There were other things to think about for now. The future could handle itself.

And the future was quickly becoming the past, as it always did, with societal changes and scientific advances intriguing enough to keep my attention for quite a while. Countries finally moved on from barbaric forms of warfare involving actual death, and agreed to compete in virtual reality arenas instead. That was fascinating enough that I spent multiple lifetimes on it – several real and many virtual – and I wondered more than once if you were in a chair somewhere, your mind lost in a digital sphere I'd never get the keys to.

But I couldn't do anything about it if you were. So I moved on.

All those hover engines I'd worked on ages ago had been refined, followed by other exciting new developments. Humanity hadn't met any aliens yet, but space travel became more sophisticated each year. There were new places to explore.

I signed up for the first colony ship.

While waiting to board, I heard your laugh.

I whirled, and you saw, and we sprinted through the crowd to embrace.

The ember in my chest glowed as bright as the sun, and nothing in the world was wrong.

As we walked up the ramp hand in hand, and buckled into adjoining seats, I reflected that we were once again helping to spread the population, this time on an astronomical scale.

But as I gazed at your smiling face, which was wearing that same adventurous grin as when we were pirates together, I knew that it would be okay.

Even if millennia passed between goodbyes and hellos, we would just have all the more stories to share when we met.

The trip to the colony world was a long one. We didn't stop talking the entire time. If the other passengers wondered about the mishmash of languages we used, then that was their mystery to figure out.

VII: THE CHARIOT

The Bastard Son by Katherine Shaw

Escape, at last.

Sweat beading on his brow, his breath already burning in his throat, Zanril was on the verge of exhaustion. He had never ventured this far from the queen's domain nestled deep within the forest, and every step away from her influence sent aches rippling through his muscles. But he couldn't stop yet.

Memories flashed across his vision, and he closed his eyes, willing them away.

It was no use.

Those eyes.

Even as her throat began to close under the weight of his fingers, that look had been unmistakable.

I was right about you all along.

Hot tears gathered behind his eyelids and he shook his head. It didn't matter now. She was breathing when he left her; she would recover. He had to keep moving.

Zanril flinched as dead leaves crunched under his leather boots. Autumn was well and truly here, and without the training given to his half-brothers and sisters, Zanril lacked the skill to pass through the forest unheard. Soon, that would be of no significance. A few more miles and he would be out of this forest, out of their realm and out of their lives. Just like they'd always wanted.

He could barely suppress a snarl as he reached the edge of the woods and the tall canopy of trees gave way to a vast indigo sky, marbled with streaks of stars. After years under the trees, the starlight was dazzling.

Zanril took a deep breath. Out here, away from the forest, the air was cool and crisp, free of the suffocation and oppression he had endured since he was a child. The others revelled in that life under the trees, flitting between branches like the woodland creatures with whom they shared a home, but not him. His mother's blood wasn't enough; it had never been enough. 'Bastard', they spat at him behind her back, 'scum'.

I'll show them.

Zanril's body felt lighter as he strode through the open grasslands, the weight of the shame and resentment he had carried all these years sloughing off him as his bright eyes followed the stars. Not that he really needed them – if there was one thing his elven heritage had gifted him, it was a flawless sense of direction. With each step, his chest lifted and his shoulders broadened. Outside the forest, he travelled in near silence, his light steps barely marking the soft grass. Away from snickering elves and the claustrophobia of endless tree trunks and crowding branches, Zanril felt powerful. Confident.

This was his domain.

Finally, as he reached the brow of the nearest hill, the starlight was dwarfed by a new light source: the city.

As the hill flattened once more into grassy lowlands, the view was dominated by a vast, sprawling settlement. Hundreds of dark wood-and-stone buildings of a variety of shapes and heights littered the land, ranging from dilapidated clusters of slums to streets of imposing, well-ordered townhouses. Despite the late hour, a great many of them were brightly lit, and even from this distance Zanril could hear the low hum of activity buzzing through the streets. His stomach fluttered with excitement.

I'm home.

He reached into his pocket and pulled out the scrap of parchment he had managed to tear out of the diary before that damn woman had barged in. He unfolded it and spoke the single word aloud.

"Danelis."

Father.

***

"Please, Father, let me help you help yourself!"

Zanril paced the small living room, heat spreading across his cheeks. When he had first tracked down Horacio Danelis, the thrill of finally meeting the human half of his parentage had overwhelmed him. But, two weeks on, the hopelessness of his father's situation was becoming too much to bear.

"You're a Danelis! That name used to mean something in this town."

"With all due respect, Son, how would you know? You hadn't stepped one foot in this place until two weeks ago."

Zanril stopped and stared down at the defeated-looking middle-aged man in the battered, old armchair. "That," he said, trying to keep his voice level. "Was not by choice." Zanril ran a hand over his face and took a breath, determined to maintain some composure. "I have done my research, Father. You – *we* – are descended from a family of status, of power. You deserve better than..." he gestured to their ramshackle surroundings, "well, *this.*"

His father's face softened and he deflated in his seat, his indignation dissolving. Zanril's bright eyes took in the older man's sagging frame and pallid features, and he realised just how tired he looked. He took a deep breath and the anger drained from him. It wasn't the old man's fault he had fallen into poverty, not really. He had done his best with what he had, but on his own, with no support and dwindling savings, he'd given up. There was still potential in the knowledge and experience he had built from his years of trading, if he only had some hope left within him to reach for it. Being alone all these years had diminished him.

Zanril knelt in front of his father's chair and took his hand in his. The time for superficial discussions was over. It had been two weeks; it was time to ask the question that had been haunting Zanril for his entire life.

"Father, when I was born, why didn't you take me home with you? Why did you leave me in that forest, where I didn't belong?"

Horacio's eyes widened and he met Zanril's gaze, radiating a passion he had not yet shown in their brief time together. "Son, when I discovered your mother was with child, I asked – no, I *begged* – her to stay with me." Zanril was surprised to see tears forming around his father's wrinkled eyes. In these two weeks with his estranged son, Horacio had remained stoic; pleased to see Zanril, but reserved in his affections. When he spoke now, his once strong voice was strained with feeling. "She refused. Said it was... *beneath* her to live with humankind. That's when I realised I meant nothing to her. I was just... just a plaything."

His head dropped, and Zanril squeezed his father's hand. It was an effort to keep his own voice free of the rising emotions whirling in his chest. He had always known his mother didn't love him – she had never tried to convince him otherwise – but as a young outcast, Zanril had at least dreamed of a whirlwind romance between star-crossed lovers that had brought him into the world.

Zanril blinked back the hot tears building behind his eyes. "I wanted to see you, Father, please believe that. I tried, but my questions always went unanswered. For twenty years, all I wanted was to see your face."

Horacio looked up once more to face his son, his own eyes moist and shining in the dim candlelight. "I believe you, Son." He breathed a heavy sigh and clasped his free hand over Zanril's, squeezing tight. "I only wish I could have lived up to your expectations. You must be so disappointed."

Zanril stood and pulled his father to his feet. A new fire kindled within him as he took in the broken man before him. Zanril had been denied half of his parentage all his life. While he was bullied and stigmatised for being different, his father was alone, and suffering. No one had benefited from the separation, except his mother, who had revelled in their misery.

No more.

Zanril drew his father closer and enveloped him in a tight embrace. "No, not disappointed, Father. I never could be."

A soft sob fell from his father's lips, breaking Zanril's heart in two. He closed his eyes and swallowed the pain, squeezing it down until it transformed, the heat of his anger galvanising it into something new.

Horacio Danelis might have descended into misfortune, abandoned by the woman he loved and destitute, but his son was back in town, and that son had something no one else had: elven blood.

"I will deliver our family to greatness, Father. I swear it."

***

Aside from the faint whistle of the wind as it crept in through the window panes, the house was silent. The hallway ahead of him was bathed in mottled shadows that didn't quite cover the full expanse of the floor. The waning moon peeked from behind the clouds, creating searchlights which seemed to constantly shift across Zanril's path. Not that it mattered; he was half-elf, and this was more than enough cover for him.

Away from the rustling annoyance of the forest floor, he glided over the soft, plush rug without making a single sound, his lean body pressed against the wall, rendering him near invisible to the naked eye. He had to suppress a laugh as he recalled the warnings about the 'tight' security at this place – he'd slipped by the two guards without breaking a sweat. Human perception was nothing compared to the keen eyes of his half-brothers and sisters, and he'd had to evade them more times than he wished to think about.

Still, he couldn't let his skills make him complacent – this was his first job, and it had to go flawlessly if he was going to secure another. Taking a deep breath to compose himself, he padded further along the corridor until he reached a set of tall, gilded double doors. His quarry was within.

Zanril tiptoed to the door and pressed a pointed ear against its surface. Silence. The target was asleep, just as he'd hoped. Zanril turned the handle and eased the door open a fraction. A shrill creak pierced the night air, sending his heart racing. He slipped through the door and darted into the corner of the bedroom, blending into the shadows. The sound didn't go unnoticed. Zanril heard movement in the large four-poster bed which dominated the centre of the room, and every muscle in his body tensed.

No, not yet. Let him come to you.

After what felt like an eternity, a figure rose from the sheets and stepped unsteadily towards the door. The room was dark, and a human would only be able to make out a shifting shadow in the gloom. Zanril was no mere human, however, and his sharp eyes presented the old man in sufficient detail to track his eye movements, revealing the opportune moment to enter his blind spot and strike.

Within seconds Zanril was behind him, and the man barely had time to notice a flash of silver before Zanril's blade tore open his throat. A terrible gurgling sound broke the silence as a crimson river erupted from the wound and the man dropped to the ground, drowning in his own blood.

Zanril watched, wide-eyed, as the life-force drained out of the man. Hot bile began to rise up his throat.

Not yet.

Chest tightening, he knelt by the body and brandished his knife once more with a trembling hand. His stomach roiled as he dug the blade into the man's soft flesh, carving a crude symbol he could barely see through a veil of tears. A snake.

With his task complete, Zanril wasted no time in fleeing the scene and escaping the house, slipping past the guards once again and running with light steps far into the night. When he was finally out of sight of the house and safely hidden within the shadows of a dirty alleyway, he gave in to his body, and the contents of his stomach spewed out onto the cobblestones in front of him.

Zanril rose to his full height, his knees trembling. He closed his eyes, and the image of a handful of gold coins flashed in his mind.

He smiled.

***

Zanril tossed the coin purse into the air and caught it again, appreciating the weight of the heavy jewels within. This had been his most profitable hit yet. He stowed it in a hidden pocket within his coat and scanned the buildings on either side of the seemingly empty side street. There was no one in any of the windows, but he adjusted his mask nonetheless to ensure his face was fully covered.

He continued to stride down the street, his soft leather boots making virtually no sound to disrupt the early evening quiet. Anyone else would have felt perfectly at ease as they neared the end of the street, but not Zanril Danelis. As he rounded the corner, he quickly turned on his heel and a knife flew from up his sleeve, crossing to the other side of the street at breakneck speed. A high-pitched yelp told Zanril he had hit his mark, and a small grin twisted the corner of his mouth.

He strode forward to see a boy, probably of sixteen or seventeen years of age, his shabby tunic pinned to a wooden door at the shoulder by Zanril's blade. At his feet lay a heavy club, forgotten where it had been dropped to the cobbles in his surprise. Zanril walked up to the boy and kicked the club far down the street before leaning in, so that their faces were only inches apart. It was a shame his assailant couldn't see the wide smirk under his reptilian mask.

"Tell your boss, when they eventually find and release you," he said with a chuckle. "That they have to try a hell of a lot harder to ambush The Cobra. Have a good evening."

The boy didn't respond, his bulging eyes and pale face saying everything. Zanril tipped his wide-brimmed hat to him, before turning and walking away.

***

Finally certain that his path hadn't been traced as he criss-crossed the city, Zanril removed his mask and stowed it beneath his cloak. He smiled as he turned the final corner onto a street that was now very familiar to him.

Home.

His father had been reluctant to leave the docks at first, but once he had moved into the townhouse Zanril procured for him, he had warmed to it immediately. Located near the centre of the city and backed by a maze of side streets and alleyways, it proved to be the perfect location for Zanril to slip in and out, any time of day or night.

He ascended the broad stone steps leading to the front door and stepped inside, the warmth of the fire very welcome after the chill of the evening. He removed his cloak, hung it on the peg by the door, and retrieved a brown paper package he had stowed behind the coat stand before leaving earlier that afternoon. As he moved towards the living room he raised his voice and called out through the house.

"Father! Are you home?"

"In here, Son!"

Zanril stepped through the doorway and smiled at his father, who sat by the fire in that old chair he had refused to throw out, attempting to sew yet another patch onto his tattered old cloak. Despite Zanril's continued offers of financial assistance, his father hadn't shaken off his frugality, making every possession and item of clothing last as long as physically possible.

"I have something for you," Zanril said, placing the package on his father's lap.

"Oh, no, you've done enough for me," Horacio protested, readying to offer it back to his son. "I don't need any more."

"Just open it." Zanril said softly, his wide eyes willing his father to accept his gift.

Horacio tore the paper gently with unsteady hands and let out a gasp as he unfolded the immaculate new coat that lay within. It was made of the finest doeskin and silks, in navy blue and trimmed with gold. The colours of the old House of Danelis.

He looked up at his son, eyes glistening with tears. Folding the coat and placing it delicately on the floor beside him, he stood and wrapped Zanril in a warm embrace. The smell of whiskey and tobacco filled Zanril's nostrils, and he squeezed his father tight, his own tears threatening to burst free.

As father and son stood in this perfect moment, a soft whisper fell from Zanril's lips.

"I love you, Father."

VIII: STRENGTH

The Game by Emily Ansell

No one knew where the game had come from. Who would've had *time* to put something together? Any mages strong enough were too busy either working on spells to patch the Bubble with magic, or trying to repair the ancient machines that had powered it since our distant ancestors first turned them on. The engineers were still working on how to get the magical patches to capture the diffuse and sporadic solar energy to turn into electricity, because every time we lost a chunk of the Bubble, we lost the old solar panels that were attached to it. And we needed every one of them, or we needed a viable alternative.

The point was, there wasn't really anyone who could've set up a game, but here it was. A *proper* game, too. Most of us had been getting by with old hacked-and-rebuilt consoles and monthly VR days, but to get right in there and play? Oh, it'd been at least a year by now.

People gathered to enter almost immediately, excitement buzzing in the air louder than an ancient generator wheezing to life. Teenagers, adults, seniors, kids, *anyone* who was into gaming seemed to be there. I loved the atmosphere; it was so nice to get people out again to play. Pax was fairly *vibrating* in line beside me, little sparkles of light dancing around her as her magic echoed her mood. It made me smile to see her so excited; the last time there'd been a game, Pax had only been eight and so had played the easy mode with the other children. This time, at ten, she'd finally get to play with the adults. Even Zay, normally the very definition of teenage stoicism, had a big grin on his face. It was so nice to do something with the whole family; often my schedule at the hospital and Kester's at the hydroponics labs made that difficult.

We stepped through the door, and Pax jumped again, delightedly. "Rooftop Courier! I love this one!"

I smiled. I wasn't the biggest fan of platformers, but this one was bright and fun and a little silly. Perfect to get everyone back in the gaming groove. And it was showing already in the jokes and lightness of the crowd.

Each person took a headset and motion controllers as they filed in, strapping on the equipment as they walked. The buzz of magic crackled as the devices powered on, connecting them to the game network. I checked over my display, ensuring everything was in place.

"Are we all good? Everything's working properly?" I asked. That earned me a round of nods. "Okay good."

"Mom, can I run this with the guys?" Zay asked, pointing to where his buddies were already gathered and were waving him over.

"Of course. We'll meet you boys at endgame, all right? Good luck. I'll watch the leaderboards to see how you do. Merc's going for the jump record this time?"

"Yeah. He's been practicing."

"Well, I think he's got the height for it now. Alright, you boys have fun, we'll see you in there."

Then Zay was off with his friends, all of them getting more animated and excited as they bragged about what records they were going to beat today. It made me smile. He was getting so big; the first time I'd been so worried letting him and his friends play together without an adult. But they were good kids, they played fair and had fun and as they'd gotten older, the worry had dissipated. And games had safeguards, so I knew that ultimately, they'd be fine.

When I turned back, it was time to enter the portal that would take us into the game. Kester, Pax, and I entered together, the magic *whooshing* around us as it transported us into the game itself. The sky was bright blue like it had apparently once been in the real world, populated with unnaturally white, fluffy clouds.

"Kes?" He hadn't spawned in with me, and neither had Pax. Bringing up the chat on my HUD, I searched Kester's screename and messaged: *Where'd you and Pax spawn? Will meet up.*

Pax not with you? He messaged back barely a second later.

No.

Not with me either. Searching now. Even in text, I could feel the tension in Kes' words.

It won't let me message her. I'm sending a ticket in. I pulled down another menu and quickly filled out the questions, hoping it was just a bug. A child playing for the first time at adult level was required to *at least* spawn in with an adult, and we'd both marked that when signing her in. I sighed. At least Pax was an experienced enough player that she should be fine on her own until we could locate her. It just made me a little sad that we wouldn't get to start together for her first adult game.

Kes popped up again. *Wyla? Found Pax. Am closer. Will meet you at first checkpoint.*

Sounds good.

So for now, I was on my own. I began to run a little, testing the feel of the game. Everything felt good, no drift or anything funky. I jumped onto the first platform, and it immediately began to wobble beneath me. Before it could fall, I jumped to the next one. That was odd, this game had never used that mechanic before. But now I was trying to get to the next building, leaping from platform to platform before they could drop out from under me. The last jump was a long one, and I put all my power behind it.

As I rolled back to my feet I heard a voice below me. "Help!"

I looked over the edge. It was Jet, the son of our head nurse. He was hanging onto the ladder on the side of the building, but the rung above him was broken. I reached down and he swung up to grab my hand. Setting my feet, I pulled him up and onto the roof.

"Doc Taratt?" He wheezed. "Thanks for that. Me and Jode missed the last jump. Bro fell, and I dunno where he went."

"He didn't respawn?"

"Nah, ma'am. He just *fell*. He's not responding to chat and the map shows him *under* the world. It's fucked up... uh, sorry."

"That's okay. Flag it, and keep going. It must be a bug. Just be extra careful and I'll keep an eye out for your brother and ping you if I see him."

"Will do, ma'am. And thanks."

He headed off to the left. I went straight ahead; the package I needed to pick up was at the top of the building in front of me. I started to climb, but the difficulty spiked about halfway up and I fell back onto the lower roof. Luckily, the fall damage was minor and I didn't have to worry about a potential respawn bug.

"What the...?" I flagged my location, and started again. "I wonder..."

Once I got to the part where it got suddenly much harder, I tested my theory. Kes hated the crouch-jump exploit, but sometimes it was the only way. It certainly was, now. Crouching and jumping at the same time, I managed to move up the building with relative ease until I was at the top.

I took a deep breath. That'd been *hard*. Way harder than an early game puzzle should have been. The difficulty was set to regular, too! I crossed the roof and picked up the floating, glowing package that waited for me. Putting it in my inventory pack, I shook my head. "I hope no one else is having this kind of trouble."

But it was still a ways to go to catch up with Kes and Pax, and now I had a package to deliver. So I pressed on, hoping for the best.

***

I had exchanged the first package for a second one, and picked up a side quest to get rid of some pigeons that had holed up in an abandoned building. Hard to argue with an easy quest and a nice chunk of XP. The only problem was that I hadn't found Pax or Kes yet, and now I couldn't get ahold of either of them. I'd even tried reaching out with my own, personal telepathy with no success.

As I rounded the corner, I saw the building up ahead where the pigeons had made their nest. It was at least a relatively short climb. Though as I got closer, I heard shrieking coming from the top. Alarmed, I pulled a power-up from my inventory and climbed the building at double speed.

At the top was a young woman of probably twenty. And at that moment, the pigeons were attacking her, mercilessly swooping and pecking. Digging through my inventory, I came upon the Pacify Animal spell that I'd found in an old car. I cast it quickly, and the birds dispersed. Ironically, it also marked my quest as completed.

"Are you alright?" I asked her, touching her shoulder. My hand came away bloody from a hole in her jacket and I stared at it.

"They attacked me!" she cried. "It's not supposed to... I'm *bleeding*!"

"Here, I can help with that. I'm a doctor. Dr. Wyla Taratt."

"Fen. And I appreciate it, thank you."

I cast my healing, my magic seeking out and closing the cuts on her hands and face and anywhere else the birds had gotten her. I couldn't take away how she was shaking, looking fearfully around her for further attacks, though I wished I could.

"Are you going to be alright, Fen? I can go with you if you want." I suggested.

She shook her head. "My friends and I are going to meet up in the town square. But thank you, Dr. Taratt."

We parted ways again. My own next stop wasn't far, dropping off the second package and picking up another one. But it was almost time to get to the checkpoint, too. At least then I could hopefully meet up with Kes and Pax.

***

The checkpoint stood at the top of a massively tall building crowned with a spire. And it was a notorious pain in the ass to climb, having to go up the fire escape, through several floors inside, and then back out to parkour the rest of the way. Everyone else who was already climbing seemed to have power-ups, but I'd used mine already and there wasn't one in here until the thirty-fifth floor. And by the Ancestors was I grateful when I finally got it, since it made the parkour section much easier.

Kes was waiting for me at the top by the checkpoint portal. I frowned.

"Where's Pax?"

He shook his head. "She's already gone through. Before I got here. She *is* really good at this part."

"Okay, then let's keep going." I tried to take a deep breath, to not scream my frustration out at Kes. None of this was his fault, after all. I'd just been hoping Pax was here, especially with all of these weird bugs.

The glowing portal *whooshed* around us, and spat us out in a new city. At least now I could see Pax on the map, and I set my HUD to track her location. I sent her a message, hoping she would get it. *Paxie, don't go past the checkpoint. We're right behind you. We'll be there soon.*

I didn't think it went through, but about five minutes later when we picked up our next packages, I got a reply. *Okay Mom. This game is weird. I don't like it. It's not the same.*

"Thank the Ancestors!" I cried, quickly messaging her back. *I know. And we're coming to you. Don't leave this level without us, okay?*

Okay Mom.

"I've got a lock on Pax. Let's go!" I nodded to Kes.

"Are we going to have enough XP for this level?"

"We'll get more when we've got Pax with us. There's something going on here, and I want her with us first."

"Right."

***

Pax was waiting for us in a diner. The NPCs greeted us with their usual lines and offers as vendors, but we pushed past. Pax's long arms squeezed around me the way the snakes in ancient videos did, crushing the air out of me.

"This game is wrong." She shook her head. "There was a gang of NPCs who tried to take my package and I thought they were really gonna hurt me."

"Oh, sweetie!" I hugged her tighter.

"Some big kid helped me; he fought them off. Said his name was Jet. He was nice, and he helped me get past that part so I could get through the checkpoint."

"I work with his mom. He's a good kid, and I'm glad he helped you. Was he with his brother?"

"No, he said he was looking for him. I hope he finds him, he looked pretty worried."

"Me too, honey." I sighed. "Let's all have a look at our quest logs and see what we still need to do. There's some real bad bugs or something and I think we need to run this quick and get out."

They both agreed and we conferred. Then we started off together, to finish up whatever we needed. I tried not to worry about Zay. He was with his friends, and they would help each other, but this game... I'd be happier when I knew he was safe.

***

The next level was a night city, plastered with neon and sparkling light spells. Platforms glowed and fireworks went off in the distance. I liked the NPCs on this level, but this time I was looking to run things quickly rather than stay and chat.

We'd just finished a long quest chain that had culminated in a boss battle where we'd had to reprogram a mail sorting bot run amok. We were now sitting on the curb, sorting loot and checking our inventories. But as we did, I heard a small groaning noise from the alley behind us.

"Mom, where are you going? That's past the end of the map!" Pax raised an eyebrow at me.

"And this game is buggy enough," Kes agreed.

"Yeah, but I know that sound. That's someone in pain. Really bad pain."

As I rounded the corner into the alley, my suspicions were confirmed. I recognized the woman lying on the ground; we'd passed each other at work and I was sure she worked in the dental wing. But right now she was clutching her head and writhing.

"Ancestors!" I knelt beside her, asking loudly, "Can you hear me? Do you need help? Can you show me where it hurts?"

"Get it off..." she moaned, pulling at a small, round metal disc stuck to her temple. "Hurts..."

"Okay, I'm going to help you." I gathered my magic and reached out with my free hand, touching both the disc and her forehead. I probed gently, trying to understand what was happening and what I could do to help.

"What in the Old World?" I said aloud. It made no sense, but at least now I could see what was happening. And I was glad I always carried a spare transmitter on me. I aimed it at the disc, not quite touching it, and channelled a different spell. It wasn't a spell I used very often, and I felt the strain a lot sooner than usual, but it was working! And it didn't take long before the disc sparked and fell off.

The woman sat up slowly, rubbing her head. "Thank you."

I picked up the disc, studying it. "This thing was pulling out the electrical signals in your brain and changing them. Why?"

"I'm not sure. I failed a mainline quest and got zapped into this weird out-of-world room and they put it on me. They said they were going to fix my gaming habit. I... I don't even game that often! My username is literally FilthiestCasual! I'm... I'm going to go back to the lobby and wait for the game to end. Thank you, for everything. I'll head to the hospital once we're done to get checked out."

"Okay, sounds good."

The woman pushed a button on her wrist pad, and winked out of the world. I quickly checked her username and saw she'd transported safely out of the level and into the waiting area. I hoped she'd be safe there.

It was then I noticed Kes and Pax watching, faces peeked around the corner. As they got closer, Kes looked at the item in my hand. "That's bad."

"Yeah. I used the healing spell to pull out the electrical signals that this thing was altering, but I worry what this'll do long-term. And how many people have already been given one. Something about all of this... this game is more than fucked. It's not even bad programming or sabotage. There's a motive here."

"Maybe we should go back to the lobby, too?" Pax slipped her hand into mine.

I squeezed hers back. "If you and Dad want to, that might be best. I have to get to the end and make sure Zay gets out alright."

Pax sounded much younger than her ten years as she whispered, "Mama, I don't want to leave you *or* Daddy. And what if the lobby isn't safe, either?"

"I don't really like the idea of us separating," Kes agreed.

Running a hand through my hair, I shrugged. "The only other option is to keep going. Keep playing. I'm not leaving while Zay is still in here and we don't know where he is."

He took a deep breath. "Me, either. Then we play, and we get out fast. I think we have enough XP that we can go to the next level. We get to the end, make sure Zay's safe and then we report this as high as we can. It's obviously not enough to go through the game's reporting system; we need to involve the police and the gaming commission. Because this is... this is something else."

***

The next level started with a train ride cutscene, but I wasn't paying attention. I was holding the little disc in my hand, thinking. *It detected the electrical signals, stored them. I pulled them out and they fried the disc. Too much electricity...*

"I've got it!" I stood up, shouting without realizing it. The other players on the train looked over at me and I sat back down, mortified.

"What have you got?" Kes asked.

"An idea. Let's get out of this game, and we'll go from there. I need to ponder it more, anyway."

***

"How are we here already?" Kes asked. The train had let us out on the final level, a timed sprint to the endgame where people liked to try and break records. But I wasn't thinking about that right now. My only concern was getting us out safely, and finding Zay and making sure he was okay.

So we ran. Pax was faster than both Kes and me, so we didn't have to worry about her. But I *was* worried about the time. Why was it going so fast? We'd only just make it at this rate!

The countdown had turned red when we reached the checkpoint, and lots of players weren't even close. As it clicked to zero, anyone not in the safe zone suddenly vanished, and the whole crowd gasped. But I was too intent on finding Zay to join them in gawking.

"Oh, the Ancestors are good!" I cried as I saw him and his friends in a small knot. They all looked haggard and hollow-eyed, like they'd seen some things. I pulled Zay into a hug and he actually hugged back.

"This game is fucked," he said calmly, but I could feel that he was shaken. "We nearly got steamrolled by a giant mail-bot. This lady pushed me out of the way. Said her name was Fen and she was paying it forward. I woulda been flat otherwise."

"Oh..." I said softly, my heart warming. I hoped Fen was still okay, because I needed to thank her in real life. Jet, too.

The endgame portal rushed to life at the top of the stairs in a swirl of bright blue magic, pulling everyone's attention to it. But a group of people came *out* of it. I began to push my way through the crowd to the front. It seemed now we would get answers.

A blonde woman with immaculately coiffured hair stood at the forefront, a datapad in her hand. I recognized her from the hospital; her name was Maggy Wenra. Her father had been in a bad accident and she came to visit him every day. Often, she came full of questions, especially about how we kept enough power for all our equipment and if her father would be okay. But why was she *here*?

She spoke calmly, a smile on her face. But it was a thin, fake smile. The kind that set your teeth on edge. "Congratulations, all of you, for making it this far. My group and I will escort you all to join the others and then when we are done we will all go home."

"Join them for what? Where did everyone else go?" someone shouted. Others followed.

I stepped forward, holding up the disc. "It's something to do with these, isn't it? What are you doing with these? Why are you changing the electrical signals in the brain?"

"Dr. Taratt?" she asked, one shocked hand rising to her chest.

"That's me. You need to tell us what's going on here, Maggy."

"*Shit*," the woman muttered. She put the smile back on. "It's just a little recalibration. After this, none of you will want to pursue this silly hobby. No more gaming, no more wasting time and resources on this pointless fucking around. Just a few zaps until the very idea repulses you."

The crowd murmured and buzzed, but I shouted over them. "Why? What's the point of that?"

Her face turned a blotchy red as she snapped, "Because it's a waste!"

"How?" I and several other voices demanded.

"You're a doctor!" She glared at me. "You, of all people, should be thinking about how to conserve our electricity! About how there are so many more important things we should be concentrating on! Don't you worry about what could happen if the hospital loses power for too long?"

"Of course I do. We all do. But look at what we have here!" I waved my arm, encompassing the group. "*This* is just as important as any procedure I do in the hospital. Look at us. We're a community. We've got folks from every walk of life, every age, every... everything! We have fun here, we collaborate, we've even made discoveries to help everyone. This is a beautiful thing, it lets us live, not just survive and scrape by. Other cities tried that, absolute austerity in the name of survival even when it wasn't necessary. And we know what happened to them. We've all seen and heard the transmissions. Why bring that here?"

"There are other things you all could be doing!" she argued weakly, as if she were trying to convince herself as much as me.

"And we have been. We haven't done a game in nearly eighteen months due to the Bubble issue. We've all been just as worried as you and your group about it. I know I can't sleep sometimes, imagining the lights flickering on and off at the hospital, worrying about the machines blipping off and hoping the alarm would still sound. I know you're worried about your father, Maggy."

"Don't bring him into this! I wouldn't have to worry about him if you lot would worry more about your jobs than using up time and power on gaming!"

I shrugged. "No one can run like that all the time. If we all burned out, there'd be nobody to do anything. But that doesn't matter. Maggy, you need to hit the button, end the game now."

"I can't." Maggy spoke very softly. "Not until you've all been tagged. Or else this is all for nothing. I can't go to jail for nothing, having changed nothing."

I climbed the steps slowly, watching Maggy. The other woman's eyes got wider and more feral with every step, but she stayed rooted to the spot. I spoke in my kindest voice, the compassionate one that delivered bad news to patients and their families. "I know. You want to change things, you want to feel like you've accomplished something. It's hard to face that maybe what you did was wrong, and maybe there'll be consequences. But Maggy, it's not all for nothing."

"How can it not be? The tags have barely begun to do their work, and none of you have one! My life is over with nothing to show for it!"

"No, Maggy. I found someone your people had tagged. I took the tag off her, and I think we can use your tags and my healing methods to solve the energy crisis!"

"*What?!*"

Everyone in the room let out a collective gasp. Then the buzz started, growing until no one could hear anything. I waved my hands at the crowd, and they began to calm down. Eventually, they'd done so enough that I could speak again.

"Okay, it's a rough idea so far, but yeah. A spell wraps around a tagged person's mind like the Bubble wraps around the city. It detects and pulls out electrical signals to recalibrate and send back into the brain. I used a medical transmitter to feed in a healing spell that pulled those electrical signals back out of the brain before they caused damage. And it pulled enough into the tag to fry it. If we recalibrate the magical parts of the bubble with larger versions of the tags that can detect and pull in the solar energy, then use a similar spell to draw out the electricity it picks up into the grid, we can turn the whole damn Bubble into a solar panel and it won't matter if we lose the old, technology-based ones that are starting to crap out anyway!"

"Ancestors! That could work!" Maggy whispered, the whites showing all around her eyes.

"We have to end the game. We need to get this to the engineers, and we've got a bunch of them here. This could change everything."

"I'm… our group, we're still going to go to jail…"

I nodded and shrugged at the same time. "Perhaps? I don't really know how things will play out. But this is a breakthrough bigger than any one of us. We have to get this into the right hands. This will save the whole city and everyone in it."

"My father will be safe…"

"If we can get this to work, we won't have to worry about power outages anymore."

"And!" a voice called from the crowd, "I work in the solar and Bubble-exterior weather monitoring. We're a long ways off from clear skies yet, but we've been keeping track and the amount of actual sunlight getting to us is increasing year-over-year. If this works, it's going to get *more* effective over time!"

Maggy swallowed hard, holding up the remote that controlled the game. "You're right. But… I'm scared. Of what'll happen."

"I know. I would be, too."

"Thank you for understanding."

We pushed the 'finish game' button together. All the spells and gadgets began to power down. An anticlimactic leaderboard trundled across everyone's visors, but for once, no one paid it any mind. They were all abuzz again as Maggy and I stepped down from the platform and began to make our way through the crowd. Pax was soon attached to my side, her arms locked around my waist again. Kester followed just behind, and even Zay stuck close. Everyone else fell in, still deep in discussion. Maggy and I didn't speak, but I took her hand and squeezed it as the exit door came into view.

We stepped out together, and found ourselves facing both a police presence and the mayor.

"Thank the Ancestors!" The mayor threw up his hands. "This game has been pinging red flags to the game oversight systems since it started. Who is responsible for this?"

Maggy stepped forward. "I am, Mr. Mayor. My group and I are."

"Alright. The lot of you are coming in for questioning, then. This was a dangerous stunt you pulled. Dr. Taratt, is anyone injured?"

I sighed. "It's very possible. The devices used should have powered off with the game ending, but we'll need mental health workers and neurologists for sure and everyone should get checked over before they leave. However, Mr. Mayor, before Ms. Wenra is taken into custody, she and I have made an accidental breakthrough we must share with you and the engineering and mages' corps."

The mayor pursed his lips. "And what did you discover that will prevent me from throwing this woman in jail right now until our investigation is complete?"

I looked at Maggy, then back at the Mayor. "We may have solved the energy crisis."

IX: THE HERMIT

For the Greater Good by Katherine Shaw

Determination powered her footsteps as Beatrice Cadogan swept through the stark grey corridors of the Grey Keep, the sound of her pounding boots echoing loudly off the cold stone. Despite an aggressive recruitment drive, the military centre of Arteminion remained half-empty; the New World propaganda was clearly becoming less effective back home.

The library, as usual, was deserted. A thick layer of dust covered the half-empty shelves, suggesting the Keep's cleaners had given up maintaining the space altogether. The room had been designed to be a grand, ornate chamber where the settlers would record all of their wondrous discoveries from the New World. Beatrice scowled as she surveyed the meagre quantity of books which the Archivist had managed to put together, each one of them a reminder of her failure. Arteminion was *her* city, and by now it should be thriving, not scraping by on what limited resources they'd been able to scavenge from the surrounding wilderness.

The Empire would not accept any more delays. She had to show progress, and soon.

Beatrice glanced over her shoulder to ensure she was truly alone before striding to the far corner of the library, where the most controversial manuscripts were kept. It was forbidden for anyone but the Archivist to enter this area, let alone to study the wickedness within, but everyone had their price, and even the wizened old man had succumbed to a bag of black rubies.

It had been dangerous to consult him, but what else could she do? She just hoped her rank would be sufficiently intimidating to secure his silence. He had certainly been accommodating, bowing so deeply his long grey beard trailed along the floor as he muttered assurances of complete obedience. *We shall see.*

She licked her lips as her eyes passed over the covers, all identically bound in cheap hide inscribed with inferior ink which would no doubt fade within a decade. Her fingers lingered over the book she had come in search of, the name emblazoned in large, scrawling letters, just as the Archivist had described:

Rituals of the Draconids

She flexed her large, muscular fingers as they hovered over the spine, hesitating for a moment as her eyes focused on the thick, golden tattoo lines which snaked around her chestnut skin. If she did this, they might call it treason. She would be going against everything those markings stood for. Finally, she snatched the book, dropping it quickly into the messenger bag she always carried.

She made a point of wearing her uniform at all times – a picture says a thousand words, and a six foot tall Officer of Erebus in full military regalia typically provoked minimal questions. She strode out of the library and walked purposefully back to her quarters, head held high.

It's the right thing to do.

"Beatrice!"

She froze, less than fifty feet away from her door. Her heart hammered against her ribs.

So close.

She turned, bracing herself for a challenge, but released a sigh of relief when she recognised the smiling face of Herman Elserbast, one of her oldest colleagues. She returned his smile warmly.

"Officer Elserbast." She nodded in recognition. "How are you?"

"Oh come on, Bea," he chuckled. "We've known each other long enough now, call me Herman."

She felt a gentle heat spread across her cheeks. *That smile.* Even after all these years, it did something to her.

"We missed you in the debrief," he continued, frowning slightly. "Where were you?"

"I was running a little late after a prolonged patrol," Beatrice gave the answer she had prepared should anyone question her whereabouts. *Nothing goes unnoticed here.* "I'd heard rumours of disturbances in the... less frequented areas of the Keep. False alarm, though. Very frustrating!"

"Ah."

Beatrice steeled herself, ready for more questioning.

"Well, perhaps I should catch you up on the latest from the General. Nothing too unusual; more pressure from the top, but I'd hate for you to get behind."

That smile again.

"Of course, thank you!" She resisted the urge to glance up the corridor towards her door. She had to get the book to safety; she could not risk being caught with it on her person.

"Excellent. Tomorrow, then? Over breakfast in the canteen?"

Beatrice tried to mask her relief as the tight knot of anxiety in her stomach began to unravel.

"Perfect – I appreciate it, Herman. Until tomorrow, then."

He nodded and swept down the corridor, striding in a perfect marching rhythm towards his own quarters. He was a true soldier, through and through. Beatrice waited for him to be safely out of sight before dashing to her own door, her desire for sanctuary overcoming her desire to prevent suspicion.

She unlocked the door and swung it open, plunging into the darkness of her office and slamming it closed behind her. She leaned back against the hard wood and took a deep breath in a vain attempt to slow her racing heart.

That was close.

***

The book was complex, and altogether too academic for Beatrice's limited formal education, but it did prove one thing she had suspected for some time – the drakes had magic.

In her heart she had known it must be true, but had not dared to speak her suspicions aloud. Magic of any kind was strictly forbidden, after all, and even discussing it publicly would have drawn attention she did not want. But now it was within her grasp, already harnessed by the indigenous beasts of this land. It certainly explained why they had been flourishing while the settlers suffered.

With magic, trees could be felled with ease, ores could be mined much more efficiently, and her army could finally wield the firepower they had so sorely missed since travelling to this wasteland. She could bring life to Arteminion at last.

She had to find out more.

***

It had been weeks, and Beatrice was getting nowhere.

She threw a report across her broad, mahogany desk, almost knocking over the dying candle she had lit hours earlier. None of her informants had brought back anything of much use. Of course, it didn't help that she had to be very selective about who she delegated these tasks to – she was well aware that some of her unit may be more loyal to the law of the Empire than to her.

Beatrice grimaced at that thought. She was not comfortable going outside of the law, but this was for the greater good. *They'll see. When I show them what we could do, they'll agree with me, I'm sure of it.*

She stood and paced the room, her quarters eerily gloomy in the faint flicker of the diminishing candlelight. As she walked, the shadows seemed to bend and twist in the corner of her eye, as if mocking her.

"They're doing something in the forest. Rituals... sacrifices... that has to be how they do it! Where the power comes from. But how? And how the hell do I get them to give it to me?"

She continued to pace, wracking her brains. There was little in Arteminion the Draconids coveted, and few of the tribes interacted with her people at all. Some of the more enterprising came into the city walls to trade, provoking stares and jeers from the settlers who gawked at their scaled skin and forked tongues, but they valued utility over wealth, only trading for commodities and foodstuffs they didn't have access to in the forests and mountains they called home. With no greed or ambition to appeal to, what could Beatrice possibly offer of equal value to knowledge of their source of power? Of their very nature?

For the first time in her life she felt useless. Meagre. She had always prided herself in being an asset to the Empire, and a rising star in the Order of Erebus, but what use was that prowess here? All her connections, her favour with the Empire, they didn't mean a thing to the Draconids.

She stomped back over to the desk and slammed her heavy fists down in frustration, sending her holster clattering to the ground and her pistol spinning into the middle of the room. Beatrice stared at it for a moment, glinting in the flickering candlelight, like a guiding star.

"That's it!"

Such weapons were prized possessions, being made up of painstakingly crafted metals scarce in the New World. Each was one of a kind, awarded to only the most deserving and trusted Officers of Erberus, and it had been one of the happiest days of Beatrice's life when she received hers. Others would kill for such a weapon, and some had. The Draconids would do even more. She was sure of it.

***

Beatrice's heart pounded as she trod through the undergrowth, eyes scanning the trees for signs of hidden dangers. She ventured into the forest on patrol occasionally, but never this deep, and always avoiding Draconid territory. Alone and this close to its centre, she was nervous. Her hand found her pistol instinctively, her fingers moulding perfectly around the grip as if it was an extension of her body. Ordinarily it would make her feel invincible, but today her heart was heavy with sadness. *It will be worth it to save Arteminion.*

As she neared the densest depths of the forest, the light dwindled almost to non-existence, and Beatrice's pace slowed to a cautious walk. If it wasn't for the faint pearlescence of the exotic undergrowth and the glow of the large fireflies bobbing around below the thick canopy above, she doubted she would be able to find her way at all.

If I didn't know what can lurk in the shadows, I might find this place beautiful.

The Draconids didn't seem to have trouble with the beasts of the Amberwood; they had a sort of kinship with them.

As will I, soon enough.

She ploughed onwards, repeating the instructions the preacher had given her over and over in her mind. She was sure she had followed them exactly, but now under the shifting darkness of the canopy, her confidence was not absolute.

Beatrice considered stopping and re-evaluating her position, but a soft chanting from up ahead urged her onwards. She strained her ears to try and identify the words, or at least the number of speakers, but it was too far away. She had to get closer.

She stepped forward, taking care to place her boots on the softer forest floor debris to minimise the noise. If these turned out to not be who she was looking for, she didn't want to make her presence known. She followed the chanting, her eyes straining in the dim light. She grimaced at her heart rapidly beating in her chest. She had fought in wars, stared death in the face without flinching, and yet now she was scared.

She froze in place as she caught sight of a large pair of eyes glinting at her through the undergrowth. She locked gazes with it, and the figure stepped forwards to reveal itself as a Draconid preacher, dressed in a hooded ankle-length purple robe. She wondered if it was the same one she had first discussed the deal with; Beatrice had always struggled to tell the reptilian creatures apart. They held out a clawed hand expectantly.

For a moment, Beatrice didn't know what they wanted, but as their eyes travelled down to her holster she realised.

Oh.

Their glowing yellow eyes continued to stare as Beatrice lifted her pistol from her holster and held it in her hand. It wasn't just a weapon, it was a symbol of everything she had achieved in her service to the Empire. It meant everything to her; it was priceless and irreplaceable, but she had to do this. She had to show them what could really be accomplished when true power was harnessed by one of their own.

Her stomach clenched in defiance as she handed the pistol over to the preacher. Their face broke into a broad smile filled with small, sharp teeth as they raised a clawed hand towards her and beckoned her forwards.

Now or never.

As Beatrice followed them, the chanting grew louder and louder, until it reached such a volume that she could barely hear herself think.

What are they saying? She only knew a handful of words in their guttural language, and she recognised none of what she heard now.

The preacher led Beatrice through the undergrowth into a small clearing lined by other Draconids, all chanting the same incomprehensible words. They seemingly took no notice of Beatrice and the preacher; their focus was entirely on a tall tree at the far end of the clearing. Its top extended beyond the tree line to the night sky beyond, but what really distinguished it was the light. Even under the suffocating darkness of the canopy above, the tree emitted a silver-blue glow from the many cracks spreading through its thick bark. The cracks snaked together, gathering in the centre of the trunk to form a crude heart which pulsed with intense ethereal light.

The Draconids formed a tight circle around Beatrice, enclosing her and the tree. She took a deep breath and braced herself for what was to come. They raised their arms and the chanting grew louder until it was almost deafening. Beatrice bowed her head, her hands trembling as she whispered her desperate plea to the Goddess of the Wood.

Instil me with your arcane power.

Instil me with your arcane power.

Instil me with your arcane power.

I beg of you.

Suddenly, she was confronted with a dazzling, blinding light. She closed her eyes, but the light seemed to be inside her head, pressing against her skull, scorching her eyelids. A great pain tore at her chest, growing until it was excruciating. She frantically tore at the front of her coat in a vain attempt to lessen the agony, to no avail. Her body swayed and her legs buckled, sending her tumbling onto her hands and knees. She fought to cling onto consciousness with all the strength she could muster, but in the end the pain overwhelmed her.

When she awoke, Beatrice was alone. She was in the same clearing, but the trees surrounding her all looked the same; the Goddess was gone. However, as her eyes adjusted, Beatrice realized she was not in total darkness. A faint, blue light seemed to emanate from where she knelt, and as she looked down, Beatrice saw that the tattoos covering her chest and arms now glowed with an arcane luminescence.

Her heart fluttered. *It worked!*

She could feel a new force pulsing through her, as if her veins were full of molten metal. And it felt good. Overjoyed, she surveyed her arms and hands, revelling in her new power. As her eyes passed over her skin, she noticed a dark object lying on the ground out of the corner of her eye. She crawled forward to get a closer look, and her newfound joy was replaced by horror. There, lying on a bed of dry leaves on the forest floor, dripping with blood, was a heart.

It couldn't be.

Her frantic fingers grasped at her neck, her wrist, her chest, desperately seeking a pulse, but there was nothing.

Her blood ran cold in her veins and she fought the urge to vomit.

Before she could process what was happening, Beatrice heard the crack of a tree branch breaking behind her, and rushed to stow the heart away in her coat. She turned, expecting to be confronted by a beast of the forest, searching for prey. Without her pistol she was vulnerable.

She froze, her stomach turning to ice as her eyes met those of someone all too familiar.

"Officer Elserbast?"

"Officer Cadogan," he announced, with a formality which in a previous life would have filled her with pride. The smile was gone, replaced with a twisted look of disgust. "I am arresting you on suspicion of treason."

"But... you don't understand. This is for the Empire! To lead Arteminion to greatness! I will—"

Her words were lost as the back of his hand struck her face with such force she was knocked down onto one knee.

"You are no longer an Officer of Erebus and you do *not* have the authority to speak."

She wiped her mouth, her fingers coming away slick with blood. From the ground she could see at least a dozen pairs of boots; he had not come alone. There was no way she could fight her way out of this. She rose, a cold dread spreading through her body. A dull ache throbbed where her racing heart should be. She stared into the eyes of her former comrade, searching for understanding.

"Herman, please."

She cringed at the desperation in her voice. He was her colleague, her equal. She should not have to beg for his mercy! For a brief moment Beatrice thought she saw a flicker of pity flash across his eyes, but any hope she had dissolved as his expression hardened into one of revulsion.

"It's over, traitor. Officers! Bind her hands, take her back to the keep and throw her in the dungeon. I don't want to look at her for one more second."

With that, he turned on his heel and marched off into the forest, leaving Beatrice frozen in place, numb.

Traitor.

***

There was no trial. There was no need for one. Once they had raided her room they found all the evidence they needed to condemn her.

She should have burned the evidence. The book, the reports, her communications with the Draconids... why had she kept them?

"Misplaced hopes of gratitude," she said aloud to herself, her bitter voice echoing off the four walls of her cramped, crumbling cell.

She had done it for *them*, for the Empire, and the starving, destitute people she had to pass every day on her patrols. They were her people; she was entrusted with their lives when they followed her to the New World. She was willing to do anything to make Arteminion flourish into something great. Her commitment was absolute, yet instead of thanks they had rewarded her with a life sentence. *It could have been much worse.* Thank the Goddess her years of service had been taken into account.

The Goddess.

Beatrice looked down at her hands, turning them slowly to study her tattoos, their pulsing iridescence shimmering over her dark skin like delicate lace. The Goddess had imbued her with the power she had desired, but it had done little good for her so far. Ripped from the bosom of the forest before she could be taught how to utilise her new-found abilities, she had been unable to put up much of a fight against Herman and his officers.

She closed her eyes and laid back on her hard stone bunk, losing herself in the suffocating silence.

"Child."

Beatrice sat upright and her eyes darted around the small cell. Dark shadows crept in from the corners where the light from her skin didn't reach, but she was certain – it was empty. She strained her ears to try and detect any movement in the corridor outside the heavy wooden door. Nothing. *I'm hearing things.* She leaned back against the wall and cursed her own paranoia.

"*Come to me, child.*"

There was no mistaking it this time; she had heard a voice. Beatrice rose to stand in the centre of the cell, turning her head to scan the area around her. She still couldn't see anything.

"Who's there?" she shouted, spinning to look behind her. "Show yourself! I'm not afraid!"

She took a deep breath to steady her breathing. She was an Officer of Erebus, no matter what they said; she was strong, and not easily frightened. She was about to speak again when a searing pain stabbed at her chest with such ferocity her knees almost gave way. She clenched her eyes shut, willing the pain to subside.

"*Embrace me, child, and you can come back.*"

The voice was beautiful, like nothing she had ever heard before. And it seemed to be coming from inside Beatrice's own head.

"What's happening?" she asked the empty room, panic starting to rise in her voice.

"*Come back to me... embrace the power I gave you.*"

The Goddess?

As if in answer, the pain in her chest subsided and she was able to stand. She glanced down at her glowing tattoos which pulsed with increasingly bright blue light. Since her arrest in the Amber Wood, Beatrice had little time to consider her newfound power, never mind attempt to use it. What was she capable of, now that the power of the Goddess of the Wood resided within her?

She walked over to the large wooden door. If her power was worth anything, it had to be capable of allowing her escape. Her eyes traversed the seemingly impenetrable surface, searching for weaknesses.

She reached her hand out to touch the wood, and let out a quiet gasp as her fingertips passed into its surface. She sharply retracted her arm, tracing a finger across her fingerprints. They were cold, unnaturally cold.

Did that really happen?

Beatrice took a deep breath and lunged forward, every fibre of her being telling her to stop, that she'll hit the door. But she didn't. She felt an overwhelming flash of cold melt over her body and before she knew it, she was standing in a dark corridor, the locked door behind her.

"What the—"

Before she could complete the thought, she was silenced by the sound of footsteps echoing further down the corridor. They were coming towards her. She sprinted off in the opposite direction, wracking her brain to remember the layout of the dungeons. It had been years since she had needed to bring a prisoner down here – she had hoped to avoid this desolate place as she rose through the Erebus ranks.

She ran to the end of the corridor, approaching a large wooden door. Against all of her well-honed self-preservation instincts, she increased her speed and charged into the door, appearing at the other side so quickly she had no time to stop herself before barrelling into an unsuspecting guard.

The man was young and inexperienced, and Beatrice was able to subdue him with relative ease. She laid his unconscious body against the wall and searched him for weapons. He was too low-ranking to be equipped with a pistol, but she recovered a heavy wooden baton which would have to do for now. Beatrice carefully removed his cloak and slung it around her own shoulders. It was light – mostly for decoration – but served to somewhat dull the eerie glow emanating from her dark skin.

She continued down the corridor, moving more carefully should any other guards appear. She recalled an exit out onto the courtyard being somewhere in the vicinity, but as her stress levels rose, she began to doubt her sense of direction. As her tension grew, she noticed the pulsating light covering her body growing even brighter, the guard's cloak no longer able to dampen its luminescence. A fresh heat seemed to surge through her veins. It made her feel strong, and powerful.

Beatrice turned a corner, and a cautious smile spread across her face as she spotted it – the exit into the city. She marched forwards, her rising power urging her onwards. Her pace quickened as the door grew closer, excitement building in her chest as her entire body thrummed with arcane energy. Beyond the door, beyond the courtyard, she would be free. Free to return to the Amber Wood, her only sanctuary.

But before Beatrice could reach the door, someone stepped out from a side corridor, their pistol pointed straight at her head. She skidded to a halt, stomach dropping. Once again, her plans were about to be thwarted by her old friend, Herman Elserbast.

She took a couple of steps back, eyes locked on his firearm. "Stand down, Officer Elserbast."

The opposing Officer didn't move a muscle, eyes blazing with hatred as he held the pistol with a steady hand. "You will return to your cell, or I will shoot."

There was no emotion in his voice, just a steely sense of purpose. Heat surged through Beatrice's body, growing as her will to escape intensified. Her hands grew hot.

"I said stand down, Herman. Don't make me do this."

She held her hands up, palms facing forward, the will of the Goddess directing her actions more than her own consciousness.

"Silence!" Herman's hands began to tremble slightly, his finger tense against the trigger. "Return to your cell, or I *will* shoot!"

"Herman..."

It all happened within a few short seconds, but time seemed to slow down around her. As the bullet left the barrel, Beatrice thought she saw a flash of regret cross over Herman's eyes, but it was too late. Streaks of bright, burning light erupted from Beatrice's open palms, incinerating the bullet and engulfing her old friend in crackling blue and yellow flames. She wanted to close her eyes, to shield herself from the horror, but she couldn't. She stood staring, in awe of it despite herself.

It was over as quickly as it began. Herman vanished with no trace, a faint wisp of charcoal smoke the only indication that anything had happened. Beatrice stood, breathing heavily and exhausted. Her skin burned all over from the release of energy and, as she stared at the spot where her comrade had fallen, she was vaguely aware of a coolness spreading down her cheeks. She was crying.

Beatrice knelt on the dusty floor and ran a hand over the space where Herman had stood. The stone was warm.

"I'm so sorry," she whispered, fresh tears freckling the ground. "If only you had understood."

The sound of approaching footsteps drew Beatrice to her feet, and without looking back she lurched forwards, passing through the wooden door into the cold, empty courtyard beyond. She wanted to rest, to take a moment to digest what was happening, but she could already hear a commotion erupting in the labyrinthine dungeon behind her. She had to keep moving.

Her eyes darted about the courtyard, fixing on the city gate. She was exhausted, but it was her only option. Striding forwards, she held her head high and took long, deep breaths, hoping to avoid suspicion.

This was dashed as the thunderous toll of the prison bell rang out over the square, alerting the whole of Arteminion to her escape. Adrenaline coursed through her, and she broke into a sprint, no longer caring who was watching.

Beatrice almost skidded to a halt when a crossbow bolt shot past her ear, only inches away from embedding in the back of her skull. They were shooting to kill. Resisting the urge to turn back, she urged her feet onwards, the gate inching closer. As she approached, the freedom of the forest seemed to call to her, and she gained a second wind, feet pounding as they carried her to the gate.

As she reached her target, she closed her eyes, ignoring her screaming survival instincts and fully trusting the Goddess to take her through. The gate was huge, much thicker than the doors in the prison, and once inside it Beatrice began to doubt whether she would get back out. She was encased in cold, unbending wood, suffocating as her lungs howled for fresh air. She wasn't going to make it; the other side was impossible to reach. She opened her mouth to scream, but nothing could make the sound come.

"Have faith, child."

The words seemed to come from everywhere and nowhere. It was the Goddess, urging her forwards. She had got her this far, surely she wouldn't fail her now. Head swimming, lungs crying out for air, she pressed onwards, deeper into the wood. Panic rose through her body, a voice in the back of her mind crying out for her to give up, but she persisted. Finally, after what felt like an eternity, her fingers felt the warm air of the land outside the wall. She stumbled forwards, almost falling onto the hard ground ahead of her.

Voices continued to ring out from within Arteminion, but they couldn't catch her now. She ran, never looking back, her feet feeling lighter with every step. As she reached the tree line of the Amber Wood, her physical self finally gave out, and she sank to her knees, gulping for air. The scent of damp earth and fallen leaves filled her nostrils, overwhelming her with a sense of calm she had never known before. The place that had once sparked deep trepidation now seemed soothing, tranquil... safe.

"Welcome home."

***

"I'm tellin' yer, she lives in them woods! I saw her with mi own two eyes."

"Stuff an' nonsense! There's nothin' in those woods but beasts, and nasty ones at that."

"I'm tellin' yer, she's there, an' she's a witch!"

The old man laughed with such volume half the occupants of the tavern turned to stare, but he didn't seem to be one who was easily embarrassed. The two of them had an air of long-time regulars who were practically part of the furniture of the place.

"You want to watch yer mouth," he said in mock warning, swilling the remnants of his ale around his tankard. "Ain't been no witches in this world for hundreds o' years, nothin' left of 'em but myths and rumours. You've gone an' hit yer head or somethin."

"She's there, Bill, and she is a sight! Ten feet tall, with bright white eyes, and pointed teeth."

At this, Beatrice failed to stifle a low laugh, and pulled the hood of her cloak further down her face as the eyes of the men fell on her. She coughed to break the silence and stared down into her own ale until they resumed their conversation, their voices lowered to avoid further eavesdropping. She didn't care – she'd heard all she needed. Word was spreading. *Good.* Pulling her cloak tighter around her shoulders, she dropped a few coins on the table and navigated her way through the tavern and out into the brisk evening air.

She strode purposefully towards the city walls, eyes darting to check for guards. Her way was clear, not that it mattered; with what she had learned from the Goddess, she was more than a match for anything the town could throw at her. She closed her eyes and took a measured step forward, her skin prickling all over. The wind rose around her, whipping her hood back from her face. She grinned – travelling was getting easier.

She opened her eyes. The city walls were gone, replaced by the empty plains separating the town from the Amber Wood. She glanced over her shoulder, at the city which had shunned her. As rumours of the Witch of the Amber Wood grew, they would come to her.

Arteminion would be saved by magic, whether they wanted it or not.

X: WHEEL OF FORTUNE

Off to Beat the Wizard by Mara Lynn Johnstone

Naomi followed the curving walkway between mailbox and house, sorting through bills without needing to watch where she stepped. Her feet knew the way. She'd redesigned this front yard herself, and she was proud of it. Even her elderly parents had said nice things on their last visit. In all their years as the adults in charge of the house, they'd never put the amount of yard work into it that Naomi and her husband did.

Ha, this one even got his name right, she thought with a huff of laughter. *Though I bet it's a typo.* She separated the credit card offer from the stack as she absently pulled the door open. Everything else addressed to him said "Leif."

"Hey Leaf," she called, depositing the rest of the mail on the dining room table. "You upstairs?" Silence. Garden it was. She passed through the kitchen and onto the back step. "Leaf?"

But he wasn't in the garden either, which was a little strange. They both made a point not to stray out of earshot without letting the other know. But he definitely wasn't among the rows of vegetables and riotous flowers, nor was he over by the beehives, communing in the bee language that he'd never managed to teach Naomi. He wasn't at the swing set that Tammy had almost outgrown, either.

Wait, where was Tammy? She'd been on her favorite swing when Naomi went out for the mail. It still moved slightly.

Naomi felt a chill. "Tammy?" she yelled. "Leaf?"

"Naomi!" called the distant voice of her husband. Footsteps said he was running closer. "It's open!"

The chill turned into an arctic freeze. "Where's Tammy?" she shouted.

Leaf pushed through bushes, his long brown hair every bit as wild as the first time she'd seen him. "She's gone! Grab the packs!"

Naomi left a trail of swear words through the house as she flung the letter in the vague direction of the dining room table, on her way to the cubbies by the front door that held the family's emergency go-bags. She strapped on her own, mentally skimming down the checklist of things in the bag and the most recent time she'd replaced the batteries and food. Everything was fine. They were ready. As ready as they could be with twenty years to prepare.

She grabbed the other two bags, one over each shoulder, and raced back outside. The door slammed behind her; she didn't even consider stopping to lock it. Every second counted.

How long since she went in? Naomi thought as she pelted madly across the yard to where Leaf had already disappeared back into the woods. *It can't be more than a minute or two. Days on that end, not weeks. I hope.*

After a few more precious seconds of sliding on leaves and dodging branches, Naomi burst into the clearing that held her worst fear: the cairn was blasted open from inside. Landscaping rocks and chunks of concrete had sprayed halfway across the clearing. Among the worry for her child and the dread of what she had to face, Naomi found indignation at the rude destruction of something she and Leaf had spent so much time on. Even the biohazard paint for scaring away hikers was wrecked, though the skull on the other side was mostly intact.

"There's still a trace," Leaf said, pulling her attention from the rocks. He grabbed his own pack from Naomi and rushed to strap it on. "Pretty sure I can do it. Ready?"

She took his hand with a nod. His hazel eyes were determined, a steadying influence that reminded her to take deep breaths. She was ready. They could do this.

They *would* do this, and nothing was going to stop them.

Leaf raised his other hand toward the dark interior of the cairn, where the original stone arch lurked. Now that she was looking for it, Naomi could just barely make out the scent of recent magic with a familiar sweetness that made her stomach turn. She focused on sharing her own energies with Leaf, what little she had.

The pendant that he never took off glowed from beneath his T-shirt, a bright green that matched the color his eyes used to be. He'd only used it twice in his time here, as far as Naomi knew – once to heal an injury in the early days when they were scared to take him to a doctor, and once when Tammy had hit her head on a paving stone while learning to walk. For the rest of the intervening decades, he'd been steadily filling the pendant with the tiniest thread of spare energy.

It was slow going with no ambient magic to work with. The pendant still wasn't close to full. But if either of them had anything to say about it, that small amount was *going* to be enough.

The recently-closed portal peeled back open until it was wide enough to admit both of them. Hand in hand, Naomi and Leaf stepped through the same doorway that had changed their lives twenty years ago and stolen their child now.

That wizard was not going to get away with it again.

***

Naomi was glad to be holding Leaf's hand, and not just because it made sure that they arrived at the same time. The portal was disorienting. When she stepped through to the bright meadow on the other side, she had to blink furiously for a moment, breathing deep and slow.

She opened her eyes just in time to watch Leaf drop the glamour that he'd been carefully maintaining the whole time he'd lived on Earth. Pointed ears looked so nice on him. When he met Naomi's gaze, his eyes were the same vivid green that she'd fallen in love with.

"Hello again," Naomi said fondly, squeezing his hand.

His bashful smile brought up all sorts of memories. "Hello, Offworlder."

Naomi tugged a backpack strap. "I've got plenty of offworld tricks ready. Let's find out what we're dealing with."

Leaf nodded, looking around, and his long hair didn't fall into his face even a little. "This is where you came through before, right? I see the old watchtower."

Naomi followed his gaze to spot crumbled stonework peeking above the trees. "Yes! That looks right." She started forward. "Let's check the view from up top."

Leaf walked by her side like when she was young, and he had the same gentle touch that turned the undergrowth aside to let them pass. Naomi remembered him taking spare moments between world-ending drama to show her how magic worked. The concept had eluded her just as much as advanced math, though she did manage to get a shaky grasp of the firefly trick.

By the time they'd needed it, she'd gotten pretty good at making her flashlight glow extra bright. It had been a challenge, but she'd given her all, and done her part to help save the kingdom from shadow monsters.

It was hard then because she was new at it. She'd spent her time since then in the magic desert known as Earth, and just like Leaf had built up his reservoir, she had practiced weaving wisps of her own life energy into glow magic.

The best she'd been able to manage at home was a firefly-bright fingertip, which was impressive for Earth. Leaf had been impressed, at least. She hadn't shown anyone else.

She tried it now as she walked. Oh, it was easy. Magic was everywhere, and she shoveled it into the spell like she was building sandcastles on a beach, after years of making do with just a tiny pile of grains shaken from a shoe.

Her right hand lit up like a floodlight, making Leaf jump. When he realized what it was, he turned a proud grin on her that was just as bright.

Naomi grinned back. "It's going to be different this time around."

"Oh yes it is," he agreed.

***

The watchtower had been in disrepair before. It was an ancient ruin now. Only the stones remained, with no sign of the creaky door and the broken railings. Naomi and Leaf had talked more than once about how time passed differently between their worlds, but they'd never been able to say with any certainty whether it was a constant rate or not. Leaf was pretty sure that whoever cast the portal could set the terms. All Naomi knew for certain was that her epic adventure had fit into the smallest sliver of an afternoon back home.

Leaf trailed one long-fingered hand along the stonework at the base of the tower. "This is a good sign." He sounded like he was trying to convince himself. "If it was the same minute-to-day ratio, then this would be just foundations, if anything. We definitely haven't been gone for millennia." He ducked inside and trotted up the winding stairs, light-footed even with the pack.

Naomi hurried to join him, with thoughts of the life her husband had left behind when he escaped with her. He'd said many times that he didn't regret it, and that there wasn't anything worth staying for even if there hadn't been a deceitful wizard trying to kill them, but she knew that some degree of homesickness was inescapable. Leaf was just brave about it.

And now here he was, at the top of the tower when she climbed up to join him, staring out at a landscape that certainly looked different from what she remembered.

"The river's bigger," he said, sounding hopeful. "Look, see how they've dug new tributaries and irrigation channels for the fields? The crops must be amazing now. And the city looks a bit wider, but not huge." He was silent for a moment, then said quietly, "They might have food for everyone now."

Naomi took his hand again, saying nothing. Then something occurred to her. "Why'd they let the watchtower fall apart?" she asked, looking at the wind-worn stones. "Even if it's all peaceful and happy, surely they'll want to keep an eye out for problems."

Leaf frowned, then looked straight up. After a moment of concentration, he broke into a delighted smile. "The dragons are back!"

"What?" Naomi didn't see anything but sky.

"They don't need watchtowers on the ground when dragons have better ones!" Leaf said. "See how those five little clouds are spaced in a perfect circle around the valley?"

Now that he pointed it out, it did look strange.

Leaf looked breathlessly upward. "I hope she's still there." Before Naomi could ask who he meant, he cupped his hands around his mouth and shouted something in a voice that reverberated off the stone. It was halfway between recognizable words and a vibrating growl that seemed to come from a larger throat than his.

Something dove off the nearest cloud. Naomi watched as the falling dart opened sudden wings, flaring silver in the light, growing larger as the dragon came in for a landing.

Wind buffeted the tower from the flapping of thunderous wings, which made Naomi squint and step back while Leaf waved both arms in joy.

"Eyescale! Do you remember me? It's Leaf! I didn't die!"

Talons scraped the ancient stones as the wind died down. Wings spread far to either side and a long silver neck arched over the edge of the tower; the dragon clung to the side since there wasn't space to land without stepping on them.

Naomi appreciated that.

"You *didn't* die!" the dragon agreed in her own vibrating voice. She looked from Leaf to Naomi and sniffed the air. A knowing grin spread along her silver snout. "You went offworld, didn't you?"

"Yes," Leaf confirmed, taking Naomi's hand. "We did. This is my wife. Naomi; Eyescale."

Naomi nodded and bent her knees in something like a curtsey; it felt like the thing to do. The great silver dragon was more than a little intimidating. "It's a pleasure to meet you."

"And you," Eyescale replied. "Now unless I miss my guess, that makes you the same offworlder who also died heroically in taking down the Shadow Lord. Did the other heroes go with you?"

"No," Naomi had to tell her. "They did die. We thought the shadowbeasts were just going to infect them, but then the Shadow Lord's hounds – wait, what happened afterward? Did Luxiferious take over?" She looked around for shadows that might have been listening.

The dragon cocked her head. "Who?"

Leaf said, "The wizard."

"The one who was helping you? I have no idea what happened to him. Why would he take over?"

Naomi exclaimed, "Because he was evil!"

"He was working with the Shadow Lord all along," Leaf explained. "We only found out at the end. It was a ruse to take out the monarchy and make him look like a conquering hero, so he could take the king's place."

"Huh. News to me," the dragon said. "No, that king recovered from the shadows just fine, and even lived long enough to have more heirs."

Naomi glanced at the distant river. "How... long ago was that?"

"Let's see." The dragon snaked her neck around in thought. "I was still out of town at the time. I got here right before Esmerelda's coronation, so that must have been... about two centuries, give or take."

Naomi looked to Leaf. He was nodding stoically, mouth a flat line. Everyone he'd known would be gone then, aside from Eyescale. Naomi had always thought it was nice that real elves had a lifespan only a little longer than humans, but now it just seemed tragic.

He did volunteer to give it all up for me, she reminded herself for the umpteenth time. *And he didn't have any close family left after the wars. And at least he's found one friend who DOES live that long.*

Eyescale was still talking. "You picked a good time to come back, actually. Well, good for the kingdom, at any rate. We could use the insights from two previous shadow-conquering heroes, since the word on the street is that they're making a return earlier than expected."

"What?" Naomi demanded.

"Why didn't you say so?" Leaf asked.

Eyescale shrugged a wing. "I just did. It's not a big deal. Dragonfire's good on shadows. No idea why the Shadow Lord is rushing to make another attempt now instead of waiting until people forget all about him like before, but it's a poor choice. There are written accounts of the last attack everywhere, not just one dusty old book."

Naomi met Leaf's eyes. "Do you think Lux is calling the shots?" she asked.

"Maybe," he said. "But he seemed to always think everything through. He would have a reason for attacking now. Something that could take the dragons out."

Eyescale scoffed. "I doubt it."

"You said you hadn't heard anything about him after last time," Naomi said. "What about another wizard, recruiting more heroes now? Is he just using a different name? Because *someone* called our daughter through the portal."

"What?" asked Eyescale. "You have a kid here? Why didn't *you* say?"

Leaf said firmly, "We're saying it now. This is all starting again, and we are *not* going to let that wizard get away with it. Not that he got away with it fully last time, which is great to hear." He looked at Naomi. "Maybe that magical dampener I hit him with actually worked better than we thought."

"Maybe!" Naomi said, thinking back. "He did say it was a really powerful one; that's why we didn't use it on the Shadow Lord right away. What with the way he was yelling about those hounds being 'cheating,' I did wonder if the dampener was also some kind of under-handed trick."

Eyescale lifted her wings. "Speculate later; we've got a kid of yours to rescue! Any guesses where she's gone?"

Naomi opened her mouth to say no, then she saw another dragon dive from a cloud. "Look!" she said instead, pointing.

Eyescale and Leaf turned. The three of them watched the dragon breathe fire toward the ground instead of landing. Just as Eyescale was starting to speak, a black tendril flashed into the sky like the arm of a kraken, wrapping the green dragon in shadow.

Naomi found herself grabbed by a large scaly hand while wings flapped madly. She was suddenly rocketing through the sky on a colli-sion course with destiny, for the second time around.

She glared into the wind, hands already glowing.

***

Instead of shadow-infected woodland creatures, they found a handful of unfamiliar little black shapes throwing dark whips around the dragon. Naomi only had a split second to take in the sight – hounds, these didn't match a familiar silhouette, and they were fully shadow, unlike the oily-black infected animals – then Eyescale was tossing her gently to the side and leveling a fiery blast between the trees.

The little implike things hadn't spotted her approach, since she came in low. They squealed like wild boars. Naomi landed awkwardly with the weight of both backpacks, but got to her feet with glowing hands, dropped the bags, and raced into the fray.

One of the imps was smoking on the ground, and two others limped, but they seemed otherwise unaffected by the fire that chased them around the clearing. Trees were going up in flames. The other dragon lay in a cocoon of shadow. Dark whips shot out at Eyescale, catching on her wings and legs no matter how much fire she breathed – they withered under the flame, but more followed.

Naomi was glowing up to her shoulders as she grabbed the first shadow whip and burned it away from Eyescale's wing. The dragon grunted something that sounded grateful, then snapped her jaws shut on an imp that had strayed too close. Another glowing figure on the other side of the clearing proved to be Leaf flinging his own whip of pure light around an imp that squealed and thrashed.

The other shadow whips dissolved as Naomi touched them with sun-bright hands. In moments, Eyescale was free and lunging after the remaining imps. Naomi ran to the fallen dragon. She ripped the bindings free like a particularly vicious child on Christmas morning.

The green dragon surged upwards, sending Naomi stumbling backward in eagerness to join the battle.

That battle was over before Naomi regained her balance. The only surviving imp was the one that Leaf had caught, which was making pitiful noises that bought it no sympathy. Unfortunately there were a number of burning trees in danger of spreading, but the two dragons worked together to dig up the forest floor and shower dirt on the flames in a surprisingly effective firefighting maneuver. Naomi guessed they had done this before.

When all that remained was blackness of the charcoal variety, the dragons joined Naomi and Leaf in looming over the captive.

Leaf spoke first, still holding the light whip, though he himself wasn't glowing anymore. "Where is the Shadow Lord?"

"In the shadows," croaked the imp, whose silhouette looked something like a frog now that Naomi thought about it.

Leaf tugged on the whip. "Which shadows? You can't tell me 'all of them.' I know he's not that strong."

"Know that, do you?" the imp laughed.

"Yes," Leaf hissed.

Naomi stepped closer, hands still glowing. "We killed him the last time. We know exactly how strong he is."

The imp seemed to be squinting. "You what? Wait, are you *those* two? What are you doing here now?"

Naomi leaned closer, fingers spread like she wanted to curl them around his neck. "Our child was dragged into this, and we want her *back.*"

The imp burst into laughter, which made Naomi straighten up in surprise. A startled look at Leaf showed that he didn't understand either. The dragons were silent, observing from very close.

"The new offworlder is *your* kid?" the imp laughed, all whimpers gone. "Oh, the Lady's broken the rules this time for sure."

"What lady?" Naomi demanded.

"The Shadow Queen. She's female this time around. Wanted a change of pace." The imp chuckled. "She also wanted to win for once, but I can tell this is going to backfire more than the timing already has. Dragons everywhere."

Eyescale took this as a cue to lower her great silver head directly into the imp's line of sight. "Why don't you start at the beginning," she rumbled. "While I decide whether or not to eat you?"

The imp leaned its head back against the dirt. "Sure, why not? This whole thing has gone so far off the rails already; let's jump it into the lake."

***

One thing they swiftly learned was that the imps were just as much of a departure from plans as the shadowhounds had been. All the legends of the Shadow Lord – or Lady, apparently – spoke of the infectious dark magic that could turn the will of innocent creatures, and even people. That was the big threat spreading across the land. But it could be defeated by purehearted heroes armed with the right kind of light, and it had been.

Those shadowhounds, though, were otherworldly things. A deadly surprise that had offended Lux, then immediately killed Ellantrika, Turnip, and Slammantha. The only good thing about their presence at the battle was the way they had shown their true allegiance by fawning at the wizard's feet. Their jaws had still dripped with the blood of his apprentices, and his reaction was most illuminating.

This imp was shaping up to be a similar font of information.

"Normally they do this every millennia or whatever," it said, surprisingly casual for someone tied up with a light whip. "Keeps things fresh, I guess. Whoever loses has to do extra chores in the shadow realm. And it may play a part in their private time too, but you didn't hear that from me. I'm not going to be the one to tell them they should soundproof the bedroom better."

Naomi held up a hand. "Hold on."

Leaf looked like she'd just beaten him to it.

"Are you telling me," Naomi asked, "That the great evil and the wizard who gathers kids to fight it are... an item?"

"Have been for about a dozen millennia," the imp said. "Almost thirteen, I think; their anniversary is coming up."

Eyescale rumbled in displeasure. "This is all a game for both of them? How *dare they?*"

The imp shrugged against the whip. "No one's stopped them yet. The last time was a mess because neither won, so they're trying again. But between you and me, they're both a bit miffed at each other."

Naomi folded her arms. "You don't say."

Leaf tugged on the whip so that the imp sat up, then he leaned in close. "You are going to help us stop them," he hissed. "Understood?"

"Sure," the imp said. "I've got stuff to do back home. Nobody asked before throwing me into this mess, though that's nothing new. But if it takes too long, just go ahead and send me back."

"How?" Naomi asked.

The imp tossed his head toward the corpses of his fellows. "A good bite ought to do it."

"Won't that kill you?" Naomi asked, though she suspected the answer.

"Nah, just this body. Honestly, I'm looking forward to leaving it behind. Flesh is so cumbersome."

Leaf tugged the whip again. "So, ignoring all that," he said, "Can you tell us where to find Luxiferious? And our daughter?"

"Ehhhh..." the imp said noncommittally, looking around.

"I can," said Eyescale. Her voice echoed more than usual.

Naomi looked up and realized where the dragon had gotten her name. One after another, the silver scales were opening into additional eyes, in every color of the rainbow and then some. Each of them was looking at her.

"Offworlder energy that way," Eyescale reported, pointing her snout to the southeast. "It thrums with a similar frequency to yours. I can smell a bit of your melody in there too, Leaf."

"Good," Leaf said. He stood, lifting the trussed-up imp like an unwieldy dog. "I've got our friend here. Naomi, can you get the packs?"

"Right," Naomi said, turning on her heel to find them among the churned-up mulch. She returned to where Eyescale waited, extra senses still flared. The green dragon was already carrying Leaf and the imp.

Eyescale picked Naomi up gently. They launched into the sky again, with a little less panic and a lot more determination.

***

The thrice-bedamned wizard had his new charges setting up a campsite at the same "mystic spring" that Naomi remembered. She could see the pond with the glowing fish from the air.

Eyes winked closed in the scales around her. Naomi had been glad to see that not all of them opened up like that – surely it would make carrying her a painful experience for the dragon – she didn't spare a thought for it now. Eyescale was making head gestures to the other dragon, who immediately dropped low to the tree line with Leaf and the imp.

Eyescale carried Naomi in from the sky, clearly visible, bellowing in that vibrating voice for the young heroes to present themselves.

Tammy was right there in the middle, and she wasn't hurt.

Naomi blinked away tears as she counted the children gathered among the wildflowers. Five, just like before. None looked injured or traumatized yet; this must be the early stages of the adventure. They peered innocently up at the winged guardian of the realm who was coming in for a landing.

Naomi saw the moment Tammy recognized her. Shock then joy traced across her young face, followed by the determined expression that she wore when she was ready to make her parents proud of her.

Naomi was pretty sure she knew who Tammy got it from.

But she didn't have time to think about it, because as Eyescale back-winged in for a landing, kicking up a mighty wind, a familiar figure stepped from between the trees.

He didn't even change his clothes in two hundred years, Naomi thought in scorn. It was the same gray cloak and pointy hat, the same white beard and proud nose. Same bastard who had gotten her friends killed, and uncountable others as well.

The last time Naomi had seen this wizard, he had lied about the portal to send her home. She remembered it clearly now, the scene playing behind her eyes as she waited for her feet to touch the ground.

"Farewell, offworlder!" Lux said with a fake smile. "Thank you for your service. I'm sure your family is wondering where you are back on Earth." He waved towards the portal that he'd just set up in the mouth of the cave, which was conveniently the only way out.

With her friends dead behind her, and homesickness strong in her heart, Naomi took a step towards the swirling colors before she remembered who had cast it. She couldn't trust him.

As she hesitated, Leaf caught her hand. He whispered, "It's not leading to Earth."

She turned to him in shock, ready to ask questions. He was already answering.

"They say one of my ancestors was a prokka; a talented dimension traveler. The magic coming from there doesn't match yours." Leaf paused, shooting a glance at the wizard waiting patiently. "He's trying to kill you."

"What about you?" Naomi whispered back. "As soon as I'm gone, you'll be alone here with him. And them."

The hounds twined around the wizard's robes, merging with his shadow in an unholy way. He didn't do a thing to ward them off.

Leaf glared at the portal. "I can make it go to Earth," he said.

Naomi kissed his cheek. "Do it," she said as he met her eyes. "I'll shine my light at him." She put her hand in her pocket for the flashlight.

Leaf reached for his own pocket – oh, he still had the magical dampener, didn't he? – then took her other hand. They faced the wizard side-by-side.

"We're going together," Naomi announced. Then she aimed the flashlight and gave it everything she had. It glowed like the sun.

As Lux exclaimed and covered his eyes, Leaf threw the crystal sphere that popped like a soap bubble to cover the wizard in a rainbow shine. The *shadowhounds whined and tried to hide behind the gray robes, getting colorful shimmer on themselves too. They yelped and hissed.*

Leaf made a dramatic gesture at the portal, clearing the swirls to show a familiar forest. He pulled her forward. The pair ran together, with Naomi's light still blasting away shadows.

They leapt through the portal and it slammed shut behind them.

Naomi sprawled onto regular brown leaves with her flashlight clattering down beside her, looking utterly normal. She sat up and stared at the trees she knew so well, the bushes that led the way home... and the elf she'd brought with her.

Leaf had let go of her hand when they fell. He looked scared now.

Naomi took his hand again, and met his eyes. "Thank you," she said. "Think you've got enough juice left for a glamour?"

He clutched his pendant. "Barely." As Naomi watched, his ears grew shorter and his eyes less bright. In moments, he looked every bit the normal human middle schooler. Well, mostly normal. He was still beautiful.

Naomi gave him an encouraging grin.

He smiled shakily back. "What now?"

Naomi pulled him to his feet. "We'll figure something out. Come meet my parents."

Hand in hand, they walked away from the portal arch and into the rest of their lives.

And now their lives had taken them back here, to face that same traitorous wizard. But this time they were prepared.

As Eyescale folded her wings and Lux stepped forward, recognition just starting to dawn in his eyes, the green dragon swooped in over the trees. A shadow whip flashed out from the imp in one hand, and a light whip from the elf in the other.

Lux cried out as the competing magics tied him tight, collapsing to his knees and then to the ground. Four of the children exclaimed in dismay.

Tammy raced into her mother's arms, and Naomi dropped the packs to hug her while dragon wingbeats blew through the meadow.

"All your stories were true!" Tammy said, face against her shirt. "Why didn't you tell me they actually happened?"

"We had a lot of conversations about that," Naomi said into her hair. "But we at least wanted you to know what to do if this ever came up."

Tammy pulled back, her expression fierce. "I didn't tell him anything. And I've got my pocket light."

"Good girl," Naomi said. "Now let's catch your friends up to speed about this traitorous bastard who is *married* to the Shadow Queen."

"He's what?" Tammy said.

The other children echoed her, coming close now that the dragon had stopped flapping. Lux glared among the wildflowers. As the green dragon set them down, the imp chuckled at the end of its shadow whip, while Leaf made Tammy do a double-take.

"Dad?!"

He looked up from his light whip. "Hi honey! We're so glad you're okay."

"Your ears!" Tammy sputtered. "And eyes!"

"All the better to see and hear you with," Leaf quipped. "We'll explain it all in a minute, okay?"

Tammy looked back at her mother. "Does this mean I'm a half-elf?"

"Yes." Naomi put a hand on her shoulder. "But let's shelve the existential crisis until we save the world again, okay?"

Tammy nodded once, and turned to face the wizard.

Eyescale did the explaining at high volume. "Luxiferious has been working with the Shadow Queen all along, arranging these large-scale conflicts as entertainment for themselves. As witnesses, we have this shadow imp—" She pointed a talon, and the imp freed a hand long enough to wave. "—And these two surviving heroes from the *last* time around."

Lux muttered something, but it sounded more like an insult than a spell.

Naomi stepped closer. "I would kick you in the face, but I don't want to soil my shoe," she spat, then she knelt to open her pack. "C'mere kids; flashlights for everybody. They're maximum wattage from Earth, more effective than whatever enchanted relics he's told you to find."

"Dibs on the good one!" Tammy said, grabbing up the handheld searchlight she hadn't been allowed to touch before.

"Just aim it away from your friends," Naomi said. She handed exotic offworld items to the other four, who looked at them with awe.

The green dragon spoke up. "I believe we have a shortcut for this farce. If you would?" He snaked his neck towards the imp, then nodded at the trees lining the meadow. "Will one of those shadows do?"

The imp kept one hand on the shadow whip, but used the other to snap its fingers casually toward the trees. "Sure thing. This is going to be hilarious. Want me to drag him in first?"

A bit of quick explanation from Leaf told Naomi and the others that the conversation they'd had in the air had led to a direct route to the lair of the Shadow Queen, who would not be expecting them. A perfect time to immobilize both of the evildoers at once.

It sounded like a fine plan to Naomi, needing just one thing. "Tammy," she said. "Did Lux give you a magical dampener, by any chance?"

"Yes!" Tammy said, pulling the glittersphere from her pocket. "He gave us each one right away!"

The imp brayed laughter at that. Lux just glared more.

"Great," Naomi said. "Can I?" When Tammy handed it to her, Naomi strode over to the wizard and threw it at the side of his head. It smashed like an egg, coating him in rainbows that would prevent any trickery. The bindings weren't affected. Good.

"Nice one," Leaf said. He hauled on the light whip. "Into the shadow portal with you. I can tell it's going to the right place."

It took a bit of shuffling to decide what order they would go in, but soon enough they were lined up to jump one after another into the tree shadow that was much darker than the surrounding ones.

The Shadow Queen really didn't see them coming.

And with this much light in her face, turning the vast cavern into an eye-searing sunny day, she couldn't see much at all. Her dramatic robes of shadow burned away into a plain black dress while the otherworldly villain collapsed onto the obsidian dais in front of her throne. The shadow hounds yelped and hid.

The shadow imp was yelling a bit too, but also laughing, so Naomi didn't feel too bad about that.

"Kids!" Leaf shouted. "Get her with an orb!"

The nearest girl stepped forward bravely to throw a magical dampener from close range. It wasn't a great shot, but it hit the Queen's shoulder and spread.

"You're not even pretty," the girl observed with a sniff as the last of the shadow magic dissipated to show a bony-looking human with black hair and an ill-fitting dress.

Naomi's flash of sympathy was brief when she remembered all the death and destruction. She pulled a rope from her bag and walked over, glowing like a sun given human form.

"Remember me?" she asked. "You probably don't. You've wronged *so* many people; how could you possibly keep track?" It wasn't difficult at all to tie the Shadow Queen's hands behind her back, then haul her to her feet. "I've spent the last twenty years thinking about what I'd like to do to you," she told her. "Sending you back home is clearly not the answer. Leaf?"

"On it," her husband replied. "Eyescale, would you do the honors and hold this bastard for a moment?" The shadow whip holding Lux had long since burned away, with the imp covering its eyes on the floor, and Leaf let his own whip disappear as soon as the dragon had one silver hand securely around the prisoner.

"My pleasurrrrre," the dragon purred ominously.

"What are you doing?" Lux yelped, speaking up for the first time.

"Sending you to a magic desert," Leaf told him. He turned toward the mouth of the tunnel that led out of the cavern, and struck a casting posture.

The wizard scoffed. "You can't do that. You're just an elf, and not even a very talented one at that."

Leaf's cocky smile was one that Naomi knew well. "They say," he said with the air of someone who's told this story before, "That one of my ancestors was a prokka."

He gestured like he was weaving something from the air, pulling magic in a way that was far more complex than that advanced math from days of yore. Swirling colors obscured the tunnel, then cleared to show a crisp view of some unassuming bushes.

Naomi dragged the Shadow Queen stumbling across the cave floor. The Queen still had her eyes closed against the light, but was starting to protest. She called for the hounds. They just whined from behind the throne.

"Hey kids," Naomi said, stopping short of the portal. "Bring over those other dampening orbs. Eyescale, let's search his pockets before chucking him through."

Naomi gave each of the villains a double dose of antimagic before telling the kids to ransack. Over loud protests, the five young heroes removed all manner of enchanted objects from the wizard's pockets and hat, then checked the Shadow Queen's unassuming dress as well. She had daggers. When Eyescale declared them both clear, using her extra sight to be sure, Naomi waved everyone back.

Leaf held the portal stable. He nodded to her. Naomi sent first the Shadow Queen and then Luxiferious through with solid kicks to their backsides. The evil pair yelled, crashing into the bushes.

The portal swirled shut. Leaf dusted his hands off with satisfaction. "All that time stargazing and studying the dimension walls sure came in handy," he said.

Tammy asked worriedly, "You didn't send them near our house, did you?"

Leaf shook his head. "San Francisco."

"San Francisco??"

Naomi told her, "They might be able to scrape a living as street performers, if it occurs to them. And if they can stoop to that level. One way or another, it ought to be a humbling experience for them both."

"I hope someone throws them off a pier," Leaf said. "I understand the water's cold."

A voice from the floor reminded them that the imp was still there. "Can you turn off those flaming lights long enough for me to send the hounds back? They've got teleporter collars."

"Oh, sure," Naomi said, extinguishing her glow and waving for the kids to shut off most of the lights. With just one flashlight pointed at the ceiling, she told the imp that it was safe.

Even acting tame, those shadowhounds brought up terrifying memories. Naomi was relieved when the imp wasted no time in activating their collars to make them disappear in wisps of darkness.

Then he waddled over to Eyescale and spread his arms. "Bite me."

She didn't waste time either. The kids made noises of alarm at the sudden violence, but at least there wasn't any blood. Only two halves of a shadow creature that the dragon spat toward the far side of the cavern.

"I declare this mess over," Eyescale said, opening some new eyes. "Everyone follow me to the way out. Careful of side tunnels." With that, she whirled in a sinuous flash of scales and ducked into the tunnel. Everyone else trailed after, with the green dragon bringing up the rear.

Leaf gave Tammy a hug. "I'm *so* glad you're okay," he said.

Tammy hugged him back, then stared at his ears. "So can we talk about that half-elf thing now?"

"I suppose we can," Leaf said, looking over her head at Naomi. "We have a bit of a walk ahead of us. I wouldn't want to go home before telling the current monarch the truth of all this."

"Do we have to?" Tammy asked. "Not the talking to the monarch thing; the going home right away. Can't we stay a bit? I have all this heritage to get in touch with! And I want to learn magic too!"

"Well," Leaf said slowly.

"What's the rush?" Naomi asked. She ran a finger along her husband's eartip. "You deserve it. And it's not like anyone will miss us."

Tammy clapped her hands together, reciting, "'And when they returned, they found that only minutes had passed!'"

"That's right," Naomi said with a fond smile. "And you know," she told Leaf, "We might just be able to find you another pendant or five to fill up before we go. So you have a stockpile for emergencies."

"Yes please," Leaf said in deep relief. "You have no idea how much I agonized over using it before. What if something worse happened the next day?"

Naomi hugged him tight. "No more of that."

Tammy hopped in front of them. "I wanna learn too!"

Leaf separated an arm and ruffled her hair. "You'll get to."

"Dad!" she complained, batting his hand away and finger-combing it back into place. He made it up to her by sparking a bit of magic to make it silky smooth, much to her delight.

"We could also," Naomi said, "Get enough of a reservoir for a return trip someday. If you want."

Leaf hugged her wordlessly. Hand in hand, they walked forward into the rest of their lives.

XI: JUSTICE

Wayward Magic by Mara Lynn Johnstone

Mot touched the child's broken arm with more than his usual gentleness. This little boy had never been healed by magic before, and had clearly spent his short life being told how evil and terrifying the mage lords were. As he should. But that did make things awkward for an escaped healer who just wanted to help.

"Hush," said the boy's mother when the boy flinched. "It's okay. Just hold still."

The boy shook his head, breath heaving, all tears and snot bubbles. He kept trying to turn away, but his mother held him in place. At this rate he was going to make the injury worse.

Mot held up one hand, fingers waggling innocently. "How many fingers do I have?" he asked in a conversational tone.

The boy stared for a moment, long enough for Mot to lay the fingers of his other hand on the broken forearm and urge the snapped bones back into place. Before the child finished counting to five, his arm was perfectly healthy.

He made a confused noise that prompted a laugh from his mother.

"There you go," Mot said. "How do *your* fingers feel? All wiggly and normal?"

While the boy tested his hand, nodding and sniffling, his mother thanked Mot. "We're so grateful. A break that bad might never have healed right otherwise."

"My pleasure," Mot said honestly. This kind of simple accident was still refreshing to deal with after so long getting slaves fixed up enough to go back to work. He stood to his full (unimpressive) height with a deep breath. "It's good luck we were here already today." He and Wayra had come on a supply run while the rest of the camp was busy, and they'd been met with more than one problem.

"We're glad to have you!" the woman said, ushering him toward the door of the little house. "I won't keep you; I'm sure they'll be wanting your input."

"Oh, Wayra has everything in hand," Mot said, but he wasted no time in saying his goodbyes and hastening down the road. Morning sunlight didn't soften the chill in the air, or maybe it was the way every person in sight moved with tense shoulders and quick feet. Smiles were strained. And they had every reason to be.

Mot found the town hall in what passed for the center of town, though forest was visible just a stone's throw away. Trees overgrew the dirt road like they were trying to eat it. Or shield it from view from above.

With a flick of his eyes at the empty sky, Mot pushed his way through the door.

Wayra was easy to spot among the townsfolk, and not just because they were all circled around, explaining their predicament to her. She towered over most of the farmers, merchants, and minor politicians. Family heritage had made her tall, while a childhood spent wrangling deer had made her strong – something that she'd only built on after the mage lords seized the ranch and sent her fleeing into the woods. She hadn't starved and died like the mage lords had intended; far from it. And Mot couldn't be more proud of her.

He made his way over quietly, admiring the figure she cut, in furs and leathers with multiple sword and dagger sheaths politely emptied into a pile on the table behind her. Her skin bore a healthy tan that put his own pallid complexion to shame, and her lips were pursed in thought. Weak sunlight from the windows lit up her hair to a color Mot would call "reddish brown" out loud, but "the hue of a mighty redwood illuminated by a blazing summer sun" in the privacy of his own mind.

Mot hadn't heard a word of the conversation on his way across the room. When Wayra flashed him a smile of greeting and made space at her side, he realized that he'd better figure out what he'd missed. He joined her with a quizzical lift of an eyebrow.

She summarized. "They've got a week to come up with a double tithe, or things start getting claimed. The question is whether to focus on gathering money or evacuating the town."

"Right." Mot nodded. "That ultimatum is a lie."

"Are you sure?" asked a gray-haired woman that the others were deferring to. "The messenger was adamant that he would return with soldiers at Sunday's dawn."

Mot shook his head. "I'm sure," he said flatly. "The mages don't even keep promises to each other; they invented backstabbing. There used to be more than seven Archons – well, six now." He turned a quiet smile toward Wayra, whose grin in return was more than a little bloodthirsty. "Anyways, my point is that they would definitely rather make an example of your town. They don't need the tithe. How quickly can you get everyone out?"

Several people answered, and the next few minutes were full of intense planning. Someone brought out writing materials to keep track; roles were assigned; other nearby towns were considered as potential refuges.

"Splitting up will definitely be your best bet," Wayra said. "Just keep track of each other, so you can get in touch if it's in the stars to rebuild eventually."

"And if anyone feels inclined to spend their days striking back instead of hiding..." Mot suggested with a glance at Wayra.

She nodded. "They're welcome to join up. But it's a traveling life of sleeping on the ground, not as cozy as a stranger's attic bed or what have you."

Mot reflected on the thick furs that he slept on, in his own private tent, which were infinitely better than the conditions in his old life. There was even enough food, and most importantly, dozens of people he could trust. He wondered if this little village held any angry youths or desperate souls who might find it similarly appealing.

Someone outside yelled, high and panicky, carrying over the sound of discussion. Then another person. Then something thumped into the side of the building with a distinctive whoosh. Mot knew what it was even before he smelled the smoke.

"They're here!" he shouted. "Wayra—!"

She was already sheathing the last dagger, with her two favorite swords ready to be grabbed. Townsfolk scattered to the windows and door. Flames licked at the doorframe. Wayra looked out a window, then declared, "It's just soldiers! Get everyone out, and leave them to me!" With that, she charged out the door, swords flashing and townsfolk leaping aside.

Mot dashed after.

Every building on this side of town was touched by flame, but the sky was clear; the enemy was on the ground with pre-enchanted firebombs. And by the looks of it, they had *not* expected a large and angry warrior to come roaring out at them. Their deer were already shying away.

When she didn't bother dodging the firebombs, simply letting them burst and flow over her like all magic did, a few of the soldiers shied too. She tore through their ranks, slashing into the soldiers and elbowing the deer in just the right place to make them buck and run. The ground was pummeled with fleeing hooves and falling humans.

Some of them stayed down. Others drew their own swords and tried to surround her. But they had been sent to face peasants, not the rebel warlord who was fast becoming the boogeyman that all of the mages' underlings scared each other with.

Mot watched from the edge of town while the tornado of violence raged and townsfolk raced to put out the fires. They weren't leaving yet. Mot dithered over whether to tell them to run for it or to help. More soldiers could be on their way.

A man ran past cradling a burnt hand. Mot grabbed him by the sleeve. "Wait!" A quick blast of healing energy, and the blistered flesh was whole again. "Go!" He shoved the man in the direction he'd been going, not giving him a chance to be grateful or afraid.

Wayra was still fighting. The number of soldiers was vastly reduced, but they'd landed hits; she favored one leg, and some of the blood looked like hers.

Mot watched, as helpless as only a healer can be when caring about a person who healing magic won't touch.

But the last soldiers were deciding to take the coward's way out – while Wayra dispatched one, two dashed off to where some of the deer had stopped short of the forest. They secured mounts and pounded away down the road.

Mot hurried forward, relieved, only to see Wayra limp off after them. "Wayra!" he called as she sweet-talked a deer that had no reason to trust her. "You're hurt!"

It was already letting her mount. "They'll send mages!" she yelled back. "I have to give everyone more time!" With a wave at the beleaguered town, she dug in her heels and disappeared in a flurry of hoofbeats.

Mot stared after her. Fire crackled; buckets splashed; people shouted directions.

Another deer peeked between the bushes.

It took him a long time to convince it to let him get close, and longer still to climb into the saddle, but then he was off like a shot. The road was a long one without any intersections. Surely the other riders wouldn't be hard to find.

After passing multiple clearings and animal trails where they could have left the road, and second-guessing each decision to press on, Mot was almost ready to turn around. But then he found a torn-up meadow, green grass splattered with red, and he jumped off the deer before it fully stopped. Stumbling, he ran toward the fallen figures in the grass.

Wayra was very still when Mot slid to her side with barely a glance for the dead men beside her. He couldn't tell if she was breathing.

Please, he thought, hands flickering from one wound to another. *Please*. He couldn't even scan her to check the damage; his magic rolled right off. The very thing that made her such a threat to the mages had given him nightmares about this exact scenario.

Tears blurred his eyes. *Maybe I'm just not trying hard enough*. With one hand on her chest and one at her cheek, he squeezed his eyes shut and focused everything he had. *Please. Just be alive.* The energies still weren't making an impact. He let out a sob and threw his own life essence at her with such force that he almost passed out.

He didn't notice the flowers blooming around him in a widening circle.

But when the body of the nearest soldier sat up, despite missing half its head, he noticed that.

Mot opened his eyes at the motion and screamed.

The dead man screamed too.

Wayra's eyes snapped open. She grabbed a sword and lopped off the soldier's head, then collapsed in a pile of swear words.

The soldier fell, forgotten, as Mot grabbed her shoulders and blinked away a haze of tears. "You're alive! Where does it hurt?"

"Ow. A few places." Wayra did some blinking of her own, gradually taking in her surroundings. She tried to sit up but reconsidered, clutching her side. "What just happened?"

"You won," Mot told her, prying her hands away to get a look at the wound. It didn't seem too deep.

"Yes," Wayra said slowly. "What *else* happened?"

At her tone, Mot looked up and noticed the flowers. He frowned, trying to remember whether they had been there before. When he turned and saw the twice-dead corpse, he flinched.

Wayra was staring at him when he met her gaze. "I already killed him once," she said. "How was he moving around again?"

Mot looked around frantically. "I don't... know?" But he suspected that he did know. And he wasn't sure he liked what it meant.

He felt something touch his cheek and turned to find Wayra wiping away a tear. Mot realized that he probably looked a mess. He sniffled and scrubbed his face with a sleeve, checking belatedly for blood.

Wayra's voice was quiet. "Did you do all this?"

Mot couldn't speak, so he just nodded once. Unwilling to meet her eyes, afraid of what he might see there, he inspected the other body behind her. Had that one moved too, and he hadn't noticed?

"Thank you for trying."

She sounded sad. Why did she sound sad? Mot turned to look.

Wayra was smiling at him in a way that made his heart seize up all over again. "I'm sorry for worrying you," she said.

"I was—" he tried. "It's just—" He stopped and cleared his throat before speaking again. "I didn't want to lose you," he said, then clamped his jaw shut.

"You didn't." The hand on his cheek felt like it was leaving a smear, but he didn't mind.

Mot smiled back for one long moment, then Wayra's arm twitched, and he remembered her injuries. "Where else are you bleeding?" he demanded. "Let me see."

It took some doing, but they found and assessed all of her wounds the old-fashioned way, cutting up both soldiers' uniforms for reasonably clean bandages. There wasn't much Mot could do for the bump on her head other than press a handful of cool mud onto it, so he did that while Wayra insisted it was nothing.

"I was only out for a moment. And nothing is broken, no punctured lungs; I'll be fine. Help me up."

That proved the hardest struggle of all, much to Mot's embarrassment. But with the aid of a sturdy branch and every ounce of strength in his undernourished frame, they got Wayra up and moving. Also wincing and grumbling, but she made a clear effort to keep that to a minimum.

The deer that Mot had ridden was still in sight. He worried that it would bolt at their approach, filthy strangers that they were, but Wayra clucked to it gently and it trotted right over.

"How do you *do* that?" Mot asked as she took the reins and stroked the deer, calm as anything.

"You've just got to show them that you're friendly," she said. "And my family sold mounts to the military even before they stole everything. This one could easily be one of ours. You're a good girl, aren't you?" She scritched the deer behind the ears, then checked the saddle straps. "Let's see if you can hold still while I get up. This isn't going to be easy."

It really wasn't. But the pair of them managed it, and Mot refused to add to the deer's load, so he walked.

"You sure you don't want a turn?" Wayra asked. "I can hobble along well enough."

"No," Mot said firmly. "You are hurt; you get to ride. No complaining about it."

There was a smile in her voice as she said, "Oh, all right. But I reserve the right to feel sorry for you having to walk the whole way."

Mot nodded. "If you like."

"I like."

He dared a look at her, and had to turn away at how she was smiling at him. The walk back to the village seemed to be long and short at the same time.

By the time they arrived, the villagers had managed to put out all of the fires, though there were many blackened timbers and a few buildings that would need to be rebuilt from the ground up.

Eventually.

"They're back!" someone called in delight. Multiple villagers stopped piling belongings into carts and rushed to greet them.

Much to Mot's relief, there were proper bandages in town, and people skilled at using them. He relinquished Wayra to their care, feeling utterly useless until more burned people approached him in hopes of a speedy recovery. The bandages couldn't do that. He felt better after helping.

He waited politely at the door of the town doctor, where Wayra limped out to meet him. "See, good as new!" she declared.

Mot gave the many bandages a judicious appraisal while she laughed about how she'd had much worse just falling off a deer as a child.

"And anyway," she said, "There's work to be d—" She cut off, stepping past him to get a look at the sky in the distance.

Heart in his mouth, Mot followed her gaze to see the distinctive shape of a mage-cloud on the horizon.

"New plan!" Wayra bellowed. "Everyone grab what you've got and run for it to the west! Stay out of sight! You've got *minutes* before the mages arrive!"

There were a few cries of distress, and the villagers rushed to speed up the evacuation. Things were thrown into carts and front doors left open. Everyone ran from the oncoming cloud. It loomed in dark purple that cast a shadow over the forest, loaded with lightning and worse.

Everyone ran, except for Wayra and Mot.

Though Mot *really* would have liked to.

"You're hurt," he reminded her as the wind picked up, blowing ash in his face. "You don't have to face them."

"I've had worse," Wayra repeated, buckling her sword belts back on. "And look at the shape of the clouds; this is *two* Archons, come to see why their thugs didn't report back." She grinned at him. "Our lucky day."

"Is that lucky?" Mot asked as she strode toward the edge of town, which was still a mess of fire damage and dead soldiers. "They can still hurt you indirectly! Archons can fling trees around if they want to!"

"Sure, but they won't start there," Wayra said, unhooking a rope from a cart that had held water buckets. "With a little distraction, they may not even think of it. And what Archon can focus properly with a lasso yanking them out of the sky?"

"What distraction?" Mot asked.

Wayra put a heavy hand on his shoulder. "My friend," she said, "I need an army."

"An army?" asked Mot, looking back at the fleeing villagers. "They're not—"

"Not them," she said. "The kind of army that only you can give me." She gestured toward the many bodies on the ground. "Are you up for it?"

Mot stared at the corpses and thought about the magic he'd worked by pure accident, sending out hesitant tendrils of power now. He looked back at the villagers, who'd be killed without help, and the oncoming mage lords, the source of everything bad that had ever happened to him.

He looked at Wayra, and thought of her facing two Archons alone. He thought of losing her for good.

Every corpse on the ground stood up around him.

Wayra grinned with all her teeth. "Excellent."

The wind blasted past them as two angry mage lords floated into view over the trees: ropes flapping, lightning crackling, and coming in low for maximum threat to the town.

Wayra charged into the storm, and Mot sent the army charging with her, into what would later be known as the first great battle in the rise of Queen Wayra the Mage-Breaker.

XII: THE HANGED MAN

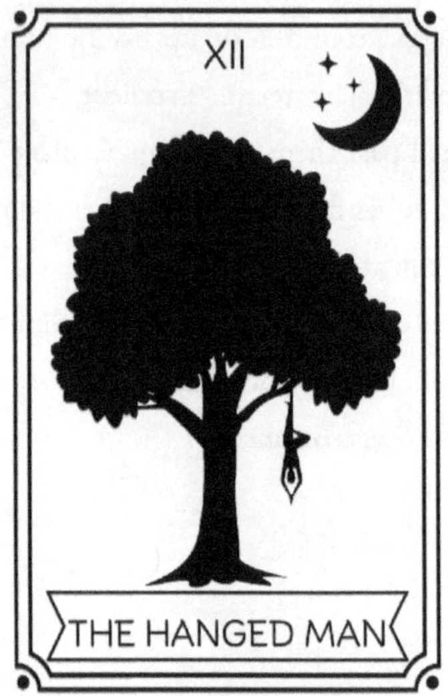

Be Still by David M. Simon

The young man made his way through Times Square, pulling a large wooden cart behind him. The contents of the cart were covered with a stained canvas tarp. He weaved between groups of excited tourists and harried businesspeople, past theaters and restaurants, falafel carts and street corner preachers. He wore a light blue shirt that read *Never Trust An Atom, They Make Up Everything*, and red sweatpants. He was barefoot.

He turned north on 8th Avenue. The sun blazed overhead, and the cart was heavy, but he showed no discomfort. His pace was slow but steady. He stared off into the distance, his face serene, beatific.

By the time he reached Columbus Circle, a small crowd followed him – teenagers who pointed and laughed, a businessman wearing an expensive suit and carrying a briefcase, an ancient homeless woman dressed in rags. A trio of whispering middle-aged nannies pushing baby carriages fell in behind him. The young man did not seem to notice. He said nothing, and continued on his way.

He exited the circle and trundled up Central Park West, his followers growing with every block. Twilight was coming on, and curious families and tourists, drawn by the sounds of the now-considerable crowd, emerged from the park shadows and melted into the throng. Most of them joined without knowing why.

When he reached the Natural History Museum, he pulled his cart into Central Park. He rolled it across a roughly bricked plaza and parked it against the trunk of an enormous elm tree. The crowd, now number-ing nearly a hundred, circled around him and sat down on the bricks. They spoke in hushed tones, speculating on what the young man was doing.

He untied and pulled back the tarp, climbed into the cart and lifted a worn plank that looked like a section of barn wood. He leaned it against the tree trunk, then reached down to take hold of a heavy mallet and a handful of long square-head nails. He propped the plank crossways against the trunk as high as he could reach, pounded a nail into the center, and added several more. The young man stepped back, hands on hips. He nodded once in apparent satisfaction.

Next came a long coil of thick braided rope. He weaved it back and forth around the plank until there were several layers, then deftly tied it off. Quickly, as if he had done it before, the young man grasped the rope in both hands, flipped himself, and hooked his right foot beneath it. Dangling upside-down, he reached into the cart.

His right hand emerged holding the mallet. In his left was a six-inch long metal spike.

Without pause, seemingly without thought, he bent up at the waist, placed the tip of the spike against the instep of his right foot, and drove it through flesh and bone into the plank and tree beneath it. The ring of metal on metal reverberated across the plaza. He struck the spike three more times, until the head nestled tight against his foot. Blood welled up around the wound, and dripped down his leg.

The young man relaxed his body until he once again hung upside-down. He dropped the mallet into the cart.

The crowd, briefly frozen in time by what they had seen, erupted. Screams filled the air. Several people moved forward to help him, but the old homeless woman who had followed the young man from the beginning stared them down, stopping the rush with one frail hand. "Leave him alone. He knows what he's doing."

A teenage girl lurched through the throng with tears streaming down her face, and fell to her knees before him. "Why did you do that?" she asked between sobs.

The young man smiled, giving her his full attention. If he was in pain, he did not show it. His voice, when it finally came, was soft and melodic. "This city. It is too busy, too loud, too fast. You are good people who live here, but this city doesn't allow you to pause and reflect, doesn't allow you time for introspection. If you're going to be your best selves, you need to stop and breathe. You need to feel the universe swirling around you."

The girl shook her head, crying even harder. "But why did you do *that*?"

"Because I had to do that" – he waved one hand at his impaled, bleeding foot – "in order to do this."

The young man closed his eyes. He bent his left foot behind his right leg, folded his arms behind his back. His body began to sway, rocking against the tree.

A low murmur rolled through the crowd like wind through long grass. "He's... glowing," a little boy said.

Bright light encircled the young man's head, pulsing gently. When he opened his eyes, they caught and reflected the light like twin stars.

"Be still," he said, and although the people gathered around him did not know it, every subway train beneath the city stopped on its tracks.

"Be still," he said, and every car, every truck, every bus and motorcycle, stopped running and coasted to a stop. Even the horns were silenced. Had they been paying attention, the crowd would have heard the sounds of minor fender benders and confusion, but they were not. They heard only him.

"Be still," he said, and the electrical grid went down, plunging the entire city into darkness.

A sliver of moon and a dusting of stars were visible through the trees above. The circle of light around the young man's head still glowed faintly. Otherwise the darkness was profound. Far-off shouts from the city floated into the park, but without traffic, without blaring horns, it was strangely quiet for a blackout.

There, beneath the sheltering branches of the elm, hands reached out blindly and found other hands, joining together. Their collective breathing slowed, synchronized, merged with the light breeze stirring the leaves. More people arrived. They wandered by, watched for a moment, sank to the ground and joined in.

The young man's face was now pale and glazed with sweat, his glow dimmed, but his smile never wavered.

The beam of a powerful flashlight pierced the dark, strobed across the crowd before coming to rest on the hanged man. "Jesus Christ! Guys, over here, bring the gurney!"

Multiple flashlight beams joined the first. A squad of police officers and rescue workers pushed through the gathering with a wheeled stretcher, moving people out of the way, but it was slow going. The people seemed confused by what was happening.

"Make a hole!"

"Get the fuck out of the way!"

"What is wrong with all of you? That man needs help."

The rescue squad reached the young man and tried to determine the best way to get him down. "Sir, can you hear me? We're going to release you just as quickly as we can and transport you to Mount Sinai, even if we have to push you all the way."

"Please don't. I'm not done yet." The young man's voice was soft but firm.

"Right, Bellevue then," an EMT said.

"Can you tell me who did this to you?" a policeman asked, glaring at the crowd.

"He did it himself," the old homeless woman said. "He did it for us. For all of us."

"Fucking hell, you're all crazy. Snyder, bring the Leatherman and a pry bar. We're bringing this wooden plank with us."

Rescue workers supported the man's body while the rope was cut away. "Easy now. Get the pry bar in there."

The plank came away from the tree with a screeching sound as the nails slid out. The young man screamed and passed out.

At that exact moment, the city awoke. The lights came back on. Vehicles roared to life. Subway cars rolled again, and with the timing off there were several collisions. Chaos roiled the streets above and below.

The young man was loaded into an ambulance and driven away. The people who had gathered around him stared at each other, dazed, many in tears. They stumbled away finally, in ones and twos.

By dawn, none of them could remember exactly what had happened to them. The hanged man was forgotten.

XII: THE HANGED MAN - REVERSED

Pater et Filius by David M. Simon

It's early on a Saturday afternoon at the Beaumont, Texas Fairgrounds, and the midway of Professor Miracle's Carnival of Wonders is already in full swing.

The pitchman lifts one corner of the worn canvas flap to let the rubes he's seduced with his spiel into The Hanged Man tent. Most have come directly from the geek show just across the sun-baked red clay of sideshow alley, where Firpo, the wild man from Borneo (actually Dave Hancock from Dayton, Ohio) had decapitated several live chickens with his teeth. It's not easy to separate a chicken's head from its neck in that way. It requires a frenzy of gnashing and shaking, a skill Firpo has not only perfected but developed as an unhinged artform over the years. Several of the locals, the ones who were closest to the mayhem, are speckled with droplets of blood, feathers in their hair. They laugh as they show their friends, simultaneously thrilled and horrified. A sense of manic excitement, like a current of electricity, ripples through the crowd.

The excitement drains away and the laughter dies in their throats when they enter the tent. The atmosphere inside is oppressive, a thick stew of stale, humid air and floating chaff from the layer of straw scattered on the ground.

Unlike the outside of the tent, the inside is absolutely devoid of ornamentation – no hyperbolic carnival advertisements, no garishly painted sideshow banners.

A stage, stoutly constructed of bare wood, spans the width of the tent. A tall gallows has been erected in the center of the stage. Thick jute rope dangles from the crossbeam, a noose at the end of it. There's a six foot stepladder centered below the noose.

The crowd, silent now, shuffles onto long wooden benches, squeezing together. The women fan themselves with the complementary Carnival of Wonders paper fans they received at the entry gate. The men doff their hats, run their fingers through sweat-slick hair. The few kids in the audience fidget, but they do it quietly, eyes never leaving the noose.

As the people settle themselves, a boy, unseen, lifts the bottom of the tent and rolls under. He stays tight to the shadows behind the benches, slaps the dust from his clothes.

Organ music begins to play, pops and scratches betraying the fact that it's a Victrola recording, but it's still effective, an ominous, spectral dirge. The spectators draw together without realizing it, squeezing toward the center of each bench. A small girl gulps a sob down, and her mother hushes her with a look.

"You are not ready," says a sonorous voice from offstage.

A massive barrel of a man dressed in the severe clothes of an undertaker strides onto the stage. He reaches the upright beam of the gallows and stops, raps it sharply with a meaty fist, then turns to face the crowd. One eyebrow raised, he surveys the anxious faces below him, a small smile at play beneath his bushy handlebar mustache. He removes his bowler, examines the crown critically, then returns it to his head.

"Ladies and gentlemen, I am Professor Miracle, and this is my Carnival of Wonders. If you've visited my other attractions, you may have noted that I do not introduce any of my other astounding performers, freaks, and oddities of whom I am undeniably proud. This is the only act I personally present.

"My friends, you may be asking yourselves why that is. I can only tell you that, of all the wonders I have found in my travels to the farthest, darkest corners of this world in search of never-before-seen wonders to bring back to you fine folks, I have never seen anything like this. And I make this sacred vow to you... you have never seen anything like this either. I am, indeed, humbled by, and more than a little frightened by, what I can only describe as a true phenomenon, a rarity unheard of in the annals of human history – a man who stands toe to toe with the grim reaper.

"Ladies and gentlemen, I ask that you direct your eyes to the gallows, and prepare yourselves, as I present – the Hanged Man." Professor Miracle bows deeply, then exits.

The man who walks barefoot onto the stage is compact, barely five feet tall. He is stripped to the waist. He wears worn, ragged canvas pants tied with a rope. His body is lean, muscled, criss-crossed with ropey scars. His face is filigreed with deep lines, his hair a bristling halo of white.

The man approaches the gallows. He looks up at the noose dangling above him, then down at the audience. He scans them slowly from side to side, as if trying to look into the eyes, into the very souls, of each and every one of them. He grasps the sides of the ladder and climbs quickly, confidently. When the man reaches the very top step he wobbles slightly, then steadies himself, finds his balance.

With practiced hands the man takes hold of the noose, pulls it down over his head, and snugs the thirteen coils of the knot tight against the back of his neck. The loose remainder of the rope hangs in a loop behind him. The man clasps his hands behind his back.

Professor Miracle takes one step out from the wing stage right, so that he is shrouded in shadows but visible. "Ladies and gentlemen, you must decide for yourselves – is the hand of our almighty God above at work in what you are about to witness, or is this a power altogether darker, more... infernal."

The professor walks to the ladder with slow, purposeful steps, directs his gaze to the man and asks, "Are you ready?" The man nods once, then looks straight ahead.

Professor Miracle rears back and kicks the ladder out from under the man. He seems to float for a moment, held in place by the horrified looks of the crowd, until gravity asserts itself and he plummets towards the stage. The rope pulls taut, jerks him upwards. The noose draws tight. He bounces, like a marionette on a string. His legs kick, causing his body to rock spastically. His hands flutter, grasp uselessly at the noose.

The man's neck stretches, then crooks at an impossible angle, accompanied by a sound like a wet branch snapping. His arms fall limply to his sides. His legs stop kicking. He hangs, the rocking of his body slowing to a gentle stop. A foul stench fills the air as his bowels release.

The crowd erupts – cries, shouts, screams and sobs. Some stand as if to leave, then sit back down, not sure what to do. A young woman in the front row doubles over, vomiting into the dust. Her husband pulls her to his chest and stares at the professor with murderous intent.

The boy at the back of the tent takes a step forward, his face eager, yearning, but he quickly steps back, glancing around to be sure he hasn't been noticed.

Two roustabouts cut the Hanged Man down, draping his body across the front of the stage. His neck is elongated, so stretched that the skin appears to be breaking in spots. When they remove the noose, his head lolls obscenely, as if on a spring. His face is the purplish red of a bruised apple. The rope has left deep imprints in the flesh of his neck, like the tracks of tractor tires.

Professor Miracle watches the chaos from just behind the Hanged Man's corpse. He holds out his hands, palms down, and gestures for calm. The crowd quiets immediately, as if they are parishioners and he a preacher.

"Ladies and gentlemen, if you are the prayin' kind, and I believe most of you fine folks are, please join me in praying for a miracle the likes of which you have never before seen." The professor removes his bowler, holds it to his chest and bows his head. As his lips move in silent prayer, the crowd mimics him. Heads are bowed, eyes closed, hands brought together. Murmured voices rise and fall.

"Mama, look!" shouts a young girl's voice. She stands, points, as the Hanged Man's head jerks to one side, then the other. His neck contracts with hollow popping sounds as his head settles into its proper position.

The Hanged Man's back arches and his chest rises with a sharp intake of breath. His eyes open and he cries out, a coarse, strangled scream. The entire audience rises as one, their screams drowning out the Hanged Man's own.

The Hanged Man climbs shakily to his feet. He staggers, nearly falls, and the professor catches him, helps him stand. The Hanged Man stands still for a moment, head down, as the professor supports him. He sucks in deep, shuddering breaths. Finally he nods, and the professor releases him.

The Hanged Man at last looks up at the audience. He smiles for the first time, and thrusts his arms up in victory. The cheers and applause from the audience are deafening in the enclosed space.

Professor Miracle grasps one of his upraised wrists, as if proclaiming the winner in a prize fight. "Ladies and gentlemen... the Hanged Man! Tell your friends and neighbors, he and the rest of my Carnival of Wonders will be here until Monday!"

The crowd chatters excitedly as they shuffle out into the brutal afternoon sunshine. Last to leave is the boy in the shadows at the back of the tent.

***

Otis McNamara is enjoying a well-deserved after-work snort of Jefferson County's finest home-brewed applejack when there's a tentative knock at the door of his wagon.

"Fuck off!" Otis pours another generous splash into his dented tin coffee cup.

Another knock, this time more insistent.

"Buster, if that's you, I'ma put a boot up your ass! You know I don't like to be bothered after a show." At the third knock, Otis storms through the narrow, cluttered confines of his wagon to the door and flings it open. "Oh, hell no."

A boy stands on the top step, hand poised to knock again. He's thin, barefoot, dressed in rags, so dirty and disheveled it looks like he's rolled in a cow pasture.

Otis rubs a hand roughly over his face and sighs. "Whadaya want, kid? You're not supposed to be back here. It may not look like much, but this is my home. You're trespassing."

"I saw your show." The boy's voice is firm, surprisingly loud. He looks Otis right in the eyes when he speaks.

"That's great. Thanks for the two bits. Now get the fuck out of here."

As Otis begins to shut the door, the boy shouts, "I'm like you!"

Otis is exhausted. All he wants is to drink himself shitfaced and collapse on his cot, but what the kid said catches his attention in spite of that. He opens the door back up. "What's that supposed to mean?"

"I can't stay dead either."

Otis laughs until it ends in a phlegmy cough. "Oh, for Christ's sake. I didn't really die. It's a trick, a gag designed to fool you country bumpkins. Seriously, get the fuck out of here before I have you tossed out on your ass. No one can cheat death."

"You can. So can I." There's something about the way the kid says it, the set of his jaw and the look in his eyes, that causes Otis to wave him into the wagon. He drops heavily into his chair and gestures for the boy to sit on a crate just inside the door.

Otis drains his cup, pours another drink. "I think I'm gonna need this. What's your name, kid? How old are you?"

"Name's Levi, sir. I'll be thirteen next month."

"Well, Levi, I'm just drunk enough to humor you. Tell me your story."

Levi sits up straight, folds his hands in his lap. "I was six years old the first time my pa killed me."

"Oh, for the love of Chri—"

Levi ignores him, just keeps on talking. "Corn prices were lower than a snake's belly, but we were getting by. Then a dust storm rolled in, lasted two whole days. When it ended, the crops were gone like they were never there, all our livestock was dead. There was no food. We were starving. My sister Eliza was ten, she could work, but a six year old weren't good for nothing. One morning Mama hugged me, crying, told me to go to my pa in the barn. I found him in the tack room with a big ol' sledgehammer in his hand. He wasn't crying, but his eyes were red like he had been. Pa didn't say a word, just pulled me into the room and turned me to face the wall. That's the last thing I remember.

"I came back to life underwater, tied up in a feed sack weighted down with rocks. I don't know how many times I drowned and came back before I tore my way out of that sack. Never did learn to swim, so I drowned three or four more times before I crawled up on the shore of Lake Caddo. I knew where I was; it was just a few miles from home. Pa used to take me there fishing for catfish before everything went to shit. The back of my head hurt, and my chest ached something fierce – I kept coughing and spitting up lake water – but I felt pretty good considering I'd died a bunch. I may have only been six, but I figured out pretty quick that Pa had put me down, and Ma was all right with him doing it. You'd think I wouldn't be in any hurry to go back there, but where else would I go? I sat there on the shore, sobbed myself dry. Then I walked home.

"Mama was in the kitchen when I come through the door. She screamed and crossed herself, called me a demon from hell. She ran clean past me, out into the yard, screaming for Pa. He came hauling ass from the barn, twelve-gauge in hand. When I walked out the door, following Mama, he shot me full in the chest, both barrels."

By this time, Otis has filled and drained his cup more than once. "Let me guess. After a while you sat up like Jesus his own self."

"Yes sir, I did. Mama and Pa were standing there, holding each other tight, and I'll remember the look on their faces 'til the day I die, if that day ever comes." Levi smiles grimly. "I don't know what possessed me to say what I did next, being just a little boy, but I was scared and pissed off, and most of all my feelings were hurt. I said, 'I'm gonna live in the hayloft. Horses and cows are dead, so you don't need to go up there for nothing. Don't kill me again, or I'll do something bad to you.' I walked right past them, head held high, into the barn and up the ladder to the loft. I think I slept for a whole day.

"I kept to myself after that. I stole food from neighboring farms, and once Eliza found out I was back alive, she snuck me bread sometimes, but Mama and Pa didn't want her coming anywhere near me.

"Papa got up the nerve to kill me again every couple of years. It got so I barely noticed. Just made me sad. Livin' like that was so lonely I wanted to kill myself, but, well, I knew how that would go. Then I saw a poster for Professor Miracle's Carnival of Wonders, and it said, big as anything, The Hanged Man. I didn't really expect you to be the real thing, but I had to see for myself." Levi finally runs out of words, sits back with a sigh.

Otis sighs right along with him. "Kid, that's a helluva story, but like I told you before, my act's just an act. It's fake. If I die, I die, and I gotta believe so do you. But like I said, helluva story."

Without another word Levi reaches into his back pocket, pulls out a baling knife. He looks Otis dead in the eye as he rips the blade across his neck. Blood bibs down his front, his eyes go soft, and his body slumps over sideways.

***

"There you are. Welcome back, kid."

Levi sits up, rubs his neck. The raw red streak there is already fading. "Like I said, I can't stay dead, and neither can you."

"Okay, fine, you got me there. What do ya want from me?"

Levi tears up, just a little. He wipes a hand across his eyes. "I want to join the carnival, be a part of your show. I want to be part of something."

"Look, kid, this ain't no way to live. You think I like this? I kill myself in front of a tent full of rubes once a night. Most times I shit myself for their pleasure, but I guess that's showbiz. The food's lousy, and I live in a broken down wooden box on wheels. We travel all year around, never stay anywhere longer than a week."

Levi sucks up a nose full of snot. "After what I been through, that sounds like paradise."

Otis is quiet for a long time, arms crossed, lost in thought. Finally he stands up, pats Levi on the back. "I'll tell ya what. No promises, but you can bunk here with me tonight, and in the morning we'll go talk to the Professor."

Levi surprises Otis with a fierce hug, then immediately sits back down on the crate, embarrassed. "Thank you, sir. Umm, can I ask you one question?"

"Sure, kid. And stop calling me sir. Name's Otis."

"Otis. Okay. Otis, how did you find out you couldn't die? How did it happen the first time?"

Otis laughs once, a sharp bark. "Civil War, second Battle of Sabine Pass. Took a Union bullet in the belly and the wound went bad. I was thirty-seven years old."

"But that was, holy fuck, a long time ago – how old are you?"

"A hundred and six next month."

"Shit. Can you die of old age? Can I?"

"Levi, I have no idea. Maybe we'll find out together. Now get some shuteye. Morning comes early here. There's an extra bedroll inside that crate you're sitting on. "

***

By the time Professor Miracle's Carnival of Wonders rolls into Nacogdoches three weeks later, the banner outside the tent reads The Hanged Man and Son, and there are two gallows on the stage.

XIII: DEATH

The Song of Ki by Emily Ansell

The City of Kir wasn't abandoned; it was dead.

Indeed, mere abandonment would have been a kindness. None had ever faced such a fate as had the doomed City of Kir, and to even speak its name was akin to speaking a curse. For fifty years it had stood as a monument to the power and the terrible mercy of the gods.

And now, it was Darra's destination.

***

The journey had begun on an otherwise unremarkable day. They had performed morning devotions and she had conducted her usual class with the novices after. It was during planning for the forthcoming Blessings Day for the farmers that her Master, Komron, had called for her to attend him. As First Acolyte, she could be commanded by very few in such a way, but all heeded the words of Komron, who even had a great influence over the king.

"You wished to see me, High Priest?" She bowed before settling at his feet, as befit both their stations.

Doom rode heavy in his voice as he replied. "Yes, Darra. I have grave news, and an even graver requirement of you."

"Of course. Speak and it is done, Master."

"You must travel to the City of Kir." The words darkened the room, and Darra recoiled. But he continued. "Not only this, but you must enter the city itself, and learn what is happening within its walls."

She sprang to her feet. "One does not travel to that place! Or enter it! That is certain death!"

"You forget your rank, my Acolyte," he chided. She sat again and he pointed a wizened finger outward. "To Kir you shall go. For something fell stirs within, and we must find out what. I am too old to make the journey, and so it falls to you. You must go."

The old priest took from around his neck a large medallion, its face carved with the image of a horned man with a farmer's scythe. He leaned down and placed it over her head, where it fell upon her chest. It radiated warmth that comforted her.

"Radas will always be with you, child," he intoned. "And he will go with you, to protect you in that cursed place. It is his will that this journey be made, that we discover what stirs there and stop it. If not, I fear the fate of that place could spread beyond its borders."

"Is such a thing possible? Have there been omens? No ill signs have come to me, Master."

"Not as such. Or perhaps I should say, not *yet*. But the works of the gods are often out of our ken. That city was destroyed by them. If something arises from the ashes, who is to say what havoc it would wreak upon our world? And so, you must leave tomorrow at daybreak, and travel with all haste. It will be a long journey, but I have faith in you. And I know that Radas will see that we succeed. I have arranged supplies and outside clothing be made for you, so go to Brother Ikar as soon as possible. He will also have a map for you, and will explain what your journey will look like. He is the most well-travelled among us, so heed his words carefully."

"Yes, High Priest. I will go at once."

***

As promised, Darra left the temple with the next sunrise. Gone were the light, billowing robes and turban she knew, replaced with thickly-woven travelling versions and a pack full of supplies. The pack was heavy, and nearly unbalanced her when she put it on.

"Don't worry, it'll get lighter!" Brother Ikar joked, watching her test it out.

"Even these clothes are heavy."

"You'll be glad for that, too. You would freeze out there in temple garb, Sister. It's not made for the outside. But come on, then. It's time."

He walked with her to the City Gate, and bid her farewell. Darra held tight to the amulet, her only link to the life she'd led up until now, and stepped out onto the road. With a murmured prayer to her patron, she took her first steps away from his city. She would now follow this road to the conclusion of her quest. It was part of the Great Highway that facilitated travel and trade. Once, that had included the doomed city. Now, at the far end of the road lay only a reminder of a past no one dared to speak of. Ikar had warned her the road had probably fallen into disrepair, and that she would need to be cautious.

The first day passed uneventfully. The road was busy so close to the city with merchants, farmers, and all manner of other people looking to sell or buy supplies and wares. They gave small bows of their heads to her as they hurried on, but none stopped to talk. That was fine. Darra instead most often watched those tending the fields on either side of the road. Radas was bringing them a good bounty this year by the look of it, and there would be plenty for the Blessings Day. That thought saddened Darra. She'd never missed a Blessings Day until now. The harvest would be finished by the time she returned, and all the celebrations with it. But so it must be, in order to safeguard her people. *That* was worth missing one festival.

By nightfall she was exhausted. Darra's demesne had consisted of the temple almost since birth, as she had been given to it at the age of three days. Life in the temple had hardly prepared her for such an undertaking; they kept fit through work and exercise, but nothing like this.

"How do others do this? Walking all day?" She spoke aloud to the darkness. But there was no one to reply. Only the barest whisper of a song drifting through the trees. A bird? It didn't sound like any bird she knew.

"Then again, how much do you know about forest birds, Darra?" She pointed out to herself. And on that, she had to admit she was right.

The days after that continued much the same. Even the initial novelty of sturdy boots in the place of slippers wore off quickly and was replaced with blisters. After that came a constant soreness even nightly salving did little to alleviate.

She did have an advantage over most travelers, however. She wore the viridian raiment of Radas, and her Master's amulet with it. Because of this, the people she met were courteous; they allowed her shelter, passage, and provision as needed. The common folk were more than happy to assist a Priestess on a pilgrimage. They never asked her destination, and she did not volunteer. To speak the name of the cursed city was anathema, and she would bring no misfortune down on a peasant for simple curiosity. Luckily, regular folk were satisfied with the explanation of 'temple business' and took no further interest. Most would only ask for a quick blessing, which she always freely gave.

Two weeks into her journey, she stopped for the night at an inn. It was a busy place, travelers and locals alike crowding around both the bar and the various tables scattered around the room. Despite this, Darra sat alone at a table the innkeeper had shooed a couple of men away from. She sat and watched. She had little experience being out and among the general public. Her only real interactions with them came during ceremonies and festivals and other blessings; she had never been afforded something like this. To actually be *among* them and see them interact.

Darra had finished her meal when she saw a woman enter. She was alone, and looked afraid. Her clothes were old and badly worn, but she held herself with as much dignity as her haunted eyes would allow. Darra watched her talk to the innkeeper for a moment, watched him shake his head and point to the fireplace. The woman's shoulders sagged, but she trudged toward the hearth anyway. Darra wondered what she was doing.

The woman didn't get that far. Darra watched four large men get up from their table and approach her. They began talking to her, smiling. But somehow it was wrong. The woman was backing up, trying to get away from them. One of them reached out and grabbed the woman's arm, trying to pull her toward him.

Before she realized what she was doing, Darra was on her feet. She strode up, standing tall beside the other woman. The men backed away, raising their hands.

"Begone." Darra spoke the word quietly, but the men broke and fled. To the other woman, she smiled. "Come, I have a table. Sit with me."

"I... yes, Priestess," the woman stammered. As they sat, Darra called the innkeeper and had some food and drink brought.

"What can I do to serve you, Priestess?" The woman glanced up over the plate in front of her.

"I... I do not require anyone to serve me. You only seemed to be in trouble, and needing something to eat. There is nothing you need do for me." The woman's words had thrown her off, and Darra wasn't sure how to answer.

"Oh. I didn't know Priestesses were nice like that."

"All the Priests and Priestesses I know would do the same."

The woman shrugged. "Maybe for one of your own."

"We are pledged to help all."

The woman only smiled thinly. "Of course. Still, I must thank you. Your clothes and that medallion you wear were enough to send those louts running, and I'm grateful. I wish I had that kind of protection while I travel."

"Where are you going? Perhaps we could travel together for a time, if our destinations are along the same way?"

"It's not far now. Just to the next village. We could get there by tomorrow afternoon."

"Then it is settled. I will travel with you to your village tomorrow."

"Thank you again, Priestess."

***

The next morning the two women struck out together, enjoying the morning coolness and the quiet of the road. The other woman sang as they walked; folk songs Darra had never heard. She enjoyed them, as well as the company after traveling alone for so long. The other woman didn't volunteer much about herself nor asked about Darra, but the travel was companionable nonetheless.

As they went, the woman's song changed. She had begun to hum a wordless tune with a complex melody. She would begin, then trail off before picking it back up again. This went on for some time before Darra asked.

"What is that song? I've never heard it before."

"Ah, just an old song. Not many know it anymore. Even the words are lost."

"That's too bad. It's very beautiful."

"It is, isn't it?"

When they reached the village, it was both larger and busier than Darra expected. The other woman turned to her as they entered the market square.

"Good luck on your journey, Priestess. Your kindness will not be forgotten." She gave a bow of the head, disappearing into the crowd. Darra looked, but couldn't even see which direction she'd taken. It was as if she'd vanished.

Now alone, Darra continued on.

***

For three more weeks she traveled, through the verdant farmlands of Radas' people, to the deep, cool forests of the followers of Warda. Again, her Master's amulet provided her passage, as only the highest of Priests would be afforded such a relic, and only one of high station would undertake a journey so far from their home temple. Warda's people lived semi-nomadic lives, and while welcoming, mainly left her to her own matters. But by this time Darra was more accustomed to travel; sturdier in mind and body, and with a level of confidence in herself she had never imagined. Though the strange woman's words would come to her from time to time, and she would wonder if it was deference, or something else that kept the people polite and any nefarious intentions away.

The road had become busier, and she knew she was close to Wardasir. And soon enough, the great ring of shops and amenities came into view. Wardasir was much different from Radasir. Inside a ring of ancient trees stood the Temple of Warda and all the trappings of a city were outside of it, bordered by more trees. Even the great road split around the central clearing, joining up with itself again on the other side.

Darra resupplied on her way through. This would be her last chance to really stock up; there was only the possibility of a few small camps before the forest's end, and there would be nothing after that. She would have to be cautious that she didn't run out, but it also meant that her journey was nearly over. Soon, she would reach that doomed city, and she would see what it held.

For now, she put it out of her mind as she rounded the ring and continued on the rejoined road. The day was fine, and birds sang in the forest. She began to whistle, not realizing at first it was that same tune the strange woman had hummed as they'd travelled together. The one whose words had been lost. It made her stop for a moment, and smile.

When she began again, a flush of heat radiated out from her chest. Raising her hand, she touched her Master's amulet. It was hot.

"What in Radas' name?" she exclaimed. But as she did, the heat was gone as if it'd never been. She turned it over in her hand. Had it grown warm from the sun, from her own body heat, or had she imagined it? She let it drop back down on her chest, but she sang no more after that.

It took two more weeks to reach the end of the forest. Now, she found herself in a sudden, jarring, openness. All around her was a rocky, bleak landscape. Little seemed to grow and it was hard to imagine that anything at all could live in this stark, desert-like place. Even with the road now in much poorer condition, few weeds sprouted between the broken stones. Desolation pervaded the land; even the sun languished, dimmed by an ever-present haze. It was said even rain dared not fall here anymore, and looking around her, she thought that was likely true.

On this barren plain, five days from the forest's edge, lay the City of Kir. She had nearly reached her destination. Then she could do as her Master bid, and discover what, if anything, had risen there. Although how anything could have come to live in this place, she could hardly imagine. To live in a land so oppressive as to feel always covered by a smothering blanket of smoke? She shuddered at the thought.

***

On the third day out of the forest, Darra crested a rise and first glimpsed the City of Kir. It sprawled over the landscape like an infected wound, blackened and foul. Even from this distance, she could see the burned remains of buildings; broken teeth jutting into the air above the expanse of the city's wall. Black specks rose and swirled around this shattered skyline, and she wondered if it was merely wind-stirred ash or something more sinister. Was this a sign of whatever foulness she'd been sent to find?

Her blood grew colder as the city grew closer. The gates were closed still, rising into the sky like sentinels, though no longer with anything left to guard. Darra had figured out that the rising specks she'd seen earlier were ravens, massive clouds of them that seemed to both orbit and occupy the city by turns.

"How can there be so many?" She asked, speaking aloud for the first time in that stagnant air. "There's nothing here for them to eat, no water. At least, none that I've seen. But there they are. Something inside the city must feed them. But what?" Darra herself had only her supplies from the ring, and the final Wardasir camp she'd encountered in the forest. There had been nothing to forage since entering this barren landscape. And yet the flock of ravens continued their flight, undeterred.

***

She now stood before the city. But, just outside of the walls were the remains of tents and habitation. What could this mean? No one had lived here after the city fell, or so anyone had ever known. And this camp was old, perhaps as old as the city's destruction or even before. Surely it couldn't be after?

"Perhaps this was survivors, people fleeing the city. But why would they stay so close?"

She wandered through the shredded remains of tents, arranged carefully in rows, though most were now little more than bare poles. The wind stirred up ashes in the long-cold fire pits as she passed. Every so often she would see some metallic ring or clasp on the ground, sometimes still attached to a length of brittle leather. But there was little else. Time had cleared away most of the detritus the people of the camp would have left behind.

"They say Kir was destroyed by the gods, but these are the trappings of men. Great Radas!" And so it was. For on the ground before her, badly weather-worn, was the pennant of her own city of Radasir. She lifted it and found two others beneath, from the cities of Oryensir and Pallosir. She gasped.

"Oryen, Pallos, and Radas. The Three Brothers. Why were their cities here?"

She slept badly that night among the camp's remains, the congress of ravens and their harsh chorus haunting her. She could swear they were singing the song, that strange song without words.

In the morning she began to explore the camp in earnest. She would glean whatever secrets she could from it before entering the city itself. She hoped it would give her some insight before she entered that cursed place, some means of preparation for whatever she would find inside.

Or perhaps it would merely give her enough time to steel herself against the fear of entering.

The camp offered little more than it had the day before. Long years had ruined most of whatever had remained behind. She still couldn't understand why they'd been here. Of the part her own people had played, there was little sign.

"Perhaps I am turned away from my task when I should not be," she sighed. "And this is a sign from Radas that I should continue my Master's mission, not pick around in the dust any longer."

A great raven passed over her head as she contemplated turning away. It cawed loudly, landing on the ground before her. It cawed again and hopped back. An invitation to follow. As she took a step forward it hopped back again. They continued this odd dance until the bird spread its wings and alighted on an ancient table, covered in papers. It hopped, bobbing its head, pointing to its perch. It only took flight again when she was close enough to touch its dusky feathers.

A book. It was worn, but so had been many of the ancient tomes in the temple archives. She knew the delicate hand it required. Nearly the entire first half was ruined, fused by some sort of damage. To her it seemed to be the result of water, but what water could have ruined it in this place? Perhaps something that had happened before the people had left? But after such a long time, the question was moot. Luckily, the rest of the book was mostly legible.

It was a journal. It seemed strange to her that someone would leave behind something so personal, but perhaps it would give her answers. It was probably the only thing here that could, and somehow that raven had known it.

"Radas would never use a raven. Who wants me to read this book, then?" She frowned, but had no answer to that. "It doesn't matter. I must know."

Despite the journal's deteriorated state, she could see the entries had been written in a crisp, precise hand. The familiarity of it turned her insides more than her proximity to the city.

16 Chavits

The siege enters its seventh month today. Those inside are becoming desperate. Surely they must see we cannot allow them out if there is a plague? I worry about that mage, Merwen. She claims she is working on a cure. I hope she's wrong.

Darra frowned. This camp had been to keep the people from leaving the city? And why would anyone be against a cure to a deadly sickness? She kept reading, carefully scanning the crumbling pages for more insight.

30 Chavits

Radas have mercy! That damned mage, Merwen, has done it! She snuck into the city, somehow. We're still looking into that. We watched her on the battlements. She says there is no illness, that we should allow the gates to be opened! That stupid woman, she's got no idea what she's done. She's ruined it all. She couldn't leave well enough alone. The other generals and I are meeting tonight, to try and sort out what to do about this. I hope the priests have something for us. We could use a sign from Radas right now.

1 Felos

Sleep is impossible. The city is rioting. They demand to be let out. I didn't know there were so many still in there! The other generals agree with me, we cannot risk it. If they cannot be pacified, it will be bad. It's already bad. What comes next will be only worse. But it is Radas' will, and I must abide by that.

2 Felos

Radas save and keep our souls! We did it. Who knew those starving and sick could be so vicious? They were trying to break out, we had no choice. We couldn't risk it. We armed our catapults, summoned our mages. We cleansed the city with fire. A small contingent will go in once the flames die down in case any have survived. Radas have mercy on those few who will give up their lives for this. The smoke rises for miles. It is black. The smell of burning fills every pore. Wish I'd brought some incense. At least the screaming's stopped.

Horrified, she scanned through the next entries. But they were sparse, terse things that told her little. She flipped the page and found herself at the final entry, dated several days later.

11 Felos

It is done. We are leaving, finally. Our men went in and checked the city. They reported no survivors before they took their lives. Safer that way, lest they bring any foulness back out with them. We can't risk that. Their sacrifice will be remembered, if only by us. It was the will of the gods, and that is how it must be known. We only did what we had to. It is so quiet now. The Song is gone. We'd all gotten so used to it coming down from their temple. I think that's where I'll go when I get home to Radasir. After this, I'm for the priesthood. The king won't hesitate to give it to me, I know that. Even if he'll be upset to lose me on the battlefield, he's got others who'll take it up. I've earned it after this mess.

Darra's eyes blurred with tears. So many things made sense now. She'd hoped that she was wrong about the handwriting, but there was the proof before her eyes. And not only that, there was also the much uglier proof that what she'd known as truth had been wrong. A lie. She turned her gaze to the city gates. It was time to see what lay behind them.

***

The sun was high now, and she was ready. There was a small side door, as the journal had said, still open. As her foot moved over the threshold, a burst of heat seared her. The amulet. It had turned hot again, but now even hotter than it had been in the forest. Hot enough that it seemed it would burst into flame.

"How am I supposed to do my Master's bidding, then?" she demanded of it. Then, before she could have second thoughts, she slipped the amulet over her head and dropped it on the ground. Something like a cry sounded in her mind, but she was already through the door.

"I've come this far; I will not stop now." Defiant as the words sounded, they were the truth. She was far past the point of turning back. She would go on, even if Radas could not or would not go with her.

This small door certainly seemed to be the one those doomed men had used when they'd entered the city after the firestorm. Ten desiccated corpses greeted her that could only have been the soldiers, because they were the only things not burned. She carefully stepped around them. She wasn't here for them.

She walked through the silent streets, the only sound her boots on the cobblestones. The road itself was wide and beautifully made. The buildings must have been as well, those broken husks all around her. This had been a city more grand than Radasir, she was sure of it. She wondered how tall some of the towers must have been, as even now they rose higher than any man-made structure she'd ever seen. They were more like the ancient trees in Warda's forest.

Occasionally, she would pass a charred body, and her heart would clench. They were too badly burned to identify as anything more than a corpse, and too delicate to examine. She discovered this after trying to touch one, only to have it collapse into ash and charcoal.

"I'm so sorry!" She raised a hand to her mouth. "I'm sorry. I won't do that again!"

Sometimes, she would see bodies that were smaller, and knew they must have been children. Some were alone, others with adults. Her throat tightened at the thought of her beloved novices falling victim to such a fate. A prickle crawled up her spine and into her skull as she looked up at the sky, almost expecting a flaming assault to come over those walls all over again and immolate her as well. But nothing came, and all she could do was press on.

There were more and more bodies as she moved up through the streets. The Great Temple stood at the highest point of the city, as did every city's house of worship. The people must have been trying to flee there. It occurred to her that she had no idea who the patron of this city was. *Kir* meant *Ki's*, much as Radasir meant Radas'. But who was Ki? She could not remember reading or hearing that name anywhere. She should've asked her Master before she'd left.

"It doesn't matter now. I'll find out soon enough."

As she climbed the hill to the temple, the going grew more difficult. There were so many corpses now, clogging the street and the sidewalks. It took her a long time to pick her way through them, hiking up her skirts and moving as carefully as she could to avoid stepping on any of the bodies. Thankfully, her concentration kept her from really looking at the sheer number of dead, or thinking about how awful their end had been.

Now out of the crowd of bodies, she found herself at the entrance to the temple. The ravens had reappeared – singing that song again – and swirling ahead of her around the charred edifice of the Great Altar. But their song was not harsh as it had once been. It called to her, to come and complete her task. To fulfill her mission. She had come for answers, and she would have them if she joined them.

She entered the temple, her eyes searching for any sign the structure was unstable. But other than charred, the building seemed sound. She crossed the atrium, ascending the stairs to the Great Altar. The ravens all flew out at once, leaving her alone with the very thing she'd come to find.

The marble statue of Ki loomed above her, illuminated by sunlight streaming in from above. The goddess had one hand lifted, her mouth open in song. But the statue was blackened, cracks spider-webbing over the expertly carved surface. The great heat of the fires had done it, but had not been enough to destroy the statue. The ravens perched above, crowding the hole in the roof, watching her. They were silent.

Darra bowed before the statue. "Great Ki, of whom I do not know, I have come to your city to seek answers. I was sent by my Master Komron, the High Priest of Radas, to seek what moves within these walls. But now I know I must seek something else. I must find the truth, for it has been shown to me that I have been told only lies. Please forgive my intrusion."

She felt a warmth in her breast, and the whisper of a tune. She raised her eyes to the statue as she scrambled to her feet, watching the cracks in the surface turn into bright veins of light. For the first time in fifty years, the goddess Ki welcomed a human being into her temple. The song burst into Darra's mind, that same song but now she heard the words as well. It was beyond beauty, beyond description. It was like nothing of this earth in its fullness. It filled her heart and soul until she felt she'd burst with it. She smiled. Tears ran from her eyes, turning to steam on her cheeks.

***

All of Radasir watched the young woman who strode through the city gate. Most didn't recognize her, but the High Priest would know his First Acolyte anywhere. Even now, in a tattered black robe that dragged through the dust yet left her arms and shoulders scandalously bare. This bareness served to highlight the terrible disfigurement of her body; she was covered in a web-like network of scars. Like heat-cracked marble. Her head was also bare, and her hair flowed behind her, black as a raven's wing. Black as soot and charcoal.

"Darra." All had gone silent at the sound of the High Priest's voice.

"Komron." She gave no bow.

"You speak above your station, First Acolyte," he growled.

She laughed. It was melodious in a way it had never been before. The scars criss-crossing her face and body flared like fire. "No, for I am your equal now, Komron. I am the High Priestess of my goddess. The first since the destruction of Kir, fifty years ago. Do you remember her, General Komron? Do you remember Her Song?"

The High Priest paled, knuckles white on the handle of his cane. "Ki the Songstress. Yes, she was the patron of Kir. Which the gods destroyed."

"Gods? Or men? What did Kir's destruction earn you? The High Priesthood, but what else? Ah, but it matters not. I did as you bid, and discovered what moves within the city. And now I have returned, and brought you a gift from my goddess. A new Song. For Ki the Songstress is no more, only Ki the Burned One. And she has not forgotten you, General."

Darra lifted her arms and brought the city into Ki's embrace. The novices danced down from the temple to the crackling rhythm of the spreading flames, embracing her. Her beloved novices! She would teach them the Song as she had been taught. Around them, the screams began. As they multiplied, she felt the warm glow of love wash through her again. She had raised a great chorus from the followers of Radas to her goddess, and her goddess was pleased.

The Song of Ki had returned to the world once again.

XIV: TEMPERANCE

Temperance by David M. Simon

The boy and girl fled into the forest.

It was early morning, and little light penetrated the forest canopy. The trees towered above them, intertwined, like the hands of giants erupted out of the ground and clasped together, shrouding them in shadow. They ran blindly, dodging between gnarled trunks that leaped out from the swirling ground mist. They climbed over deadfalls and slipped beneath the tangled branches of downed trees. They ran until their legs and chests burned, until their breath came in ragged gasps. They ran with only one thought between them: get away.

They finally stopped when the boy tripped over tree roots hidden beneath the blanket of fallen leaves and tumbled to the ground. Until that point he had pushed himself, had held his own. But he was only six years old, after all, and the fear that had fueled him, that had allowed his tiny body to push on, was subsumed by pain from his scraped palms and his twisted ankle, by exhaustion, by overwhelming sadness. He rolled into a tight ball, arms wrapped around his knees, and he cried.

His sister dropped down beside him and rubbed his back, her hand riding up and down with each shuddering sob. "It's okay, Caleb. We can rest for a while. We're pretty far away now, and he's probably given up looking for us already. The search was eating into his drinking time."

"Thanks, Ad," he managed to choke out through his tears. "I just need a few minutes, and we can keep going."

Adelaide was nine years old, and she was not fueled by fear, but by rage. A rage so incandescent, it was a wonder the cabin they had so recently shared with their father had not burst into flames long ago.

Their father was a bad man who had chased away their older siblings one by one. He was prone to drinking, and prone to using his heavy fists to address even the smallest of infractions. Their mother, a kind but frail woman, tried to protect them, and had taken the brunt of his punishments until the day she disappeared. He swore to the two of them up and down, tears in his eyes, that she had left them all, had run away with a traveling peddler. Only, Adelaide had noticed the freshly turned earth at the back of the garden the very next morning.

Caleb endured another beating soon after that, and Adelaide vowed to him that they would leave together. While their father snored mere steps away, she filled a knapsack with the meager contents of their pantry, and they snuck away through the root cellar.

***

As night fell, they staggered out of the trees and spilled down a shallow embankment, landing in a tangle at the edge of a stream. They were cold and wet, and the setting sun wrapped them in long fingers of shadow. Too tired to stand, Adelaide and Caleb crawled away from the water, settling into a hollow beneath the embankment.

"Ad, I'm hungry," Caleb said.

"I know, little brother. It's been a long day, and you've done so well." Adelaide dug through the knapsack. She unwrapped a crust of bread and some hard sheep's milk cheese, and they ate in silence. Adelaide pulled a jug of water from the knapsack and they shared it until it was empty, then she refilled it in the cold, fast-moving stream.

It was soon full dark, the stars like handfuls of glittering pebbles thrown against the black sky. The brother and sister leaned into each other and nestled as best they could against the rocks and dirt at their backs. Caleb did his best to ignore his throbbing ankle.

Just when Adelaide thought Caleb had fallen asleep, she heard his small voice say, "If Papa finds us, he'll kill us."

Adelaide sighed, and for the first time that day she felt tears sting her eyes. "He won't find us, Caleb. I won't let him. Besides, he's lazy. He'll probably be happy that he doesn't have to feed us any more."

Caleb was quiet after that. Adelaide wrapped her arm around his narrow shoulders, and she felt them shake as he cried himself to sleep.

The next morning they ate the rest of the bread and cheese, and each had one of the small, sour apples that grew wild on their property. "Are you ready, Caleb? We need to keep going, just to be safe," Adelaide said.

Caleb took a few steps on his twisted ankle. It hurt enough to make him wince, but it supported him. He nodded solemnly. "I'm good, Ad. Let's go."

Adelaide gave him an encouraging smile. "We'll follow this up-stream. It should be easier than walking through the forest. And a little less scary, huh?"

Caleb set off along the stream bank. He looked back at Adelaide and said, "Nothing's as scary as home." Adelaide nodded once and followed him.

They stayed with the stream through the day, keeping to the bank, walking in the water when the bank was impassable. The rocks were moss-covered and slick. The sun, when it managed to pierce the narrow gap between the trees on both sides of the waterway, was fierce. They came to a waterfall and were forced to scale the small cliff the water tumbled over, searching for perilous footholds, grasping at exposed tree roots. When they reached the cliff top they found that the going from there was steadily uphill, and there was a mountain visible in the distance. The sun, perched between the twin peaks of the mountain, draped the rocky slopes in ribbons of gold.

Too exhausted for words, Adelaide and Caleb shared a grim smile and a shake of the head, and carried on. They had water to spare, but no more food, save a few of the apples that twisted their stomachs more than filled them.

With dusk settling like a hazy grey shroud, the stream widened, the current slowed, the land flattened out, and the forest crept back to form a large clearing, a meadow rainbowed with wild flowers. In the clearing next to the stream sat a small cottage. It was squat and round, built of river stones, with a thatched straw roof. Candle light danced and flickered in the windows, and smoke curled from the chimney. Next to the cottage was a lush vegetable garden, and behind it a pen where goats grazed.

The brother and sister watched the cottage from the edge of the forest, hidden, fearful of who might live there. The door finally opened, and a person in a long white robe walked out. They walked toward the stream, a large golden cup in each hand. When they reached the bank, they placed one foot in the water, then reached down to fill one of the cups.

Caleb began to stand, but Adelaide stopped him with a cautious hand on his shoulder. "Wait," she said. "I want to see what they're doing." Caleb dropped back down to his knees, but his entire body was tensed, ready to spring forward.

The person held the two cups up to the sky, as if in offering, then stopped suddenly and looked in their direction. They raised a hand in greeting and called out, in a voice that was soft and sweet yet carried across the clearing, "Are you hungry?"

This time Adelaide failed to stop Caleb as he burst into a run, and she had to race to catch up to him.

***

The brother and sister were shy at first, saying little. But walking into the little cottage felt like being enveloped in a warm hug, their host was gentle and welcoming, and the rustic round table at the center of the room was laden with mouth-watering food and a jug of sweet clover tea. Their bellies were soon filled to bursting. They said little, giving halting answers to the sympathetic questions they were asked, but before long the food and drink had loosened both their tongues. Grateful to have an adult who listened without ridicule, the words spilled out of them.

"I think Papa killed Mama and buried her in the garden. And I was afraid that if we stayed with him, he would kill Caleb, and me as well. So we left, not knowing where we were going. It didn't matter. All that mattered was leaving." Adelaide finished, sighed, and sat back in her chair, as if the story had exhausted her as much as the journey.

Caleb had contributed to the story here and there, but mostly listened. More than once he started to speak, seemed to think better of it, and remained silent. Finally he looked up at their host and said, "Can I ask you a question?"

"Of course! You can ask me anything."

"Are you a boy or a girl?"

"Caleb, that's rude," Adelaide said.

"It's fine, Adelaide, not rude at all. It was an honest question. Caleb, how about this... you can call me Temperance, and we'll leave it at that. Will that work for you?"

"Temperance. I like that," Caleb said.

Temperance reached out and joined hands with each of them. "I can't imagine what you've been through, the strength and resilience it took for you to leave home. Adelaide, I am humbled by the love you have for your brother, to keep him safe no matter the cost. And Caleb, you are the bravest little boy I have ever met.

"I live a simple life here, one of contemplation and balance. I live for small joys. The way the sunlight dances on the water outside my door, the satisfaction of growing my own food, the pleasure of reading a good book read by the light of a roaring fire. It may not sound very exciting—"

"It sounds wonderful," Adelaide whispered.

"I have not heard the laughter of children in this home for a very long time, and I would welcome it. If you're agreeable, I would be honored to have you live here with me, for as long as you desire."

Adelaide and Caleb looked at each other and nodded simultaneously. "Yes, please," Caleb said.

"There is one thing I must ask of you," Temperance said. "Each evening I perform a ceremony of sorts on the bank of the stream. In fact, that's what I was about to do when the two of you showed up. It's my way of thanking the Mother, of finding harmony and equilibrium in all things, in the earth and water beneath my feet and the sky above my head. It's personal, and I'm not ready to share it. That may change over time, but not yet.

"So, I would ask that you both rest by the fire – I'm sure you're exhausted after your long journey – and not look out the front windows until I return. Can you do that?"

Adelaide wrapped her thin, strong arms around Temperance in a hug, and Caleb quickly joined in. "We won't watch," Adelaide said. "You have my word. Come on, Caleb, I see some books there on the shelf. I'll read to you."

Temperance smiled. "I believe you. Thank you." Adelaide and Caleb settled together in front of the fireplace, feeling safe for the first time that either could remember.

Life in the little cottage in the meadow was good. Temperance was a patient, generous teacher, and the two children learned to fish in the stream, work the soil in the garden, and tend the goats. But they also learned to chase tadpoles, and turn cartwheels through the wild flowers, and lie still in the grass, soaking up sunshine like the laziest of cats. They learned to laugh and be kids again. Caleb released the fear that had for so long coiled in his ribcage, squeezing his heart. The anger that burned like a hot coal in Adelaide's soul cooled, then wafted away on the breeze like ash from a fire. At night Adelaide curled up with a book while Temperance taught Caleb to read.

True to their word, the brother and sister never once peeked out the window when they were not supposed to.

***

"Temperance, Ad, he's here!" Caleb burst through the door of the cottage, wild eyed.

"Who's here?" Adelaide asked, though she knew by the sudden flare of heat inside her who he meant.

"Papa! He just walked out of the forest, heading this way. And he has an axe!"

Temperance placed a calming hand on Caleb's cheek, touched Adelaide lightly on her shoulder. "Stay in the cottage. I'll deal with your father. I promise no harm will come to you."

"He's a dangerous man," Adelaide said.

"He has a big axe," Caleb added.

Temperance surprised them both by laughing. "I've dealt with dangerous men and bullies before. You just need to remain calm and rational, and show them that you are not frightened. There's almost always a scared little child inside the bluster, ready to flee when confronted. Please stay inside."

"May we watch?" Caleb asked.

Temperance thought for a moment, then smiled. "You may, from the window." Temperance strode out through the door. Adelaide and Caleb scurried to the window and huddled together.

The children's father stopped at the edge of the garden, just a few steps from where Temperance stood, taking the axe down from his shoulder. "Give me my brats. I know they're here; I saw the little shit running to hide. Send them out now, and I won't have to tear your little hovel down to the ground."

"No."

The father towered over Temperance, his fist white-knuckled on the handle of the axe, but with that one word, said with quiet conviction, he seemed to shrink just a little.

"Those brats are mine to do with as I wish. Stand aside." He stepped forward, hefting the axe.

"I said no!" Great feathered wings burst from Temperance's back and unfurled. With one mighty thrust, the wings drove Temperance into the sky, and the powerful wind they created buffeted the man to the ground. The axe flew from his hand, tumbling end over end into the stream.

Temperance hovered there above him, wings roiling the air. The wind turned warm, then hot, the grass around him beginning to scorch and wither. "Leave now, sir, and never return. This will be your only warning."

Adelaide and Caleb watched in wonder as their father stumbled to his feet and ran towards the forest without looking back. When Temperance walked through the door a moment later, they were waiting with open arms.

"Who's hungry?" Temperance asked.

As the three of them prepared dinner together, Caleb asked, "What happened to your wings?"

Temperance smiled. "I'll tell you what, Caleb. Tonight, why don't you and Adelaide both join me outside. I think I'm ready to share my ritual with you, and I promise my wings will make an appearance."

XV: THE DEVIL

The Devil and the Department Store by Craig Rathbone

The Evergreen Glades Shopping Centre was bustling. Crowds of sweaty people thronged the ostentatious concourse, peering into shop windows, leaving stores with bags of clothes or expensive kitchen appliances. Some were sat around the food court, filling their faces with sandwiches, chips and ice cream. Parents clucked at their unruly children, miserable staff members tried to survive another summer Saturday, and old couples tutted and shook their heads at noisy teenagers who had come to the shops to hang around and not buy a thing.

One such trio of teenagers was currently mooching around the front of the arcade, chafing that they hadn't thought to bring any money with them. The undisputed ringleader, a skinny girl with a shock of wild red hair, was teasing one of her friends in a loud, screeching tone, drawing the ire of said pensioners. "Oooh, look at me! I'm Wesley and I'm *above* searching the arcade floor for loose change! I don't *want* to play *Mortal Kombat* in case my mum finds out and makes me go to confession for ripping a ninja's spine out!" she crowed in a none-too-flattering accent.

The recipient rolled his eyes behind round-framed glasses, which glinted chrome against his dark skin. "I told you, Ginger, I am not scurrying around on that dirty floor! People have trod all sorts in there, not to mention dropped food, drinks – I wouldn't be surprised if people have, well, you know, *done it* on that floor," he fired back, in a somewhat more measured tone to avoid any further dirty looks. The third member of the group giggled from behind a large planter, having sought a hiding place out of the line of sight as she often did when Ginger insisted on being noisy and attracting unwanted attention. "And you can stop laughing, Gen; you're just encouraging her!"

Ginger rolled her eyes, throwing her hands wide in exasperation. "Oh, fine then. We'll just wander around without a plan instead, same as last weekend and the one before that. Maybe we'll see something funny like Billy Fuller falling over again. I bet Gen wanted to play *Mortal Kombat* though, she's actually unbeatable on *Street Fighter 2*. Isn't that right?" she asked as they moved away from the tutting pensioners. As was often the case, Wesley walked slightly behind the girls, the ever-awkward Gen sticking to Ginger's side like glue, wringing her hands anxiously. To Ginger's question regarding video games, Gen just nodded a response.

Wesley wasn't sure how Genevieve Lloyd had fallen into their gang, upgrading a duo of outcasts to a trio of losers, but he was happy to have her aboard. While Ginger was assertive and bossy and he was studious and fussy, Gen was mousy and near-silent, always looking as if she was about to walk in front of a firing squad. It didn't help that she had a terrible stammer, or that she'd been bullied and pushed around by far too many of the other kids at school, at least until Ginger had gone after a group of boys with a length of lead pipe one afternoon after school. She'd saved Gen from a beating that day, and the girl had hung around with them since.

The usual shops looked to be drawing the crowds. CDs and cassettes flew off the shelves in Virgin Megastore, the designer clothes shops full of young men and women looking to spend megabucks on threads that would probably be out of fashion within six months. While it wasn't one of those massive *malls* the size of a small town they had in the USA, Evergreen Glades was doing pretty well for itself, just a fifteen-minute bus journey from picturesque Charlton-on-Sea. "Look at all of those posers in there, those shell suits are *awful* and I bet they catch fire so easily," said Wesley snidely as a nattering group of adults emerged from one of the clothes outlets. Wesley's family had worked hard to provide him with whatever he wanted in life, though he'd never lost his disdain for fads and trends.

"Right? Those things will probably still be in fashion in, like, the year two thousand as well," cackled Ginger, loud enough to attract some venomous glances from the shell suit gang. "Everyone rustling around in their dumb, colourful jackets and pants. If I were them I'd just get a lighter and—"

Gen and Wesley almost slammed into the back of her, such was the harshness of her sudden braking, the soles of her battered trainers squeaking on the polished floor. Wesley stepped past her irritably to see what the hubbub was about. On the ground, paces away from them, was a very old-looking ring. It may have been shining silver once, though the passage of time had rendered it a scratched and grubby grey. Different coloured jewels adorned it, glittering in the artificial light of the concourse.

"Holy *shit*! Would you look at this little beauty," said Ginger as she stooped down and collected the errant piece of jewellery. "Reckon these diamonds are real? We could take it down to *Money Generators* and trade it in for a small *fortune*!"

Wesley and Gen exchanged a nervous glance as Ginger cooed over the ring. They knew when an *Argument with Ginger* was incoming and suspected that they wouldn't win this one either. Still, they tried. "S-shouldn't we h-hand it in to s-s-security?" tried Gen meekly, her willpower to resist her redheaded friend not as eroded as Wesley's.

Ginger placed a hand on one hip, fixing Gen with a playful yet stern expression. "We *could* do that, but what do you suppose they'd do with it? They'd just trade it in themselves and spend all the money on beer or cigarettes or, I don't know, awful shell suits. Far better it stays with us and we get all the arcade money we could ever want, and maybe enough left over for a *MacSweeneys*. Come on, don't be losers!" she tried, noting from her friend's resolute expressions that she wasn't winning them over.

Wesley held his hand out for the ring, radiating real *disapproving parent* vibes. "You know that isn't the right thing to do. I am *not* getting into trouble over a tatty old ring; it's probably fake anyway. Besides, *Money Generators* won't serve kids, so unless you intend for me to grow a moustache a couple of years early, we're out of luck."

Much to their relief, Ginger gave up on her idea, rolling her eyes dramatically at their iron-like sensibility. "Alright, fine. We'll give it to the fake cops. Not like I need a couple of hundred quid anyway, it's only my house that's falling to bits. Can I at least try it on first? Is that alright with you?" she pouted, placing the ring onto her finger with a theatrical flourish.

The air pressure in the shopping centre rapidly changed, and time slowed to a halt around them. Shoppers froze like statues mid-walk, a parent turned into a tableau of misery as she wiped a toddler's sausage roll-covered mouth and a nearby security guard's eyes glazed over, his walkie-talkie held to his mouth. "W-wh-wh-what the—" squeaked Gen, terror palpable in her voice and her saucer-like eyes. Wesley turned in a slow circle, his ever-active mind taking stock of the unusual situation.

"It's been months since the last weird thing happened, Ginger. You *promised* that we wouldn't get ourselves dragged into any more supernatural adventures. You. Promised!" he snapped, rounding on Ginger, who took a step back in surprise before her usual aggressive attitude recovered and placed her onto the offensive, her natural habitat.

"*Excuse me,* Wesley? How is this my fault? All I did was put this bloody ring on!"

"Everybody knows that putting on weird jewellery you find on the floor is dangerous," Wesley retorted hotly. "I know you don't like reading books, but surely you've seen a few movies or played a bloody video game?"

Ginger's face flushed crimson as she closed the gap to her friend, poking his chest with a long finger. "Oh sorry if I missed that lesson in Gandalf's survival school, you nerd! He never mentioned that magical jewellery could exist in shopping centres!" she hissed like a polecat, the ring glowing ever brighter on her hand as it jabbed at Wesley.

"Stop whinging and *take it off*, you moron!" Wesley roared in response, watching wild-eyed as his friend tried and failed to do so, panic in her eyes as the cursed item refused to move past her bony knuckle. "You're useless, you know that? I *knew* I should have stayed in bed this morning—"

"S-st-*STOP IT*!" Gen screamed over the top of their argument, snapping them back into reality and away from over a decade of childish disputes. As shocking as the whole frozen-time situation was, being scolded by their newest friend was even more unexpected, for she was usually as meek as a lamb. Not that she could be accused of such at that moment. Her usually pale face was even redder than Ginger's, her limp hands balled into fists of rage at her sides. Wesley and Ginger exchanged guilty looks, having completely forgotten about her needs in the heat of their argument.

"Sorry Gen, didn't mean to go all bitch mode there, I just got freaked out 'bout the whole time-stopping thing. This kind of event really fucks up my weekend, you know?" Ginger said soothingly, placing her arm around her friend's shaking shoulders.

Wesley stepped closer too, a hangdog look on his round face. "And I'm sorry for being a dick too, I just freaked out a little, you know?" he added helpfully.

An awkward few seconds passed while Gen fought back tears, her two friends comforting her in their way; Ginger hugging her while Wesley made a lame joke about never wearing things you find on the ground. Eventually, Gen nodded her head and gently extricated herself from Ginger's embrace, which was like being embraced by a scarecrow made of coat hangers. "Th-that's okay, I know you w-wouldn't kill each other really," she said, a gentle smile on her face, "but this is r-r-really scary. What's going on?"

Wesley exchanged a knowing look with Ginger, the redheaded girl nodding her permission for what he was about to tell the newest member of their gang. "Well Gen, this is going to sound really weird, but Ginger and myself, we've seen some proper unusual shit the last few months, shit that you wouldn't even believe. Remember when the school had that gas leak and got all fire damaged last autumn?" he asked, receiving a slow and dubious nod in return. "Well it was no leaky pipe. We befriended an actual chi—"

He was interrupted by an alarming *crash*, as if thunder were somehow occurring inside the shopping centre. A blast of pressure sent them flailing, Wesley managing to catch Gen before she toppled over onto the dirty floor. The other shoppers remained frozen in place as the three friends recovered their equilibrium, only to find a new arrival standing before them. A tall man, dark-skinned and handsome, had popped into existence, bedecked in a perfectly tailored suit of red. His beard was immaculately shaped and groomed, his long hair flowing down his back. Golden eyes shone hungrily above a wolfish smile.

"Finally, somebody put on my ring. I've been waiting for a very, *very* long time for that to happen!" the man said smoothly, his strange eyes fixed upon the glowing ring upon Ginger's hand. "It does suit you, Kerry Wells of Charlton-on-Sea. Now, what say we get to work changing people's lives for the better?"

Ginger took a step back, moving closer to her friends and away from the strange new arrival who apparently owned the ring. "Hey, only my teachers and my dad get to call me Kerry, alright? And I hate to break it to you, pal, but I'm only fifteen so you can't go around inviting me out to do *work* with you, alright? There are laws against that kind of thing," she replied, fixing him with a rather accusing glare.

If the man was troubled by Ginger's revelation, he didn't show it, laughing long and loudly instead before stepping closer toward them. "No law applies to the great Beelzebub, child. Besides, I have no interest in anything like *that*. I merely wish to give these greedy, vain fools what they wish for the most – material wealth. Wouldn't it be nice if I just clicked my fingers and the rule of law no longer applied here? All of these drones could simply take whatever they wanted, without consequence from lawmakers or those who enforce their will. Even you three piglets could net yourselves the latest in fashion, a new video games console, or if you wish to *truly* live, enough food and drink to throw a feast of your very own," he oozed, his words dripping with promise.

Wesley, Gen still attached to his arm with a look of wide-eyed terror on her face, saw Ginger falter at the idea of infinite wealth without consequence, the thought of owning everything she ever needed overriding the very obvious problem that a mysterious man called Beelzebub had just popped into existence to tempt a whole shopping centre into some kind of Faustian pact.

"So what's the catch? You'll give us the world in exchange for our souls?" he asked, trying to keep his voice from wavering, wanting to sound courageous for Gen's sake as she looked completely out of her depth. He could feel her shaking against his arm.

Beelzebub fixed Wesley with a predatory glance, the smile never leaving his face. "Wesley Lewis, you always were the shrewd, cautious type. I should have known you'd be digging for *What's in it for Beelzebub?* It's a simple one. Let these idiots shop until they drop, sow enough harm and spite to last a century, and return home before suppertime. They get what they want, I get mine, it's a deal made in Hel – *heaven!*"

"I-I d-don't like the sound of th-this," Gen breathed, appealing to her friends to perhaps not go along with the apparition's plan. Wesley nodded in agreement, but Ginger hesitated, her eyes flicking between Beelzebub and the various shops that surrounded them. Her friends could see the cogs turning in her head, and sense the conflict. Her family had never been particularly well off, and things had only become worse since her mother's death the previous year. If any member of the trio would be tempted to take the deal, it would be her.

Thankfully it was Ginger's more infamous characteristic that shone through: her stubbornness. "I think we're going to pass on that, thanks, mate. No amount of video games and food is worth bringing hate into the world, or whatever it was you said. Nah, I just reckon me and my friends here will go back home and *not* take some weird deal with a golden-eyed dude that just popped into existence and *froze* a bloody shopping centre," she spat defiantly, shoulders back and chin raised. Wesley could have cheered at her resolve if he wasn't deeply concerned about the unusual situation.

Beezlebub shrugged laconically, unmoved by her defiance. "Oh, that is fine. I don't actually need three fifteen-year-olds to give me permission, you see. These fools will give in to their greed and murder each other over material baubles with or without you. The Philosopher, the Pauper and the Witch," he reeled off, pointing to Wesley, Ginger and Gen in turn. "All will die in this place. Shoppers – *kill them!*"

The apparition clicked his fingers, causing their ears to pop as time oozed back into motion. The three friends looked around wide-eyed as the throngs of shoppers began to move again, this time toward them, deep hatred reflected in their eyes. Beezlebub laughed heartily as he stepped back into the approaching crowd, which was now pressing the trio up against the frontage of a discount clothes shop.

"What's wrong with you all? You're really listening to that arsehole? You're going to kill three kids because some weirdo told you to? You can *have* all this shit, we don't even care!" Ginger shouted, her voice cracking. Their eyes were glazed, empty apart from feral hatred. Behind the crowd, on the upper level, other shoppers were already rioting, smashing windows and taking handfuls of goods in a frenzy. Some were even turning on each other, a middle-aged woman shoving a burly-looking man to the ground to steal what looked to be a handful of action figures.

"I don't think they're listening. Let's get out of here!" Wesley yelped, grabbing Ginger's arm to get her attention, pointing into the big discount clothes shop where they could perhaps lose the crowd. Ginger locked eyes with Gen. The poor girl was terrified; they would need to protect her and keep up their tough fronts as best they could for her sake.

"Right you are, fuck this lot!" she replied to Wesley and, together as one, the friends turned tail and fled into the shop behind them. The mob followed them to the door, but no further. Some even dispersed, scurrying off to other shops to join in on the looting. But there was to be no respite for them, as the lovers of discount clothing inside the store were also on the rampage, tackling each other over displays and straight-up fighting in the aisles over clothes that were way too high in polyester.

"Isn't th-there a s-side entrance here? Onto the c-cookie store?" asked Gen, pointing past a group of pensioners filling baskets with cheap suits (the kind that never quite fit anybody properly).

Wesley nodded enthusiastically. "That's right! If we can get there, then maybe we can lose this mob of zombie shoppers!" he cried, casting his eye around to find the best route through the chaos. Things were steadily getting worse in the store. More shoppers were gravitating toward the melee and even the staff were now laying into the stock, and each other.

It was Ginger who broke the hesitation, much to nobody's surprise. "Well it's not getting any quieter, let's make a run for it; I *hate* clothes shops anyway!" She grabbed Gen by the hand and moved further into the warzone. Together the trio weaved through the shelves and up-turned tables, stepping over strewn-about cheap neon apparel as they avoided the zombie-like shoppers, making their way toward the side entrance and in the hopes that Beelzebub's executioners weren't there too. After some backtracking and rerouting, they managed to reach their chance at escape, breathing a sigh of relief that the entryway was mostly clear, with just one elderly woman trying to fill her cardigan pockets with packets of tissues.

Wesley watched the woman's antics for a moment from around the side of an aisle before turning back to the others hiding behind him. "Just one granny. We should be able to squeeze past her, I think. Ginger, please don't punch her or anything. It looks like these people are under some kind of spell, so it isn't their fault," he lectured, not liking the crooked smile that had appeared on her face.

"Screw you, Grandad! I wouldn't punch your wife; chill out!" Ginger sniped in response, pushing past him, still trailing Gen by the hand. The latter fixed Wesley with a *help me* glance as they disappeared around the end of the shelving.

Wesley hadn't liked having Gen around at first; he'd been used to having Ginger's attention to himself for most of his life, and found it jarring to have a new personality thrust into the middle of them. But it was hard to dislike the girl, even if she was incredibly quiet. Not only was she into the same things as they were, but she was also as bookish and academic as him, so he finally had a homework partner that took the job seriously. But the best part of it all was how much her presence improved Ginger's often dark, abrasive mood. The redhead seemed to speak for both of them, and the two had become joined at the hip in the last few months. Wesley had grown to find the whole thing rather sweet.

"Oi, bellend, move it!" hissed Ginger, sticking her head back around the corner. Wesley snapped out of his thoughts, muttered an apology and rushed after them, his trainers squeaking on the floor. The old lady was still at the tissue display, now trying without luck to stuff further tissue packets into her mouth, so they were able to successfully sneak past her and back out into the concourse.

Unfortunately for them, the main floor was just as hellish. On their wild flight toward the exit, they passed entire families fighting (a child attempting to apply a chokehold to their father being a highlight) and even a woman trying to drown an uprooted store mannequin in the fountain. The trio moved as quickly as they dared, avoiding all manner of spilt condiments and debris in their path, until the grand entrance to the shopping centre loomed ahead, blessedly devoid of any possessed, psychotic shoppers.

"See you in Hell, sucke—" Ginger started to shout as she passed through the archway to the car park beyond, only to be sent sprawling backwards onto the dirty floor by some unseen force.

Wesley and Gen rushed to her side, eyeing up the impassable exit warily. "Wh-what the heck just h-happened?" wailed Gen hysterically as Wesley helped Ginger into a sitting position. The redhead was blinking back tears but otherwise didn't seem too affected by the unusual phenomenon as she scurried back to her feet.

"That golden-eyed, beardy *shit* blocked the exit with a bloody force field or whatever, that's what," she growled in a wavering voice. "When I see that loser, I'm going to rip his nipples off, I swear!"

Whether she would get the chance was, however, quite up for debate. The shoppers had ceased their internal struggle, no doubt alerted by Ginger's collision with the magical barrier, and were now converging on their position. While some were slowed down by their bags of stolen goods, others were travelling somewhat closer and moved to close the gap quickly, murder in their eyes.

"Time to go, I think, *time to go*!" Wesley barked, ushering the girls in front of him as they fled for the escalators to the upper floor, the only escape route left to them as the foyer became a sea of dangerous zombies. They took the steps as fast as they could, Ginger pulling Gen by the hand as always while Wesley broke his own rules of chivalry by pushing her from behind, the horde trying to follow them up but falling over each other in their haste. As soon as they reached the top of the escalator they were off again, flat out running and avoiding the odd looter as they went.

"We can't keep running! We need a plan!" gasped Wesley, casting his bespectacled eyes around for any sanctuary they could use. But there was none to be had; every store had become a desperate melee as the last scraps of valuable goods were fought over. They even passed several unconscious bodies (well, hopefully they were unconscious) until, in a flurry of panic, they slid into the middle of the food court.

The open space was trashed, but surprisingly clear of the actively possessed. A few lay around the place, sound asleep and covered in condiments and crumbs where they had gorged themselves under the suggestion of the mysterious Beelzebub, but otherwise, they had the space to themselves – at least until the horde from the foyer caught them up. "O-ok-okay, ideas! We n-need ideas, now!" Gen gasped, unable to tear her eyes off the way they had come.

"I'm with her on this one; if we can't escape then we're going to need a way to find this Beelzebub arsehole and get him to end this madness," Wesley agreed, "Come on, there must be some way to get him to reappear, then we can bargain with him to end it!"

Ginger snarled, kicking an empty paper cup across the food court in impotent rage, "*Bargain?* I'm going to punch that smarmy dickhead so hard that this ring gets jammed in his fucking *windpipe!* Make me run into a magic door, will you?" she ranted, kicking various other items of refuse in her impotent fury. While it did little to calm her, it did give Wesley an idea that hit his brain like a thunderbolt.

"The ring, of course! Ginger, get some washing-up liquid on it and take it off, quickly. I suspect that removing it *might* break the spell, it's worth a try at least," he ordered, having to raise his voice over the sound of the approaching mob, who had thankfully been waylaid by further looting. There were a few more shops between them and the food court, so at least they had some time.

Ginger slapped her forehead in frustration. "Of course, what can't washing-up liquid solve?" she said in something between a scream and a laugh, hurtling over to a churro stand and grabbing an industri-ally-sized bottle of green liquid, pouring it over her hand with great urgency.

The bustle of the crowd was closer still. Wesley and Gen were able to see them ransacking a nearby television shop, one man attempting to carry away a unit as heavy as a car and failing miserably. "H-hurry up

Ginger, they're almost h-here!" Gen called, unable to look away from the ever-approaching danger.

"Doing my best here, but the bloody thing is *stuck*! It's not even too small for me, it just won't let go of my skin! *Bastard*!" Ginger wailed in reply, the mob now pouring into the other end of the food court. They would be on them in seconds. Wesley and Gen backed up to the struggling Ginger, Wesley stopping to pick up a discarded yard brush on the way, brandishing it like a club as the first possessed shoppers spotted them and ran to close the distance.

But they never reached the three friends, instead slowing to a halt as time froze once again.

"I told you, resistance is futile," said Beelzebub, leaning against the side of a doughnut cart as if he'd been there all along. "And you'll never get that ring off. Do you know how very *dull* humanity has become over the centuries? There's hardly any magic left in the world. You frittered it all away, insisted on carrying a light in the dark and finding an answer for everything."

"You'd rather what, exactly?" Wesley spat defiantly. "That we remained Neanderthals afraid of shadows? Or dirty peasants blaming illness on spirits? You're just an old demon, Beelzebub. A bully who's been toying with humanity for centuries. You're actually a bit of a loser." He brandished the brush like a spear before him.

Beelzebub laughed long and hard at his efforts, unmoved by his passion. "You're a fool, boy. Your ancestors suffered at the yoke of those of your friends here. They chained them into ships and sailed them across the sea as their property, and yet you claim to harbour no hatred toward them? No *spite*? Just give in to it, Little Philosopher, agree to my terms and let's spread some real *unpleasantness*!"

Wesley gripped the brush with renewed vigour, taking another step closer to the apparition. "Really? You're trying to turn me on my friends by pointing out that racism exists? You'll have to do better than that. I love my friends, and I know they love me too, so try again, you utter *creep*!"

Beelzebub rolled his shining eyes in response and, with a gentle flick of a wrist, sent Wesley sailing backwards into a table covered in food waste, sprawling to the floor in a tangle of limbs. Ginger screamed in rage and tried to charge the demon, only to be frozen to the spot by another gentle gesture. "Oh, stay there and be quiet, peasant. I already told you; only magic can break my curse. A dirty, skinny wretch like you would never have a chance."

While Ginger stood frozen, able only to glare at their attacker, and Wesley lay groaning on the ground, Gen seemed to be marshalling her panic into an idea. Ginger had seen that face before, usually when her antics had got the three of them into trouble and Gen came up with a cunning way to get back out of it, an event that seemed to happen all too often.

"The Peasant, the Philosopher and t-the *Witch*!" she breathed, darting across to Ginger's immobilised form before the demon could react and, in one smooth move, lifted the ring from her frozen finger.

Beelzebub's golden eyes went wide as the air pressure changed again and a huge crack of thunder peeled through the shopping centre. The demon was lifted off his feet by an invisible force, his lower extremities already turning to an impossibly black smoke that whipped away in an unnatural gale that sent food packets flying in a tornado. Gen stood before him defiantly, the demon's increasingly inhuman-sounding insults and cursing washing over her usually timid countenance as if they were nothing more than dust.

"One r-ring to r-rule the mall, *motherfucker!*" she screamed, holding the tarnished jewellery item aloft until Beelzebub was gone for good, his golden eyes the last to fade into nothingness, pupils altered and snakelike.

Ginger fell to her knees as the wind died away. The shoppers looked around in confusion, piles of stolen goods dropping from their hands onto the floor.

Wesley slowly climbed to his feet and limped over. "That really bloody hurt. What an absolute tosser he was," he moaned, holding out a hand to help Ginger back to her feet.

For once, his best friend took the offer of help as she wiped the washing-up liquid on her pants and then got shakily back up, both of them looking at Gen with pure admiration.

"That was absolutely *mint*; how did you get that evil thing off my hand? And what was that cool thing you said to him? That sounded absolutely *mental!*" Ginger laughed, collecting a rather overwhelmed Gen in a powerful hug. If Gen was expecting help from Wesley, she was sorely disappointed, as he encompassed the both of them in a back-breaking hug of his own before disengaging, a grin on his bruised face.

"I *knew* you never read *The Lord of the Rings,* Ginger," Wesley said. "It's a really famous line from those books. Glad you have taste though, Gen. Maybe you can convince her to read it," he laughed.

Ginger stuck her tongue out at him before striding toward the food court exit, forcing the others to fall in behind her. "Good luck with that! I'm more interested in the fact that Gen is a *witch* and can apparently break ancient curses. The weird few months we've had, that'll come in very handy."

Gen smiled as she followed them out, still riding high from a combination of adrenaline and the wild fact that she had just used magic, *real* magic to break a curse and save everybody's lives. Clutching the warm ring in her fist, she let the back and forth of her friends' bantering wash over her.

***

Gen didn't believe Wesley and Ginger at first, about the strange regularity of their adventures in the supernatural. But she soon would, as they ran into a golem and a hobgoblin before the end of that summer. More adventures would follow. While she still hid in the shadows at school, she ended up being rather effective at using her newfound powers against these supernatural menaces.

As for the incident at the shopping centre, it was closed off by a strange military unit dressed in all black, *Bellerophon* emblazoned on their insignia patches. The confused shoppers were told the same as the local council, the same excuse secret agencies always seem to use.

There was no devil; it was just a gas leak.

XVI: THE TOWER

Yellow Eyes by Peter Linton

I halted at the top of the pass. Before me lay a broad, untamed valley of broken boulders and stunted trees. I had about twenty miles to go and I had to travel it on foot... blindfolded.

My name is Phyrra and I am an elf-sorcerer. I was one of those whose powers shone through their eyes, an appreciable yellow-on-yellow glow marking my birthright. No one, not even my mother, knew the natural color of my eye's iris. Even my pupils were hidden. Most people are taken aback, or even threatened by my visage. Though that wasn't what concerned me now. In the dark of night, they pin-pointed me from far away. So tonight, I closed them and tied a black bandana over them, the triangle tails hanging down upon my face.

Jynx would be my eyes.

An elf-sorcerer doesn't select their own magic. Spells are chosen for us whether by chance or fate. We discover them by time and trial. And we're stuck with what we have.

And I had the magic for a familiar and possessed an exceptional mastery of it as well.

His name was Jynx. I usually chose a hawk as the animal form for him. As my familiar, I possessed scrying eyes through him and I heard what he heard. If I so desired, I could see a mouse a mile away and listen to its chirp if Jynx approached. He has a mind of his own, but he always obeys my thoughts and commands. Pity, perhaps, that he couldn't protect me or fight for me like a summoned beast. I'm on my own should any combat take place.

I removed my backpack and waterskin, and ate a few bites of travel cake. That would be the last bit of food I would have for an uncounted number of days. Likewise, I would not carry any water. Jynx would have to find that necessary substance for me. For this was not some sightseeing excursion. If I was going to achieve retribution, I had to move fast and stealthily. So armed with merely a dagger and some treated rope tied to a grappling hook, I quickened my pace to a run.

***

"What did he do to you?" I asked.

"He led me into his chambers and…" Myrra replied, squinting her eyes as if she were staring into the sun… or in pain.

I stood, regarding her a moment before turning away. Whatever anguish she was attempting to share might best be told without my yellow glare.

"The room was lavishly adorned with many pillows. Part of me knew I should leave, but a fog entered my mind, and glittering lights appeared before my face. "Do you like my suite?" he asked. "It is sweetly scented and gently lit, and here we may rest undisturbed."

***

I took my first steps down the mountainside.

Orienting myself in Jynx's eyes took just a moment. I had linked his sight to my steps an uncounted number of times. He flew above me, but close enough to clearly mark the details of the path before me, scanning the terrain and guiding my steps.

The pass itself was fairly easy to negotiate. Long ago it was cleared by dwarves making the mountain top accessible to gain access to the valley. They uprooted the trees and excavated the earth, and were quite thorough in the execution. Even now, centuries later, when the dwarven realm had come to an end and its people moved on, the pass and the mountainside trail remained traversable by foot or horseback by any solitary traveler.

They named it Torevir's Approach for the clan's first chief. Lore has it that the clan kept regular contact with elves beyond, in what is still called Berevan Valley. Yet just as the dwarves came to an end, so did the kindly elf domain. The Berevian elves who lived here now were arrogant and conceited.

Some had guessed that at one time they engaged in dark and forbidden magic, even demon worship. Yet there was no trace of evil in their faces. Just a hubris that comes from being walled in with privilege and wealth. Indeed, from my perspective, they looked down upon those of us who wandered the wide world and instead claimed a home in hidden forests outside their great valley. They focused only on themselves.

Oh, yes, I've had interactions with them. None with more aspersion than with their crowned head, Dayrelie.

Standing above all those before him, Dayrelie was taller than any other elf I knew. His skin and blond hair emanated a golden sheen. He looked upon you with his amber eyes set inside a slim face with high cheekbones. Indeed, he was handsome by any standard. I, on the other hand, come with a rounder face with plain features. And like any elf of the deep woods, my dull skin color matches the gray-brown bark of mountain oak.

Like me, he was an elf-sorcerer, but one of greater faculty. He once had the effrontery to try to seduce me to his bed. By virtue of my own powers, I was able to repel his magic seductions, leaving me only with his scorn, saying my yellow eyes were the result of my being weak, ill-bred and uncouth. Still, some things once seen can never be unseen, and that's putting it politely.

I was younger then, younger by many years, and could not challenge him for his abusive intention. Yet, the memory was now forever ingrained in my mind, it seemed. Long have I imagined a satisfying redress. Triggered now by the staining of my sister's probity, I would seek it.

***

"I breathed in a fine rose-like smoke. I parted my lips to say something, but my thoughts were broken. I grew dizzy and my sight blurred. I blinked my eyes shut. When they opened, my vision had cleared. Standing before me was an eidolon visage of him. Sparkles of gold and silver light spun around his head and face. I grew entranced."

***

I trekked more than half of the miles between the pass and the Berevian Tower. That was my first night's plan. Jynx located an appropriate tree for me to hide in for the day, perhaps even to rest in the elf fashion. Elves do not sleep in the normal course of night. Instead, we rest for a short period of time in a vital function simply called 'transire'. The length of time varies, but typically for about four hours we must remain in a semiconscious state as our minds mist and dream.

I stopped at a creek to scope my surroundings. All I heard was the ruffle of leaves, tweets of birds, and the lapping of water. I felt the sunlight on my skin and took a drink. Then I climbed the tree, balancing myself on an appropriate branch.

***

"He came up to me and embraced me, kissing me full on the lips with a honeyed mouth. I was taken. I stroked his hair as he toyed and pecked. 'My doxy, I will keep you,' he said. I felt my clothing slip away. I saw lights and breathed roses."

***

In truth, I was impatient to continue. The anger I felt urged me forward. Yet I knew my body would fail me if I did not give it ample rest.

***

"Sparkles became torches, then bright lamps; multiple suns spiraled in my mind like fire." She paused.

I was still turned away, gazing out the window towards the mountains. I knew where this story was leading me.

"A quiet followed," she continued. "I settled and caught my breath. I found myself on my elbows. A shudder ran through my spine. I closed my legs and sat on the edge of the bed, turning away from him.

'I got carried away,' he said. 'I hope you don't mind.'"

***

I couldn't rest, as much as I tried. Myrra's words burned into my heart.

***

"Then he dressed me. I trembled at his touch. He left the room. I was all alone. I cried and fled, terrified he would find me, but my horse was strangely ready for me and the gate opened."

"He abandoned you," I said. "He wanted you to leave."

"But why? Why would he do that?"

"His heart is dark," I answered, "as is any rapist's."

***

'And I'm going to kill him,' I thought, bringing my mind to the present.

Two Berevian elves appeared in Jynx's eyesight. They were heading in my general direction. I magicked Jynx into a smaller bird and he flew near them, watching and listening. The Berevians stopped at the stream and calmly took a repose beside a tree.

"Well," began one of them, "time to fill the waterskins."

"And take a short one for our feet," answered the second.

"I told you to wear comfortable boots."

"Oh, they're comfortable enough. We still have many miles before us."

"Indeed, here we rest from our wench quest."

"The King doesn't like such words," replied the second. "Maybe I should report you," he added with a grin.

"Oh, you won't do that," answered the first.

Whatever brought these two to this part of the valley, it was not because of me. Though their purpose became clear.

"Hah! No. I'd lose my best friend. Just call the females 'lovers for King Dayrelie' and not wenches."

"Or cocottes or harlots or strumpets," laughed the first Berevian.

"No, don't you dare!"

"Ah, well, if the King wants to spread his seed around as they say in the plow field, then who are we to label his 'lovers'?"

"They don't say that about *him*. They'd all be in prison if they talked that way about *him*."

"Either way, he pays us." The Berevian looked westward, holding his hand at his forehead. "We should be at our base by nightfall."

"Hmmpf. Traversing the mountains is tiring. Why doesn't the King just make love with other Berevians?"

"I don't know."

"Maybe because he doesn't want any illegitimate youngster to come and claim the throne."

"Whatever," said the first Berevian, filling his waterskin. "Let's be on our way."

"Like as not, I'm coming."

The Berevians journeyed on. I remained vigilant while Jynx watched them from afar. How they would 'garner' any elves beyond the valley I didn't know, but I guessed it was with either lies or magic, or a mix of them both. Yet now I knew how my sister came into the King's clutches. I vowed to kill these two if I found them with any future victims. But not now.

The afternoon drove away the morning. There was no further activity near me, Berevian or otherwise. Thus, I was able to transire after all.

I roused near sunset. By accident or design, that worked well for me. It was late enough for me to journey quickly and not be seen. I gritted my teeth, determined to finish what I had begun.

Perhaps that was because I am an elf. We normally prefer negotiation to force, kindness to ferocity, yet we can be relentless in principle. We are slow to make enemies of others, yet once made, we never forget them. Serious injury has consequences. We will pursue justice with a vengeance. Leastways, that is what I told myself.

***

The time was well past midnight when I arrived at the King's tower. Rain was falling. That too was good. I could move more easily under the cover of rain drops.

He lived in a wooden and square castle-like structure that had one corner tower. In their foolish conceit, the Berevians did not design guard stations that overlooked the base of the tower. I slowed and crept quietly among the rocks and bushes up to the base.

The tower was tall, but I could scale it easily with my length of rope and hook. Living within the forest, I was accustomed to climbing many kinds of twine ladders.

His room was near the top. No windows were built along the sides of the tower.

I magicked Jynx into a sparrow. He flew up the height of the tower and scoped his quarters.

First, the balcony deck. Rounded newels adorned a railing roughly four feet tall. The balusters lined up evenly beneath the top railing with a spacing of about three inches – too narrow for my grappling hook. I would have to fasten my rope to the top railing, preferably beside a corner newel.

Beyond the railing, the entrance and the two accompanying side windows were wooden-framed glass from floor to ceiling. The deck door was closed. I thanked the gods that Jynx did not see a lock. I magicked Jynx into the tiniest of ants to crawl under the door. He was now free to check on the room's inhabitant. The room was unlit and he heard no breaths of an elf in transire. For whatever reason, the King was not inside.

Quickly, I threw the grappling hook up to his deck. It failed to latch and came crashing down, landing with a dull thud. I hesitated for a long moment, panicked to see if the noise had been noticed. It hadn't. Everything around me was still dark and silent.

I tossed the rope a second time. It stayed up. Jynx confirmed that the hook had grasped the top rails and was firmly in place. I tested it anyway after climbing five feet. I didn't want to suddenly fall from any height. Not that the impact would be fatal. It wouldn't, but casting the magic to slow a fall would produce a bright light and be clearly audible.

Reaching the top, I climbed spider-like over the rail. Before I tried the door, I tied the rope to the railing. To my relief, the glass door opened like any normal door – it was not magicked against entry.

I removed my head scarf to give me ample light from my eyes. Despite their yellow glow, I observed the world in its normal colors. In this dim room, I discerned a bed long and wide enough for several elves as the main feature. Over-sized, billowy pillows lay strewn about the room. Random cherry-red curtains hung along the walls beside tapestries depicting naked and embracing elves. There was no antechamber or adjoining rooms. *'He must use this solely for his pleasure,'* I thought. The sight sickened me.

It wasn't long before I heard footsteps outside the interior entrance. Alarmed, I returned the scarf to my eyes and hid behind a curtain near the deck door. My hope was to surprise him, even kill him, before he knew what hit him.

The interior entrance opened with a slam.

"Okay," his voice sounded. "Who's in here?'"

I froze in place. It was Dayrelie. My surprise was spoiled.

Dayrelie took a few cautious paces inside. "Did you honestly think I would leave my suite unwatched?" he jeered. "Simple magic is all it took to alert me that my room had been entered."

Quickly I formed a new plan. Jynx would lure him in. I metamorphosed him into a butterfly fluttering about the room in front of Dayrelie.

"What's this?" Dayrelie said, taking a few more steps. "A butterfly? A bright yellow one at that."

It was working. Jynx was leading him my way. With my blood racing and my muscles tensing, I drew out my dagger.

Jynx slowed beside my hiding spot.

A hand reached out for him – Dayrelie's hand.

I quickly pushed aside the curtain swinging my dagger down on his wrist. The blade sliced through his arm, but it vanished. I had cut through an illusion.

A painful jolt suddenly ran through my body. I grimaced and moaned in shocked disbelief.

"Foolish cur," he hissed. "That's two times you've underestimated me."

He grabbed me by the throat and hoisted me up. His strength was undeniable. Then he removed the scarf over my eyes.

"I know you," he said. "You're that insolent sorcerer that rejected me once. Why are you here?"

His hands tightened on my neck, choking my throat closed.

"No matter," he sneered. "This time I will have you."

I couldn't breathe. Jynx was powerless to help. I had one move. I grabbed onto his shirt and pulled him in. In a backwards somersault I kicked him off me and through the glass. The door shattered in a storm of slivers. He hurled through the air grasping the deck's top rail. I ran over to him to push him down. The rain had increased.

He was holding on with one hand. I cast a ray of weakness, but he laughed, blocking my spell with a magic shield.

I pried at his fingers, but he laughed again.

Suddenly, giant wings sprouted from his back and he flew out from the balcony. He shot a bolt of bright blue light at me. The lightning juddered through my whole body, teetering me to my knees.

"That's three times!" he shouted. "A charming end, wouldn't you say?"

My enervated body went limp; my magic was no match for his. I saw my death in his eyes. Yet, I still had a risky play.

I leapt from the deck and grabbed onto him. His flight faltered from the additional weight, and we struggled mid-air. I held onto the hair behind his neck and he tried to push me off and away, but I still had a free hand. I quickly raised my dagger and plunged it into his heart.

A gasp of surprise came from his face as we fell to the ground. We landed with a slam, the crack of his bones resonating through my hands and arms. He shuddered his last breath, his body twitching. In aching pain, I stiffly rose.

I didn't have time to gloat. Our brief battle was sure to have been noticed, but I had a planned distraction to stymy any chase.

I went over to my hanging rope. With a snap from my fingers, it caught fire. I had prepared it to burn rapidly, and flames climbed up it as quick as a jackrabbit. Soon, the chamber would be aflame.

Yet, I didn't stay to watch. I closed my eyes and limped away as fast as I could manage, hacking and coughing.

After about a mile, I halted and caught my breath. I magicked Jynx into an owl and directed him back to the tower. I saw it on fire. Even with the rain, Berevian elves armed with mere blankets tried in vain to put it out. Other Berevians were commiserating over their dead King. There was no immediate sign of pursuit, but one would soon begin.

I had to get away from the Berevan Valley.

***

Fortunately, my legs were intact and I was not bleeding. Drenched as I was, I was still able to hobble through the night and into the morning. The bolts he racked me with had left their mark and I would walk with a slight limp to the end of my days.

Yet, I escaped. I was able to evade even the best trackers with Jynx watching my back. And any that came too close I trapped with a spell or two.

I crossed the pass and found my hidden backpack. Now with food in my stomach, I made it home.

Our house was a modest edifice with one flight of steps. The wood that constructed it came from trees that had died during a beetle infestation hundreds of years ago. The tiny trails of the insects could still be seen inside the planks. Glass windows lined up along the four sides of the building. A nearby stream provided running water; its plumbing pipes needed to be replaced every few decades. Oil lanterns hung from the ceiling, lighting up the magically composed portraits of the family's ancestors.

Afternoon sun bathed the structure when I arrived. My parents were seated for a late lunch when I entered. They questioned me, but I lied to them as to where I had been and did my best to hide my limp. They gave me questioning looks, but dismissed me when I said I needed rest. They were loving parents, but traditional, conservative, and it did not sit well with them that their daughters had independent thoughts.

I climbed the steps and found Myrra in our shared bedroom.

"Where have you been?" she began.

"Out and away," I answered. I didn't want this conversation to begin with what I had done. Yet, she saw me limp.

"You're injured," she followed up. "How did that happen?"

I exhaled a breath before answering. Haltingly, I said, "I ventured into the Berevan Valley."

Her eyes widened with surprise. "Why did you do that?" she asked.

Again, I paused. The decision to bring my wrath to the Berevian King was mine alone. "Sister, I pray for your healing."

"What do you mean?"

"And closure," I said.

"Phyrra! Tell me straight. What are you talking about?" she said with a firm tone.

Taking another breath, I answered, "I have slain your rapist."

Her eyes shot open with astonishment, but she kept hers locked onto mine. "What did you say?"

"I think you heard me. I journeyed to his tower and killed him in battle."

"Why?" she asked, her face breaking. "Why did you do that?"

"As punishment for his crimes."

"You acted as judge and sentenced him to death?"

"Perhaps I would rephrase that, but yes. I took it upon myself to serve retribution for your sake."

She put her face in her hand. "No, tell me you didn't do that."

"I did," I said. "I will not lie to you, dearest sibling."

Her body shook as she suppressed a sob. "No. No."

I scowled, surprised by Myrra's reaction. "I didn't think you'd be sad," I said.

She faltered and her lips trembled. Her eyes went to the floor. "Phyrra," she began. "I might have needed him."

A flash of anger ran through my head. "Egad, he's no more than a rapist."

"Stop calling him that!"

I stepped back from her rebuke. "But why? It's true."

"It's too late," she said, shaking her head. "Now it's too late."

"Too late for what?" I asked.

"For a father," Myrra answered. "Because of you it's too late."

My eyes widened at the implication of what she said.

"There is a life growing inside me," she said gently.

"You mean you're pregnant?" I replied.

"Yes," she answered, bowing her head.

I sat beside her and folded my hands. "You'll have to end the pregnancy," I said looking at her.

She still held her view to the floor. "I-I don't know if I can."

"Of course you can," I said. "I'll find someone with the right magic."

"No, you don't understand. I don't know if *I* can."

I furrowed my brow. "Do you mean that you wish to carry the child to birth?" I said. "Your rapist's child? You want to mother... this child?"

She let out a muffled sob. "The baby is innocent."

I stood up and looked away. My eyes teared hearing Myrra cry, but I had to think. *'This child? Her rapist's child,'* I repeatedly thought. *'Now a fatherless child.'* I fisted my hands with a rage that threatened to overcome me. I could not at first believe what she said. Yet even as long as we have to live, we elves cherish life in all its forms. And however she rationalized it, she believed a new life had begun.

I sat down beside her. She no longer suppressed her weeping. "Father will expel me," she said.

"But I won't," I answered.

"Even with my bastard child?"

However much I hated Dayrelie, my choice to kill him put me in this spot. "Your innocent child," I answered. "I will never abandon you, Myrra. Please believe that. I will be here beside you and we shall raise this child together and they will learn love."

Myrra leaned her head on my shoulder and I hugged her through her tears.

***

In due time, Myrra gave birth to a daughter. Born on a windy day, Myrra chose the name of Xefuros, which in old elvish means 'a warm breeze'.

Like her father, Xefuros had golden hair and like her mother, her skin was the gray-brown color of an oak, but with the additional feature of a bronze sheen. She grew to be a beautiful elf with noble features and a tall bearing. And also like her father, she was a born sorcerer. Yet, her eyes manifested the same yellow-on-yellow glimmer as did mine. I took it upon myself to be her mentor as well as her aunt.

As Myrra guessed, we were expelled from our parent's house, the only abode we had ever known. Our younger brother would now inherit the property. Far away, the three of us managed to build a different kind of home. We often joked that we would be the foundation of a new realm, but it would be years before Myrra or I would trust any male elf – especially considering Xefuros.

But how that came about is another story.

XVII: THE STAR

Keen Vengeance by D. S. Levey

The water was ice cold as Moira Donnelly placed her right foot into the pond. She glanced at her reflection, noting idly the constellation Pleiades hovering directly overhead. It had been a symbol of mourning for her ancestors, and it seemed fitting that it shone so brightly over her now. Her brilliant red hair seemed also to glow as she gazed at her manifestation in the serene water.

Clothed only in the light of the full moon, she braced herself for the next steps, and pondered all that had taken place to bring her to this point...

***

She came of true Irish stock, a bloodline of rebels going back generations. Her grandfather had done his time in the cages during The Troubles in the 1970s. His grandfather fought from the General Post Office in the Easter Rising of 1916. Before that came Fenians, United Irishmen, and so on. And yet, all that lineage was at risk of disappearing forever.

Her father was gone, the result of a fishing accident off St. John's Point in her home of Donegal when Moira was just a baby. Her mother had suffered medical complications during the great pandemic of 2020, just a few short years ago. Her passing had left Moira all alone in the world. The one unique aspect of her family was the lack of cousins, uncles, and aunts that most others seemed to have. Both of her parents had been only children, and the same had been true with her grandparents and great-grandparents.

And so, while there was certainly no particular shortage of the name Donnelly on the Emerald Isle, she was all that was left of her particular line. She was only twenty-three, with plenty of time to settle down and raise a family of her own. She knew though, that in the traditional and patriarchal way of things, the odds were good that she was, at the very least, the last Donnelly of her branch.

She lamented often about the lack of a brother. It hurt her to think of her line being annexed into someone else's family tree; merely a footnote of historical curiosity. Her friend Jenny had tried multiple times to tell her that a marriage and name change wouldn't lessen her own family history, but Moira herself could never quite bring herself to believe it. She was a Donnelly. She wanted to remain a Donnelly. It was really that simple.

She knew she could marry if she wanted to. Her looks were far above average, with a pleasing overall shape, and long red tresses framing an ethereal face. She had had any number of suitors over the years; no one who had captured her attention, however.

No one, that is, until Tommy Russell.

His name alone had pulled her up short. While there was no relation whatsoever to the famous United Irishman, Thomas Russell, his parents had purposely named him so in a fit of patriotic pride. And he had spent his twenty years on Earth trying to live up to it.

Tommy Russell was a member of one of the larger socialistic societies in Ireland. He believed in the independent spirit of the island and the need for self determination over all of its thirty-two counties; but only in a republic that would treat all men and women equally. He believed firmly in the words of another United Irishman, Theobald Wolfe Tone, regarding the need to 'substitute the common name of Irishmen in place of... Protestant, Catholic, and Dissenter'. He felt equally strongly about those who treated others poorly based on religion, race, etc. and felt that those who acted so had no place on his island home.

Moira first met Tommy at a small march of commemoration for the deaths of some young men killed during The Troubles. Fifty years had passed since those terrible times, yet the memories of the martyrs created then lived on every day in the hearts of countless Irish men and women. Many vowed to continue the struggle, in one form or another, until the six counties that comprised the North of Ireland were rejoined with the twenty-six in the Irish Republic.

One of those killed in this particular incident had been a good friend of Moira's own grandfather. He had said to her more than once that had he not been on a mission himself that day he would likely have been there with them.

She had joined the march with some friends and was duly introduced to Tommy. While his name interested her from the get-go, she truly took notice when the young man was asked to speak. Moira had been to many marches in her young life and knew the routine well. Speaker ages ranged greatly of course, but it was unusual for a lad of only nineteen (as he had been at the time) to be asked to perform a major speech; and he had nailed it.

The speech lasted between ten and fifteen minutes, and the passion and eloquence had seared it into Moira's soul. She found herself captivated by his words, but took just a long enough glance around to see that everyone else seemed to feel the same. He *believed* in what he was saying; and persuaded his listeners to believe it as well.

Moira and Tommy met again at another meeting soon afterward, and hesitantly exchanged phone numbers. Tommy promised her he would call the next Thursday, and Moira was pleasantly surprised when he followed up on that promise. She knew that young men often liked to play games when it came to courting, but in Tommy she sensed only sincerity in all he said.

Within the time of a few weeks they had cemented themselves into a definite relationship, and within a few months they were nigh on inseparable. Though they enjoyed walks around many of the trails and sights of the island, they never failed to show at meetings or marches representing the continued struggle for Irish Independence.

The day before their six month anniversary had been spent at a well-attended march in county Tyrone. This one had many of the usual trappings of a border-town event. The local police were out in force to watch the proceedings. Some were in an armored van taking pictures of those who had gathered. Moira had seen this plenty of times before and had no doubt that both she and Tommy had files in a database somewhere. The thought never really bothered her. It was just part of the territory for standing up to the established order.

The commemoration went off well and everyone had gone their separate ways. Tommy was driving Moira back to Donegal and they were discussing their plans for the next day when he noticed a large van coming up behind them.

"They're really hauling ass," he noted out loud to himself.

"What's that?" Moira responded.

"There's somebody coming up behind us really fast," he replied.

The young woman turned to look from the passenger seat and gasped. "What are they thinking?" she asked aloud. "You better turn off or move over; they're headed straight for us."

Tommy looked for a place to go, but there was no shoulder along this lonely stretch of road, and no turn-offs coming up.

"Well, there's no place to go," he began, "but there's no cars coming from the other direction either. If it comes to it, I'll jump in the on-coming traffic lane to avoid them."

It was less than a minute later when Tommy judged he should move over to avoid being struck. He watched the rear-view mirror anxiously as he slid his car into the other lane. The van closed the remaining distance in no time, and at the last possible moment it moved over as well. The young couple barely had time to realize what was happening when the van struck their rear bumper at full speed. The car jolted as the back end crumpled. Tommy desperately tried to hold the wheel straight, but the little vehicle careened first to the right edge of the road, and then went into a skid towards the opposite side.

The car spun multiple times along the road before finally coming to a shuddering stop, facing the way they had come.

Miraculously, neither of them appeared to be seriously hurt; although they were both extremely shaken up.

"Are... are you ok?" Tommy asked.

"I think so," she replied. "How about you?"

"I'm good," he said. "But I'm going to kill that jerk! What the hell is wrong with that guy!?"

They both unfastened their seatbelts and hesitantly exited the wrecked vehicle. Each of them noticed new aches and pains from their muscles as they did so. The van responsible was parked about one hundred meters back along the road. Moira noted with confusion that the front bumper appeared to have been heavily modified to sustain an impact such as had just occurred.

The van started towards them at a low rate of speed while the young couple watched in trepidation. It finally stopped again with only about twenty meters between them. It was then that Moira noticed the driver was wearing a balaclava mask.

"Oh shit!" muttered Tommy. "Get your phone and call 999! I'll try and stall them! Hopefully someone will come in time..."

Moira backed up, searching for her phone. She was still shaken up and processing the collision, the masked driver, and the whole situation in general when she found her cellular. It was at that moment that the side of the van opened up.

Five men, all dressed in similar fashion and wearing balaclavas of their own, stepped out one after the other. All of them were armed in one way or another. Two of them held cricket bats; another pair had a small knife each, and the final man had a knuckleduster on his fist.

Moira finally realized the gravity of what was happening. She desperately tried to dial 999 but her phone didn't have any signal.

Tommy began speaking. "What the hell is this then?" he shouted at the oncoming men. "Real brave to have a whole load of you like this!"

The man in the lead pointed his cricket bat at Tommy. "To Hell with you, Fenian bastard! You and your little bitch have done more than enough talking! Ye fuckin' Taigs are all the same. Think you're better than us! You think we're gonna give up the North? To Hell with that!

"The six counties belong to Ireland!" Tommy responded. "England can't hold them forever! You and yours better get used to that reality! Our day will come, and you can either be part of it or piss off over to England."

"That'll never happen on our watch!" the masked man shouted back. "But people start believing it can when you run your mouth so much. It's time to shut that mouth up for good!"

The man was nearly within striking distance of Tommy now. Moira still couldn't get any reception and stood in stunned disbelief at the events unfolding before her.

What happened next occurred both quickly, and yet as slowly as a bad dream one can't wake up from. It was an eternity of Hell for Moira.

The leading man swung his bat. Tommy somehow blocked it with his forearm, and returned the strike with a punch of his own to the man's face, knocking him back. The next man rushed forward, swiping a small knife at Tommy's arm. Moira heard Tommy's hiss of pain and knew that the blade had hit its mark. It was Tommy's turn to reel backward. He clutched his right arm, his left hand quickly being covered in blood.

Moira started towards him when the man with the knuckles intervened. He grabbed her with a firm grip and yanked her away from Tommy. Then he wrapped his arms around her, pinning her arms, and held on tightly.

"Ah, ah, ah my sweet," he crooned. "This is between the men."

Tommy turned towards his girlfriend, ready to challenge the man. Moira could see the fear and anger mixed in his eyes. But before he had a chance to reach her, the first man struck again with his bat.

Moira could do nothing but watch as Tommy was struck on the back of the head. The sound of the smack was sickening. Tommy collapsed immediately, barely getting his arms out in time to break his fall. Moira screamed and broke loose from her captor only to be yanked right back by the arm. Through tears she saw Tommy trying valiantly to rise from the dust as the first man spoke again.

"Put her to sleep and let's finish this without all the noise," the man ordered.

She had just enough time to turn to her own assailant and realize the knuckles were coming at her, but no time to react. In an instant, she was knocked out.

***

Moira awoke in pain and confusion. She was lying on a hard bed in a small space. Someone was sitting to her left. There was the sensation of movement, somehow, as well. It took her a full minute to realize she must be in an ambulance.

"Tommy," she breathed. "Where's Tommy?"

She struggled to sit up, but found herself restrained somehow. She turned to the figure next to her, who she now realized to be a medic. "Please, where's Tommy? What did they do to him?"

The young woman looked at her sadly. Before she could speak, Moira knew.

"Just lie back there, dear," the woman spoke softly. "First, let's get you to the hospital. There'll be time to discuss him later. Right now, we have to worry about you."

"He's gone, isn't he?" Moira asked through brimming tears. "Those assholes killed him, didn't they?"

The medic seemed to be having an internal conflict about how much to say to her patient. "Just rest hon," she started.

"Tell me!" Moira sobbed. "Please!" she begged through her tears.

"Yeah, hon..." the young medic was barely breathing out her words. "He's gone."

***

The next day, Moira was discharged from the hospital into a political firestorm. The brazen attack on a prominent young Irish activist had made news across the island. Pundits weighed in on the history of the organization he had been a part of as well as his own personal history, short as it was.

People who had never even heard of Tommy were suddenly analyzing his speeches as well as any other detail of his life that they could dig up. Most just chalked his demise up as another meaningless death in the never ending conflict surrounding the northern six counties of the island. Some honored his memory and listed him as another martyr for "The Cause". Practically overnight a mural went up in West Belfast with his likeness and a quote from one of his orations. Conversely, there was a section of the population who actively cheered his death as the acceptable outcome for any Irish Republican. Many of the latter voiced their pleasure of the attack on message boards and social media.

There were reporters everywhere Moira went, every one of them looking to get an exclusive interview with the injured girlfriend of the recently deceased. Grieving was a difficult enough task as it was; doing so while being hounded for a scoop was torturous. She found what solace she could by spending time alone in the privacy of her small flat, but even that was not a safe space for her mental health.

She relived the ambush a thousand times in her head. Each replay brought with it not just the anguish of the loss, but an oppressive guilt telling her that it was somehow her fault. She came up with countless irrational reasons to blame herself; she should have fought harder, she should have struggled more, she should have taken self-defense when she was younger, she should have asked him to temper his speeches, she should have... she should have...

The days went by quickly leading up to the funeral. Moira wept silently as she sat next to Tommy's parents and siblings. Dressed in black, the tears streamed openly down her face. Looking around at the mourners, she had a sudden realization; it was not her fault.

It was not his parents' fault for raising him to love Ireland. It was not the fault of his brother or sister for supporting him as he found his path. And it was not her fault, even though she had been there at the horrible end.

There was nothing she could have done to change things. She knew her support and encouragement had been a positive in his life, but he would have made his speeches whether she encouraged him or not. It was just who he was. Not speaking up for justice and freedom was anathema to his nature. In the end, the same enemies would have come for him; only without her, there would be no witnesses.

Moira understood then the mistake the attackers had made. They had left her alive with nothing to cling to but hatred and vengeance.

She was determined that one way or another they would pay, and pay dearly, for what they had done.

Around her the tears of the mourners continued to flow, but within her breast the seed of a terrible resolve had been planted. A fire began to burn that she could barely contain. At that moment she wanted nothing more than to begin her quest for justice, but the same steely determination for retribution gave her the strength to get through the remainder of the day.

The funeral itself was followed by a reception of Tommy's friends and family. Thankfully some acquaintances had volunteered to act as security due to the nature of his passing, to say nothing of the media interest in the situation. This worked out for the best as they ended up thwarting more than one attempt by an unscrupulous reporter to gain inside access to the solemn event.

After the long and emotional day, Moira was nothing short of relieved to finally get home. For the first time since she could remember, she found the silence comforting. She had come to a critical epiphany today, and was determined that tomorrow her quest for revenge would begin in earnest.

***

She awoke to the feeling of a presence. There was no noise, yet something told her she was not alone. Her eyes strained, but they were unable to trace any discernible shape in the pitch dark room. She slowly picked her phone up from the nightstand, noting the time as she turned it on: 3:01 am. The witching hour had just begun.

Brushing aside the superstitious thought, Moira turned on the flashlight function of her cellular. The light shone out starkly against the prevailing gloom. Whipping the beam throughout her room, the young woman let out a gasp at a shadowy figure standing at the foot of her bed.

The stream of light from her phone shook in response to the trembling of her hands. Meanwhile, the figure stood motionless. She could see only that they appeared to be in an enveloping cloak, with their head down and shrouded by a cowl. The light from her cellular seemed to flow around the intruder rather than glance off of them. It was as though the air surrounding the being was impenetrable by brightness of any kind.

"Who... who are you?" asked Moira tremulously. "What do you want with me?"

The figure remained completely still. The moments felt like a heavy eternity to the frightened young woman.

Then, the head lifted.

Moira found herself staring at what could only be described as an old crone. Streams of thin white hair flowed from beneath the dark cowl. The gaunt cheeks framed eyes as black as obsidian. Every detail was reminiscent of a classical sorceress or wise woman.

As Moira's shaken brain tried to process all this, the woman spoke.

"Want with you?" a voice began. It was dry and brittle, but each word sounded stark and clear to Moira's anxious ears. "My dear, I want nothing from you. I come to offer you... an opportunity, shall we say?"

"An opportunity?" Moira muttered in confusion, more to herself than to the woman. She began to wonder if she was still asleep and this was some sort of dream.

"An opportunity," the woman said again, with firmness. "I know your story, young lady. I know the pain you have been through of losing your love. Of being beaten senseless while they ripped the life away from him. I know the anger you feel towards those who perpetrated this horrendous deed. But most of all I know…" The woman paused for a brief moment before finishing her sentence with a fierceness that belied her fragile seeming frame. "I know that nothing will come of it!"

This speech only added to Moira's bewilderment. But the old woman wasn't done.

"You want vengeance, young one. I could see it in your eyes at the funeral today. Yes," she drawled out as she answered the shocked look on Moira's face. "I was there today. I saw your sorrow turn to anger; and your anger to resolution! You want revenge on those that have wronged you. Rightfully so, I may add."

Moira was mystified. How could this woman have been at the funeral without anyone knowing? How could she pinpoint exactly how Moira's emotions had gone this day?

"But do you truly believe that justice will find those young men that attacked you? Even if they were to be identified by the law, they would not be held to account. And if they somehow were brought to court and sent to prison, they would become heroes in the eyes of their peers. You know this as well as I."

It took only an instant for Moira to recognize that the stranger was correct. She could name a dozen different incidents that had gone unpunished just off the top of her head. She knew of families that had fought for decades with no resolution yet to be found. Martyrs were easy to find in Ireland; lawful reckoning was not.

The old woman saw the realization come home and continued her spiel.

"I can offer you a way not only to get your vengeance, but to continue meting justice out as you see fit for a very long time."

Thoughts of retribution came rushing back to Moira. The callousness with which Tommy had been brought down screamed at her. How dare they! How dare they take this man away from her. And not just her; the whole island was less for his being gone. He had been making a difference. And because he was making a difference these cowards had destroyed him! If reprisal was being offered her in the form of this old woman, then damn it Moira would not turn down that chance!

"Come with me, my dear. Come with me and harness the power of your ancestors! For generations your people have been fighters. Now is the time to stand above them all and strike home against those who have done you wrong!"

Moira found herself both confused and inspired by this strange speech. "How, then?" she began. "How am I to 'harness' this power you speak of? I don't understand!"

"Come with me child, and you will. But know this... once you come down this path vengeance will be yours for the taking, but your old life will be left behind for good. There is no coming back from this choice. I believe though, that this is the destiny you were meant for. That is why I have come to offer it to you." She paused briefly before continuing. "I know this is a lot to take in, but you must choose now... power and vengeance, or helplessness and regret. Your sorrow will be with you always, but on my path, you can have the solace of raining retribution on those who so deserve it!"

Moira was still bewildered by this old woman in her room. Her thoughts continued to swirl. Was this a trick? A dream? A delusion brought on by grief? Or was this a genuine opportunity to pay back those who had wronged her? In the end the choice was easy. She had no living family to concern herself with and had just lost the only love she could ever imagine having in her life. She wanted one thing only now. Justice. And if she could deal it out herself, all the better.

She stared into the old hag's abyssal gaze. "I'll go," she answered.

A thin smile crept upon the woman's ancient face. "Then close your eyes and let us begin," was the response.

Moira didn't understand, but she did as she was told, and soon felt a change in the air pressure around her. A slow wind seemed to whirl around her room, and strange sounds reached her ears. She fought hard against the temptation to open her eyes and see what was going on.

Finally, the old woman bade her open her eyes, and Moira was shocked to discover that she was no longer in her room at home. She was now standing in a little glade with a full moon reflecting off the surface of a nearby pond. The stars were brighter than any she could remember seeing. She noted, too, figures similar to the old woman surrounding the glade. At least a dozen more beings were shrouded in the shadows at the edge of the clearing.

"You are moments away from harnessing the ancient power of your homeland. You have but to remove your clothing and enter the sacred pool. Immerse yourself completely and, should you survive, you will emerge triumphant. A member of our order... the Ban-Shee!"

The pronouncement struck Moira as the reality and the weight of what she was about to do descended upon her. And what did the woman mean by 'if' she survived? This was all happening so fast. Yet she was not afraid. Not anymore. She knew the woman was right about any justice she could expect from the political institutions. If she wanted reprisal she would have to do it on her own, and this was likely to be the only option for her.

She stood and walked slowly to the edge of the water, shedding her clothes as she did so. She hesitated just a moment before placing her right foot in the icy pond. Noting the Pleiades over her reflection, she thought grimly of all that had brought her here.

But now it was time to put that aside. She knew instinctively that this was an opportunity afforded to a precious few. Once she took this plunge, she would arise from the water forever changed. She may not understand yet all the implications of this moment, but she pressed forward with one purpose on her mind: the knowledge that her revenge would now become inevitable.

She continued her journey into the pool, one foot after another. Persevering through the icy cold, she waded onward. She was soon submerged up to her shoulders. Shutting her eyes tight, and drawing in one last mortal breath, Moira Donnelly pulled her head completely under the water.

The feeling was instantaneous. Pins and needles seemed to prod every inch of Moira's skin for what felt like an eternity. Her very blood felt aflame. Her body thrashed spasmodically under the water as oblivion itself tore at every fiber of her being. She resisted the impulse to try pulling herself to shore and possible safety. Instinct told her that she couldn't raise herself from the water; not yet.

And then, in an instant... it stopped.

A light pierced through Moira's closed eyelids and she felt her temperature climb considerably. Not only was she no longer icy, she found herself, in fact, warm all over.

She raised her head from the water, threw her hair back from her face, and let out a strident, bloodcurdling shriek. This was instantly taken up by all the shadowy beings she had seen before.

Moira felt exhilarated. A newfound power coursed through her. It was raw. It was primal. And it gave the sweet promise of unstoppable vengeance.

She turned and waded back to the edge of the water where the old crone who had brought her here waited patiently. The ancient woman handed Moira a towel, some dark garments, and a cloak that seemed the twin of the one the old hag herself wore.

Once she was dry and clothed, Moira finished off her new ensemble with the dark cloak. Power coursed through her as she stood in front of her benefactor.

"You have done well," the ancient woman began. "Not all who take the plunge survive, but I knew you had the strength for the trial."

The woman continued, "There are a few things you must learn before handing out the justice you yearn for. You will find that many of your new capabilities are instinctive, but be patient and heed my advice first, then you will fulfill your destiny.

"Now... let us begin."

***

Billy Ingram was laughing to himself as he left the pub. He and the boys had had a hell of a night carousing. It was one month since their expedition to off the loudmouth Fenian, and no one outside of their group had any idea it was them; no one who would say anything anyway. They had gotten away free as birds.

He'd been a little worried that they'd left the woman alive. A couple of the lads had wanted to do her in as well, but Jimmy Smythe had stopped them. After all, she wasn't the one making all the speeches. It wasn't like she could identify them anyway, and the last they'd heard she had disappeared. It had all gone off perfectly and that little bitch was probably crying her eyes out far from the North by this time. They had certainly taught her a lesson!

Walking along, Billy pulled his coat a little closer to his body. The night had suddenly gone chill, and very, very quiet.

As he neared his van in the lot, the young man quickened his staggered steps. His keys fumbled in his fingers while he unlocked the door. Trying to calm himself, he became aware of a presence behind him. He could feel the hair on the back of his neck stand on end. Turning suddenly, he saw only someone in a cloak standing at the end of the van.

Drunk and now quite a bit frightened by this strange encounter, Billy was about to try blustering his way out of whatever this situation was when the stranger raised their head. Billy immediately recognized the Fenian woman they had beat up last month and almost laughed. Almost but not quite.

There was something wrong. Her face was the same, and her red hair flowed out from the cowl framing her head. Her eyes, however, were now a pitch black; seeming to absorb any light that came near. It was the most terrifying thing that he had ever seen.

It took a moment for Billy's inebriated mind to register all this, and it was only when the recognition and fear came to his face that Moira opened her mouth... and screamed.

The shriek was piercing. Billy fell to his knees, clapping his hands to the sides of his head. He was vaguely aware of the feeling of blood running out of his ears. His entire skull throbbed. It was like no pain he had ever felt before. Then, just as suddenly, the awful shrieking stopped.

Trembling, Billy looked up to see the young woman taking slow steps towards him. She raised a hand in the moonlight with nails that were inches long. The last thing Billy Ingram ever saw was the slice of Moira Donnelly's arm as those nails whipped across his eyes. His world went instantly dark, but nothing else mattered to him at that moment except the pain. His eyes. His ears. His brain itself. They were all on fire in a level of torment he could never have imagined possible. The young man tried to scream. It was a futile gesture however, as he felt the sting of the nails across his throat next.

With that, Billy Ingram knew no more.

The lifeless body crumpled to the ground at the young woman's feet. She felt a thrill as her first victim fell. The next ones would have to wait... a little while at least. There couldn't be a risk of discovery. The neophyte understood that these new powers must be kept secret at all cost. She would have to be more circumspect with the remainder of the group; but this death would send a message.

In the end she would get them all. She had been remade into the stuff of legend; her rebirth giving her all she needed to achieve her retribution. And after that... she didn't know. The one thing she was certain of was that this... was only the beginning.

XVIII: THE MOON

The Moonlight Bathing by Imelda Taylor

Year after year, Tia's mother Pilar wished to bathe in the moonlight. The night finally arrived. Pilar basked under the full moon – but not how she would have wanted to spend it. Not alone, not lying in the dark with her husband's ashes.

Mesmerised by the beauty of the full moon, her vision blurred and tears trickled down her temple. A gentle breeze dried her eyes quickly. "I feel your spirit, Pedro. Even in the afterlife, you wipe away my tears," Pilar whispered. "Is there any more to life when you are not by my side?"

Pilar rolled on her side and traced the epitaph on Pedro's urn: *Father, husband, dreamer*, and the memories came flooding in.

***

After many a full moon came and went, Pilar walked the paths she had once travelled with her beloved, and ate the food they loved to share. Now, the dishes were dull and flavourless. Pilar continued to smile and laugh, but her pillow knew her sorrows.

"Shall I come with you on your next holiday, Mum?" Tia asked as she snapped Pilar out of her thoughts, growing more and more unsettled each time Pilar went away. Tia had flashbacks of a recurring nightmare about her mum on an oarless boat drifting in still dark water before the fog finally engulfed her into nothingness.

Of all four siblings, only Tia knew – felt – her mum's broken heart. After a life of reclusion, they were glad their mother was back doing the thing she loved: travelling. It was a welcome sight that she was enjoying life once again.

Tia tried to speak to her siblings about her concerns, but they all said their mother was happy. *She's fine, give her space, leave her alone*, they would say. None understood why Tia was constantly anxious and unsettled about their mother going away on her own. Tia was haunted by an unexplainable feeling that her mother needed to be rescued, to be protected from something she couldn't identify.

"Where are you off to next?" she carried on badgering.

"Tia, you don't have to. You won't be interested in the things I do when I travel. It's for old people. Why don't you go with your sister or your friends? Or go out on a date again? It's been months since your divorce. You deserve to have a good time and stop worrying about your ageing mother."

"Why do you always say you're ageing? I just want to spend time with you, Mum. Things always happen and I want – I need to spend time with you. Please?"

"Come on, Tia, you're a grown woman."

"Life is short, Mum..."

Pilar paused as Tia's statement hit her. She took a deep breath and held back tears.

"Please, Mum?"

"Alright, Tia! Geesh you're forty, not four."

"Maybe we can go on my forty-first birthday if I can book it off?"

"Alright..." defeated, Pilar agreed half-heartedly.

***

Sitting next to her mother on the plane heading to their holiday destination, Tia couldn't help but feel like a child again. It was the first time Tia had sat in the middle row. She always liked sitting by the window, but this time, Tia didn't mind. She was just glad to be with her mum.

"Now, Tia, just remember I need to have some alone time, okay?" Pilar reminded her after the pilot announced a sunny clear sky, ready for landing. Perfect holiday weather.

"Sure, Mum," Tia agreed. She understood it was important for her mother to spend time how she wanted. However, she couldn't help but imagine having adventures together. "But you are spending my birthday with me, right?" Having sensed the uncertainty in Tia's voice, Pilar reassured her they would be together on the day.

"Mum, when did you realise you liked travelling alone? When we were little, you said it was sad to travel alone. Those places and experiences should be shared."

"Yes, but in life, one should try and leave their comfort zone."

"Fair enough. But, I can come with you any time now, you know, when I can of course?"

"No, you need to rebuild your life, darling. Start over again."

"But I have started, Mum." Tia's frustration was rising. However, an unexplainable sense came over her, a feeling, an energy perhaps, that didn't belong to her. "Mum, are you happy? You never really talk about your adventures. You used to take lots of pictures and there was a sparkle in your eyes when you told people about your travels, even the annoying things that my siblings and I used to do."

Tia noticed Pilar's expression hardened. She waited for her mother to answer patiently, but she understood. She was hoping she did anyway. Tia rubbed her mother's back and rested her head on her shoulder knowing she wouldn't get an answer.

***

Pilar led Tia to a restaurant where she had once spent time with Pedro. She chose the table in a corner under a stained glass window. Tia couldn't blame her mum for choosing the restaurant that was once a church. Its gothic carvings and wall painting remained with a few modern twists, including a bar with an impressive array of drinks. In the middle was a large round frosted glass window. Iron chandeliers hung from the ceiling with flickering lights that looked like candles. The whole place was anachronistic, yet tasteful.

"Wow, this place looks great, Mum," Tia tried to break the silence. Pilar gave her a little nod while she carried on scrolling through her phone. "What do you want to drink?"

"Don't worry about me; it's your birthday. I'll get myself something in a minute." Pilar replied but didn't look at Tia and carried on tapping on her phone. Tia held her tongue, not wanting to give Pilar a reason to regret taking her.

"It's fine; I'm getting something anyway. Let me look after you sometimes." Tia longed to spoil her mum but Pilar didn't give her any opportunity. She would tell her and her other siblings not to spend money on her for presents or that she was capable of doing things herself and didn't need looking after. Pilar always insisted on paying for her meal every time she went out with her children, oblivious to the fact that it was making Tia feel disappointed and rejected.

"What are you looking at, Mum?"

"Just some old pictures."

"Can I see?" Tia asked. She smiled when she saw it was a picture of her parents at the very same spot they were sitting. Both of them looked happy.

After their lunch, the mother and daughter had a look around. As they walked along the plaza, a colourful canopy caught Tia's eyes. It had a mystic feel to it, a mash-up of Arabian, Moroccan and Bohemian themes. The smell of incense wafted in the air as if inviting them.

"Have you had your fortune told, Mum?" Tia asked as she noticed several fortune-tellers offering their services.

"Oh no, those things scare me."

One in particular stood out, and Tia was drawn to the woman running the stall as if she was under a spell.

"Have your fortunes told, ladies?" the woman asked as she caught Tia looking. Her blue eyeshadow sparkled in the sunlight, her magenta lipstick shimmered like a pearl, and her wavy ginger hair framed her flawlessly sculpted cheekbones. There was something about her green eyes that flirted with them. Everything was a stereotypical fortune teller: the headwrap, the large hoop earrings... but those eyes said there was something unique to her.

Before Pilar said "No thank you," The woman spoke. "I know what you're thinking... because I'm a psychic, right?" She laughed at her own joke, and Tia and Pilar couldn't help but join her. "Many people come to me and have their fortune told on their birthday, you know?"

Tia's jaw dropped and she wondered if the woman knew it was her birthday.

"I know, I'm good," the Mystic said.

Tia was tempted, but having seen how much the woman charged, she kindly declined, explaining they had a budget.

"OK, because it's your birthday, you can choose a card and just Google what it means. My treat, but a tip will be much appreciated." She spread out a deck of tarot cards facing down on a purple velvet table.

Tia pulled a card from the deck that the woman fanned out and turned it. The Moon. As she handed it back, the woman nodded and kept silent.

"If you need answers, give me a call." With a wink, the woman gave them her card: Madame Elisa, The Mystic Priestess.

Pilar gave the woman a small amount of change for entertaining them. Then off they went sightseeing.

The sun was setting, but there was one last activity for Pilar and Tia.

"Why did you choose this place, Mum?"

"It's a good place for moonlight bathing."

"What is that?"

"The name says it all. Like sunbathing but with the moonlight."

"Nice! What is it meant to do?"

"Nothing. You just stare at the moon and... that's just about it, I think. Your dad says it's magical, though. We often visited this place but never had the chance to moon bathe... nor in other places he said we would." Pilar said under her breath.

"Wow, I've never heard of it."

"Your dad probably made it up. You know what he's like and his stories..."

"I love his stories, though. They were magical to me when I was a little girl. Like when he battled a humanoid monster with a horse's head to get a pearl that dropped from a banana bloom on a full moon." Tia smiled as she visualised the moment in her head.

"Yes, the pearl that gave him superpowers," Pilar added.

"Did he have superpowers?" Tia asked jovially.

"Not sure about that. There had been something about the moon that fascinated your father. He was always drawn to it, always curious, as if they were connected. From the moment we met many moons ago, he talked about moonlight bathing and how it recharged his 'powers', the power that he gained when he took the pearl. He promised he would take me with him one day. Until life took over. Then, the day came when Pedro had to join the moon in heaven."

"Can I go moon bathing with you, Mum?" Tia's suggestion made Pilar freeze. A flashback of her time with Pedro once again overcame her. But this time, Tia's voice broke the shell Pilar only shed alone before sleep.

***

Mats on the ground, mother and daughter watched the moon align at their perfect spot. From the moment Tia spotted its ascent late in the afternoon, something brewed inside her. She kept clutching the pendant resting on her chest. In it were some of her father's ashes. All of her siblings and her mother owned a piece of jewellery with their father's ashes. It was meant to keep them together, yet their lives were divided. Only Tia had the desire to keep the family's relationship alive.

As they lay in silence under the full moon, their gaze was fixed on its mystic beauty. Tia noticed her mother's eyes were closed, so she dared not disturb her. Clutching the pendant, she thought of her father. This was how he would have wanted it – quiet and peaceful. She reached for her mother's hand and to her surprise, her mother held her hand back.

The pendant felt warm in her hand, but the breeze was cool. Her hair tickled her ear at a puff of wind, as if someone blew on it, teasing her.

Tia looked up. Towering above her was a humanoid horse looking down with fiery eyes, and a thick coarse mane resting on its shoulders. Its muscular chest heaved as it breathed. At the end of its tensed rangy arms were its clenched fists. It stood on dark heavy hooves that made a crunching sound on the ground.

She rolled and scrambled, and there lying next to her was her own body, as well as her mother's.

An overwhelming thought gushed through Tia's guts: the monster might have killed both of them.

"You are not Pedro," the creature spoke in a deep gruff voice that rippled.

"How did you know my father?" Tia asked.

"Your father? I'm his servant."

The moment became more and more bewildering. Was she dead or was she having a nightmare?

"I only serve one master and to be my master, one must prove worthy." As soon as the creature spoke those words, he charged at Tia. Her movement was quick, but it distanced her from the bodies on the ground. Sensing the creature would charge again, she moved quickly.

Tia wanted to run away, but was afraid to leave her body. She thought if she tried to go back, she would wake up or return to life. But the creature's next move was cunning. It leapt near where her body was, ready to snatch it. To Tia's surprise, the creature deflected as if it hit something solid. Upon realising, Tia dashed to the bodies knowing she would be safe there from the creature's blow.

She dived into her body while the creature was down. However, she couldn't go back in. The creature was up and tried to grab her, but a force field stopped the beast from coming closer. It was furious; she could see the vein on its neck popping, and the mighty blows with its arms were strong but useless. Tia wanted to get back to her body but couldn't. She screamed, she wriggled, and she even prayed and called on God.

There was shaking and rumbling. A faint voice familiar to Tia slowly distracted her from the horror. The voice got louder. Tia opened her eyes, gasping for air, and saw her mother. "You were having a nightmare," Pilar said.

Disoriented and in a cold sweat, Tia tried to process what had just happened. It was only a nightmare, her mother said, and that was what she wanted to believe.

The answer to her question was within reach. As she shoved her hand in her pocket, she felt the lady's card from the plaza. Maybe she would know? Maybe it was time to make a phone call. Maybe it was meant to be...

The next day, Tia told her mum she was going to explore on her own.

Pilar was pleased to hear Tia was willing to spend time on her own while she did the same. Yet, there was something about that morning that didn't feel right in the pit of her stomach. As Tia sipped her coffee, it reminded Pilar of the time Tia had her first coffee when she was fourteen, and the way she made a face when she had taken it black. Then when Pilar added milk and sugar to it, Tia was hooked. Pilar clutched her pendant, wishing she was holding Pedro's hand instead.

"See you later, Mum! Love you," Tia said as she kissed her mum on the cheek. She flung her backpack over her shoulders and waved at Pilar when she was halfway through the door. At that time, Pilar didn't see a grown woman. She saw her little girl going to school for the first time, a little girl free from suffering caused by others, a little girl who only felt gentle touches from loved ones, whose pain was from grazed knees and not unkind hands. It was the time when a broken heart was caused by the loss of a pet and not their unborn child. There were many occasions when she told Tia to be strong, but could not remember the time she told her daughter that she was strong and that she was proud of her.

After many years, Pilar wished she had taken Tia to school that day. She should have said 'I love you' back. When Tia finally left, tears fell uncontrollably down Pilar's cheeks.

Tia arrived at the address Madame Elisa gave her, although she wasn't sure if she was at the right place. She stood in front of a heavy black gate. Behind it was a well-kept modern-looking house with a balcony. Its door was made of dark wood with carvings of a phoenix. The garden reminded Tia of something she had seen in magazines: lush green grass and exotic-looking plants outside the grand house. No way Madame Elisa lived there, thought Tia. It could be that she worked there. Embarrassed by her thoughts, Tia caught herself stereotyping Madame Elisa and quickly shook them away.

The heavy gate clanked as it slowly opened automatically. After being let through, Tia approached the front door and admired it up close. Not a minute had passed when the door opened, but there was nobody behind it.

"Come in," echoed a familiar voice.

Tia made her way inside a bright hall. Abstract paintings adorned neutral walls, and the cornflower rug over the marbled floor felt soft under Tia's footsteps. She thought she should have taken her shoes off, but it was too late.

She found Madame Elisa lounging on a Chesterfield sofa, tapping on her phone.

"Have a seat." Madame Elisa gestured at a nearby chair.

"Lovely place you have here," Tia said.

"Not bad for a street fortune teller, ey?" Madame Elisa remarked. Tia shook her head. "It's not all from fortune telling, if you're wondering, which I know you are."

Tia blushed at Madame Elisa's remark. "So, I guess you already know why I'm here?" she asked.

Madame Elisa nodded with a sideward grin. Tia didn't know how to go forward.

"The creature wasn't a dream," Madame Elisa revealed. "Let's talk about it over tea and cards." She got up and left even before Tia could answer. Tia felt slightly embarrassed but she still couldn't believe how accurate Madame Elisa was with her thoughts. Was she right about the creature too?

Madame Elisa came back carrying a tray with an elegant tea set. The smell of tea was fresh and glorious. Steam rose as Madame Elisa poured. Although she was not so keen on tea, Tia found the experience pleasant. She lifted the cup near her nose, inhaling the floral scent.

"The card," Madame Elisa said. "The one you chose the first time we met, you remember?"

"Yes."

"It's all about fears, worries – deception..."

"That doesn't sound good..."

"We'll see. People's actions change the outcome of their fortune sometimes, but some things were meant to be. Take a card."

Tia did as instructed and turned it over. The Roman numeral at the bottom, the moon between two towers, the two dogs and a pool with a lobster were all familiar. The moon card again, but this time reversed!

"Is that good or bad?"

"It depends... it means things will be revealed. There was a reason why you came to me, why we met."

"What has this got to do with the creature?"

"Everything. Come to my office and I will tell you."

Madame Elisa led Tia down a short flight of stairs into a dimly lit basement. A round table sat in the middle with a black velvet tablecloth. Behind was a heavy purple curtain which Madame Elisa pulled back to reveal the door to her office. Once inside, Tia was drawn to the collection of alcoholic beverages in sophisticated bottles displayed on a shelf.

"Drink?" Madame Elisa offered. "What would you like?"

Tia was surprised that Madame Elisa had to ask. For sure she would have known.

"Would you like to try some mead?" Madame Elisa suggested.

Tia had only heard of mead from documentaries. Before she could accept, she was handed a crystal goblet filled with an amber liquid.

She gazed at it and said, "My father used to tell us a story that he fought a creature once – it sounded very similar to this one. It said to me

I should prove myself worthy. Then it attacked me. You said it wasn't a dream. I don't understand. This is freaking me out. Is this going to kill me?"

"Not while your father is protecting you."

"What?"

"You carry a piece of your father, and you are his flesh. Only your father can see the creature. He is in you. But, you don't possess the golden strand."

"What is that?"

"A Tikbalang has one strand of golden hair. To survive a challenge from a Tikbalang, one must conquer it and to conquer it, one must pluck its single golden strand. Your father was the worthy one."

Tia was filled with pride but still confused.

"Will this creature come back?"

"Yes, now that you have soaked the moonlight."

"What should I do? Fight it?"

"It only has one golden strand. And your father had it. If you show him the strand, it will be your forever servant."

"If I can't, I'm as good as dead?"

"No, weren't you listening? Your father is protecting you, his ashes are protecting you. And yes, you're as good as dead without the ashes. Come with me. I'll show you something." Madame Elisa led Tia to her garden. The moon was still full and looked as beautiful as it had the night before. Madame Elisa instructed Tia to wait while she fetched something. Tia sat on a luxurious garden chair with a velvety cushion, yet it did not help her feel comfortable.

Madame Elisa came back with a locket. "Open it," she said.

Tia did as she was told and was astonished to see a picture of a couple. One was her dad, but the other one wasn't her mother.

"They're my parents," Madame Elisa revealed. "Your father wasn't as perfect as you thought. And, no, your mother doesn't know." Madame Elisa answered Tia's questions in her head before she could ask. "Nice to meet you, sis," she added.

Tia's head spun.

"Here's another drink; you need it." Madame Elisa handed Tia another glass of a spirit that Tia could not identify, but Madame Elisa was right. She needed it. The bittersweet liquid touched her lips.

Soon, the potion served its purpose.

Madame Elisa looked up at the sky. "We don't really have much time, so I'll make it quick. You are here because I needed our father's ashes. You see, I have the golden hair. It was a gift to my mother. Tonight might be the only chance I have to conquer the Tikbalang." As Madame Elisa said these words, Tia's vision started to blur, her head spun and her mouth dried up. Her last vision was of Madame Elisa's silhouette on a hazy white light.

Madame Elisa took the ashes from Tia's lifeless body, her mouth agape and her eyes half open. Madame Elisa placed the chain around her neck with the locket containing their father's ashes sandwiched between her chest and palm.

She waited.

An illuminated smoke swirled in front of her like a mini tornado, growing, growling.

As the smoke of energy disappeared, the Tikbalang rose and bowed down before Madame Elisa.

XIX: THE SUN

Just Something About My Liane by A. R. K. Horton

I don't remember when I met Liane, but I'm sure I've always known her. Right? For some reason, the memories I have of her feel like dreams, but there are so many of them they must be real.

She leans against my truck with a piece of straw between her perfect, smirking lips. Her eyes shine at me like lucky pennies. I want to believe anything she has to say.

Pulling the straw from her mouth and letting it drop, Liane greets me. "Hi Charlie."

"Hi Liane."

I tip my hat. It's the gentlemanly thing to do. She giggles, because she loves it when I'm the quintessential cowboy.

"It was some kinda harvest, huh?"

I get the feeling that she's fishing for some kind of compliment instead of making a statement. It was a lucky year, that's all. Yeah, we worked hard, but some years we bust our asses only to fall to some fungus or storm.

Liane slides her hand into mine. It's always so warm when she touches me, like that first bite of a buttery, syrup-drenched griddle cake. Everything else about her lights me up inside too – braided flaxen pigtails, her honey eyes, her golden-brown tan. All she needs is a bottle of some brand name beer to be the All American Girl.

And for some reason, she's crazy about me.

"Wanna beer?" she asks and I wonder if she heard my thoughts.

Like Jason Voorhees in Friday the Thirteenth, she pulls out a surprise from some unknowable space behind her back. However, instead of a chainsaw, she's holding a bottle of my favorite brew. I don't think too hard about how that's possible, because she pops off the cap with an effortless flick of her thumb. I happily take it to discover it's ice-cold. The first sip is perfection.

We arrive at the Fourth of July picnic to find the festivities already swinging. Smoke plumes from the grills, tempting every nose in Texas. A cover band is playing all the best hits, songs I belt out when no one's around, that bring up my best memories. Everyone's dancing, smiling, and laughing.

"I thought this thing just started. Don't parties take a while to really kick off?"

Liane shrugs. "As soon as people got here, they were ready to party."

The closer we get, the more I feel it, the reason why someone could jump right into the swing of things the moment they set foot here. It feels like Liane when she's stolen my hat while straddling my lap.

Before I know it, Liane is pulling me to join the other dancers. And I just go. Me. The man who usually sits quietly in the corner, hoping he looks mysterious.

The other dancers have lost all their inhibitions. They've all taken that 'dance like nobody's watching' advice to heart. Liane and I bust out laughing at Old Lady Bertha. She almost got to break dancing right on the dusty ground.

Everyone's so free that I lose all embarrassment of letting my body enjoy music the way it wants to. I flow and twirl, like I've always secretly longed to. It feels so *good*.

I only stop when Liane whispers in my ear, "Let's get something to eat."

I don't want to leave, but she tugs at me. I'm pulled away from the dance floor like a suction cup. I can almost hear the pop.

Liane is right, though. My stomach's growling something awful. Feels like I haven't eaten in days. And it's hot, so hot. I think I already have a sunburn. I tear into the short ribs with wolf-like ferocity and drain my beer right down my parched throat.

"God, Liane," I say, grabbing a hot dog from the buffet table. "I must have been dancing for longer than I thought. I've never felt so hungry and tired."

"Tired?!" Liane's eyes flash wide open. "Don't you go sleeping on me, Charlie! There's still fun to be had!" She shoves a soda at me. "You need less beer and more caffeine."

Suddenly a bottle of pop sounds like Heaven. I laugh as I toss my hot dog aside and chug the soda down. With one last sip and one loud burp, I feel more alive than I've ever felt before.

"Let's go dancing again, Liane. I feel like I could spin you around for years and years."

Liane laughs a little too brilliantly. "No, baby, I want to do much more than dance with you."

I hoot right then. I know what that means, and I'm not surprised when she leads me to the barn. It's been cleaned well for the day's events. Instead of smelling like manure, it smells like gardenias on a hot summer day.

But gardenias don't grow so well here. So why—?

Liane pushes me onto a hay stack and takes my hat. I don't mind. She looks better wearing it anyway. She doesn't hesitate to unzip my jeans and my body's already ready for what she has planned.

When she slides onto me, I almost burst right then. But I don't. I don't know why, but there's always been something magic about her that keeps me going for hours. This time's no different. She seems to be enjoying it even more than usual.

When Liane screams, I don't even care if anyone hears her or if we're caught. I'm just happy I can satisfy her. I swear it seems like she's lit up like a glowbug, but that must be my dopamine-addled brain seeing things.

When I finally climax, she trembles so hard the hay bale beneath me shakes with her. There's a flutter, just a wink of gossamer wings, behind her back. Am I imagining that?

I reach out to touch whatever I must have seen, but Liane bats my hand away.

"What are you doing?" Liane's eyes are sharp; all her features are. I've never seen her anything but sweet and charming. She almost doesn't look like the same girl at all.

"I thought I saw…" I shake my head. "Too much beer."

Liane's face brightens again and she winks. "Not that it slowed you down any."

She gets off my lap and straightens her skirt, while I zip up my jeans. "Want more to eat?"

I almost say 'no.' After all, when I left the buffet table, I'd finished a heap of short ribs, burgers, and hot dogs. But I realize I'm famished. It really feels like I haven't eaten in days again.

"Yeah, let's do that."

I almost can't see the buffet table because everyone's crowded around it like ants on roadkill. I don't let that stop me, though. I get in line and grab a paper plate. I realize too late that it's the last one, and I feel guilty.

"Here, Liane," I say, passing her the plate. "You should have it."

Liane pushes it back. "I'm not gonna eat. Gotta watch my figure." She puts her hands on her waist and swivels her hips to show off the rockin' bod she is maintaining.

I finally get to the food and have to bat a swarm of flies away. "Jesus, where did these come from?"

The flies are forgotten the moment I notice Bill, right next to me at the buffet line, shoveling pulled pork into his mouth.

"Bill, at least take the food to your table before you—"

Liane tosses corn on the cob, coleslaw, and what feels like a pound of brisket onto my feeble little paper plate. I struggle to keep it from toppling over.

"Let's go get a table!" She beams at me, a little too brightly, and we make our way over. She watches me intently.

I take a bite of the coleslaw first, and spit it out immediately. "What the Hell did Tina put in that?" I wiped the residue off my lips. "Her slaw is usually perfect."

Liane taps the edge of my plate. "I'm sure that was just your bitter beer. Take another bite."

But I haven't had any beer since she'd told me to switch to soda. And the slaw didn't taste bitter. It tasted off, like rot.

I take another bite, though. Liane told me to and I always listen to her. This forkful is perfection. "Oh my God, this is the best she's ever made!"

"See?" Liane smiles at me. "I told you. Now keep eating so I can screw your brains out again."

Remembering my gnawing hunger, I inhale my meal until I could rupture. I lay back in my seat in a near food coma.

"Oh no, you're getting sleepy again. Let me get you some more pop."

Liane jumps from her seat and races back to the buffet without me. I watch her bouncing bottom, barely covered by her skirt the whole way. Gotta love a girl who doesn't believe in underwear.

I see more than her now, though. I see the other people at the buffet table, and in my haze, I see them differently. They're so sunburnt their skin is blistering. Their eyes are red and they're slathered with sauce all around their mouths. They never stop eating, even to take a sip. It's like they're vultures tearing apart roadkill.

Disgusted, I turn away to look at the band. They're playing still, but their motions are robotic now, as if someone's forcing them to move. The singer's grown so hoarse that he's barely more than a whisper now.

The dancers? They're spinning around and around like crazy. Their shoes are worn, at least those that are still on their feet. Their smiles splinter across their red faces. Their manic eyes match their shrill, screaming laughs.

"What the hell is happening?"

"What's that?" Liane asks as she presses a bottle of soda into my hand. It's hot. The plastic must have been baking in the sun all day. But we've only been here an hour, two hours tops.

"Does everyone seem kinda strange to you?"

"Strange?" She shakes her head at me, worry in her eyes. "You've been drinking too much beer again."

"I stopped drinking beer before we even went to the barn."

At the mention of the barn, her smile curves wickedly. "Wanna go again?"

I suddenly do very much, but my stomach turns over and all at once I hurl onto the table. Liane doesn't even blink. She just grabs some napkins with a smile and says, "Here you go, Charlie."

"Why do I feel so god awful?"

I look down at my plate and push away from the table as fast as I can. Maggots. My plate is crawling with maggots.

"Oh no..." Liane looks crestfallen, genuinely so. She's not pouting or upset with me. She's heartbroken. "You're not supposed to see this. You're supposed to go easy."

"Go easy? Go where?"

Liane doesn't answer, but I see her wings again. They're drooping now, but still shimmering. Her eyes are no longer amber, but void black all the way up to her lash line. She's shining as bright as the sun, which burns so hot I think I might die.

I take a look around her and see that the grass has turned brown. There are dead leaves drifting by on a blessedly cool breeze.

Bill collapses at the buffet table. No one stirs; they just keep eating as though they hadn't had anything in days. It might have actually been days, even months, because it's autumn now, not summer.

The question in my mind claws into me, not content with Liane's silence.

"Go where, Liane?"

That's when I see one of her hands caressing the curve of her round belly. She reaches over the table to take my hand, my bony, sallow hand.

"I looked at you all and I liked you the best," she says. "Everyone seemed really nice. So I wanted to make sure the whole county died happy. Having the best. Day. Ever."

I realize I've never met Liane before, not before I came to this party. I had remembered a girl I never knew.

"Who are you?"

"I liked you the best though, so..." Liane turns her attention down to her swollen abdomen. "I wanted this one to be yours." She casts her crooked smile at me, seeming more sinister now than enticing. "I figure it was an even trade for this year's harvest."

I'm so hungry, so hungry, but the pain of losing this beautiful sunny day feels even worse.

"Go easy, Liane?"

She nods.

"Can you make me believe it again?"

It's such a beautiful day! The band is playing all the songs from my favorite memories. Everyone's laughing and singing. This brisket tastes better than anything I've ever had before.

"Want another beer?" Liane asks.

"Boy, do I!" I hastily grab the bottle as my gorgeous girl giggles at me. "You feel that sun, Liane? God, I've never had such a wonderful day. I could die happy like this."

Liane leans over the table and kisses me the way she always does, like honey and whiskey and everything beautiful. "I know, Babe. I know."

XX: JUDGEMENT

A Mother's Judgment by Gregory Coley

Moonlight illuminated the inside of the carriage, making it feel like a mausoleum. Lips traced the woman's jawline down to the wounds on her neck, savoring the final slow beats of her heart. The sightless eyes of her new husband watched, his head slumped back into the blood-soaked collar of his tuxedo.

Leon pulled the handkerchief from the dead groom's pocket and wiped the blood from his mouth. "Driver, stop here!"

Without a word, the carriage rolled to a stop on the dusty road. The vampire stepped out into the cold air with a jingle of spurs, leaving the gruesome scene inside. As he closed the door, the scent of fear-piss accosted his senses from the direction of the driver.

"Leave," Leon said, tossing a small bag of gold in the driver's direction.

The satchel never reached the driver. With a flick of the reins, the horses tore off, working themselves into a lather, dragging the terrified human with them. The wagon wheel wrenched the bag open.

Coins spilled across the earth. With a chuckle, Leon shrugged. He pulled his wolf's pelt cloak tighter around himself, and he set off into town.

It being so early in the evening, the small thoroughfare couldn't have hosted more than a couple dozen people. He stalked the storefronts. Some glowed softly by candlelight, while others were boarded up, long abandoned. Sickness was a recent visitor to these parts. Most of the area was dead, and the rest was dying or eagerly awaiting it.

The stench of death hung heavy as a shroud. He wouldn't find any food worth partaking in here. Still, he could grab a drink. Walking up the wooden steps to his left, he stood before a pair of swinging saloon doors.

He stepped through, his spurs rattling on the dusty wooden planks. The forlorn music that whispered of lost opportunities stopped as the musician in the corner looked over his shoulder at the newcomer. His sunken eyes blinked slowly before turning back and beginning to play again.

The doors swung closed behind Leon as he removed the wolf-skin cloak. Underneath he wore a three-piece suit, and a duster that had seen better decades. He brushed his long blond hair behind his ears, and he scanned the room for exits in case any danger arose. Just the main entrance and another behind the bar. Half a dozen people dotted the tables, and four were playing poker.

Strolling to the bar, he removed his Stetson and placed it on a stool before sitting on the one next to it.

The bartender smiled at him, his gaunt face looking like death warmed over. "What can I get ya, son?"

"The most expensive thing ya got," said Leon sliding a gold coin across the bar to the bartender.

"Very well, very well."

The bartender pulled an amber liquid off the shelf that looked like all the half full bottles around it, and filled a glass halfway before sliding it over.

Leon nodded. "Obliged. So, where am I anyway?"

The bartender stared into the distance, the milky discoloration of his pupils unregistering as if he were listening to a far-off noise. Unmoving, and unresponsive. Leon waved his hand in his field of vision. The bartender jumped as if startled.

"What brings you here?" he said as if he had no memory of the last few moments.

Leon furrowed his brows. How peculiar. Leaning on the bar and glancing at his drink, he sighed. "Work."

"Strange accent there. Deep. Old. Not from around here?"

Leon nodded. "Once upon a time, yeah," he chuckled.

"Bit far from home all alone."

Leon swirled the liquid in his glass, seemingly lost in thought. "Let's just say I overstayed my welco—"

"Yes, Mother," mumbled the bartender, staring blankly into the distance.

His milky eyes said more than his words. They seemed pleading as he focused on something Leon couldn't see.

Leon felt the patrons of the bar staring at him. "You know what... thanks, but I believe I'll move on to—"

"Yes, Mother," said everyone in unison, their heads turning as one to face Leon.

The bartender dropped the glass he was cleaning. It rolled across the wooden planks underfoot. Not taking his eyes off Leon, he moved rigidly, like a poorly built marionette. He lunged.

Leon leapt backward, knocking his stool over in the process. He turned to leave, but found himself face to face with the card players reaching for him.

"Alright then. Violence it is," muttered Leon, driving his forehead into the nose of the nearest one.

The nose caved into the face like wet newspaper. Stumbling briefly, the patron reached for Leon as if nothing had happened. Leon cursed under his breath, hitting him in the chest with a front kick. The ribs snapped, sending the man backward over the table of cards. Brightly colored rectangles painted with shapes and numbers flew into the air before fluttering to the ground like raven's feathers. Then to Leon's annoyance, the patron returned to his feet.

The music stopped as the pianist climbed to his feet. "Yes, Mother."

Leon drove his shoulder into another patron, sending him stumbling back through the window and onto the walkway in a rain of glass shards.

Leon pushed through the others and careened through the swinging doors. To his right, the fallen patron climbed to his feet, glass shards embedded in his face.

The patron turned and walked in the other direction. "Coming, Mother."

Leon sighed, relieved. A wave of bodies lurched through the door behind him. Weaving to avoid their grasping hands, he stumbled out into the thoroughfare of ice and mud. More residents exited the buildings, heading towards him. They all wore the same mask of confused agony.

Leon's pulse would have quickened if he had one. He may have been a powerful creature of the night, but he could still fall victim to the numbers game. He slammed his elbow into the jaw of another as he scrambled away so they couldn't surround him. With his back against the outside wall of the general store, he began to throw punches. Left. Right. Elbow. Kick. It was futile.

He lunged forward and bit into the neck of the nearest resident of the town. Black, coagulated blood flowed into his mouth. Dead, useless blood. Pushing away from his intended victim, he spat the viscous fluid on the moon-drenched ground.

His eyes widened in realization. The gaunt faces. The sunken eyes. They were dead. All of them. The growing horde surrounded him, trapping him against the wall. They grabbed at him, ripping his long leather duster off his shoulders.

Leon took a chance and turned his back on them. He began to climb the wooden planks of the general store. He had nearly reached the top when his escape was thwarted by several hands grabbing hold of his spurs, wrenching him down. He lost his grip and fell back. The waiting embrace of the dead residents welcomed him hungrily.

To his surprise, they did not attack him, or harm him in any way. He warily gave up the fight. They lifted him onto their shoulders like he was a coffin in a funeral procession. He expected to hear the ghostly lamentation of a funeral dirge floating through the still, chilly night air. Instead, the night was filled with the excited exclamations of "Mother" as they carried him through the center of town.

The procession moved through the main drag and up the faded white wooden steps of a church. The double-doors stood wide open, welcoming him like the stretching maw of some imposing beast.

If he hadn't seen the outside, he would never have known this was a church. All trappings of religion were gone. The walls were blank like a canvas awaiting paint. The stained glass high above the dais was shattered, only a few shards still clinging to the edges. Where past Padres preached the gospel stood a metal platform. At the sight of it, he began to fight to free himself again.

No matter how hard he fought, the many arms kept him restricted. The masses surrounded the platform, lowering him into place. He struggled into a sitting position and tried to escape the table, to no avail. Dozens of hands reached for him, forcing him back down. They wrapped him in thick leather straps that held him tightly in place.

Once he was secured, they released him and moved as a single-minded hive back down the aisle. Through the open doors and down the steps they trudged. The final resident to step through the doors stopped and turned.

"Thank you, Mother," she said, her ghastly toothy grin the last thing Leon saw before the doors closed and latched in place with a heavy thud.

***

Leon relaxed on the table. It was useless to fight against the leather straps that held him.

"Who was Mother?"

He had a sinking feeling in his stomach he would find out sooner rather than later.

The night dragged on as he lay there, bathed in the scent of death. Minutes to hours, and hours to minutes. He could predict the coming of the light before he could see it. It was a sensation similar to that of being watched. It couldn't kill him, but it would weaken, and burn him badly. At first he dreaded it, but when he thought of who Mother could be, his centuries of undead life at last seemed long enough.

The sky through the broken stained-glass window lightened to gray. The vibrant stars and distant planets faded like a dream after waking. Yet, this nightmare wasn't ending. The sun rose over the frozen landscape. Beams shone through the windows, bathing the broken and disheveled pews in agonizingly dazzling light.

It wasn't until the unfiltered rays peeked through the broken stained glass like an antelope checking for the lioness that the sun's scorching rays caressed Leon. It began slowly, as most torture does. Sunlight across his forearm. A twinge. A sting. Evolving into a burning sensation. Pain, like getting too close to a campfire and being pushed in.

He bared his fangs, howling in pain as the skin of his forearms bubbled, erupted into clear pustules before they burst, their clear fluid running down his arm to the table.

"Knock knock," came a voice out of his view.

The tenor of the voice was raspy. Not a child, but still it held a hint of playfulness.

Leon looked around as much as he could. Movement by a door near the dais. "Who's there?"

"Oh, I am *so* excited. My children brought me a gift. They truly are so thoughtful," said the voice with a sigh.

"I assume you're Mother."

The voice changed, becoming harsher. "You don't get to call me that! I didn't raise you from the shackles of the earth!"

"Fine. Then what do I call you?"

She entered wearing a black dress. Simple. Unassuming. Sunken olive eyes and terracotta skin. Black hair in a bun that was coming loose. She looked like a disheveled nun without her habit.

"Evelyn. Evie. Eve. Any of them will d— Oh dear, you are hurt, aren't you my little pequeñito? Nasty sun! Shoo. Be gone."

"Pequeñito?" Leon asked.

"Hah! Such a gringo. It means you are my little one."

She waved her hand dismissively and a heavy fog formed near the rafters, blocking the light from the broken window. Striding over to him, she leaned close to his arm, grimacing at the smell of burning flesh. In an exaggerated motion she bent to the side, raising her palm over her head before lowering her finger to touch the wound.

Tendrils of green, grey, and black spread from her fingertips through the wound. They danced across Leon's flesh, blending like shadows. The skin grew tough. Black. Husklike. Removing her finger from his arm, she drew closer, touching her tongue to the blackened skin. She blew cool, damp breath that smelled of earth across the arm and the husk flaked off, blowing away, scattering in the morning light like ash.

"All done, pequeñito."

"I... thank you," Leon said, eyeing her warily. "Are you a priestess?"

She straightened suddenly. Tilting her head to the side and pursing her lips, considering the question. "No. But also yes. I once was in another life before your kind tainted these shores. Lucky for you I am not though, pequeñito."

Relaxing, Leon chuckled. "Why is that?"

"Priests mourn the dead. I heal them," she smiled, eyes turning black as ink.

"What are you then?"

"Oh... tsk tsk. Naughty child. You know the answer to that. You're nearly as old as I am. Healed many of your kind I have. They used to search me out in the jungle temples. I can still hear their voices in here." She tapped her temple. "Mother, oooh Mother. Where are you? The sun has nearly risen. Heal my wounds for coin and I will leave thee be. To think they could hurt me? Vampires are dead and death is my plaything!" She raised her hand as if she were holding a marionette. She cocked her head to the side, wiggling her fingers. "Dance for Mother, pequeñito."

Out of his control, Leon's arms moved as if by an outside force. His hands pulled free of the leather straps. In the process, the straps broke every bone in his hands and stripped chunks of flesh away. His eyes watered as he sat up, lifting his gnarled hands and wiggling his finger in a gruesome shadow play of Evelyn's movements. Tears ran down his cheeks as he tried to scream in pain but no sounds came from the body he no longer controlled.

***

Leon collapsed back onto the table. Evelyn touched each of his hands. The same green and black magic waltzed around the gruesome injuries before turning black and drying. She again blew on them and the wounds floated away with the ash-like husk. The pain was gone, and his hands were whole.

"Necromancer," wheezed Leon, his red-rimmed eyes wide with horror.

She nodded. Necromancy. It was dark magic that had been around since the dawn of time.

Leon had heard whispers, but thought they were mostly rumors. It was forbidden in most places, though some welcomed it in the forgotten lands, the town and hovels left after the war when the remaining humans banded together. A badlands that filled the space between high-tech human settlements. In the places where the supernatural was forced to hide... that was where necromancers were revered.

Priests stayed to the bright lights of the cities. They clung to their god of daylight. Necromancers healed what should never live. That included vampires. They could raise the dead, with limitations. Ghouls could live autonomously but always felt a pull to the necromancer that raised them.

Mother's ghouls were different. They seemed devoted fully to her, like a cult leader. Maybe it was devotion, or maybe it was fear. Leon could understand that.

"What do you want me for?" asked Leon, not daring to move.

"I am going to heal you."

Leon scoffed. "You've healed me enough, all from wounds you inflicted."

Evelyn leaned against the table and her powers held him in place. "You misunderstand. When I say I want to heal you, I mean I want to *cure* you."

"Of what?" he asked skeptically.

"Do you know what vampirism is? At its core?"

"Well it—"

"It is a disease, vampire. When you are murdered by the vampire and forced to drink its blood then you ingest the disease. A demonic symbiote. A supernatural leech. It releases a part of itself with the blood and inhabits the new host. That is why you live. The symbiote keeps you alive. An all too willing host. You ingest the blood, which nourishes the symbiote. In return, you live. With every new sire it releases more of itself into a multitude of hosts," she said, almost condescendingly.

"If you're right, and that's a big if... how do vampires ever die?"

"You separate the symbiote from the host body," she said, drawing an imaginary line across her throat with her finger.

"Why heal me?"

She thought for a moment. "Clout. Research. Nobody has ever cured vampirism. Not even a necromancer."

"What makes you think you can?"

"Centuries of failed attempts. Don't get me wrong, it won't be easy, and it may take a few tries but—"

Leon sat up and immediately lost control of his body. With a flourish of Eve's left hand, he was slammed back onto the surface of the table. "What if I don't want to be cured?" he snarled.

"You're sick. You need to be cured. Mother's orders." she said, stretching the fingers of her right hand out.

Dusty, charcoal black vines broke free from the floorboards underneath him. They coiled around the base of the table. Across his body they crawled like inky serpents. Securing him, the vines reached his neck. They wrapped around his throat, tightening their grip. He could hear the blood pulsing in his ears. It felt like an elephant was sitting on his chest. The burn as the vines cut into his neck, blood running over his shoulders and chest. Pooling on the table beneath him, the stench of the metallic crimson was overpowering. His vision swam. His spine snapped, darkening the world.

He was nothing. A disembodied… thing. He floated above his body, strange and dreamlike. He watched the vines recede, leaving his head detached from the body.

How? Was he a ghost? A spirit? Did souls really exist? The staggering implications of this experience would come later because right now he was in shock. His ghostly body vibrated.

Body? Is that accurate? he thought.

He wasn't sure if he had a true body. Either way he flew at Evelyn. He nearly reached her when a force stopped him. He pushed and fought, but he could not move any closer.

Without looking up from his body, she spoke slowly and deliberately. "I know you're there. I feel you. Do not forget, I can control the dead. Body or not, dead is dead. Be patient. The experience will be… momentary."

As she moved her fingers like she was knitting, more blackened vines rose from the ground. Before Leon's eyes, they broke his flesh again and again, sewing his head back to his body as if they were yarn. Once done, they coiled around his neck and turned into a husk before blowing away in a sea of blackened particles.

He felt himself pulled downward. The mouth of his corpse opened and welcomed his spirit like a long-lost friend. As it reabsorbed him, it was over. He opened his eyes, sitting bolt upright.

"You killed me, you witch!"

She waved her hand dismissively. "Only briefly. Besides. You're human now."

"I… what?"

With a wave of her hand, the dark cloud covering the broken window dissipated. Sunlight bathed Leon. Shielding his eyes, he let the light warm him. It felt wonderful… until his skin began to blister and burn. He tried to move but her powers still held him down. It didn't last long. The fog was in place in front of the window almost immediately.

Evelyn shrugged. "We have another way to cure vampirism."

She once again summoned decaying, dying nature to heal Leon's new wounds. It reminded him of diseased nature magic. He wondered briefly if she had once been a druid. He didn't want to be cured, and he was her guinea pig, but he had to admit that he was curious to see if she could actually do it. If she could, he would be able to walk in the sunlight again. Eat real food. Be part of the changing world. He would also age and die. He wasn't sure if he wanted that. Nevertheless, he couldn't help but feel a bit of admiration for this necromancer.

"What now?" he asked, looking at his newly healed wounds.

She narrowed her eyes suspiciously. "There is one more thing I could try if you are willing."

"Why worry about that now?"

She froze for a moment, her eyes darting around as she thought. "This will be very intricate and will require more focus, so I need a willing participant."

Leon thought about it for a moment. "I was once a man of science, and I have to admit that I am most intrigued. If you cure me, will I be free to walk away?"

"Almost definitely."

Leon ran his fingers through his hair. "Let's get this over with. What do I need to do?"

"Nothing," she smiled supernaturally broadly. "I will... extract... the vampiric symbiote. Yes. That is the word I will use. Just... don't move or you will... hmm, it doesn't matter. You won't be alive to know."

I should run, he thought. *But the sense of wonder, and possibly my inner masochist, won't let me.*

Beads of sweat rolled down his face as Leon lay down on the slab, and Evelyn placed the restraints back on him. Black vines broke free from the dry, cracked earth below the floorboard and slid upward, much finer this time and crawling like worms. His palms began to sweat and panic grew in every fiber of his being. Closer, they inched to his face. Moment by moment, heartbeat by heartbeat.

The vine split into half a dozen. Two went into his ears. Two went into his nose. Then a fifth went into his mouth. He gasped. Clawing at his restraints like a bound animal, Leon regretted his decision not to run, as his muffled screams filled the inside of the church.

"Calm. The pain will be brief as the symbiote fights the coming of the light."

He felt the vines, thorns and all, make their way up into his skull. They wiggled around like worms behind his eyes. A sharp pain stabbed at the base of his neck, then the wiggling vines all moved to that spot, pulling and wrenching. The worst headache of his life.

He rolled to his side the best he could as the vines receded back into the ground. Bile rose and he threw up blood and black ichor. The same oily black substance oozed from his ears, eyes and nose. He gasped for air as Evelyn released him from his bindings. He sat up, letting his legs hang off the table. Chest heaving, he breathed in the air. His blood and ichor-stained clothes seemed looser. Gulping in the air, his lungs burned. Breathing. He was breathing.

"It worked," he gasped, brushing his hair out of his face.

She smiled broadly. "I am the greatest necromancer to ever exist. Not only can I control death, but I can cure the curse of immortality." She cackled wildly.

He felt something he had not felt in a very long time. His heart beat against his ribcage and his pulse quickened with... what was that sensation? Fear.

"You said I could leave," said Leon, his voice shaking as he slid off the table.

"I said I would not stop you. I am a woman of my word. Go. Live the time you have left," she said, continuing to laugh and dance around.

***

Leon's hair flew back as he hurried down the aisle between the pews at a full run. He slammed into the doors, bursting out into the sunlight. Falling to his knees, he looked into the sky. The sun washed over him, warming his body and soul. The smell of death and the sound of shuffling steps brought him back to reality. He stood, face to face with the undead residents waiting outside the church.

A blow to his back knocked him back down. Another blow, and another. Every time he tried to stand, more fists bludgeoned his body. Bones broke, and organs burst.

"You said you would let me go!" he screamed, blood pouring from his mouth.

Evelyn stepped out into the sunlight, her hair now loose and wild. "I said I wouldn't stop you. I didn't say anything about my children."

They closed in on him. More blows until he felt nothing. The world went dark.

Moments later, the darkness was lifted. The ghouls stepped back, allowing a space for Mother. The love he felt when he saw his Mother was immeasurable. She moved her fingers and his newly dead body shambled toward her.

"See? I cured you, Leon."

He nodded, his broken jaw hanging loose. "Thank you... Mother."

XXI: THE WORLD

The Wondrous Traveling Spectacular by A. R. K. Horton

It's been almost a year since Mom died. Yet something will happen and I'll reach for my phone to call her and tell her how funny or sad or hopeful it was. Then it hits me all over again that she's not going to answer when it rings. She never will.

All the moments I wanted to have with her will never happen. She'll never see me get my graduate degree or walk down the aisle. Life has now become a list of things empty of her presence.

So when my father emailed me, I was more accepting of him reaching out than I ever thought I'd be. You see, I've never met him before. All I know about him are the stories Mom used to tell me. She'd used to go on about how handsome and charming he was.

One time, I snooped through her bedroom to see if I could steal a look at what present she kept tucked away for my birthday. That's when I found the box of love poems and a sole photo of the man. She was right, he *was* a striking sweet talker, so much so that she also kept a diary in the box to record how much she missed him for years and years later.

The man compared her to constellations and spoke of his love as having the depths of ancient oceans. Then he left her the moment she told him she was pregnant. She never got over it. No other could capture her heart after that.

I wonder what it's like to love like that. Ever since I found those letters, I've daydreamed about what it might mean to have a soulmate. But I've also woken from countless nightmares about heartbreak. How can I long for something that terrifies me to my core?

While Mom forgave my father, I never could. Especially when I look at my reflection. His eyes, green with golden brown ringing around the pupils, mirror mine. Sometimes, when I stare long enough, I feel as though I can reach through and touch my soul – *his* soul. And we're both dark and cloying.

I'll never be him. I refuse.

Still, he reached out to me after finding out that she died, and my traitorous self took his invitation to form a relationship just so I could have another piece of Mom. We've spent weeks now sharing superficial details about our lives.

I told him that I had one more semester before getting my graduate degree in musical theory. I expected him to be like everyone else and tell me I should have chosen something more reliable. Instead, he shared that my love of music must come from him because he'd played the fiddle for circus acts ever since he dropped out of high school.

Mom never told me that and I admit it intrigued me, enough so that I agreed to stay with him for a few days at the circus he works for – Obe's Wondrous Traveling Spectacular!

I've been to circuses before, a lot of them actually. Knowing what I know now, I think Mom was secretly hoping she'd run into my father. This one isn't anything like the ones I've been to.

For starters, it's not just one giant tent. It's a series of tents. In the center, there's a slightly bigger tent made of brilliant blue and gold satin woven and stitched together to create a pattern of oxes, eagles, and lions. At the pinnacle is a small golden classical statue of a nude person. I can't tell if it's a man or a woman, not from ground level. Surrounding that are lots of moderately sized tents of various colors – blood red, emerald green, amethyst purple, and more. They're all also made of satin. I can't help to wonder how they could afford so much satin and how any of it resists leaking and water damage.

It's also not built on some mall parking lot. No, this is stationed where a long dirt road ends at the edge of an oak forest. Their marketing must be impeccable, because there's no way people are lured in by driving past it.

Everything is so grand that it's hard not to gawk at it all. However, as my father gives me a tour of the place, I find myself just as fascinated by him. I saw that photo of him when I was a little girl. I expected him to look different now, but it's like he stepped right out of the Polaroid.

In many ways, I see myself in my father. We're both on the short side, except that he's so thin I felt like I might accidentally break his bones during our awkward greeting hug. We also have the same pert nose. However, I can tell there are some things that I obviously didn't inherit from him, like my red hair and pale, freckled skin.

My father's hair is almost black. He keeps it short and styled with pomade. His skin is tanned and slightly sun-damaged from working outdoors frequently. His lips are thin and perpetually raised in a devil-may-care smile.

Despite how frail he looks, he proves his strength by chipping in while the circus gets everything prepared for their opening night. He even keeps up with the muscle men putting together all the heavy structures. He reminds me of those ants who can carry ten times their weight.

Then, the people my father's helping realize that I, the woman who is staring at them, am his daughter. They shoo him away so he can introduce me to everyone else. First he takes me to the other musicians who are rehearsing. Then, he moves on to the acrobats and clowns practicing their acts.

They all take my breath away. There's very little that fills me with childlike wonder anymore, but this does. Everyone smiles when they notice my wide eyes and dropped jaw. When my father tells them who I am, their voices rise in excitement to meet the daughter he's been talking about for weeks.

"You're just as beautiful as he described!" says a woman dressed in a red spandex leotard and sparkling gold tights.

"I heard you're getting an *actual* graduate degree," says a congenial man who is chest level with me, despite my petite size. "You must be so smart."

Twins somehow hold a conversation with me while juggling metal rings with each other. Mostly, they go on about how much my eyes resemble my father's. They tell me their names are Jessa and Becca and then ask me for mine.

"Eve," I tell them.

"That's a sign," says Jessa.

"Of what?" I ask.

Becca darts her sister a cutting glance and then looks at me with a softened expression. "Ignore Jessa," she says. "She just likes to sound mysterious."

Jessa giggles and they both return their focus on passing rings between their hands with a breathtaking, aerial grace.

A lanky man pauses his hypnotic bongo beats to barrage me with a string of questions. "You like music? Do you play an instrument?"

"Yes," I say. "I'm a violinist."

His smile broadens. "Violins and fiddles are the same thing, right?"

"Well, technically," I answer, "it's really the style of music that makes the difference. I'm classically trained while my father probably plays folk music."

The man's obsidian eyes sparkle. "You'd be surprised at what all he can play."

Throughout the day, I receive heaps of praise from these strangers. My father keeps saying things like, "Isn't she just amazing?" and "I told you she was smart!" while beaming at me. It's all a little embarrassing but also causes my heart to swell, because my father, who seemingly never wanted me, is obviously proud of me now. Does he regret all those years he'll never get back with me? Does he miss my mother? I try not to dwell on those questions, because I don't want to taint what will surely be three days of magic and wonder.

My father has his own trailer, which surprises me, since almost everyone else shares space in the larger trailers. My father isn't the ringmaster. I met that guy. His name was Obe and he definitely has more authority than my father, who is just the fiddler who accompanies various acts. The tall man walks around in a black pinstripe suit and a top hat, like he might bump into an unexpected audience at any moment.

There are two beds in our trailer. One is wider and on the floor. The other is more like a cot and placed on a sort of loft above the other.

"You can have the big one," he says. "I'm used to a small bed in one of the group trailers."

"Oh, this trailer isn't yours?"

My father shakes his head. "No, our newest star act is letting me borrow his while you visit."

"Do all the star acts get their own trailer?" I ask.

"No, not all of them. He sells out a lot of shows, though, so he gets special treatment." His face brightens. "Let me introduce the two of you. Such a generous man. You'll love him!"

My father dashes out of the trailer and I have to rush to catch up with him. He only slows when he gets near a group of folks who are totally transfixed by a man dancing with fire and breathing it too. Looking at him, I don't think it's his talents that have everyone so enraptured. He's the most beautiful person I've ever seen in my life.

A mess of wavy, honey blond hair crowns his head, looking like a lucky accident. One lock falls across the tawny skin of his forehead to rest between his eyebrows, which are a slightly darker shade than the rest of his hair. He's almost as golden as the statue at the peak of the big tent, but his eyes are a dazzling aquamarine. And his body? He looks as strong as all the people putting together the heavier structures.

"Goddamn," I whisper to myself.

My father glances at me with a twinkle in his eyes and my cheeks succumb to a heat wave of embarrassment.

"Adam!" my father calls out to him, catching the man's attention immediately. "Come meet my daughter!"

Adam? Oh God, this is too perfect.

The golden hunk walks over, crooking a lopsided grin that contrasts with his strong, symmetrical jaw. When he reaches me, he takes my hand in his. The moment he does, I feel the sweetest song sweep against my heart.

"Nice to meet you, Lovely," he says and gives my knuckles a chivalrous peck. "I'm afraid Conner here never told me your name."

Conner? Oh, yeah, that's my father. How did I forget my own father's name?

I'm forgetting a lot at the moment because he's still holding my hand and his strong, calloused thumb is stroking my knuckles. I wish it was stroking me in so many other places.

"Um, I'm Eve."

Adam's brows lift and his smile broadens. "How funny is that? Adam and Eve meeting at a circus of all places."

I laugh in a way that isn't natural in the least. It's nervous, fearful even, because it's all I can do not to melt onto the leaf-littered ground.

"I believe you two have more than a Bible story in common," my father says. "For instance, Eve is getting her graduate degree so she can become a music teacher."

"Oh really?" Adam says. "My dad was a music teacher. Taught me how to play the piano. I'm terrible at it, but still..."

A shrill whistle breaks the trance of Adam's gaze and I look over to find the source. It's the ringmaster and he's beckoning my father to him.

"I gotta see what that's about," my father says. "You two talk about piano lessons or something."

Once my father is out of earshot, Adam steps closer. "You look a little like Conner," he says. "But I'm guessing you got those plump lips and fiery hair from somewhere else."

"My mom," I tell him.

"If she looks anything like you, Conner is a very lucky man."

Suddenly, the heat that's been uncoiling within me cools, because he's talking about Mom in the present tense.

Adam's perfect eyebrows furrow. "Did I say something wrong?"

I shake my head. "No, it's just that... Well, she died and sometimes just thinking about her..."

"Oh, I see," he says. "I understand that."

"You do?"

A brief shadow of grief passes over Adam's face like a dark cloud blocking the sun. "My dad died a couple of years ago. I never knew my mom, so he was my only family."

"Until my father reached out to me a few weeks ago, my mom was my only family, too."

The initial attraction I felt the moment I saw Adam seems miniscule compared to what I'm experiencing now. There's something special about shared heartbreak. Adam must be reflecting on the same thing, because he squeezes my hand and offers me a sad smile.

His charms aren't all for show now. A real connection has formed between us within a matter of minutes. I never expected to encounter magic like this at a circus.

"I know this is going to sound too forward, but..." Adam clears his throat, looking a little shy. "I feel like we—"

"Hey!" my father shouts as he approaches us carrying two styrofoam take-out boxes. "The ringmaster ordered us some Thai food!"

I gasp, both delighted at the surprise and touched that my father remembered how I told him it was my favorite. "That's so kind of him!"

"How about we go eat at the trailer and catch up?" my father asks.

An incredibly self-centered and infatuated reaction hits me and I look at Adam. "Oh, well, I thought we could eat with the rest of the circus..."

"Oh, they mostly eat on their own too," my father explains.

Adam nods. "Yeah, I typically eat alone in my trailer." He leans in to whisper. "Kinda hard to digest when there are so many people flirting with me, and I think you'd have the same problem."

As a fair-skinned redhead, I know how obvious my blushing is but it's too late to cover it up. Adam smirks, knowing just how he's made me feel.

He lets go of my hand and turns his attention to my father. "The acrobats have been trying to get me to eat with them for a while," he says. "I suppose it's time for me to take a break from my loner nature."

My father lets out a bark of a laugh. "You? A loner? Never heard such a lie."

"Things aren't always as they seem," Adam says.

"Very true," my father responds with a serious expression. It's the first time I've seen him without a bright smile on his face.

For an awkward moment, I wonder if he's trying out that whole overprotective father thing. He has no right to, given that only now is he even interested in my existence, but I have no desire to bring that up in front of others.

Adam doesn't let my father's tone deter him. He gives me a long look, this one with genuine depth. His lips are parted in awe and his eyebrows are pressed together in tenderness. My heart threatens to pull out of my chest and I resist the urge to throw my arms around him.

"You'll find me tomorrow, right?" he asks. "Please?"

I find myself nodding.

"Thank God," he responds in a breathy whisper and then clears his throat. "Have a good night."

"Good night," I say, unable to tear my gaze from him.

"Bye, Adam!" my father calls out and puts his hand on my shoulder to turn me toward the trailer.

My father's saying something or other, but I don't hear a word of it. My head is swimming with Adam. Is this what love at first sight feels like? I've had boyfriends, remarkable ones, most of them attractive and interesting, but I've never felt this intense surge of emotions.

Suddenly, soulmates seem possible and it's more thrilling and horrifying than I ever expected it to be.

***

As my father and I eat our Thai take out, he shares stories about how he met Mom.

His circus was in town. He spotted Mom staring at him as he played the fiddle and he fell in love with her at once. He toyed with the idea of leaving his wanderer life to 'settle down'. Yet, the more he shared about his experiences with her, the more he realized that was where he belonged and he felt it was wrong to force such a wonderful woman and their child into that kind of life.

I hear his story for the tapestry of pathetic excuses it is. The whole time I feel like tossing my curry at him. I keep listening, though, because the way he talks about her is almost lyrical. Her hair, so much like my own, flickered like the bonfires she danced around. Instead of a delicate giggle, she threw her whole head back to laugh as loud as a trumpet. In his eyes, she was the goddess of life – one he preferred to worship from a distance.

I only soften to him when he admits that he never moved on from her. He never even entertained flirtations with others. My parents didn't have a romance; they had a tragedy, soulmates fated to live forever in different worlds.

Still, he could have sent the occasional letter.

My stomach is full and it's been a long day. That must be why I feel so... foggy. I want to keep talking to him about Mom, but when my father leaves to discuss some things with the other musicians, I can't fight sleep.

My mind wanders to Adam as I trip over my feet to the bed. I can see loving him the way Mom loved my father. I don't think I could survive if he left me. Only the top half of my body reaches the mattress when my eyes close and I drift off.

***

A bittersweet dream haunts me. Mom dances around a bonfire. She's in the forest, *this* forest. The folks I've met at the circus are there. They look exactly as they do now, laughing with her and studying her when she looks away.

My father pulls her by the waist, bringing them so close their lips almost touch. "We could do this forever, Jane," he says. "Dancing and laughing and never growing old."

"Never growing old?" Mom asks, but she doesn't wait for an answer. Instead, she shakes her head and says. "One day, I want my hair to turn silver and I want to carry grandchildren on my hip. Being young forever seems so *boring*."

She never got her wish. Her hair was as bright as always when the police found her on the floor with an empty oxycodone bottle just beyond her icy blue fingertips. How did she even get it? What drove her to it? I can only imagine she finally gave in to the unbearable weight of her heartbreak.

I want to hate my father, but there's a sorrowful sheen in his eyes. "I love you," he whispers and tears roll down his cheeks as his lips touch hers.

That's when I notice that he doesn't look any different from now. He's ageless somehow with no blush of youth and an ancient depth in his green and brown eyes, but not one wrinkle or grey hair. How old was he when they met? They must have both been so young, because if not—

A slam of a trailer door jolts me out of my slumber. It's not our trailer's, but one that must be further down. Then I hear my father shout, "No!"

I'm still weary, but I have to know what has him so upset. I crack open the small window in the cramped kitchenette and peek outside. My father and the ringmaster are locked in an intense stare.

My father stands with his arms crossed over his chest. There's a scowl on his face as he stares up at his boss. It's like watching a terrier stand up to a mastiff. "You promised if I kept finding light fae, we could take a break this year," my father says. "That she'd be safe."

"I truly thought we could, but I was wrong," the ringmaster replies in a firm but calm voice. "The hunger is getting out of control. The clowns took a *child*. You know that's going to make people around here suspicious."

"I don't care!" my father shouts, throwing his arms up in frustration. "Anyway, she's only half dark fae. This won't work."

"Half and half will do. Her half dark and his half light will—"

"Two halves don't make a whole, Obe," my father interrupts. He's on his toes, trying to get in the ringmaster's face.

The ringmaster's eyebrows tent in sympathy as he puts a hand on my father's right shoulder to gently nudge the man away. "I know you want to believe that, but it's worked before. Two half fae *can* complete the cycle. And if we don't do it, we're stuck here, giving in to our darkest urges."

"She's too pure." My father's voice trembles, as if he doesn't believe his own words.

"Anyone with even a drop of dark fae in them is far from pure," the ringmaster says. "You saw the way they looked at each other. Their love has already sparked. The dark in your child is drawn to his light. It was destined to happen this year."

A short, tense moment of silence passes between them and then my father takes a step backward, his head shaking slowly. "Jane didn't do it, did she? It was you."

"I let her live when you fell for her," the ringmaster says. "And she got to raise your child, just like you wanted. It was time for her cycle to end, though. To make way for Eve."

I gasp.

The ringmaster's head snaps in my direction and he stares right through the screen of the open window I'm using to spy on him. His eyes narrow and his jaw tenses.

"Shit!" he hisses. "That dinner was supposed to knock her out all night!"

I stumble backward, wincing as my hip slams into the table. I rub at the sore spot, but I know I can't stay there and nurse it. They were talking about *me*. I'm not sure what they were saying exactly, but I don't like the sound of children and hunger and dark urges. And how Mom died...

I don't bother to grab anything. There's no time. Instead, I open the door and sprint away. I don't know where I'm going, but I plan to put as much distance between me and the circus as I can. Memories of the dream dance around the edges of my panicked mind as I race through the forest. Perhaps I should have taken the road, but I'm hoping the oak trees will make it harder for them to see me.

The lights of houses glisten between the distant branches and my breath catches on a swell of hope. If I can get there, I can ask someone to call the police or—

My toe collides with a root, causing me to topple face forward. I brace myself for the fall, but before I hit the ground there's a shattering sensation on the back of my head and I'm blinded by sparks of pain.

***

My world is cast in a sapphire glow. It takes me a moment to realize why. Above me is a canopy of blue and gold satin. I'm laying flat on my back staring at the ceiling of the big tent. How did I wind up here?

I had been dashing through the forest, my hip aching with every stride. I'd heard a conversation about me and I had been scared. I don't remember what it was, but... I feel fine now. There's no pain anywhere on my body and my heart is at ease. Better than that, love hums in my chest.

I turn on my side and see the reason why. Adam sleeps next to me, a peaceful smile on his face. There isn't one stitch of clothing on his perfect body. I realize only then that I'm nude as well.

Did we? No, I'm too clean and dry. Instead of the musky scent of sex, we both smell of bergamot and jasmine.

Adam's long lashes flutter open, revealing his aquamarine eyes. Though he seems as groggy as I am, a broad smile spreads across his face at the sight of me.

"Hi, Lovely," he says in a sleepy whisper. "I dreamed about you."

A song weaves through my soul. "You did?"

His calloused hand brushes a tendril of my hair from my cheek. "You were reading poems from a box and they made you sad."

I laugh. "Poems from a box? Why would that ever make me sad?" I ask, but some melancholy familiarity tugs at me. That feeling is gone the instant Adam's thumb sweeps across my bottom lip.

"You're the most beautiful woman I've ever seen," Adam says. "The moment I saw you, I just knew. My whole body thrummed."

"It did?" I ask. When he nods, I say, "You make me tremble. I look at you and my entire being is consumed by a song."

Adam's eyebrows press together in such tenderness that my heart aches for him. "I know that song."

He presses his lips to mine; they're so soft and yet so firm. I open my mouth, inviting him to deepen our kiss and he doesn't hesitate. The kiss is warm, sweet, and syrupy.

Adam pulls away for a second to lock eyes with me. "Honey. You taste like honey." His lips collide with mine again, this time fiercer, as if he's starving.

Calloused palms roam all over me, stroking the swell of my breasts and the curve of my bottom, before roughly grasping my hip. I respond with a sharp, delighted gasp against his lips. He rolls on top of me and reclaims my mouth with an even more ravenous kiss.

My left hand drifts down the muscles on his back until it cups his rear. The fingers on my right hand weave through his golden locks, as I buck my hips against him.

"Fuck," he whispers into our kiss and then pulls away to lock eyes with me. "I couldn't stop even if I tried. But I won't try, because I want this. I want this so bad I might die."

He's so right. There's an urgency to this that I can't deny. Parting from him will kill me. I just know it.

Hooking one arm behind my knee, he parts my thighs in one fluid motion so that he can enter me. *Oh, God!* This is everything. This is life and death and every wonderful, wicked moment in between.

I don't even notice our bodies moving, just the concert of our manic energy. Our lips part so that we can gaze at each other, touching souls. Am I calling out his name? I think he's calling out mine. I can't tell because I feel like I'm under some delirious spell.

It feels like there are other hands involved now. Maybe it's just because he can't stop touching me everywhere. Even if there was an audience, it wouldn't matter. The two of us are all that exists right now and my entire world is the joining of our bodies.

Wait, he's not on top of me anymore. I'm straddling him as we both sit on a... throne? I'm so confused.

Adam focuses on me as he chants, "I love you. I love you. I love you."

Gone are the questions that briefly troubled me.

"I love you, too!" I cry out, as the steady, rapid motion of our love-making makes my thighs tremble from exhaustion.

It feels like we've been doing this for hours. Have we? What are those voices?

Suddenly, I'm gripping onto a cold, metal cylinder so tight that my hand aches. I break eye contact long enough to see what it is. My fingers are curled around the handle of a dagger.

I turn to Adam, my heart thumping with not just love, but also terror. "What's happening?"

"I don't care." His hazy eyes are so lost in mine that he doesn't even see what I'm talking about. "I don't want to stop. I *can't*."

I can't either, but now that's seizing me with panic, because I'm fighting the urge to bring that dagger down to his heart. No, that's not me I'm straining against. Someone put this dagger in my hand and now they're trying to force my arm downward.

I look around the room and find row upon row of witnesses. I know these faces. They were smiling at me yesterday.

A fog lifts and memories open up like a flip book. This is the circus. My father brought me here.

"Where's my father?" I ask my audience.

They reply with cackles and nothing more. I remember him fighting with the ringmaster. If he's not here, then... Oh, God.

My arm continues to shake against the force someone is applying to it. I look up to see the ringmaster. His teeth grit together in determination. I try to let go of the dagger, but his other hand has my fingers clamped on the hilt.

If I can just get off Adam's lap, I can push the ringmaster away. I have to try. I need to save Adam! I love him! But when I pull away, Adam rolls with me, unable to break from our euphoric dance.

I look back at my lover. My breast is in his mouth as he moans. My gaze lowers to where we're chained together. We've been so distracted by our lovemaking that we didn't even notice.

"Adam!" His name comes out like a growl as I struggle to keep my arm from striking him with the blade in my hand. "Snap out of it!"

He doesn't hear me.

"Eve!" he cries out as he shudders beneath me and, God help me, that sends me right over the edge too.

We orgasm together and Adam grabs onto me, his breath coming out ragged as he lays his weary head against my chest. Something bright glows where we are joined. It's warm and soothing and *right*, filling me completely.

"I love you," he whispers.

My arm buckles and the dagger, still tight in my grasp, slams into Adam's heart.

A rough, guttural scream erupts from my lover and he looks up at me with heartbreaking eyes and a mouth spilling blood by the buckets.

"I love you, too," I whimper between sobs, keeping eyes locked on Adam's, as the ringmaster forces me to bury the dagger even deeper.

Adam's head droops. I can't feel our song anymore. That's how I know he's dead.

The ringmaster releases me. I wrap my shaking arms around Adam.

"Now the cycle is complete," the ringmaster shouts to the audience of circus workers. "His death gives way to the life he put in her womb."

Their smiles are jubilant and vicious as they cheer in response. The ringmaster looks at me with an affection that one might give a relative. But, he's not, is he? I wonder again where my father is, but I know deep down that he's dead. Just as soon as I met him, he was lost to me.

The ringmaster cups my cheek tenderly. "Our dark fae child has returned to us and she carries the seed of the light, so that we won't give in to our most dangerous urges."

I startle when there are more whoops from the circus workers.

"Death gives way to life," the ringmaster continues. "The heavens touch the earth. Man and woman become one. We are sated for another year." His smile grows unnaturally wide. "And it looks like we have a replacement for our fiddler, too."

My love and grief for Adam hollows out my heart, making room for something twisted and hungry. The darkness within me sighs with relief that it's finally broken out of its cage.

Acknowledgements

I would like to thank the talented authors who have made this anthology possible. When I came to them with the idea of a dark fantasy anthology based on the major arcana tarot cards, I did not expect to be met with such enthusiasm and immediate commitment to what has turned out to be a lengthy project. Their hard work and boundless creativity has both impressed and humbled me, and I'm very grateful.

A special thanks goes to Dave M. Simon for his terrific cover art – I could never make anything so amazing.

A huge thanks also to Dave M. Simon and Mara Lynn Johnstone for carrying out copy edits of the stories – no mean feat with such a chunky book!

Finally, thanks to you – the reader. Thank you for taking a chance on us. It means the world.

If you enjoyed *THE MAJOR ARCANA*, please consider leaving a review on Goodreads and Amazon.

Every review helps us get this book into the hands of more readers.